GIRL FROM SOLDIER CREEK

A NOVEL

For more information:
Stephen F. Austin State University Press
P.O. Box 13007 SFA Station
Nacogdoches, Texas 75962
sfapress@sfasu.edu
www.sfasu.edu/sfapress

Book design: Shaina Hawkins
Cover design: David Wilder
Distributed by Texas A&M Consortium
www.tamupress.com

LIBRARY OF CONGRESS CATALOGING-IN-PUBLICATION DATA
Foster, Patricia
Girl From Soldier Creek/Patricia Foster

ISBN: 978-1-62288-125-3

FOR JEAN, KATE, SUSIE, WYLINE, AMY, AND THE LATE LOUISE
BOUZAN

GIRL FROM SOLDIER CREEK

A NOVEL

PATRICIA FOSTER

Stephen F. Austin State University

PROLOGUE

It's silence that soothes me, comforts me as I dive into the glossy blue water, then glide around the deep stillness of the tank. Always I feel a soft hum in my chest as I flip toward the picture window then lengthen my body as if lounging on a couch, my arms folded neatly behind my head, my feet kicking in quiet, steady waves. When I somersault backward, water rushes around me in a fine skin of bubbles. My arms look ghostly white, my fingernails and toenails glitter like scarlet jewels. Sometimes I move slowly, each stroke deliberate, intimate as if I'm swimming in the creek, but other times I plunge to the bottom, then ricochet up to the surface for air. It depends on the routine. On what Earl Ray wants us to do. Now I swim toward the window, raising my arms like a swan fluttering her wings, then press my breasts against the glass, splaying my hands, palms flat, in a gesture of helplessness. I'm supposed to snuggle against the glass, to kiss the window, but that feels so ridiculous I turn my cheek to the side and close my eyes.

I never think about the men behind the window, men staring at me, gawking, as I float toward them, my breasts bulging from the tiny bikini top, my thighs long and slim, my perfectly painted toes. I never think about the neon sign that blinks rhythmically against the window, throwing off a swarm of golden light: *Earl Ray's Bar.* I never think about Earl Ray, watching at the bar, dressed in beige linen pants and a crisp white shirt, his blonde ponytail smoothed to sleek perfection.

I think instead about my sister Amanda and our home in Soldier Creek, Alabama, though neither of us is there anymore.

"It's just us," she used to say to me on the nights we ran breathlessly over wet grass and sticky pine straw, our cotton nightgowns billowing around us until we stood panting outside the back door. What I remember is a sultry evening in late August when the moon floated out from behind the clouds and we watched a lizard scamper like a black smear across the screen door. *"Touch it,"* Amanda whispered with a six-year-old's fierceness. I tried to pull my hand away, some part of me dashing into the darkness where the crickets sang and the tide shifted while another part stood silent and terrified as my sister jerked my hand up to touch the lizard's tail. "You *touched* it and now you'll start turning into a lizard," she insisted, but when I began to cry, she turned suddenly, leaping at the window to grab the lizard before it scampered away. "There," she said, bringing her hand close to mine. "I touched it too. Now we'll both be lizards." And I understood then the reward of my loyalty: *she might frighten me, but she'd never desert me.*

No, it was I who deserted, I who changed directions, following the lizard as it slipped into darkness. One night in early December I got on a bus in a little town in Alabama and didn't get off until there was nowhere else to land.

PART I

JIT SOLDIER

1

"Okay, mermaids!" Earl Ray clapped his hands. "Let's go. *Let's go!"*

We hurried into line, suited up in silvery blues and greens so that the men sitting at the bar drinking whiskey and bourbon and watching us through the magnified picture window would see us as sexy and romantic, but I got the job because swimming was the only thing I knew how to do.

We waited, silent, edgy as he went down the line, asking to see fingernails, calves, the inside of a thigh. "What's this, Judy? Whaddaya doing to yourself? Banging into furniture?"

"Just a bruise, Mr. Ray. Gotta haul groceries, you know. Musta hit a chair."

"Step out," he said. That meant no swimming. No paycheck. Late rent and extra worry.

"Ahhh, com'on."

"Step out!"

We were expected to be perfect, flawless, our toenails and fingernails expertly painted, no chipping, no flaking, no streaking, no peeling. Good legs. Full breasts. White teeth. *Law according to Earl Ray.* It was common gossip that he had spent time in Vietnam, and the older girls swore he knew punishments that would shock us.

"All right. Get to work."

As I breast-stroked through the half-light of the tank, I saw nothing but a swell of water as my partner, Lisa, dove into the pool. We swam together, supple as mermaids, our movements synchronized, attuned, legs together like a shiny flash of tail. As she swam, Lisa's blonde hair floated and tangled like seaweed. My own hair shivered like leaves. Lisa smiled as she flutter-kicked toward me and we joined hands, circling, until for a single instant, I rose into the air and saw not Lisa, but Amanda, her gaze locked possessively to mine. *Where are you? Come home.*

And then it was over. On cue, I surface dove, swift as a torpedo, my thighs as straight and sure as a ballerina's. After thirty minutes, we were replaced by two other girls who swam while we rested, Lisa and I wrapped up in big terry cloth bathrobes and huddled in old, ragged beach chairs, small cups of water in our hands. We were allowed only two snacks and a glass of water "meted out in doses," Lisa said, "so we won't have to pee."

After our break, we did our next routine, circling each other like lovers, parting and connecting, holding hands as we flipped backward, our knees pulled tight to our chests, our free hands brushing through the water. Sometimes I really did feel like a ballerina, as if my body in water were as fluid and graceful as a swan. My arms and legs became stronger, quicker, and when I twirled in the water, I imagined there was a real purpose for this, some reason beyond survival that bound me to this job.

I was thinking this as I followed Lisa up the ladder out of the pool at 10:30 p.m., not really paying much attention to anything except the water dripping in a cascade from her back onto my arms as she shimmied a little, shaking herself like a wet dog. She turned and laughed at me, flicking water in my face. I didn't see Earl Ray standing in the shadows, waiting, a drink in his hand, until I was almost to the dressing room and he stepped in front of me, blocking my path.

I jerked back, surprised, flinging water from my hair.

"Come with me," he said, confident, in control. He had changed into a fresh white shirt and stood silently observing me. He was tall with hooded eyes and a pale white scar, a tiny fishhook, just above his lip. "Got some extra work for you."

Like the other girls, I knew that to keep my job I had to do what Earl Ray demanded, but I'd never been singled out before, never been asked to do anything extra other than cut my shoulder-length hair into a short, pixyish style because he had me pegged as a young, kittenish Gina Lollobrigida. Obediently, I followed him into his office where the door was partly open, where I heard a whirring noise, a vibrating buzz, a sound both familiar and strange and unsettling. Earl Ray swung wide the door, and as he did a man in a wheelchair spun around, his skin oily and pale, creased on one side of his face with tiny scars that bubbled up like blisters. He was thick-lipped, leering, his eyes blatantly scanning my body. I stopped just outside the door, unable to move.

"Come in, come in," Earl Ray coached, reaching behind me to shut the door. The room was as cold as a refrigerator, the air-conditioning blowing streams of freezing air. Goose bumps prickled my skin. The man, I noticed, was drinking a frosty beer.

"Well, Randy, I've got the one. She's first-rate. She'll give you a good show."

The wheelchair buzzed with motion, and before I could move again, the man's knees were almost touching mine, his upper body big and muscular beneath a bright Hawaiian print shirt that opened as he leaned toward me, revealing a bulge of white skin. He stared at me with intense blue eyes, narrowed at the corners. "She's good, huh?" he threw back over his shoulder at Earl Ray, his gaze still fastened on me.

A shiver started at the back of my knees and pulsed through my thighs. I couldn't take my eyes off the man, though I knew such staring was the worst thing I could do. His eyes were flat and hardened like bullets trained on a target.

"One of the best," Earl Ray smiled, coming back from around his desk and handing the man a cigar.

"Just a special assignment," he said, nodding at me as if there were no room for refusal. "I'll put you in a practice room," he said. "Just do one of your routines and Randy here will be much obliged."

The man's fingers touched my thigh. They were as cold and dry as winter grass. Abruptly, he motored backward and I saw that one foot was missing, the pants leg hanging open, empty, collapsed from the knee.

As if he just noticed my noticing, Randy bunched his lips together and blew me a kiss. "Prima donna," he said, making it a slur. And then both he and Earl Ray laughed as if it were the funniest thing they'd ever heard. "Primmmma donnn-nna," Randy repeated and saluted me with his beer.

"Go on," Earl Ray said when he saw me hesitate. "Go into the practice room and do your stuff."

I backed out quickly. I tried not to think of the man Randy, his empty pants leg, the way his mouth drooped, how he stared at me as if I weren't human. I didn't feel quite human as I entered the room sealed off from the bar. Usually this pool wasn't lit, was merely a deep aqua swimming pool where we swam laps, where we practiced or rehearsed for special assignments. The windows fronted Earl Ray's office. But now the pool was lit and I saw its ugliness: sides stained a greasy brown like mud, the bottom murky and gray, tiny cracks like veins rupturing the concrete. There was no one in the room, only the faint strains of "Moon River" floating through the stereo system, and for a single instant I stood silent and still, unable to move. I didn't know why I thought of Mother, of the way she looked at me that night Amanda called from Trinity College, the night in December when everything in my life got turned around. What I remembered was how Mother's eyes flashed a single instant of triumph, a look that seared me, making me want to run.

I couldn't move.

"Go on. Do your routine," Earl Ray's voice crooned softly over the intercom, almost endearing, as if he knew I'd need convincing, and the next minute I was in the water, swimming like an automaton, diving deep to the bottom and then swirling my way around the glass, swimming close to it as Earl Ray had taught us to do, splaying my body against the picture window, hugging it with breasts and hips and hands, and then flipping backward, turning smoothly, effortlessly. Though I wasn't aware of anything I did, I was so sure of my movements I could have been performing a stylized ballet, but for the first time I knew I was doing something dirty, something vulgar and disgusting. For the first time I cursed my long, slender legs, the smooth sheath of bare skin between my bikini top and bottom. I hated my tan belly, my unblemished cheeks, my toenails painted a bright cranberry red. I don't know how long I swam before a bubble burst in front of me and as suddenly I saw not this awful pool in Los Angeles, but the soft, gray curve of Soldier Creek where two porpoises leapt near the bow of our boat, their black, oily bodies moving in perfect rhythm through the air, and then dark shadows swollen beneath the water.

I no longer thought about my body, about my movements. I no longer worried about what I was doing. Earl Ray was gone. The man Randy was gone. The mermaids were gone. Los Angeles was gone. I was just a girl from Soldier Creek swimming around the little island twenty feet from our pier, following the tides, my arms moss-coated, my hair threaded with seaweed, schools of minnows tickling my legs.

And then, as suddenly, it was over, the routine finished, my mind trapped between geographies, between the margins of dream and reality. I lifted my head out of the water. I floated on my back as if I had died and been brought back to life. Soft strains of "Moon River" drifted above me, and in the background I heard the hiss of the showers, the mumble of voices. New girls had arrived, but I continued to float.

It wasn't until I climbed up the ladder that I heard again that strange sound, the whirr of Randy's chair. I felt a quiver of panic. A shudder. A sensation like a nail scraping on cement. When I looked up, Randy was sitting at the top of the ladder, his wheelchair blocking my way out. When he looked at me with those flat lizard eyes, it was as if he didn't see me, but followed only the movement of my rib cage and the water streaming down the fabric of my suit. I watched a drop make its slow descent down my belly, a liquid star collapsing into the stretchy material of my bikini bottom. Randy watched it too. For a moment we remained absolutely still like characters in a frieze, me caught between the third and second step, he with his wheel butted up against the chrome railing.

"So, that was pretty good, was it?" His voice was belligerent as if I'd cheated him somehow.

I stared at my feet, white and distorted beneath the water, my toenails broken chips of scarlet.

"What's wrong, cat got your tongue? You some kind of mute?"

"Sorry," I mumbled.

"What?" he said irritably. "What are *you* sorry for?"

"I mean . . . if the routine wasn't what you wanted."

"How would you know what I want?"

I had to make myself look at his eyes. Though they were narrow and piercing, for an instant he flinched, and I realized he didn't like this any more than I did . . . but something kept him there, blocking my path, demanding my attention. "I don't know . . . I don't know what you want." I made my voice as calm as I could. "I . . . I don't know what anyone wants."

And to my surprise, Randy laughed, his eyes loosening their hold. "Well, darlin'," he said, leaning toward me, almost friendly. "I think you've just woken from your princess sleep."

Though I had no idea what he was talking about, I told myself to think about Soldier Creek, to see porpoises leaping in smooth, silvery arcs though watery air and even the swaying beauty of jellyfish, and then Randy's hand reached out to touch my thigh, to trace a drop of water as it trickled down the length of my leg. I stiffened and stood absolutely still, his dry fingers like the bristles of a brush against my skin. He was stroking, long, slow sweeps with two fingers, as if he were drying up the water, suctioning each drop from my thigh. He never took his eyes off me. He didn't blink. The briefest silence dropped down between us, while in me a breathless panic fluttered up, choking off my air. I thought I was going to scream. Or faint. Or do something crazy. To my surprise, Amanda came to me, rising effortlessly inside me, her voice quiet and controlled, as steady as a ticking clock. "Baby," she said, "be still. That's right, don't react. He wants you to be frightened. That's what he *needs*." And I listened to that voice. I made myself take little sips of air. I didn't scream or faint. I remained very still, my body coiled, and yet I worried what would happen next, what he would try to do, whether I should leap into the water, whether—

"Why lookie here, if it isn't Mr. Randy Carter!" Suzanne waltzed out of the dressing room, calling out in her flirtatious voice. "Now what brings your handsome self to town?"

Suzanne was loud, sexy, her voice like a whistle beckoning. She smiled at Randy as if she knew some inside joke. She walked slowly, swinging her hips, swaying on strong, fleshy legs. Only when he turned his wheelchair toward her did a wedge open between us. Quickly, I squeezed through the space, sucking in my breath, my thighs pinched by the cold bite of chrome. But as quickly, he wheeled around, catching my knee so that I flinched. "Gotcha!" he said, winking at me, his eyes darting back to Suzanne. She bent over and planted a big, smacking kiss on the good side of his face, then wiggled her hips. He reached over to tug on her suit. "Why, Mr. Carter," she pulled away, "we don't handle the merchandise." And when he burst out laughing, the chair moved slightly, barely an inch. But enough.

2

Six blocks from the bus stop. Four blocks. Two. Trash blew around me, spinning like pinwheels in the stiff ocean breeze. I had changed into my street clothes, not bothering to shower, barely drying off, not even tying my shoes. It was February in Los Angeles—February 1968—and the sky was a slate gray, the color of ash. During the day it was never blue, but white and dead, an unnatural blankness. This night rain fell in clean, cold drips, and when I lifted my face, the sky was a flat emptiness, the leaves rustling furtively on the trees. Cars flashed by, horns beeping, tires squealing on the slick wet streets. "Hey you!" somebody yelled. "Yeah, you!" An old man with a spiked stick walked slowly along piercing McDonald's wrappers and Dairy Queen cups, tossing them into a black plastic bag, but all I could think about were Randy's eyes, the way he knew I didn't belong there.

"*Gone?*" I imagined Flo Hinton, the town gossip, whispered to Officer Budd after I left Soldier Creek. "What do you mean she's gone?"

"Done run away, that's what. Her mama hasn't seen her since midnight."

"A shame." Flo would instinctively tuck stray hairs into her beehive hairdo before turning toward her ancient black phone. "Running away at sixteen. It's not right."

But that's exactly what I did, though it felt more like drowning, like going down deep, swirled into blackness, never coming back up, the world just a thick wave of water. I never planned to run away, never planned to live anywhere else but Soldier Creek, Alabama, where the water is glassy smooth, shimmering against sun-heated banks, where at night a mist floats low, swallowing up the creek, leaving an ache in my chest. I never planned to desert Amanda, to end up in such a restless, hungry place, so big and noisy, so dirty and bright. Even as I thought this, the Number 12 slid to a stop, water splashing against the curb, spraying toward me in a drizzly arc. A man pushed against me, jostling my arm. I stiffened, then remembered that it meant nothing. Just someone hurrying to get on. Hurrying to a bottle or a fish dinner or three sleeping kids. "What's up, Sister?" he turned to me, breathy voice in my ear. "Don't you know God loves you, and the spirit blesses you?"

Then I saw the yellow tract he was trying to give me. I shook my head and squeezed past him, but he dropped the yellow paper into my hands.

At Lincoln Boulevard, I got off, sloshing through surface water, hurrying past the Cash and Carry, past the Chinese Laundry, past Los Feliz Tattoos, though I told myself never to run but to move slowly, slowly. That night, I ran.

Once inside my tiny room, I bolted the door then picked up the phone and dialed Amanda's dorm at Trinity College, her number branded on the inside of my brain. All I could think about was hearing her voice, the sudden exhale of breath when she said my name: *Jit,* like a button popped off a tight blouse. At first, she'd laugh out loud, and then she'd shout at me: *Goddamn you. Where are you, Jit? You get your ass back here. Right now.*

"Right now," I said aloud. I wanted to giggle because Soldier Creek is exactly where I wanted to be. I remembered Amanda's plaid bathing suit, the elastic loose in one leg, hanging on the back line, and the stalky ends of the palmetto pricking her as she ran to get it. "Beat ya!" she'd yell at me, and I'd run as fast as my child's legs could go, but Amanda always raced past me and got to the creek first where she stopped dead still as I plunged in. "Com'on, com'on. Please," I'd say. But she never would.

"Please," I said to myself, glancing at the clock where I saw my last sand dollar propped up on the bare table, round and white and whole. And then before I could stop myself I saw that other scene: the shambles of my old room the night I left, my prized sand dollars crushed into fine white powder carpeting the floor, my clothes flung across the lamps, jammed beneath chairs, dangling from the curtains, the dresser. My pictures torn. My bathing suit ripped.

Mother did that.

I dropped the phone. *Mother did that.*

Out the window eucalyptus trees bent and thrashed in the wind. The leaves were water-spattered, trembling, and now I was trembling too, shaking all over because I needed to call Amanda. I wanted to ask her what had happened and what I should do. She'd be quick, incisive. She'd tell me the story so that it had a beginning, a middle, and an end, one that made sense, the shadows brightened, all uncertainty burned away. Except . . . except Amanda wasn't in Soldier Creek that night. Amanda was in North Carolina at Trinity College, and I was the only one who could figure out what happened between Mother and me and everything good and bad that led up to it.

Even as I was thinking this, I heard a woman crooning, a voice that drank up the air and emptied it clean and hungry in my lap. It was coming from somewhere beneath the trees. I moved closer to the window, listening.

Down home, body can't be free, missy . . .

A freedom song. I leaned out into the night, listening. I let the first tears fall.

But I didn't cry long. I let all the hurt and worry come up inside me, and then I sat very quietly on my bed and told myself to think like Amanda. "Don't be a scaredy cat," I heard her say. "Don't let the world gobble you up. But don't stay here alone either." And I knew it was true. I didn't want to be alone. I had to try to find my Aunt Katy. Katy Harper—not even blood kin, only my aunt by marriage, but I had a letter that said she was here somewhere, trapped in this city, dressed maybe in a long peasant dress with wooden beads around her neck or maybe in a beige pantsuit, looking tailored and trim and carrying a smart leather purse. She might have long hair by now or a soft double chin. She might be sitting behind a desk marking papers or breathing heavily into a phone. I had no idea. I hadn't seen her in six years, but if I could just find her I believed she would help me make sense of it all. Years ago she took my face in her hands and said gently, "Oh, honey, you're living in a minefield."

I grabbed the phone book and looked through all the listings for Harper. I'd already done this once, called all the numbers, listened to phones click off, listened to maids speaking Spanish, listened to men shouting and women saying, "No, senorita, I don't know no Mrs. Katy Harper."

That night I wrote down not just the phone numbers, but the addresses. Other people might know her. Neighbors. Storekeepers. Know where she was. I knew I'd have to go in search. I'd have to find Aunt Katy on foot. I picked out three addresses near Venice because Aunt Katy always liked water. I put stars beside those. And then I lay down on my bed, curled onto my side, and listened to a dog barking in the street, a door slamming, a squeaky window opening. And far below, I heard that soft crooning.

3

I woke to sparrows squawking in the catalpa tree. Outside my window gulls flew over the ocean, swooping suddenly to the sea and then rising effortlessly. A door banged across the hall, and I heard water running somewhere above me. The night before I had gone to sleep with the phone book tight in my arms, the only thing I had to hold onto. Now I fixed cereal and sat down to the three names on my list. I had four hours to look for Aunt Katy before I went to work at Earl Ray's. That thought made me hurry, quickly splashing water on my face and getting dressed.

Still, I took time to get out the little slip of paper from my purse. *My name is Katherine Soldier, but please call me Jit because that's what my father calls me.* I wrote that down on a card when I first arrived in Los Angeles just in case I went blank with fear, my throat splintered, when someone asked me who I was. The truth is, I never used it. But it was my security blanket, my safety net. Next to it I wrote this sentence: *I'm trying to find my Aunt Katy. Will you help me?*

When I stepped off the bus at Ocean Park, I saw a group of surfers leaning against the thick, bright colors of a mural decorating the side of a building. They were drinking sodas and turning their bronze faces to the sun. They ignored me, and I was relieved as I crossed the street and checked my paper. The first address was on 3rd Street. For good luck, I thought about Aunt Katy's golden curls falling over a red dress and her low, thrilling laugh, the way she leaned toward me once and said, "I don't ever want to eat another chicken part in my life!"

The outside of the building was splotched and faded, but there were three stories of motel-style apartments with dark green doors and a generous balcony at the top. I imagined Aunt Katy living on that third floor, walking out onto that balcony in the evening sun and staring at the Pacific Ocean as the sun spread its golden arms over the water. *Ridiculous!* I could hear Amanda say, but the truth is, I could imagine the two of us doing just that, me sipping a Coke and leaning on the railing while Aunt Katy told me a story about her childhood.

I had to force myself to knock on the door. It was one thing to stand in the street and imagine Aunt Katy welcoming me into her life and another to wait patiently in front of a closed door, not knowing who would open it. The apartment listed in the phone book wasn't the one at the top with a view, but a first-floor apartment that faced the dark alley.

I knocked and then stepped back, staring at my tennis shoes, noticing for the first time that they were gray with dirt. I'd barely made this assessment when the door flew open and a short, fat man with an unruly mop of black hair confronted me. "What? What you want?"

He was wearing a beach towel of faded mermaids wrapped around his middle, so I kept my eyes on his face, on his dark, anxious eyes and furrowed brow. "I'm looking for my Aunt Katy," I said. "Katy Harper . . . from Alabama."

"Well, you are, are you?" And then he smiled and turned back into the apartment. "It's okay, honey," he said to someone in another room. "Well, I don't know no Katy Harper."

"The phone book says it's this address." For some reason I felt compelled to show him the address I had listed on my notebook as if that would validate the interruption.

"Musta moved," he said. "People in and out of here like flies."

I took the bus up Sepulveda and got off before a row of green and blue and lavender bungalows, houses that looked about the size of one room with a roof slapped down on top. But they were pleasant and colorful and I stopped at a corner stand to buy a carton of orange juice with a straw, watching the wind tousle the branches of the palm trees and working up my courage to go and knock.

Before I could, two dark-haired kids pushed through the door, jostling each other. "It's my turn, get outta the way," the boy said. They were wearing swimsuits and flip-flops, and when they saw me, the girl said, "We're going out to get frogs. *Rana temporaria* is what they're called."

"Com'on," her brother yelled.

"You wanna go?" she asked, sliding one foot in and out of her flip-flop. "We have to get earthworms too." She held up a kitchen fork and a sand shovel.

I looked closely to see if there was any resemblance to Aunt Katy— that creamy skin? Large, gray eyes?—then asked if this was the Harper residence. "We're Benedicts," the girl said, tugging on her suit. "And we gotta get our frogs." She ran past me, arms swinging, almost tripping on the garden hose, then righting herself and yelling to her brother to wait up.

Disappointed, I started back toward the bus stop, seeing Aunt Katy as I first saw her that Thanksgiving Day in Soldier Creek. "You gotta see her," Amanda yelled at me from the upstairs window. "She doesn't look like anyone here in Soldier Creek." Then she laughed, her face squinched up. "She looks like Christmas." And I saw a woman lean her head back against the seat of a Plymouth, her mop of blonde curls framing a delicate face. Even from the distance of the window, I saw her lips were painted hibiscus red, her skin the soft white of a gardenia. She looked like a movie star, a goddess from another planet. Maybe I fell in love with her that day.

I told myself not to be discouraged as I ducked under the bus shelter awning where an old black woman sat upright on the bench in a straw sun hat and blue woolen gloves. I wondered why she wore the gloves since it was way too hot for winter clothes. She was pulling at her pants, picking lint off the navy blue jersey, and making humming sounds to herself. When I sat at the opposite end of the bench, she scooted over and tugged at my shirt, agitated and frowning, trying to say something. "Shhh-tut," she got out, patting my arm frantically.

"I don't understand," I said. "I'm sorry."

But she kept pulling at me, blinking and nodding her head. She tried again, the words not quite words, just garbled sounds that made no sense. I saw that she had no teeth and that the straw hat was unraveling around the edge. She grabbed my hand and kept nodding at me, then looked down at her feet.

I saw the sparkly ballet slippers, faded blue with silvery sequins, on the wrong feet.

"Okay, I can help." And I knelt down, ready to lift one foot.

"Shooooooes," she said, drawing out the word, and before I could prepare myself, a spasm jerked my stomach, sending quivers through my bowels.

Don't, I thought. *Oh, don't.*

But already I heard Mother's voice, the way it sounded when I was three: soft and wooing, like a whisper in the grass.

"Shooooooes," Mother said, holding up a pair of my sandals and pointing to my bare feet. That day the sky was a wash of pink, and we stood on the pier, a slight east wind kneeling at our backs, churning the water into ruffles of white. "Shooooes," she said it slowly, carefully. As if I were deaf. Though I understood what she wanted, at age three, I didn't talk. Not one word. I don't know why. Maybe I loved silence. Maybe I only wanted her to keep talking, to move closer so I could touch her thick, shiny hair. As a little girl I was always trying to find some way to get closer to her body, to fold myself into her arms, to seep into her skin. "Shooooes," she repeated, her mouth bunched up like a budding rose. She stared hopefully at me, her eyes wide and clear beneath a dark fringe of lashes, and when she leaned nearer, I rushed forward to touch her smooth, white hand. But as quickly, she jerked away.

Surprised, I stood very still, pressing my feet into the splintery wood until Amanda said softly, "Come here, baby. Come on, let me put on your shoes."

Even today I can feel the scratchy hardness of those boards, can see the waves lapping against the pilings and Amanda's hand holding up my scuffed white sandal. Her hands were barely larger or more agile than mine, but it was my sister who tended me, mothered me while my mother stood aside, watching, a little frightened, as if I were an animal caught in a trap, an animal whose captivity made her feel guilty.

Amanda held out my shoe. I took it gratefully while Mother watched, embarrassed and relieved. Between us, something was settled, a bargain struck. Mother had her guilt. I had my longing. What we both had was the solace of Amanda.

Though she was only two years older than me, Amanda always tried to explain the world outside Soldier Creek as if she were drawing a map, pulling me out of my small, improvised self. "In every social order there's a code of rightness, a seal of approval," she said one day as we waited for the school bus, "everyone jostling everyone else to achieve it. At college, I'll begin my upward climb. It's necessary, Jit." She gave me a piercing look. "We can't stay on the bottom forever." Then she looked away. "At least, I can't." And I believed her, believed that Amanda would do what Daddy couldn't do, believed that she'd save us from instability and obscurity, believed that she'd go to college, become educated, and then we'd all start to rise.

I could see her sitting in a classroom, her eyes glued to the words in a book. She would sit very still as if what was happening on the page was more real than real life. And more important. If I could whisper in her ear she'd say, "What?" not really looking up, only flicking at me with her hand as if I were a gnat flitting in her line of vision. But at that moment, I wasn't even sure if Amanda was in school at Trinity College or back home in Soldier Creek. I wasn't sure there was any such thing as a seal of approval, a code of rightness . . . or wrongness, for that matter. Everything I once believed had been blasted out of me. The only thing I was sure about was swimming.

"Hey, Dreamy, you're with me today." Suzanne sat across from me in the

dressing room at Earl Ray's, pulling her t-shirt over her head. Her wild, curly black hair sprang out of its clasp, tumbling over her shoulders, and she tossed her head, then gathered the hair back in a wide barrette. The girls had nicknamed me Dreamy; they said I lived in a world of my own.

"Okay." I didn't want to look at her, to be reminded of the day before. I was tired and nervous.

"Yesterday was a bitch," she said, unhooking her bra, "but you gotta know the deal with Randy. He's harmless, really."

"He doesn't seem harmless."

Suzanne laughed. "You gotta treat him like he's normal. If you treat him—"

"But he's not!"

"Yeah, but he wants to think he is. He wants everything to seem okay. Don't you know what that's like?" I could feel her looking at me.

"I don't want to see him again."

"Well, there's plenty more where he comes from. Listen, Dreamy," and now Suzanne sat down beside me, so close our bare legs almost touched. "You've gotta be smart about people, know what the hell's going on."

I looked away, embarrassed. I wanted to say if I knew how to be smart I wouldn't be here.

"Didn't they teach you none of that down home?"

I was about to tell Suzanne the truth about what they taught me when Earl Ray's voice buzzed over the intercom. "Ten minutes, girls."

Instinctively, I tensed and pulled on my bikini bottoms, bright red and so small I dared not look at myself in the mirror.

"Stay with me," Suzanne said as if we'd worked something out. "It's just us together here."

I nodded but didn't move. Those words: *just us*. Amanda used to say that all the time, binding the two of us together. "It's just us. Jit and Amanda. Amanda and Jit. The girls from Soldier Creek."

But she was wrong. It wasn't just us. It never was. There were four of us. Daddy, Mother, Amanda, and me. The Soldiers of Soldier Creek. And there were others, Josie at the One-Stop and Mr. Hesse at the high school, Toby Reznick and Johnny Turner and Teddy Ashirsch, all who played a part in what happened to me, what led up to that night when everything changed.

I closed my eyes and heard again the pulse of the waves, the shiver of wind through the longleaf pines, the damp hiss of bugs against the screens. And always, there was the creek. Soldier Creek.

How our story began.

4

"Paradise," Daddy said when he first saw those high bluffs above the creek, the woods full of titi and chinquapin and pines hidden in the little toe of Alabama. When he came down here in the late forties, the land was still raw and undeveloped, the ditches bright yellow with dandelions and goldenrod, the fields sweet with alfalfa and clover. Soldier Creek was mostly wilderness in the fifties and sixties, full of uncharted water and animals scurrying back into the brush. For people, we went ten miles into Moss Point where there was a public high school and a slew of churches, and in June the Speckled Trout Rodeo Queen parade with flashy majorettes and rusty go-carts and a brass marching band full of trombones and tubas. Moss Point was hardly big enough to scratch around in, but it was here that Amanda said we'd learn the ways of the world—how to be smart and pretty—while in Soldier Creek we were nobodies, like ordinary goldfish dropped in a jar. But the truth is, we weren't completely alone at the creek.

Across the water where a finger of sand jutted out, there was the One-Stop, nothing more than an old fishing shack painted a shiny gray like an oily sardine, built under the shade of an old oak tree. It had a porch around three sides and a tin roof that made the afternoon rain sound like evening music. Josie McLaughlin lived there and kept the store going by selling bait and groceries, renting boats to city fishermen who came down from Atlanta and Macon and Montgomery. Sometimes she went out with the men because she knew the waterways and the tides, where the fish were biting and how to sit quiet for hours waiting for the magic of the river to work. Then she'd bring the men in, clean the fish herself and bury their guts deep in the woods so her dogs wouldn't dig them up. She'd shake the grouper or red snapper in cornmeal and fry them in a skillet to a delicious golden brown while the men sat on her porch, drinking beer, then eating fish and hush puppies until their bellies sagged. After Josie collected their money, she sent them packing back to Macon or Montgomery or whatever small city they'd crawled out of.

Mother claimed Josie didn't always send them home. Sometimes Mother would walk out to the bluff beneath the swaying pines and stare hard at Josie's house, like a sentinel watching for a storm. Not that there was much you could see from this distance, but in the afternoon you could tell whether there was a car or truck parked under the shade tree, though from here it would appear no bigger than a child's toy. If Mother saw one, she'd look smug and satisfied. She'd hated Josie from the minute she laid eyes on her because Josie was everything Mother wasn't: bold and outspoken, tall and sharp-featured, with a halo of kinky hair the color of a waffle. Before meeting Josie, she'd been optimistic. The day Mother heard there was another woman at Soldier Creek, she was so excited she got dressed up in a tea dress and stockings, hoping the other woman would have ideas about how to keep your hair curly in the damp weather and what catalogues featured colonial bedspreads and Tiffany lamp kits. She said she imagined two women sipping iced tea and gossiping as they licked their green stamps and worried about their petunias and the sad streaks in their pound cakes. But when Mother arrived at the One-Stop, Josie was dressed in a t-shirt and men's boxer shorts, bathing her dogs and herself as well. She was wet in all the wrong places and when Mother got out of the car, Josie swung the hose around and splashed Mother's new white sling-back shoes. Mother screamed, but Josie laughed, and I think it was the laugh that cinched the bitterness.

But to be fair, Mother had never wanted to come to Soldier Creek, never wanted to leave the city of Birmingham where she had grown up as a little girl, where there were movies and restaurants and music. No, Soldier Creek was my father's dream.

He'd hitched down here when he was just a kid of nineteen, working on a construction crew, building a bridge across Perdido Bay. He's told me the story so many times I can see it as if it's my memory and not his. He was a bachelor then, working hard and sleeping deep, long days of physical labor, sunup to sundown, before he hightailed it through the thick piney woods the day Tom McCauley's arm was smashed by a piling of concrete, blood spurting like a fountain.

Frightened, Daddy ran up a riverbed, through woods full of water oaks and chinquapin and palmettos, not paying the slightest bit of attention to where he was headed until the trees thinned out and he was standing on a bluff overlooking water the color of a mackerel, waves lapping the shore. Beyond him, a point of white sand jutted out like a truce flag, dividing the creek from the bay. He actually thought he'd discovered it, thought it was his since his name was William Soldier. In that moment he swore he'd have it. Soldier Creek. It took him another two minutes to realize he was standing smack in the middle of a red ant bed and he danced, howling, into the water.

To Mother and Amanda, Soldier Creek was only a place of heat and bugs, of interminable boredom, full of loneliness and solitude and the invasion of nature. When you opened the doors in summer, locusts leapt out of the darkness, their pale shiny skin an eerie green in the dim porch light. Families of roaches flew across the kitchen, landing on the curtain, the crisp sound of a nail brush, then a mad dash for the tiny crack in the window. Spiders, big as your palm, hid on the top shelves in the bathroom and danced across your vision while you were stuck on the toilet. There were snakes—water moccasins, cottonmouths, rattlesnakes—and possums and raccoons and mice. Wasps and ticks and lizards and turtles. Eels and catfish swam in the creek. As did barracuda, crabs, and stinging jellyfish.

But Daddy saw none of this. Like me, he was a dreamer. He believed that fortune had turned its pale silver light on us, holding the moon firmly in the sky while our world gathered strength and order and we claimed what was best for us. Surely his spec houses would be built and sold so effortlessly that the land at Soldier Creek would be unequivocally ours. Surely the wilderness surrounding us would not be tamed, but Mother's gardens would flourish, magnificent with daffodils and irises and dew-drenched summer roses, pale yellow, soft pink, and dark, vivid red. Amanda might leave us, her energy catapulting her into the wider, tempting world, but she would always come back, perhaps to write about us, embellishing our story in Soldier Creek.

And me? All I ever wanted was the creek, the place where I shed my outer darkness, became quiet and still, a remarkable kind of creature. It was that simple.

Only Mother, it turned out, believed in divine justice. Only Mother believed our fate was sealed.

5

"It's a punishment," Mother whispered as we walked down the bluff to the creek. "A punishment from God." It was the summer of 1955, and it drove Mother crazy that I didn't talk, that, at age three, I might be a mute, a freak.

"God loves everybody," Amanda piped up, tugging on Mother's skirt so she'd listen. "God's going to teach her to say boo. Boo, Baby. Say *boooooooo!*"

"No, she'll never talk," Mother said, adamant, ashamed.

"Hush now," Daddy said, lifting me to his shoulders where I sat straight and tall with his hands clasped firmly to my knees. "Don't start."

And Mother didn't start. Instead, she pulled Amanda tight against her skirts, pushing Amanda's head into the soft cotton cloth so all I could see was her body squirming and twisting in Mother like a headless doll. "Mmmmm-mmh, Mama's smart one, Mama's little brainchild," Mother crooned, hugging Amanda to her as if she were a big teddy bear. Amanda giggled, holding onto Mother's skirt, but then she pushed away, skipping the few steps to Daddy and me, laughing over her shoulder at Mother just as Dodo, the big blue heron, our perennial visitor, swooped down from the top of a pine and landed at the edge of the pier. Dodo dipped her head and stood perfectly still, white feathers quivering, long neck extended. I reached for Dodo, needing to touch her, to feel her soft, perfect smoothness.

Beyond us, insects screeched. A mullet jumped. Then Daddy let me down so I could run to Dodo. "Give Dodo a fish," he said. "Go and feed her the fish, baby. Dodo's hungry."

"Hungry?" Mother laughed, her head thrown back, her neck white and arched like Dodo's. "Everyone's hungry. I just didn't know it. Papa could have traded me in that store. It wouldn't have made much difference because men all want the same thing. But I've won. Now I can sleep alone."

Because we had no idea what mother was talking about—*What store? And why would Grandpa Harper want to trade her?*—there was a sudden silence as if the air had sucked out our breath until Amanda's curiosity sprung her loose. "Who's going to sleep with Daddy?" she asked as easily as picking up a shiny thread. She looked from one to the other.

"Anybody who wants to," Daddy said, eyeing Mother.

Amanda clapped her hands. "Me and baby," she yelled, then tried to pull on my leg, but I was watching the seaweed float and drift beneath the water like secret hair. It tangled and untangled while silent fish floated by, open-mouthed, hungry. I wanted to touch them.

"Hush now," Mother said softly to Amanda. "It's just that I can't sleep at night. Things bother me and I can't sleep."

And then we were all quiet, listening to the crickets in the trees and the frogs in the bushes, until Mother broke the silence, her voice so low and troubled it frightened me. "Why didn't you tell me it would be so hard to live here, Will? These long nights when the heat won't let go and I'm—." There were tears in her eyes.

"Maggie," Daddy said gently. He eased toward her as if she were a china bowl he might break. "Honey, I'm sorry. I'm—." He opened his arms and she stepped closer.

"She won't talk. I try, even though the doctor said it wasn't my fault." She lay against him, limp and unbending like a piece of paper stuck to his chest. "I try, Will. You see I do."

I put my thumb in my mouth—it smelled like fish—and watched Mother and Daddy, their hands fitted together, their bodies uncertain, the wet on Mother's face and in her eyes. Gnats flew in a cloud around my head, but I couldn't move, couldn't flick them away. I stood in a trance, dizzy, paralyzed until Amanda bumped me and I could move again. "Com'on, baby," she said. "Say good night to Dodo. Nighty-night, bird. Nighty-night, creek."

There were times like that, I reminded myself as I swam laps for Earl Ray, when it seemed that everything that had broken loose between us would be knit back together, that Mother and Daddy would find their equilibrium, balancing like graceful dancers on the top of a music box. Our dreams would surely come true. Then all that was soft and hopeful would flutter around the room, drifting before our eyes like a cloud of gnats, and Amanda and I would grow up strong and resilient and giddy with love. But even as I watched Mother, I knew that something was deeply wrong. It wasn't just my silence she didn't like. There was something she was afraid of in me, something that leapt out of her when I reached toward her as I did that evening in late August.

It seemed like any other Sunday in our lives, with Daddy listening to the cheerleaders yelling "Go-Bama, Go-Bama, Go-Bama-Go," while the football players came running back, grim-faced, with muscles bulging, like ancient warriors rushing onto the field. Mother had been in her room, already putting on her nightgown, her hair spread out long across her shoulders so that she looked young and beautiful. Through the sheer cloth her breasts were round and white and full. Amanda and I were playing in the middle of the floor, and Amanda picked up a sock, stuck her hand in it to make a mouth. She opened and closed it with her fingers inside. "This is a wolf," she said, eyeing me suspiciously, "and it's going to *eat you up*," and then the sock was eating up my hair, my ears, my nose, and because I was startled, I began to cry, pushing at the wolf, flailing at Amanda. She looked startled. Then, seeing my distress, she reached around me with her small arms to hug me close. "Baby want hug, want hug, baby?" she crooned, and I felt a swirl of her hair on my face. Then she turned to Mother. "Look, Mama. Baby want hug. Hug her, Mama."

I put my hands out toward Mother, waving my fingers in the air, for Mother was all softness and curves and cotton dresses and whatever was cautious and fragile in me had stumbled to its knees, knocked flat by desire. I saw Mother sitting near, and I wanted that hug. Wanted it the way a mosquito wants blood.

But Mother didn't move. She looked straight ahead as if she'd just seen a shadow on the wall, something that demanded all her attention. Amanda said, "Mama?" then, "*Mama?*" more insistently, but still Mother didn't move while my fingers grabbed at air.

"Maggie," Daddy said, looking up from the TV. His voice was sharp, disapproving. Behind him players piled on top of each other in a mass of tangled bodies.

Mother turned to Daddy and surprised us all by the shy smile on her face.

"Hug her, Maggie," Daddy said, his voice low and urgent, though his face looked calm as if he were telling her he wanted more iced tea.

Mother leaned her body toward me as if she were about to comply, but then her shoulders slumped, her hands dropped limp in her lap, and she whispered, "I'm sorry." Her face gave itself over to sadness and despair, and Daddy stiffened, then got up abruptly and walked into the kitchen, making a lot of noise opening the refrigerator and taking out ice trays.

I couldn't have known at the time that one of the hard spots between them was Daddy's drinking. When he was drinking, he was like a runaway horse without restraint or direction, only the desire to keep going. I couldn't have known that he'd been in a dry spell for months, hoping to regain Mother's affection by his good behavior, by getting a loan from Mr. Turner and planning to build houses he was sure to sell to all the northern people moving down South to get warm. I couldn't have known that they were two people struggling to keep moving in the dark. Though Daddy often left after their fights, he always came back. All I knew was that it was Amanda who grabbed my hands, Amanda who stood beside me while they quarreled, excitement leaping between us, creeping from her skin to mine.

I wanted to say the same for Daddy, to believe he was there through thick and thin, but when he started drinking, as he did that night in late August, he became as slippery as smoke. He found a bottle he must have saved for just this sort of dilemma and within minutes he was gone, lurching out of our house as if he'd just been readmitted to the kingdom. That left Mother and Amanda and me sitting in the living room, Mother staring at me as if I were a foreign guest.

What happened next—after Daddy drove away—is that Amanda demanded ice cream as if sugar could cure any sadness. All I remember is that Amanda stood in the open doorway with her bowl full of chocolate ice cream, looking out at the backyard where Daddy had just driven away. She gazed out into the blackness. Bugs flew in, moths and stinkbugs drawn to the light. They whirled and dove in a flutter of wings. "Is Daddy going to hell?" she asked, turning toward Mother, her spoon halted halfway to her mouth.

"Yes," Mother said, looking white and pale as if she were going to be sick.

"Yes," I whispered, but neither of them heard me. I was turned away, staring at a moth skittering up the wall.

6

Eventually Daddy did go to hell. Before he lost everything, each morning I'd go down to sit with him on the pier while he drank his coffee and I practiced my spelling words, the two of us watching the movement of the creek and the way the sun spread its fiery fingers across the sky. We didn't talk much because we didn't need to. We believed we could see through the pampas grass into the very workings of the island where turtles spawned and mosquitoes lay violent and breathing in the sandy mud.

And then one morning in the middle of October, the year I was ten, Daddy didn't show up. I stood on the pier alone, my notebook splotched with water stains, dried and wrinkled in places, smooth in others. I sat down and waited, though I'd never had to wait before. Daddy was usually there ahead of me, coffee steaming in the air, the newspaper spread out on his lap. I dangled my feet near the water, playing with the idea of dipping the toe of one shoe in the creek, but resisted, knowing Mother would notice. I printed out my spelling words—*casual, chemical, coda, colonial, cucumber*— erased my mistakes, not worrying until the sun flashed bright over the trees, and I knew it was late. When I turned toward the house, I saw Daddy stumbling down the bluff as if his legs no longer supported him. As he came nearer, he looked haggard, pale, his blondness grayed by exhaustion. He stopped before he got to me, gazing back at the house.

"I've lost it," he muttered to himself. He kept repeating that sentence until I knew, without really knowing how or why, that he'd lost Soldier Creek. I heard the frogs in the marsh singing, the gulls crying above my head. Insects nipped at my bare arms as my hands loosened and my spelling words slid from my lap into the creek. I watched the pages thicken, darken, then sink like stones. I stared hard into the water and watched *casual, chemical, coda, colonial, cucumber* drift in shivery lines at the bottom of the creek.

"He was reckless," Amanda said later, stabbing the air with her fist; when it came to Daddy, she was merciless in assigning blame.

And the truth is, he gambled on the future and lost. In 1955 he'd built five houses in Moss Point, and in 1960 he mortgaged our land to build five more, then ran out of money, the houses half-finished, pitiful, like half-dressed mourners. Weeks later we saw the notices—ten months of them—stuffed in the back of his closet like old, dirty laundry. Almost as suddenly he lost Mother and moved to an old fishing shack five miles away at Perdido Bay. Mother and Amanda and I stayed in Soldier Creek, renting the house we'd once owned from Mr. Turner, the local banker in Moss Point.

As these things were happening to Amanda and me, they seemed random, without pattern or meaning, a freak occurrence like a hurricane in December or a snowstorm in June, but now I wonder if they weren't bound up in the secret suffering of our parents. After Daddy left us, I couldn't sleep but would lie in my bed at night, worrying, staring out the window at the creek as if he might come paddling along in a boat just to say hello. But he didn't. During the daytime I was sleepy and clumsy, spilling my milk, dropping off in a doze in the middle of my crowder peas. It was then that I learned one of their secrets and set myself irrevocably on a course.

It was one warm Sunday afternoon in late October, and Mother was helping Amanda make a Halloween costume—Amanda insisted on being a pirate with a curved cardboard sword and a black, swashbuckling-style cape. "I want the cape lined in red taffeta," Amanda said, and Mother, with pins in her mouth, nodded. *Oh yes, you'll do whatever Amanda needs you to do*, I thought, surprising myself with rage against Amanda. Scissors and black thread sat waiting on the chair. Red taffeta would be purchased tomorrow.

"I think I'll be a hummingbird," I said, inching closer.

No sooner had I mentioned this, than Amanda turned and said dramatically, "Don't be *stupid*. It's Halloween. You have to be something scary."

Mother raised her eyebrows and nodded at me.

"Scary," Amanda repeated. "A bandit or a city orphan."

And then they huddled together over the cape as if I'd never been in the room.

Deftly, unseen by either of them, I picked up the scissors and fled, dropping them in the azalea bushes by the pear tree. *There*, I thought, *that will show them*. I started out through the woods to Daddy's cabin, pushing through saw palmettos and slash pines, stepping over raccoon tracks and deer scat.

When I arrived, Daddy was repairing a crab trap, down on his hands and knees, fixing a loose, bent wire. He'd gotten a job at Mitchell's Sawmill outside Moss Point, working Tuesdays through Saturdays. Now he was squatting in the grass, hunched over, intent on his work. When he saw me, he pushed the trap to one side and pulled me into his lap, holding me close. He smelled of machine oil and pine straw. So familiar, I started to cry.

"Now, what's this? What's got my girl from Soldier Creek all tied up in a knot?" He jiggled me, trying to make me laugh.

"It's not the same without you," I whispered. "Mother makes me nervous."

Daddy went quiet and still. He let me loose and stood up, looking out past the scrubland and marsh grass to where our skiff undulated in the roll of the tide. "Things have never been right with your mother," he said abruptly, then stood looking at the bay as if making a decision. "After her mother died when she was eight, she idolized her father. He was all she had."

I nodded. I knew this. It was family history. To Mother, Grandpa Harper was a saint. But there must have been a sadness in my face that hinted at alarm because Daddy said softly, "Let's go out in the boat." And I didn't know if that was the end of the story. When he gunned the motor, diesel fumes filled my nostrils and I watched as the gasoline spread through the water in a flood of colors. We sped across Perdido Bay to Soldier Creek, the wind chilling our faces, blowing our hair, until we reached the Narrows where we dropped anchor in the thick, marshy reeds with their bleached yellow tips. We both put out our lines and waited for the fish to find us. We were quiet. When Daddy started talking again, his voice was gentle as if he'd just awakened from a nap.

"Your mother had a hard childhood," he said, looking up quickly at me, then as quickly into the depths of the water. "There was a lot of damage done." It was the closest he ever came to condemning Mother, and now I so wanted to hear the story that I too stared at the reeds, hoping distraction would hide my eagerness.

"It's her story," he said, "but I'm going to tell you what I know about it." As if uncertain about this telling, he slumped forward, brooding, letting his line dangle loose. If we caught a fish we'd have been surprised and irritated, bothered by the interruption. Daddy sighed and started again, telling me that when Mother was about my age her father went to work for a mining company in Birmingham, a company dead set on busting the unions. "Grandpa Harper was hired as a spy who could get the goods on the miners, find out where the weak links were. They sent him up to Walker County."

As Daddy talked, I stared at the still water, which looked like a sheet of stained glass with seaweed lying strangled and dark underneath. Nothing moved except the gnats and a dragonfly buzzing just above our heads.

"Your mother said she was frightened that first day," Daddy continued, looking out over the reeds shining a golden rust in the afternoon light. "She said it was so foreign, so ugly, she didn't even want to breathe. The air was thick with dust, the mountains bare, strip-mined. She knew they were going to the general store so her father could talk to the men, but she didn't know why. She only understood that she wasn't to speak, wasn't to interrupt his work, no matter *what* was said.

"When they got to the store, your mother . . . she was a girl no bigger than you are . . . and her brother, Buddy, stuck to Grandpa Harper like flies," Daddy said. "Grandpa Harper just looked at the men slumped around a wooden table in the middle of the room playing poker. They were a hard bunch, poor and illiterate. You can imagine their faces—pinched, dirty, a mouthful of bad teeth. Except one. Your mother said he looked soft, with pink skin and hair so thick the grease couldn't hold it flat. 'Course, the men didn't bother to look at them directly, only through the haze of cigarette smoke. But Grandpa Harper pulled out a chair and sat down." I could imagine Mother sitting very still, very quiet in that country store, her dress pulled tightly over her knees, the way she sat each Sunday in church. And I knew she would be watching, waiting . . . just as I would have been . . . for something bad to happen.

"The men were playing seven card draw, using matchsticks for chips and cards so old some of the numbers were rubbed off. They kept playing, smoking and spitting, ignoring Grandpa Harper and the kids until Grandpa Harper leaned over and said something to them. Then those men looked up fast, but all he did was touch the top of your mother's head. "And the girl," he said. "I'll play for the girl."

The girl. I saw the men's mouths open. Funny black holes. Tongues like fat gray worms inching out of darkness. And then I saw Mother. Her jaw clamped shut. Eyes wide as saucers.

"Your mother said he didn't mean it. Said he was joking."

Daddy jerked his pole as if he wanted to make sure no fish were getting curious and hungry, anxious for lunch. He cleared his throat and stared hard at the sky. "Then that damn Harper just waited for the next round to begin. Only the pink-cheeked one stood up. 'This ain't right, you sorry sonsofbitches. Ain't but a girl.' The other men looked over at your mother and started laughing." When Daddy paused, I could imagine them cackling, snickering, showing their yellow, crooked teeth. "Well, they waited. They wanted to see what your Grandpa Harper would do. And that didn't take long. 'Stand up, girl. Stand up and let down your pretty hair.'"

"That's right," Daddy nodded. "That's what he made her do, and don't you know she went pale as a sheet. She didn't move until he pulled her up himself. She had these long thick braids across each shoulder, and you can just see her standing before them like she was being examined under a bright light. 'Go on now,' Grandpa Harper said. 'Let it loose.' And she did it real slow, looking all the time at her father, who kept nodding at her until it all spilled across her back and shoulders, all that long, pretty, chestnut brown hair.

"'Ain't right,' the greasy-haired fellow said again. But no one was listening. They were waiting to see what Grandpa Harper would do. And what he did was look at his open card and raise the next bet four more matchsticks."

I couldn't look away from Daddy though he was staring into the water as if memorizing the current. "That scoundrel," he muttered, "made her trust him, then took—" but he didn't finish. Instead, he stiffened as if he were seeing something terrible. I wondered if he saw what I saw: a little girl standing next to her father, her hair spreading across her shoulders, its beauty suddenly hateful, embarrassing. Were those nasty men allowed to touch Mother's hair? I felt sick to my stomach. I thought of Mother's hair now, how she kept it pinned up and never let me touch it.

"He didn't even make the showdown," Daddy went on. "Those men probably laughed at him, but old Harper wouldn't quit. The next round he had a queen of diamonds and a two and three of hearts showing, a jack and a four of hearts as pocket cards, but still he refused to fold. And your mother standing there the whole time, the walls like painted soot, the floor as much mud as wood. Then she had to go to the bathroom. Said she couldn't help it. All that attention. All that anxiety. You can imagine what it was like." Daddy was quiet for a minute, and I had no choice but to see my mother standing there, pressing her legs tight together, begging her body to be still, then feeling the trickle down her thighs, and the inevitable puddle.

"She started crying," Daddy said. "And all Grandpa Harper said was, 'Hush now. Don't be doing that.'"

Daddy looked at me. I felt my mother's humiliation. And what would the men do to her if Grandpa Harper lost? I was confused, but something prevented me from asking Daddy. I saw her—a girl like myself—being made to clean up after them, to wash their dirty clothes and scrub their grimy feet. There was something worse, some possibility too horrible to get my mind around.

What Daddy said next about that game I remember only in snatches, something about those scrawny old men playing for another hour. Then another half hour. He said Grandpa Harper never smiled, never frowned, even when the men stared openly at Mother, their eyes curious, their gold rimmed teeth flashing when they pulled on a plug of tobacco.

"After another hour," Daddy said, "damn if Grandpa Harper's luck didn't change with a pair of kings and a flush. Now he picked up more matchsticks. Sat up straighter. At the end of three hours, he scooped up the pot, took hold of your mother's hand and without a word, walked both children out the door."

Daddy looked away from me, his shoulders slumped in exhaustion as if he'd just climbed a mountain. He sighed and fiddled with the weight of his pole. "And you know what your mother said about that day?"

I shook my head.

"She said that bastard saved her, *saved her*, and she never once asked why he'd offered her up in the first place."

Daddy gave me this story as if it were a revelation about my mother, a story that might protect me from my fears. *Mother isn't right. She doesn't understand betrayal. Or is it danger she misunderstands?* Later in my life I would understand the sexual nature of this story, something I understood only instinctively then.

When I got home that evening, I stood in the doorway to the kitchen watching as Mother rearranged the cupboards above the sink. She stood on a stool and pulled out all the cans, stacking them in neat, distinct piles. She was humming to herself and didn't know I was there. I wanted suddenly to help her, to be the one who handed her the tomato soups so she didn't have to bend down for them.

When I took a step toward her, she turned and almost lost her balance before grabbing hold of the cabinet door.

"Goodness, you scared me," she said, steadying herself. "I wasn't paying the least bit of attention..." but then she stopped as if she'd just realized I wasn't Amanda. "Hand me those soups," she said, and dutifully I did.

Three days later I got up early in the morning when only the sparrows and starlings were awake, when the creek shimmered like a black field of glass. I'd found an old toothbrush and with a jar of soapy water I got down on my hands and knees and began scrubbing the kitchen floor. I started at the sink where the grime sometimes darkened the seams of the linoleum and left shadowy spots of stain. I worked the soap into the floor with the bristles of my brush, scouring in little circles until the soapy water became gray and flecked with dirt. When the light brightened behind me, I worked faster, my arm pushing hard into the floor, rushing to get it all done before Mother and Amanda got up.

I was in the middle of the kitchen, my back to the door when I felt her behind me. My hand still moved in circles, but the rest of me stiffened. I longed to turn and say, "You don't have to do any of it!" But the next instant she was gone. The sound of the birds came back. Light suddenly swept across the kitchen floor. I stood up quickly and poured the jar of water into the sink and tucked the toothbrush into my pocket.

"What are you doing?" Amanda asked a few minutes later as I knelt to wipe up the suds. She eyed me suspiciously. "Mother said you're doing something weird." Amanda picked up a doughnut off the counter, stuffing half of it in her mouth, sugary crumbs crusting on her lip.

"I was helping Mother," I said, knotting up the rag.

"Oh, silly," Amanda said, yanking the rag from me and wiping her hands. "Mother doesn't need any help." And then she leaned nearer and whispered. *"This is what she does all day. Do you want her to think she doesn't do it well enough?"*

I winced. Had I gotten it all wrong again?

Mother came into the kitchen, tying the sash of her old green robe and picking up a glass of milk Amanda had let sour on the table. "For heaven's sake, we can't afford to waste food!" Mother frowned but her voice was light, easy. She ignored me as I crouched still on the floor.

I got up and went to my room. A different image came into my head. It was of Mother cleaning up after her father, picking up his dirty socks, his soiled underwear, wiping up the yellow stains from the toilet seat, picking up wet towels, and then bringing him a cup of tea, some Vicks VapoRub, maybe a hot water bottle, its bloated red belly held out like a prize. What if she liked it? Thought he was special? A "scoundrel," Daddy had called him. And that's when something stubborn came up in me. If Grandpa Harper did what Daddy said he'd done, how could Mother love him?

From that day onward, I protected the distance that existed between my mother and me. Before that, I'd yearned to close it, hoped for her eyes to light up when I came in the room as they did for Amanda. But now I insisted on that distance, made it my own. I was obedient and prompt, kept my room exceptionally neat, hung my clothes in sober groupings, lined up my sand dollars like quarters on the windowsill. I made up my bed every day, did my homework out on the pier.

And it was all right because Amanda was there, diverting us with her constant talk of school and books and food. "Let's get some ice cream! I've gotta have some ice cream!" she'd demand, rushing Mother and me into the car for a trip to the Piggly Wiggly in Moss Point. Amanda was our safety net. "I'll do something *marvelous*! You wait and see."

I believed her. At night I sat on the back porch, listening to the waves beat against the pier and dreamed about our lives once Amanda had risen to the top of the heap.

7

Sometimes when I swam at Earl Ray's, I wished I had a friend in L.A., someone I could talk to about my childhood in Soldier Creek. Or maybe I'd start in the middle, maybe with that day in late March when the wind whipped through the mimosa trees and swept pine needles across the lawn, the day the big hand of fate reached down and turned us in another direction. I was sixteen. Amanda was barely eighteen.

"You won't believe this!" Amanda yelled as she ran past me into the kitchen, waving a letter in her hand. When she stopped, she did a little jig, dancing in a circle. "I got it, Mother. I got it . . . the scholarship!" And then she leapt onto a chair and raised the letter in triumph.

It wasn't just any old scholarship, but a big, fat scholarship to the best college in the south: Trinity College in North Carolina. Amanda hugged herself. She was ecstatic.

As suddenly Mother started crying, a kind of violent weeping that made Amanda go silent and still. Amanda let the letter drop from her hand, then stepped down from the chair. She seemed suddenly weary, old, her forehead wrinkled in a puzzled frown. Then she bent to pick up the letter, and when she looked up I saw, for the first time, something stony and hard in her face. "Mother, don't. Don't ruin this for me." And I was glad to see Mother rebuffed, took my own stony satisfaction from Amanda's reproach.

Without another word, Amanda walked out of the room, the letter left facedown on the kitchen table.

Of course Mother rushed after her, the letter gripped in her hand. "I'm sorry," she said, and I heard them talking in the living room, their voices thick with emotion, but now it was Amanda who was crying, Amanda who was saying, "But don't you *see?* Don't you get it? This is our chance. Don't you want me to succeed?"

I stared out the kitchen window at the scuppernong arbor, at the thick mass of green and the tiny orange fruit that tasted so tart against my tongue. I should be out there picking the fruit, hiding in the shadows while

Mother reassured Amanda. Of course she must go to Trinity College.

And yet as I swam with Lisa around the tank, back-flipping through the water, my eyes closed as if lost in a slippery dream, what I remembered even more vividly than the day of the scholarship was the day Amanda left Soldier Creek and there were only two of us, the day the world turned its back on Mother and me.

It was a hot, stuffy Sunday afternoon in late August, no breeze blowing, only a suffocating airlessness rising like dust from the ground. "Dog days," Amanda said, and I knew she was thrilled to be escaping Soldier Creek.

At the airport, she held tight to Mother and me even while cruising the windows for her plane. And then we all saw it, a small DC-9 that would take her straight up to North Carolina, a place she'd never been. When they announced her flight, Amanda hugged us again. She whispered something to Mother and laughed happily, kissing her on the cheek before she turned to me. "Now, don't be too good," she said, squeezing me, and giving us both a big, infectious smile. Then she hitched up her shoulder bag and rushed out the door before any of us could work up a good cry. Mother and I watched until all we saw was her red sleeve waving from the plane, then the plane took off, slipping into the clouds like a fish diving into moss.

Alone with Mother in the car, we were so quiet I could hear the clock ticking away every second, could feel the pressure of Mother's toe on the accelerator, her mind going tight and busy with worry. I couldn't think yet, my life still bound up with Amanda's leaving and my staying, and I simply repeated her last words to me, "Don't be too good," but what I really thought was *I'm on my own now.*

The truth is, once Amanda left, I thought the whole world would change as if a mountain you glimpsed every morning would suddenly vanish from sight. You'd walk out of your house, glance toward what should have been there and realize nothing would ever be the same. And yet the bus ride to school the next day was no different than it had always been. Little seventh-grade boys sent spit balls whizzing through the air, while the older boys said, "Fuuu-ck," real low and sweet as if it were a two-syllable endearment. Four kids got on at Finley Road, elbowing their way to the back, already sweating in the late August heat.

I was relieved to have homeroom and first period with the same teacher, but anxious because Mr. Hesse had been Amanda's journalism advisor on the newspaper. To him, she was the smartest thing since Emily Dickinson. All last year I watched him talking with Amanda outside the editorial offices, his short neat body clothed in wrinkled khaki pants or gray woolen trousers, the back pocket twisted inside out, wet grass stuck to his cuffs, a button missing. Always I wanted to go up and straighten the pocket, pat it flat to his buttocks, pick off the blades of grass. Today Mr. Hesse's back pocket was bunched up as if it hadn't been properly ironed, wadded in a ball, and I felt oddly satisfied as I watched him talk to a dark-haired boy in wire-rimmed glasses. When the boy turned away, I noticed that his left ear was strange, like a folded apricot squashed flat against his skin. When he caught me staring, he quickly flicked his longish hair over that ear, then sat down in an empty desk across from me and looked out the window.

When the second bell rang, I was leaving with the herd when Mr. Hesse looked up from his desk, his clear blue eyes freezing me in place. "You're Amanda's sister, aren't you?"

For a rebellious moment, I wanted to say no—"No, I'm me!"—but then I saw that his shirt collar was turned under on one side and a giddy rush of tenderness burst inside me, squeezing out all protest. I nodded yes, mentally straightening his collar. My fingers held it smooth.

"Well, that's fine," he said, smiling. "It will be my pleasure to get to know you."

To get to know me. I wondered what that meant.

While Mr. Hesse talked about *Jane Eyre* and nineteenth-century British education in the second week of school, I hunched over my desk, making furious wave patterns across my page. Below them, I drew a clump, and wrote BRITAIN, sunk into the sea, a rocklike hunk of coral. Jane Eyre was a small fluttering fish, feeding innocently off the coral while in its more hidden crevices lurked Rochester, an octopus, one tentacle squeezing the life out of a bloody but colorful fish. His other tentacles were relaxed, waiting for the next prey. I wanted to put Helen Burns somewhere, a pale, transparent fish, her internal organs exposed, and then the crab, St. John Rivers.

When the bell rang, I looked up from my drawing into the dark intensity of Toby Reznick's brown eyes. Then my gaze went to his ear, the skin delicate and white, bleached at the fold as if empty of blood. Blushing, I jumped up, fumbling with notebooks and papers, and rushed out of the room.

In Algebra II, he was already seated when I arrived, his tall frame hunched in the seat, his white t-shirt stained with half moons of sweat. When I sat down, I didn't see the piece of paper held out to me.

"Here." His voice was deep and hollow as if it came from inside a long tube. "You dropped this." I saw the scrawl of water and rocks; mortified, I quickly folded the picture. But Toby flicked the hair over his ear and smiled—a flash of perfect white teeth, his wire-rimmed glasses moving up a fraction on his nose. Relief flowed through me. *He likes me. I don't have to worry about staring at his ear.*

That evening when I arrived home, Mother was in the kitchen stirring soup in a pot. "I've bought you something," she said quietly. She seemed anxious but also pleased with herself as she fastened her eyes to my body. "I've noticed you're outgrowing your clothes, getting a shape." "*Boobs,*" Amanda would have hooted. *"They're boobs, Mother."* Embarrassed, I crossed my arms over my breasts and looked down at my shoes. I had on a yellow sun dress with a square neck and full skirt, a little tight under the arms, but still roomy in the waist. It was bright and cheerful. "Come see," Mother said and there on the sofa in the living room were three long-sleeved dresses in pink and blue and dark green. Each had a white Peter Pan collar with a little ribbon bow in the center and four buttons down the front. *"Sixth grade!"* Amanda would have crowed, but I couldn't get away with that.

"Thank you," I said and touched the fabric.

"Well, take them up to your room," she said. "I'm sure they'll fit. And then you won't be embarrassed anymore."

I carried the dresses upstairs and hung them in my closet. On impulse, I turned off the light, stepped inside, holding them, hugging them close to my body. I put my face into the cloth as if they were beautiful, colorful and daring, imagining myself praised and admired, my whole self changed by something I had no inkling of. *A pleasure to get to know you*, Mr. Hesse had said. And yet what happened instead was that all the longing I'd stored up as a little girl came roaring back. I saw my mother sitting still and frightened in the room, unable to touch me, and despite all my good intentions, I began to cry. I sat down in the floor of my closet, wondering what I'd done to hurt my mother. It must have been something awful in childhood, something I couldn't see, couldn't stop. Tears wet my cheeks, my chin. I couldn't help myself. And for the first time since she'd left, I desperately missed Amanda. "Come home," I actually said out loud. *Come home.* If she were here, Amanda would sit next to me, our knees quietly touching, the spill of clothes brushing our hair. She'd lean against me and whisper the truth. "You can't change Mother. She is the way she is."

During homeroom the next day, Mr. Hesse lingered beside my desk, his khaki pants stained with tiny ink marks that blurred into blobs. "Could you stay a minute after first period, Jit? I promise not to make you late for your next class." He smiled a shy, hopeful smile, and I nodded, dizzy with happiness.

I wore the blue dress Mother had bought—it was loose and shapeless—but no one seemed to notice how absurd I looked. Maybe no one saw me at all.

But when I glanced over at Toby, he was staring at me, not the kind of relaxed connection we'd made in Algebra II, but with a question in his eyes. Confused, I looked away, out the window where squirrels dashed furiously up and down the trees, then stopped furtively, their bushy tails still.

"There's a student council election coming up, and I thought you might help," Mr. Hesse said when I stood before his desk after class. He looked particularly vulnerable to me sitting down at his teacher's desk, a cowlick sticking straight up from the part in his hair like a rooster's comb. I wanted to pat it back down, smooth out the edges.

Before I could stop myself, I nodded yes. I could help make posters and hand out flyers. "Good," he said, marking something on his paper before he looked up again to catch my eye. "I knew this was the kind of thing you'd be helpful with. And I'm going to ask a special favor of you. Toby Reznick, who sits beside you, is a real whizz at math. Mr. Schultz and I have been encouraging him to run for treasurer, and we've got him ninety-five percent convinced, but because he's new, he doesn't have anyone to give his introductory speech"—Mr. Hesse had not released me from his slate blue eyes—"and immediately, I thought of you."

I squirmed out from under his gaze, looking instead at an enlarged pore just above his eyebrow, a huge gaping hole around which skin puckered. He didn't say why he'd immediately thought of me. Was he trying to trap me? Was this some trick?

"I know you'll do a good job, and he seems to feel comfortable with you. That'll make things a little easier for him." Then the bell rang and Mr. Hesse said quickly, "That's all from me. But check with Toby. The introductions will be given next Friday."

I walked out into the air as if I'd been slapped. My skull pressed tight against the skin, trying to break loose. *Make a speech!* The thought made me feel huge, like a loud lettered sign, something that said *STOP! LOOK!* I ducked into the girls' bathroom where three senior girls leaned against the sinks, smoking, pale smoke drifting lazily toward the ceiling. They looked suspiciously at me, then dismissed me as irrelevant and went back to their conversation. Behind them the concrete walls sweated like bleeding stones. I escaped into a stall, lifted my dress and sat. Mr. Hesse was thinking of Amanda. Of course, that was it! Eventually it had to come out: the comparison, as if being sisters implied any connection other than the accident of blood. For one hot moment I hated her, despised her. She was the cause of this new humiliation. Now I was caught. If I refused to do the speech, Mr. Hesse would think me a coward, someone who had gone back on my word, but at the same time I *couldn't* do it, couldn't get up on stage and speak.

Late to Algebra II, I slipped in while Mr. Schultz was at the board, his back to the class. Though I couldn't look at Toby, I could feel his gaze burning through me like a hot flame, asking the question. So that was what he wanted. Chill bumps burst out on my arms. Then for a single instant, I saw myself standing up on stage, as willful and confident as Amanda, the student body gaping in awe as I gave my speech. Me, Jit Soldier. And in that moment, I knew I had to try.

Now that the decision was made, I was less horrified, but more anxious. When I got home Mother wasn't upstairs ironing as she usually was, but in the kitchen taking wadded-up paper out of a box and bunching it on the counter.

"I've got to make a speech at school," I blurted, trying to imagine how Amanda would announce it—grabbing for potato chips, kicking off her shoes, giving quotes and speaking alliterative first sentences to attract Mother's attention.

Mother stopped pulling out balls of paper and looked quickly at me. She smiled. "Well," she said absentmindedly, then she leaned over the box and silence exploded between us. I prayed she'd look at me again, see that I'd worn the blue dress and say something hopeful about my speech.

"It's for student council," I said louder, tapping my foot. "Remember last year when Amanda—"

"Dead!" Mother leapt back, a shocked look on her face as if she'd just witnessed a terrifying event. "They're all dead."

I looked where Mother was staring and saw two roaches turned over on their backs inside the box, legs crimped to their body, a reddish shine to their papery wings.

"Student council," I repeated softly, still staring at the dead bugs.

"I was going to use this box to send Amanda—"

"Next Friday."

"—some special thing."

Neither of us moved. Neither of us made an effort to remove the bugs from the box. I turned toward the stairs, feeling heavy and awkward as if my bones had thickened, my head gone light. It wasn't really the students I'd imagined watching me up on stage, but Mother standing at the back of the auditorium, listening intently to my speech.

Three nights later Mother was still fixing up a box for Amanda. She'd made chocolate chip cookies with walnuts and had wrapped them in aluminum foil. When I came down from my room at 8:00, Mother had an old apron over her dress, the kitchen was a mess, and yet she looked more alive than she had in days. Her face was practically shining.

Encouraged, I said, "Tomorrow's my speech," from the distance of the door. I'd worked on the speech every afternoon, alone in my room, always seeing Toby at the blackboard, self-absorbed and focused. That's what I decided to emphasize: *he was focused.* Now I stood on one foot, then the other, the free foot stubbing lightly against the wood molding.

"Tomorrow?" she said. A streak of flour painted one side of her nose.

"Yes."

I dug my nails into my palms, held my breath, waiting, but she only looked into the depths of the box, rearranging something she'd already put in. "I hope I've got this packed right."

I felt the heat of the stove, heard the drip of the faucet. I waited a bit longer, holding my speech in my hand, not waving it around, but folded over, all those careful words tucked inside. But when Mother turned to me, her eyes were distant, cloudy, and I knew then she was missing Amanda.

I went back up to my room and without thinking snatched the blue dress off its hanger. A button popped off and rolled under my bed. The ribbon bow came untied. Before I could stop myself, I put my fingers in the arm seams and pulled. One sleeve began to tear. I pulled harder until loose threads spilled into my hands. I felt something so close to pleasure I was frightened and threw the dress back into the closet. I thought of Mr. Hesse staring at me from the emptiness of the doorway. He looked both puzzled and shocked. What kind of girl was I? What kind of girl?

At school the next day I was exhausted and anxious, but as I walked into Mr. Hesse's room, a jolt of energy flooded my veins. The air exploded with tension. Mr. Hesse looked up and smiled at me, a smile that warmed my heart, before he turned back to Henry Lewis, the guy running for president. When I saw Toby, he looked as nervous and awkward as I did in his stiff white shirt already stuck to his back with streaks of sweat. First period had been canceled in order to have the assembly, and homeroom was chaotic. Mr. Hesse seemed disorganized, distracted. A dot of dried blood bloomed on his chin, and his cowlick stuck straight up, revealing what I'd never noticed before: a small, neat bald spot. When the bell rang, we rose in a chorus of noise because assemblies meant time away from books and teachers, time to gossip with friends.

I picked up my books, leaving with the rest, the first catch of nervousness in my stomach like little butterflies trapped in a jar. My speech on note cards lay stacked perfectly on top of my books, and as I walked by Mr. Hesse's desk, he looked up with his penetrating blue eyes, looked deeply into my own as if he could walk right into my soul. *It will be a pleasure to get to know you.* I gasped, felt myself float on air. For the first time, I looked directly back at him as if we were living on the same planet.

Then he stood and smiled at me. *Me.* I felt a thrill of recognition.

He held out his hand and smiled. "Give them your best, Amanda!" he said, pulsing a little on the balls of his feet as if he too might rise further in the air.

He neither recognized nor corrected his mistake. Instead he looked to the next person behind me. "Good luck, Toby."

I couldn't get my breath. *Breathe*, I told myself, walking slowly forward out of Room 22, but something inside me knotted and balked. I could feel it dislodging, the bile rising and sneaking into my throat, and I rushed away from the crowd, into the restroom where I entered a stall, lifted the toilet seat and heaved until there was nothing left but hollow sound.

From the distance, I heard the muted strains of "The Star-Spangled Banner." I wiped my mouth and tried to calm myself, to move in the direction of the auditorium. Applause spilled from the windows as I began to run toward the auditorium door. I saw all the people turned toward the stage, actually paying attention, and when I thought about getting up and speaking my words, I saw Mother staring at me in that pool of silence and then turning away in the kitchen. Quickly, I knelt in the grass, throwing up nothing but empty air.

8

I spent the rest of the morning in the nurse's office, a wet cloth plastered to my head. Too embarrassed to move, I moaned when she asked how I was and begged for more aspirin. "Please," I said, trying to be polite.

That afternoon on the bus to Soldier Creek, I looked at the oak trees shadowing the road and then into the bright sunlight when the branches separated and the tall skinny pines flattened against the sky. I stared at the ditches on the side of the road, a smear of red dirt stealing through the blackberry vines. All around me kids threw paper wads and yanked on each other's books while couples made out in the backseat, a coat draped over their heads. I sat quiet and still. When the bus stopped at the creek road, fear bloomed in my chest. I didn't want to get off, to admit that I'd failed.

I walked slowly, crunching oyster shells with my shoes. I hoped that Mother would be in Amanda's room taking a nap, but when I came through the back door she stood at the sink, peeling potatoes, her head tilted forward, her hand scraping the skin.

"Well?" she asked, and for the first time in days she smiled at me, her eyes bright and interested, one brow lifted. She seemed happy, content, and I wondered if she'd just gotten a letter from Amanda, a long newsy letter, full of gossip. I couldn't look at Mother but stared into the brightness of the window where I saw not the tangle of vines, but me leaning into the grass, my head lowered to the ground.

"How did it go?" she asked.

"Fine," I held my books close to my chest.

"Well, that's wonderful." And she stared at me, still smiling. "I know you're relieved. Was there a lot of applause?"

"Oh yes," I said. "Mr. Hesse said I was the best." I couldn't seem to stop myself until she turned back to the sink and picked up another potato. I needed to get away. Quickly I put my books in my room then fled out the back door, running not toward the creek, but through swampy woods to Daddy's cabin, a place I walked to every week.

When I was a little girl, Daddy used to carry me high on his shoulders into the water while I squealed with delight. Then he laid me on my back and showed me how to float. *"There,"* he said softly, putting his hands under my body to anchor me. *"Now just let the water hold you up, baby. Let yourself float. Let yourself relax."*

That's what I needed: support.

When I saw the cabin, I stopped running. I kept a package of hot chocolate at his cabin, and I imagined we'd sit together in the late afternoon sun while I told him about my disaster. I needed someone to understand that it wasn't entirely my fault. I knew what Daddy would do. He'd listen closely, then pull me toward him, saying it was all right, everybody makes mistakes, everybody falls down. Then he'd say it was only natural that I'd be compared with Amanda, but that what was natural wasn't always necessary. I had my own life, my own ways. I had to listen to them. *Listen closely*, he'd say, *because the heart can be a stranger.*

Then I heard a ragged voice barking out sounds. "Here comes Swifty!" followed by a hearty laugh. I stood in the doorway watching Daddy cackle as if he were witnessing a comical scene, moving his arm parallel to the table, then snatching it back, hiding his fist in his lap. He seemed caught in his vision, like a child in the middle of an imaginary game, and for a moment I didn't interrupt him. "Bing!" he cried out. I wasn't frightened that he was talking to himself. I did that too. I believed it was the way of lonely people. Instead, I stood quietly, staring at his profile, hoping that when he turned his head, his eyes would be clear and blue and that he'd laugh and say, "Ah, don't pay one bit of attention to me."

"Daddy?"

Once again his hand sliced the air. But then he stopped, his hand held out as if it had been reprimanded midstroke. When he turned toward me, I saw a glazed, dreamy look in his eye, the glittery shield of whiskey.

"Baby," he said with purring delight. And I heard then the cloying heat of his drunkenness which sat like a third party in the room. Still, I moved forward, anxious, staring at his familiar, silvery blond hair. I could still make the hot chocolate, could give it a try. He leaned toward me and very softly touched my arm. "You should have seen them run," he continued, skidding one hand against the other, making the motion of quick speed. His eyes refocused for distance.

"What, Daddy?"

"Greyhounds, baby. Fast, bee-u-ful dogs. B-u-ful dogs. At the tracks, honey. I bet the Quinella every time, and there . . . hey, hey, there they . . . go!"

His voice grew excited, loud, and he rose then and held out a fistful of money. "Here," he said. He dropped the money in my lap. He was smiling a slick, careless smile as he stumbled closer to me. Drunk. But that was Amanda's word. Confused. Slipping. *Helpless.* That word throbbed inside my skull. But if he were helpless, then he couldn't help me. He slumped back down, and I sat in a heap beside him, seeing a plate of fish bones on the table beside a letter. Idly, I looked at the address. Katy Harper, 406 . . . Boulevard, Los Angeles, California, the street name blurred by a water stain. I remembered Aunt Katy visiting us years ago, remembered how I'd loved her soft blonde curls, the way she'd hugged me as we sat together on the pier. She and Daddy had got on famously, and even as a little girl I could see that Katy admired Daddy as a man who could laugh at the ridiculous world.

"What's this?" I pointed to the letter, but he didn't understand.

"Greyhounds," he said. "You shoulda seen them run." He looked out the window at the silent ruffle of clouds and became wistful. "Here comes Swifty," he whispered to the wordless pines. *"Here comes Swifty!"*

I dropped the letter and the money and ran so fast I didn't look where I was going. I moved through the trees, dodging puddles and brush, running toward the road.

9

When I got to the front of Josie's One-Stop, the dogs were asleep on the porch, mouths open, pink tongues hanging out, their eyes heavy lidded and twitching with dreams. One farted and flapped his tail against the boards, his collar jingling. "Stinking dogs," I said, walking past them. "Stupid, stinking dogs."

"You criticizing my dogs?" Josie stuck her head out the screen door. She wore a bandana over her frizzy hair and her shirt, the sleeves rolled up, was stained with grease. "'Cause if you are, go away." She pulled her head back inside the door like a turtle retreating into its shell.

"They stink too much to bother with," I said. "They stink to high heaven, and if you don't wash them, nobody's gonna come in this store at all, not even summer riffraff."

"What does Miss Fancy Pants know about summer riffraff?" Her head bobbed out.

For a moment I was embarrassed. It was Mother who talked about summer riffraff hanging out at the store: crude people from up north who wandered down here to fish, picking their teeth with toothpicks, guzzling beer and burping majestically, but looking at us as if we were losers and hicks. "I heard you talking about them to Daddy," I said pointedly, "about how they use all their fancy equipment to fish the creeks dry."

Josie looked severely at me as she wiped her hands on her shirt. "I'm not going to listen to some damn fool girl tell me what her daddy said last summer or the summer before or anytime at all, for that matter. And furthermore, my dogs don't stink. You oughta get your head examined." Josie pulled the screen door closed. I saw her snatch off the bandana and wipe at the stains climbing up her shirt.

Miserable, I sat down on the porch steps. One of the smelly dogs woke and sidled up behind me, sniffing, reeking with the stink of the woods, and without thinking I started petting him, leaning my head against his coat, scratching the smooth fur behind his ears, under his chin. His toenails clinked on the boards as he pushed closer, stretching out his dank, smelly neck as if he might purr with pleasure. Then I could feel Josie behind me at the screen door, watching, breathing in short, raspy sighs from smoking too many Camels.

"Listen, I shouldn't have said that," she said sharply, stepping out onto the porch, her hands on her hips. "I'm just sensitive about my dogs. They're all I have in this world. You know that, so you oughta be more careful." Josie sat down deliberately beside me; the older hound raised up so she could pull on his ears. "Good Shoot, good boy," Josie said and dropped a piece of bologna on the porch. Shoot and Jacob scrambled for it, confusing each other in their mild, bewildering paranoia.

I had no idea why I'd come here, what I wanted. I'd just started running. But in a funny way it was a familiar path because Daddy and I had come here so often to pick up Josie and head out to the bay. On our fishing trips she always turned toward the deep as if it were a sacred place, as if only in the middle of the bay could she be content and alone and independent. Mostly she was silent, her words as sparse as oracles, but when she spoke, she spoke fiercely, intent on what she said. I liked that, though I couldn't have said exactly why back then.

Now I sat bent over, studying my shoes.

"What's taken the thunder outta you?" Josie asked, wiping at her shirt. "Last time I saw anybody with a face that long they were coming back from a funeral."

"Nothing."

"Uh huh," Josie nodded. "Does this nothing have a name, or am I supposed to guess?"

I looked into Josie's coal-black eyes, eyes that didn't flinch from direct contact, but I couldn't speak. My silence could probably be felt in the next county.

Josie nodded again. "Well, come on in the store and have a root beer and let's get a look at this nothing." Not waiting for an answer, she kicked the screen door open and walked back to the rusted cooler that held the cold drinks. "I got to have me a cold one to think at all now in the afternoons. Must be something drying out or heating up inside me, but you might as well have one, too."

I took the cold drink Josie offered, popped the cap, throwing it into the round barrel she used for a garbage can, but I couldn't look at her. I was too embarrassed, too spent with emotion. Instead, I drank the sweet taste of root beer while Josie coughed and swallowed a couple of times, no words passing between us. We sat slumped and silent. Josie wormed a cigarette out of the crumpled package stuck in her belt. "I'm not good at this," she said, thumping the cigarette. "Let's go catch some fish." And relief settled in me as I helped Josie carry the familiar poles and the fishing line. I grabbed the jar of night crawlers she kept ready on the back stoop. We picked up mildewy life jackets with raveled ties to stash in the bottom of the boat, and Josie put a special fly—a smashed-up beetle—in her pocket next to two packs of Camels. Together we headed for the point.

The water lay around us like a gray mirror, a flat, pale face, all its autumn flash drawn out by the still afternoon air. Josie flung an old sweater at me; it must have been pink at one time, but now it was a dusty beige, pitted with small pilled balls that made it nubby to touch. "Put that on so you don't catch cold," she said, but I'd already picked up an oar and I didn't stop rowing, just held the sweater limp in my lap.

When we were in the middle of the creek, we dropped anchor and took out the poles. I threaded a worm onto my hook and cast the line out into the silver shimmer of water, then with one hand fixed the old sweater over my shoulders. The ugly pain in my stomach began to ease as if a knot were unraveling. The school speech disaster already felt like a long time ago; what scared me now was that my daddy was losing ground, sinking fast in a way I couldn't understand. I'd always forgiven him when he went off on a binge, felt relieved when he came back, sober and sensible, taking me for a walk along the back roads of the creek, naming the birds as we went—cardinal, finch, sparrow, starling, lark, blue jay, crow—talking about preserving the land, keeping out the greedy developers who wanted only a slick, easy profit. But now I needed help in a different way.

"Pull, girl," Josie whispered, her voice low and husky. "Pull steady now. Don't let supper get away."

I snapped back to the present, glad for the tension of a fish and for the effort of pulling it in. I let it drag the line out and tire itself just as Daddy had taught me to do. The fish struggled to the left, to the right and then out again into the gray stillness. Instinctively, Josie was beside me with the net, her hawk eyes scanning the surface of the water as my fish labored against me. "That's it," she whispered. "Lay him in easy. He's a grouper all right. A good ole grouper."

She scooped him up in the net, her hand firm on the handle while the fish shivered and flopped against the mesh, splashing us with water.

After we put him in the bucket—his cold, dark, unblinking fish eye staring straight up at the sky—Josie and I sat back, pleased with ourselves. Josie lit the Camel that had been dangling from her lip and blew smoke out in one long, sensuous puff as if nothing in her life had ever been so good.

Her flowered skirt barely covered her pale, whiskery legs, bare of stockings; the sweater she wore looked as thin as a dishrag, but she held her shoulders straight as if what was on her body didn't really matter. It occurred to me that Josie had led a secret life I knew nothing about. She gave the impression of not having to please anybody but herself, but I knew that couldn't be true. She'd once tried to please my daddy. Embarrassed at such a thought, I looked down at the fish. It wasn't struggling anymore. "Did you grow up here, Josie?"

Josie cocked her head as though I'd pointed a gun at her. "No." She blew out smoke. Coughed, then inhaled again, the stream of blue-gray smoke drifting off behind us into the chilly air.

"Where'd you grow up?"

"In hell," she said, then laughed, her eyes jumping at the joke. "Actually, in the hills outside of Knoxville, Tennessee, if you want to be picky about it." Josie dragged on her cigarette, staring at its fiery tip. "It was like Egypt during the famine, everybody hungry and waiting for the bad dream to end and the good one to begin. But after the famine, comes the plague, you know, and the good dreams were said to be in the glory of heaven. You were supposed to wait for it, blessing yourself for your bad luck 'cause you'd be first in line." She took another long drag. "We used to hear about Jacob wrestling with the angel, and I always thought of myself as Jacob wrestling with that place."

"How'd you get out of there and come down here?"

"Ah, well, that's a long story," Josie said, dipping her hands in the water as if checking the temperature. But I knew it was a dodge and wouldn't let her off that easy.

"We've already got supper so you might as well tell me."

We let the boat drift awhile, and I pulled the sweater on, clutching it tight around my shoulders as if for warmth.

Josie ran a hand through her hair, flattening it, her fingers working the kinky curls while behind her the blood-red sun was sinking in the western sky. I settled into myself, shivering a little but also waiting for whatever would push me outside my own skin. Josie coughed again, then said, "When I was seventeen, my mama stood me buck naked in front of a mirror and said, 'There's your birthright. Now go use it.'"

My stomach tightened. I felt my skin heat up, a flush somewhere deep inside.

"And she meant it too," Josie said. "If I didn't find someone to take me outta there, my mother would find someone to load me down with babies, and I couldn't see them hanging all over me, squashing my dreams.

I used to lie in bed at night listening to the trucks going up the grade to the quarry, the old gears shifting, always downshifting, hard like they were panting, squeezing just a little more life outta those rigs. Then, after they were gone, I could hear the wind howling through the mountains, banging screen doors and windows and anything else that wasn't tied down. I thought I couldn't bear it."

Josie stopped talking and looked over at the One-Stop and frowned. "So, when this mattress salesman came around that spring, I started talking to him about Knoxville and how much it'd cost to live there. I wasn't intending anything but to get out the best way I could. I would've jumped off the mountain if he'd said that was the way to go. But by the end of May, he asked me to come with him—he was a traveling man, he'd been to Boston and Philadelphia, places I'd only heard about, and he lived not too far from some mills in Knoxville. There was work there. I stood myself in front of the mirror again, and I decided that if you stored up longing it would become hate, and hate was worse than not loving somebody. So I went with him." She took a knife from under her seat and slashed the fish wide open, its hot, stringy guts steaming before they spilled into the water.

"Did you stay married to him?"

Josie's eyes shifted toward the water, and she spoke as if there were someone behind her she was really talking to. "No, I didn't. I found out there are some things worse than hate. Hate, at least, is a clear emotion. Some things aren't. Especially in marriage."

"Like what?"

"You'll find out when you get there," she said. "Now, get me a worm. Get me a wiggly one."

I held the jar but wouldn't put my finger in to pull one out, wondering whether Mother hated Daddy or what murkier emotions existed between them. "Why does everyone quit talking when you get to parts like this? What if I need to know now?"

I could feel Josie studying me, her hand still holding the jar as if it had become part of her. "Okay," she nodded, "that's fair," and she started on another story about Luther—"that was his name"—how he wasn't a bad man, not bad in the sense of hurting anyone or wanting to cause harm or trouble, but he became like those trucks, only traveling on her. "You see, sometimes a person wants to keep you in a situation that you don't want to be in anymore and, in fact, makes things so hard you can't get out." She paused, looked beyond me to the water. "So I started hating him, but at the same time I understood him and knew that what I did to him, marrying him in the first place, had been wrong. Dead wrong. See, I was running a truck over him too. So, I was stuck, and the more stuck I got, the more I wanted to break outta there, wanted him to let me go, let me fly free. But he wouldn't. To him, I was his. Till death do us part. But the thought of freedom started eating on me, and I struck back at him, but it was like punching a tar baby. If somebody wants to keep you a wife, they can make it plenty hard to get free. They can work on you in a number of ways, and one of the best ways is to plain wear you down, just drag the thing out, hoping you'll give in from exhaustion."

I looked across the creek. You could just see the roof of our house, the bluff a sienna red in the evening sun. For a moment I held on tight.

"But you can't conjure love," Josie said. She wasn't looking at me now or even talking to me. She seemed alone on the creek, talking to herself. "You can learn sympathy and patience, I expect, but you can't learn love. That was what he wanted, that poor man. Poor Luther. He just wanted me to love him and I couldn't. He'd even say that to me, 'Why can't you just love me?' and it would break my heart. The thing about it was, it wasn't all straight and clear what I did feel. I was grateful to him. If that had been enough, well, who knows." She looked at me finally. "Do you understand what I'm saying?"

I nodded, but of course she was right. I didn't really understand. Not then.

"But grateful wasn't enough and finally I did what I had to do. I walked out. After a few years I came down here and rented the One-Stop from your dad, then bought it a few years later." Josie took a towel and cleaned the knife, wrapped it in tinfoil and put it back under the seat.

"Was he different then, my daddy?"

Josie looked at me from under lowered lids. "He was both different and the same, honey. He was generous, if that's what you mean. He wouldn't let a person drown if he could help it, and if you're a poor woman, alone, there are mighty few men who will lift a finger when they see you going under." Josie smiled at the thought as if she were remembering her younger self.

"But did Daddy drink then, Josie?" My voice sounded pinched, barely squeezed out of my throat. I was afraid I'd cry so I looked hard at the fish, its body limp and lifeless, unflaggingly dead.

"He drank then too, hon. There's no use lying about that. But it seemed like back then he could drink and hightail it around here and still be on top of things." Josie stared out at the water, her profile softened so that she seemed younger, almost beautiful in a funny way. "Now it seems like he's lost his way. I guess he didn't think things would bust up like they did. I think losing the house and the land took him by surprise and he never got over it. I don't mean the actual selling of it, but the fact that he'd have to make do."

I pulled the sweater tighter around me, stunned by the same hollowness in my stomach I'd felt at the shack. Maybe it was a mistake to even bring up Daddy, to try to figure it out. "I wish he'd quit," I said, and before I could stop myself, I was sobbing, tears splashing out as if the thunderstorm inside had finally broken loose.

Josie wiped her hands on her skirt and reached over to clasp my hand. I felt silly grabbing hold, but I didn't let go.

"Doesn't mean he don't love you," Josie spoke quietly, her breath tart with the smell of cigarettes. "It just means he can't help you much. But down deep he's still feeling for you. I know he is. He's only tried to numb out the bad feelings about himself, not about you."

I lowered my forehead to our clasped hands even though my face was wet and blubbery. "But what am I supposed to do when I need him?"

Josie's hand tightened around mine. "Oh, love, I don't know what to tell you about that. Sometimes when you lose people, when they can't be there, you have to find them in yourself . . . because, well, in a way they are actually there."

I felt the tears well up again. I would have to work hard to let him go in the flesh, not to want his comfort, his sadness, the way he wrapped me in his arms, the way he made me know I belonged. I squeezed Josie's hand, listening to her raspy swallowing, the scent of sardines and cigarettes. Then Josie was pulling away, picking up the oars, touching my knees. "Com'on, hon, pick up the other oar and help me out here. It's getting dark now, and we've got to go in and cook us a supper we won't forget."

After I left Josie's that evening, I put Daddy in another world, one that was separate from the rest of us, with its own set of rules. It was the only way I could remain loyal, and more than anything I needed that. Not to him, but the memory of him. In my own way, I let him slip into that other world while I held onto the memory of him standing beside me at the end of the pier, staring at the water as if he'd seen a vision. As I watched, the melancholy left his face and he stood taller, straighter, and smiled as if he were telling himself a good story, one with a happy ending. He liked happy endings, liked silly movies like *Pillow Talk* and *Goldfinger*, where all the loose ends fit together and all the noise of unhappiness was slapped shut and resolved. And I guess I liked them too or this memory wouldn't hold such power.

I never did get a chance to talk to anybody about the student council disaster. Of course, Toby lost the election, and I can still see him sitting stranded on stage, flipping his hair over his ear, nervous and embarrassed because I'd deserted him. For months I couldn't bring myself to look at him; he moved back two desks in Algebra II and kept his head down over his paper. I couldn't look at Mr. Hesse either, even when I confessed that on that day I'd gotten violently ill. All that fall I thought that if I could talk to Amanda she'd see through this mess, would look into her crystal ball and say, do this, don't do that, and it would all become perfectly clear.

Now as I walked through the crowded streets of Santa Monica looking for Aunt Katy, I wondered why I had so much faith in Amanda. What was it about her? Of course, to me, she'd always been older and trustworthy in a way that my parents never were. It was Amanda who showed me how to tie my shoes, Amanda who said, "That's your bed," pointing to the one by the window, "and this is mine because I'm older and I have to sleep beside the door," letting me know where I belonged and why. She must be next to the door in case something terrible happened and she had to run tell. At least, this is how I understood it, that Amanda was the daughter in charge, the one who would make things understood to our parents while I, the sentry, stood guard, waiting for whatever was wrong to be set right. I sat on my bed by the window and looked out at the creek and knew it was my place, the mist rising like steam from all that slippery wetness, content and unruffled. But it was also much more than that: it was what Amanda had and I didn't, what I saw as absent in me. What she had was certainty, a sense that she mattered, that she took up necessary space.

On Sundays when we talked to Amanda, Mother always hogged the phone and never left my side when it was my turn so that I mumbled the ordinary stuff about school and the creek, never telling her the real mess I was in. What I really wanted to say was I'm scared. Come home. But I couldn't say that. And I was too embarrassed to tell her about Mr. Hesse or Johnny Turner. But in a way what happened with both of them was pivotal: Mr. Hesse never did get to know me, and Johnny Turner took me up to the old Parker place where I lost that blue sweater. Who would ever think such small things would change the course of my life?

10

My first school dance. I wasn't trying to be one of the popular girls who danced every dance, but I'd do anything to avoid the strained silence of another Friday night with Mother in front of the TV, even if it meant sitting in the bleachers watching the other couples and listening to Buddy Holly, the Beach Boys, Ray Charles, and Roy Orbison.

I dressed that night in Amanda's blue sweater, a jolting violet-blue that brightened my eyes and fit close to my body, making my breasts look soft and touchable. Maybe it fit too close, I thought, but when I heard Angie at the door, saying, "Hello, Mrs. Soldier, how are you?" I was afraid Mother would change her mind, so I rushed out and grabbed Angie's hand. For the first part of the night, we did sit in the bleachers, giggling at the chaperones, Mr. Peeper Creeper talking to Lois Lane, whose sweater was baggy around her boobs. "Needs a little titty lift," Angie whispered, as we watched them shuffling together, almost touching, then jerking apart. I probably would have stayed in the bleachers all night if Johnny Turner, a boy from the class ahead of Amanda, hadn't waltzed in out of the humid darkness, then stood at the doorway, surveying us all. In the stark entrance light, he seemed bigger than ever, with football shoulders and those long Turner legs that people said could outrun anybody on the basketball court. "A snake," Amanda once called him, but all the girls turned to see his crooked smile and wavy black hair. He looked dangerous, as if he didn't have a care in the world.

"Looking for bait," Angie whispered, but I turned away, thinking only that his daddy owned our house in Soldier Creek, though secretly I believed Amanda would get it back. I was thinking about this when my gaze met Jimmy Stokes, who asked so hopefully if I wanted to dance, I didn't have the heart to say no. Jimmy was fat and sweaty and gripped me like a sack of potatoes as we fought a little battle with his right hand. "Don't," I kept whispering, but he was stronger than I suspected, and when the song ended, I jerked free, propelling myself right into Johnny Turner, who was so close

I could smell the Clorox in his jeans. They were bleached to a pulpy blue.

"Oh, I'm sorry," I said, but he seemed not to notice. He was talking, telling a dirty joke, and I heard the punch line: ". . .some guy's dick. . ."

Everyone laughed, and I turned back to the bleachers until Johnny caught my arm, pulling me around. "What's wrong with you? Don't you think that's funny?"

I couldn't look at him. My head went dark with worry. I loosened my arm and walked away, back toward Angie, toward safety. I could have gotten away with it too if he hadn't followed me, tugging on my sleeve, looking at me with a strange, imploring curiosity. "Hey, you're Amanda's little sister, aren't you?"

I nodded, not surprised. Everyone knew Amanda.

"You know"—he shook his finger at me—"I couldn't place you at first 'cause you're so different from that smart fucker of a sister. You two don't look a thing alike."

"Yes, we do," I said, surprised at my boldness. Secretly I always thought there was something alike about Amanda and me, though I knew it wasn't our features because Amanda's were sharper, more angular, and mine rounder, softer. Maybe it was just that we both revealed a sense of desperation, though in Amanda it came out as a swagger and in me an apology. Still, it was the same furrowing of brows, the same sharp intake of breath, the same drumming of our fingers on the table, the same restless hope that got us through the day.

"Nah, I don't think so," Johnny said in a teasing voice, giving me the once-over, his eyes lingering meaningfully on my sweater. "I bet you look like your Mother."

I crossed my arms over my chest. "Amanda's at college. On scholarship," I added, bristling.

He fisted both hands in his pockets. "Well, my, my, my, my. Isn't that something?"

It was his sarcasm that made me speak, made me leap out of my old anonymous self. "She couldn't wait to get away. I guess you're different."

Suddenly he looked defensive, his forehead creased in a scowl. "I can see now you're Amanda's sister. Me? I work for the old man on Saturdays. You do what the old bastard says or you're out on your ear."

"I bet you like the money," I said, forgetting I should be afraid. Already I had waded out into deep water and felt the pull of the tides. Maybe it was like swimming, a matter of keeping your balance and perfecting your stroke. Besides, I liked him better on the defensive, sullen and silent, a pulse quivering steady at his temple. Everyone said his father, Mr. Turner, president of the bank, was piling up money for Johnny if only he'd straighten out and fly right. Which meant Johnny might someday own our house.

"I can spend it," he said and smiled again a boyish smile, eager and embarrassed, his eyebrows lifting, a dimple deepening in one cheek. It was his smile that crept into my bones, jarring loose my lips so that I smiled too, feeling a strange heat jump between us, puddling in my stomach, creeping up my spine. I'd never flirted before, but now it seemed natural, like floating on my back in the creek.

"You mean you come down here just to get out of the house?"

"Sure, where else do you go in this one-horse town?"

"I don't know," I said, looking around at Lois Lane doing the twist with the Peeper Creeper. The Peeper Creeper didn't move his legs, only swiveled his hips from side to side like the rotator in a washing machine. He smiled at Lois Lane, and even in the flickering light, I could see she was grinning like a teenager. Other people were shaking and twisting, fluttering their hands in the air. I glanced up to where I'd been sitting with Angie, but her place was empty, only a blank space near the windows, her coat bunched up next to mine.

"Saw her go out with Twilly," Johnny said. He pulled a Chap Stick out of his pocket and twisted off the cap. "Just to get some air." He laughed and swished it across his bottom lip.

But now I was worried. Angie had this monster crush on Twilly, so she was probably necking in his car. I had a curfew, and since Soldier Creek was fifteen miles east of Moss Point, we had to leave earlier than the town kids.

"If she doesn't come back, don't worry," he said softly, his face earnest, serious as if he understood my dilemma. "I can take you home . . . if that's what's bothering you."

I nodded, turning away from him, moving back up into the bleachers to sit alone.

Of course, our coming together was fragmented, fragile, arbitrary. Alone, outside of the school gymnasium, Johnny and I were both shy, and I like to think a little frightened of each other. Driving the fifteen miles to Soldier Creek, Johnny hummed quietly to himself while I stared out the window at bushes so matted together they formed a solid wall of darkness. It was flat here, the highway just a strip of straight black ribbon, the ground overgrown with kudzu and weeds. Beyond, a thicket of oaks and pines made a dark, ragged splotch against the night.

"You're almost finished with school, aren't you?" he asked suddenly, his voice coming rich and deep out of the darkness.

"Next year."

"I thought you were older."

"No, just sixteen."

Then he stopped talking and we both stared at the narrow road. It was one of those inky nights, the sky a spill of stars. I didn't know what to do about this kind of awkwardness, so I didn't do anything, only listened to our breathing and pressed my knees tight together so I could feel their soft, even heat.

"What next?" he asked, after a period of quiet. "I mean, after high school."

"I don't know," I said, because I couldn't imagine my life after Soldier Creek. I wasn't like Amanda, who wanted to make a big, noisy splash. I needed the quiet. "I guess I'll know when I'm there," I said. And I was surprised to see Johnny smile as if he was pleased with this answer, as if my uncertain ambition was a point in my favor. "What about you? You coming back here, planning to take over for your father?"

"Maybe." He looked directly at me, but now his face was solemn, grim. And for the first time I realized it might not be so wonderful to be the son of the richest man in town. Mr. Turner was arrogant, sneaky, known to hold grudges. I'd seen him rise up in the stands at baseball games and cuss out the umpires while Johnny, at the pitcher's mound, started pitching wilder and wilder until the coach had no choice but to take him out. "I guess I just sorta let things happen, but the old man's determined I get through college, though he thinks they're jerking me around."

"Why's that?"

"Oh, you know, all those papers you have to write about somebody in another century, somebody not even real, just a made-up character from a book you have to figure out. It drives the old man up a wall. 'Stories! Goddammit! What good's that going to do you in business?'" And Johnny laughed. "But there's nothing he can do about it because it's required."

Listening to him, I'd turned toward him, watching the shadows play against his face, flattening his cheek so that it looked angled and sharp, but when I glanced out the window, I saw we'd missed the creek road. "I think you've passed my turnoff. It's right back there." I saw the reflector at the edge of the road glowing dimly in the foggy distance. "You can turn around up at the old Parker place." The Parker place was set back on a red dirt road, potato fields on either side, wild corn so tall you could barely see the porch of the house. It had been abandoned in the fifties and nobody lived there except Mexican migrant laborers in the summer, busting in the screen doors, living with lighted candles and flashlights and an old outhouse in the backyard.

The drive was dark, edged with bushes and palmettoes and honeysuckle vines that twisted in strangled knots from the trees. "You don't have to pull so far in," I said. "It gets muddy up further and it's easier to turn around here."

"Why don't we stop a minute."

I felt that quiver between us and thought of the pulpy blue of his jeans. "No," I said quickly, staring straight ahead, feeling the door handle behind my back. "I have to get home." Even in the dark I could see Mother's glare, a sharp anger in her eyes. Boys, she said, were trouble. But then what did she know, a woman who didn't love my father?

"But I wanna talk to you," he said, scooting closer.

"Well, you can't," I said, automatically putting my hands up to push at him in the dark. I imagined Mother sitting at the kitchen table, waiting, her eyes fixed on the door just as I felt his hands reaching between mine, touching my sweater. "I want to go home."

"No you don't," he whispered, his breath on my face. So near, his face looked solemn, sincere, and I felt the way I did when I first dove into the water, as if anything could happen, the whole force of me released, revealed.

"I do." But already his arms were closing around me like a noose, one that felt oddly nice, almost safe. Actually I didn't want to go home, but I turned my face away.

"Aw, com'on," he whispered. He looked pleading, uncertain, and for a moment I shivered with pleasure. Again Mother's eyes swam before me.

"Please," I finally got out, but then he reached up and turned my face to his, his mouth warm and sweet and despite myself I opened my mouth to him. I didn't mean to. I knew I shouldn't. I could hear Amanda crowing at how stupid I was, but the next minute I didn't care, his hand moving in slow circles across my chest. I let him for a little while, then pushed his hand away.

"Com'on," he whispered. "I like you."

And I felt in that moment that he did. His eyes smoothed me out, turned me upside down. A force whirled through me, something hungry and loose turning scary and thick. The sky lowered itself, darkening, a cloud shadowing the moon. I couldn't see his eyes, could only feel his hands, searching, searching as his lips moved closer.

"Stop," I said, suddenly frightened. And then he looked at me, pulling away.

"Why? I like you," he whispered again. He looked lost, a little frightened himself.

"No, please," but he kept coming, moving closer. And then I was frightened of myself. I could feel his intent and with each movement, I lost more ground, became more pliant as if I were diving into the creek, letting the water surround me, pull me into a deeper darkness. But I wasn't in the water, and I knew then what I had to do. I had to take control. I'd read about it in a book, how a woman could cast a spell over a man. "If you promise to take me home," I whispered, "I'll show you."

He leaned closer, his breath soft on my neck. "Okay," he said, and I closed my eyes. I couldn't look at him, couldn't think about what I was about to do. Maybe it was silly, but what else could I do?

"Remember that you promised," I whispered as if he were a Boy Scout learning about the dangers of fire. As I spoke, I saw a lizard dart across the windshield and stop, frozen on the glass. And slowly I lifted the blue sweater, pulling it over my face, the night air cool and wet on my skin, a breeze of softness, like a spray of lilies fluttering across my chest until I realized that the coolness wasn't coolness at all, but Johnny's tongue pressed against my breast, his hand pulling the sweater up over my head. It was only then that I snapped awake as if I'd been lost in a dream. I don't know if I jumped first or screamed, but in seconds I was out of the car. My sweater fell to the ground. And then I was running, racing toward the highway, rushing down the drive, caught by vines and briars, the red, powdery dirt thick against my bare legs.

11

It was already past my curfew. As I got nearer to the house I saw a light on upstairs in the back of the house. Amanda's room.

At the back door I made myself stop. I tried to still the shivering, standing there in my skirt and bra, my lipstick smudged, my thighs scratched. Very carefully, I opened the screen, pinching the wood with my thumb to keep it from squeaking, but a moth fluttered hot against my cheek and I screamed, letting the door bang shut. I was sure I was lost, a goner, and yet as I waited, nothing happened—no lights, no voice—and I pushed the door open and stepped inside. I stood in the thin darkness, breathing, listening, still waiting to be punished. But there was no sound, so I went to the laundry basket and dragged out an old t-shirt, smoothing it down with my hands. I listened, hearing nothing. Maybe I was safe.

I started up the stairs and was surprised to see Mother sitting on Amanda's bed, smiling at something she held in her hands.

"Look, Amanda's old red shoes," she said, holding them out. "She forgot them. Now I'll have to send them to her." Her face was flushed a high, feverish color, her eyes a little too bright, too excited. She was still dressed in her clothes, a streak of tomato sauce down one sleeve. "You remember how much she loved them, don't you, how she wouldn't take them off after she got them?"

I nodded, but I could see that they were scuffed and scarred, and I knew Amanda had left them intentionally.

"Do you think I should send them?" she asked, looking up wistfully.

"I guess." I was suddenly tired, afraid I'd start trembling again. I wondered if I had leaves in my hair. I saw a streak of dirt down one leg.

"She'll just think I'm sentimental," Mother said, and then she looked up at me as if only now did she realize who I was. "You'd better get ready for bed."

When I came back in my nightgown, Mother was taking the shoes off her hands. One fell to the floor between us. "I don't want to do anything silly."

I picked up the dropped shoe and stared at its faded color. Last year when Amanda bought them I'd been jealous because she and Mother made such a silly fuss over them. Nobody ever made a fuss about me . . . and then I saw Johnny's hands, the way they moved as if through water, pulling something out of me, pulling . . . and I dropped the shoe.

"Well, pick it up just in case I might."

I stooped to pick up the shoe, and when I rose, Mother was looking at me, staring, her eyes squinting as if seeing through me, knowing what she couldn't possibly know. "It's past midnight," she said quietly. "You were late."

I nodded, staring at my bare feet.

And to my surprise, Mother didn't say anything more, just turned abruptly, leaving me alone in Amanda's room with the sound of the wind picking up, blowing the leaves off the trees.

For what seemed like hours I stared at the creek, holding Amanda's red shoe. And then very deliberately, I brought it up to my face and whacked myself hard until my lip puffed up and bled, and I relaxed to the sweetness of punishment, my tongue lapping at the blood, my cheeks numb, my legs trembling. Relieved, I picked up the other red shoe and held it close, coddling it as if it were valuable. I remembered the way Amanda used to be crazy about these shoes, dancing around the room in them before she went to a party, then falling on her bed afterward, the shoes dropped to the floor with a thud. She'd laugh when Mother scolded her for being so careless with good things, insisting instead that Mother sit right beside her, "Right here, Mama," and hear all the party gossip. "Michelle Turkey-Chin tried to flirt with Bob Tarkington, but he didn't even notice her creepy little smile," Amanda would say. "He's smarter than you think." They'd laugh and tease about everybody in Amanda's class. Old Snoopy-Face and the Hatchet Man, two reporters on the paper with Amanda, who loved nothing better than to get the scoop on the popular crowd, the athletes and cheerleaders and homecoming queens. But after Mother left, Amanda would go quiet as if all her shiny brightness was depleted. Sometimes she simply turned her face to the wall and told me to shut off the light. Other times, she didn't move, only stared out the window into the darkness as if she could see something she'd never wanted to see. "We've gotta get outta here, baby," she'd whisper then. "Whatever happens, we've gotta leave. Fly to the moon."

But I never wanted to leave.

That night I sat down on Amanda's bed and put on the red shoes. They fit me perfectly. They could have been mine. I lay back against her pillow, closing my eyes, floating my tongue over the bubble of my lip, wondering what it would feel like to have Mother love me as she loved Amanda. It was then that the strangest thing happened: Amanda came to me. I could see her hovering above me, a hushed, frightened look on her face, a look that said she had to leave. Had to, baby.

Quickly, I removed the red shoes and wrapped them carefully, tidily in a pillowcase as if they were precious objects, delicate cargo. Walking very slowly in the darkness, I crept down the stairs, stopping often so the steps wouldn't creak.

The grass was wet beneath my feet, the trees black against a dark bruise of a sky. I walked slowly, feeling my way, something rotten mushing beneath my feet, maybe a crab apple or a toad gone soft with the heat. Frogs croaked in the trees, and I heard them leaping in the grass. An owl hooted, hoooo-hoooo, and I stopped, hugging the shoes to my chest. Was that a warning? I looked back at the house. Only darkness. The night went silent again, and I moved on like a ghost in the mist. I was near water now. It shimmered on the surface, shiny like satin, rippling against the pier. A tart, seaweedy smell drew me closer.

Out on the pier, the moon slid from behind clouds, a glossy white beach ball thrown up in the sky. For a moment I felt myself rising too, losing myself in the night as I unwrapped the pillowcase and flung the shoes into the creek, the current carrying them, bobbing and dipping, a toe, a heel, a sole, before they slipped below the surface, lost to the night. In that silent stillness, I imagined that we were both free.

12

It was late afternoon when I arrived in North Carolina, dragging my raggedy-ass suitcases behind me, making my way toward my dorm. I knew that this private college—we called it the Harvard of the South—was the first and perhaps the most important leg in my journey, and more than anything, I wanted to enjoy every inch of that green velvety lawn beneath a canopy of oaks and maples and cedars. Even the landscape seemed tended and old, like good rugs, worn but given exquisite care. Much later after our troubles began, Trinity College would seem like a mirage, something vague and shimmering, blurring into the dwindling darkness, but that first day it was beautiful.

I stopped to stare at the limestone entryway of my dorm just as the front doors swung open and three girls with long straight hair and short skirts sauntered out, their bracelets jangling like the sound of money. They were talking and giggling, and they walked right past me as if I were invisible; I knew then my stockings were bagging around my knees, my shoes scuffed, my hair hanging limp down my sweaty back. For a brief moment I was frightened, embarrassed, until I remembered a day when I was a little girl riding my first banana-seated bicycle down the road at Soldier Creek, pedaling hard in the still, quiet air, the sun rising fast in a blazing blue sky, the dew just melting from the crabgrass sprouting alongside the road. I was wearing an obnoxiously bright pink shirt, one I insisted on buying, and as I rode down the long, flat blacktop, I knew I could let my hands lift from the handlebars like wings, floating out to my side. I could do anything! Standing in front of my dorm, I did just that—lifted my arms as if I might fly. Then I grabbed my suitcases and rushed into the building.

As I hauled my bags up the stairs, a gypsyish-looking woman with long, red hair and thick eyebrows darted out of a nearby room. "Welcome to a forgotten circle of Dante's hell," she said, smiling, pushing a loose strand of hair out of her face. Her front teeth overlapped slightly, and her eyes were large and gray, alive with pleasure.

I smiled, dropping one of my bags to greet her. "Amanda Soldier," I said, holding out my hand.

She laughed and gave me a quick, firm shake. "Elizabeth Goldman, but call me Beth." She picked up one of my suitcases. "I've been all over this damn barracks. Where's your room? You better hope it's not near the bathrooms. Toilets sound like Niagara Falls."

"208," I said.

Beth jerked her head. "This way."

When we opened the door, sunlight streamed through the windows, lighting up a scarred desk, a single bed and oak dresser on worn, pine floors. The mattress was bare, the blue ticking forlorn-looking, naked, but it was a corner room with double windows through which afternoon light splashed everywhere in unbroken brilliance. I thought it the most wonderful place in the world. "Ohmygod!"

"Ta-da! The scholarship wing. Nice, huh?"

"It's perfect!" I said. "But I don't have a new bedspread." And then I clamped my hand over my mouth; I hadn't meant to say that. It was Mother whispering in my ear.

"Neither do I," Beth confessed. We stared solemnly at each other, then as suddenly we burst out laughing. "I'm starting off secondhand. An old pink comforter from Aunt Rachel in Brooklyn."

"My mother," I began.

"Don't even say the word. Mine's already sent bagels. She thinks they won't feed me here. 'Who can tell what's under all that gravy, sweetheart,' she said at the airport."

I dropped my bags on the bed. "There isn't anything under the gravy," I smiled, walking to the window, my hands touching the sill, the white wooden blinds, even the newly washed panes of glass. "It's just flour and bacon grease. A Southern plot."

"Exactly," Beth nodded, grinning.

After Beth left, I closed the door and sat on the unmade bed, hugging myself. But I couldn't stay still. Instead, I jumped up and opened the closet, fingering all the hangers, bunching them together then spreading them apart. I opened the drawers to my desk, felt into each dark, clean space, my hands already sweaty with excitement. Next the dresser. Two large drawers and two smaller ones. Underwear. Socks. I even flicked the lamp on and off, touching the silk shade, then kicked off my shoes and lay back on the mattress, the pillow under my head. The ceiling was smooth cream, no cracks or water spots, no faded discolorations, no spider webs caught in the corners. I ran my hand down the wall and sighed with relief. No one here could possibly have heard of Soldier Creek. I imagined all the other girls would be from exciting places like Philadelphia or New York, and I couldn't wait to be from somewhere else too.

The next morning I fingered the course schedule cards in one pocket, the scholarship check in the other as I stood in line at the administration building, looking out the window into the bright September sunshine, where parents in Bermuda shorts were still unpacking their cars and two boys threw a football back and forth in long curving arcs. The day was soft and warm and pleasant, and as I waited, I daydreamed myself speaking eloquently to a mesmerized crowd. I leaned forward, caught in the thrill of my own fervor—

"Next," the secretary called, and someone nudged me from behind.

"Oh . . . sorry." I felt flustered and silly as I hurried to sit in the chair the last student had vacated. Portraits of stern old men in high collars and double-breasted suits lined the walls, and a bouquet of lilies draped over the secretary's desk.

"Amanda Soldier," the woman said, pulling out my file. She was short and pudgy, and she smiled. "Your course schedule is complete, my dear, but are you sure you want this honors class with Dr. McKune? It's an upper-level class on the other side of campus and doesn't get out until seven o'clock on Friday evenings. Friday is the big worry," she winked at me, humor etched in her eyes. "Now you could also take a three o'clock with Dr. Bismark. Nineteenth-century American literature with Whitman and Dickinson and Poe." She smiled briskly, pencil poised, but I looked at my schedule as if it were a sacred thing. I'd selected a major known as "Progressive Studies."

I shook my head. *The course I was interested in was literary modernism: This course will reflect a conflict between the forces of T. S. Eliot, Ezra Pound, and James Joyce on the one hand and Virginia Woolf, W. C. Williams, and Gertrude Stein on the other.* A feast! And I could eat out of every pot. It had taken me four years to get here, four years of work supervised by diligent, bemused Mr. Hesse, who said I'd make it if anybody could.

Back home I used to get a quart of chocolate ice cream and sit alone in the dark, daydreaming about what I'd be when my brains paid off. And yet all I could imagine were the boys in their daddy's chicken trucks and the old men on their riding lawnmowers waving and whistling at me as I drove through Moss Point—known and famous and important—on my way back to Soldier Creek. I saw Flo Hinton in a pink polyester pantsuit smiling her tiny-teeth smile and telling everyone that I no longer sweat or had athlete's foot or warts or moles. "They take care of those things when you're famous," she'd say, and I'd nod because there were no sweat stains anywhere on me and my bra straps were clean and white and no longer held together with safety pins. Everything about me would be high class and polished, and I'd nod politely to Josie in her pilled-up, faded old sweater and baggy dungarees, and pretend we didn't wish each other crawling on the moon. Of course, Mr. Hesse would shyly ask me about *Ulysses* and *Absalom! Absalom!*, his cowlick sticking straight up, a little fever blister erupting on his bottom lip. Before I got to the rose petals strewn out in welcome in our drive at Soldier Creek, I began to get a little worried, wondering if "becoming important" might not be as easy as everyone seemed to think. On hot, sultry nights when the humidity made my hair stick to my neck, when the bugs smashed and fluttered against the screen and my pajamas were damp with sweat, I knew deep in my bones that it was going to be downright hard.

Secretly, I wanted it to be hard. I wanted to push against something bigger than myself, something firm and decisive and conquerable. I knew I'd found it when I rushed into my third class, the honors seminar with Professor McKune. He walked into the room with a satchel under one arm, looking as if he'd been built for mountain climbing. I had to pinch myself to calm down as I watched him methodically take out books and papers from his worn leather briefcase, his fine-boned face, the kind I could imagine on St. Francis of Assisi or Judas. He stood before us, silent, maybe musing on some private delight, letting us absorb him as if he were a divine odor in the air.

"Modernism is not just a period in time," he began slowly, emphasizing each word, "a movement that galvanized the world after World War I, but a sensibility, a fully contemporary art form that attacked the linear plot structure of naturalism and realism." As he talked, he paced the room, stopping occasionally to catch the eyes of a particular student, then putting his hands in his pockets and musing to himself. "What had been held dear— the family, the nation, the moneyed class, as well as a certainty about the order of things—was now held up to ironic scrutiny. What the naturalists, particularly Dreiser and Norris, tried to do in terms of narrative, the high modernists tried to undo." He stopped pacing and stood before the lectern, his hands, which were square and surprisingly small, rubbing the edge of the wood. "So you see, we'll be looking at narratives which are fragmented, circular, and juxtaposed in time as opposed to those that are symmetrical and sequential. Just to give you an example, we'll spend much of our class work exploring Joyce's epiphany and stream of consciousness narrative, Gertrude Stein's continuous present, and Virginia Woolf's tunneling."

In class I wrote down everything he said, but there were such gaps in my understanding, I wasn't sure what most of it meant. What was a circular plot structure? Who was Norris? I didn't know what naturalism was, had never heard of Gertrude Stein, much less Virginia Woolf's idea of tunneling. Tunneling? What in the world could that mean? Professor McKune mentioned the imagists, someone named H. D.—was that a male or a female?—as well as Freud, Jung, and William James. He ended the lecture by saying that he hoped we would all "be fond of sentences" by the end of the term, and he smiled a sly-looking smile. A few students smiled back as if he'd spoken in code, but I had no idea what he meant.

Immediately I went to Holden Library where haloes of light glowed from polished globes. Somewhere behind me I heard the murmur of low voices, the tap-tap of a cane. What should I look up first? "Start with background," my history professor had told us that morning at 9:00. So I looked up naturalism since Professor McKune had said that modernism challenged naturalism and realism. But when I pulled out the card drawer for naturalism, there were so many entries that after writing down ten, I shoved the drawer back into its slot and went on to the next unknown: Gertrude Stein. God, what an ugly name. I hoped poor Gertrude would rise above this moniker. I hoped she'd surprise me with something good. By the time I got to Virginia Woolf, it was 10:30 at night and my enthusiasm was waning, My stomach growled. I hadn't eaten since 4:00 when I'd grabbed a hamburger from the union before rushing to Dr. McKune's class. While in the stacks, I decided to read *To the Lighthouse* because the title appealed to me and I'd found it on the shelf.

I wanted to start reading the minute I got back to my dorm, but just outside the library, I saw Beth, her arms also full of books. "Let's go over to the Sweet Shop," she said. "I'm dead without more carbohydrates. I need calories to crack these guys." And she thumped her books.

"Sure." I shifted the load in my arms.

"Machiavelli!" Beth held up *The Prince*. "Monster or realist? That's our first assignment."

I was too ashamed to admit I didn't know who Machiavelli was or what he thought, and mentally added that name to the list growing tall as a skyscraper in my head.

"It will be a relief to get to Rousseau," Beth said, shifting her books to the other arm. "What have you got?"

"Literary criticism and a novel. *To the Lighthouse*."

"Oooooh, don't you love Woolf? I couldn't get enough of her in high school."

"Absolutely," I nodded and put that one on top.

13

One month of college taught me the brevity of my education, the rudimentary perimeter I'd drawn with Mr. Hesse like notching out the first hole on a big man's leather belt. What I longed for was a private conversation with Professor McKune. If only I could meet him one on one, surely I could discuss Mrs. Ramsey in *To the Lighthouse*, surely my determination to take issue with the past would blaze through my words. *And yes, we have a new marvelous student*, he'd say. But in class, I never opened my mouth, never spoke. Quickly, I understood the distance between being the best in a small-town high school and becoming educated.

But to Mother and Jit, I only bragged. "I made an A minus on my first American History exam," I told them over the phone, then gave glowing and comic descriptions of my teachers. Dr. Hanbury wore a toupee and spoke ardently about the Gettysburg Address and Lincoln's re-interpretation of the constitution. Dr. Winthrop, once a minister, made each lecture a sermon, appealing to the "good citizen and fellow traveler" in each of us, yet he had such severe post-nasal drip that in the middle of a passionate point he'd stop and snort into his handkerchief, then stare at it intensely before continuing his lecture. I saved my most glowing praise for Dr. McKune. "Mother, I'd marry the man tomorrow if he didn't have gray hair and knobby knees."

For our first essay in McKune's class, we were "invited" (I laughed to Beth about that word) to respond to an issue of modernism and explore its influence through one of the books we'd read. Easy enough. But to my surprise, I was the only student who hadn't read all the books for the class though it was only the second month of school. Still high from reading *To the Lighthouse*, and spurred on by Beth, who was doing a paper about Mary Cassett for art history, I decided to write on the defiant plight of the woman artist.

Our essays were due on Friday. Although I'd made notes on index cards, I'd never written this type of paper before, and as I sat at my desk typing out my thoughts, I felt as if I were sitting on top of a vast building in a new city, trying to describe what I saw. It was a little like being God, omniscient and proud, sending a flash of light into the darkness, watching as the shadows receded and trees grew huge, green, luminous leaves. As I described Mrs. Ramsey, pictures of Mother sitting on the porch at Soldier Creek, her flyswatter in her hand, interrupted my thoughts, and I'd find myself saying, "It's all right, Mother. Really, it will be all right," until she faded back to the periphery of my mind. She'd called last night to talk, but I was too busy with my paper and told her to call on Sunday at 5:00, then I got back to Mrs. Ramsey and Lily Briscoe. When I finished writing at 2:00 a.m., I fell into bed, exhausted but with a delicious sense of triumph: I too had put my tree further in the middle! My own little modernist rebellion.

When I answered the phone the following Sunday, Mother sounded frantic, distraught. Something hidden strangled the air. "What happened?" she asked. Though I couldn't see her, I knew her hands gripped the phone.

"Why nothing, Mother. What's wrong?" I imagined Jit sitting on the pier, refusing to go to school or Mother with her arm in a sling, unable to work in her garden. I saw Daddy drunk and passed out at work. "What is it?" I repeated, trying to calm down. I slumped cross-legged to the floor.

"It's 5:30," she said. "You weren't there when I called. You said to call at 5:00, and the dorm counselor . . . well, she didn't know where you were."

I stood up so fast I felt dizzy. "Jesus Christ, Mother, I was just down the hall. I . . . I forgot, I'm sorry. I wasn't looking at the time but checking my biology notes with another girl." Of course, I was gossiping, sitting on Beth's bed, discussing the quirks and pettiness of the other girls, but what did it matter?

"Well," Mother said, and I could hear the sadness in her voice, a sense of hurt as if I'd betrayed something much bigger than thirty minutes. "I know you need to study, but I thought we'd agreed on a time. I thought it was important to you . . . and you know how I depend on that."

I sighed. I twisted the phone cord around my arm. "I won't let it happen again."

But irritation must have crept into my voice. "Oh, honey, I'm being . . . awful," Mother began to apologize. "I know I am, but don't you miss me? Don't you want to know what Mrs. Shelton said about you at church?"

I looked down at the polished pine floors. I remembered the day Mother told Mrs. Shelton in the produce aisle at the Piggly Wiggly that I'd gotten a scholarship to Trinity College. Mrs. Shelton's eyes widened with such envy and respect, Mother walked triumphantly away, her head held high, her groceries completely forgotten so that we had to go back twenty minutes later and find them. Now I giggled, excitement racing through my nerves. "Of course, I miss you, and guess what?" I burst out. "I'm reading the most wonderful book!"

"Well, I know you are," Mother said, "and listen, everyone is talking about you. Mrs. Shelton wanted to know if you were taking logic, and Mr. Ellis said you must study calculus. He says we'll be teaching it in the high schools soon if we're ever going to put a man on Mars."

"The moon," I said. "We're trying to put a man on the moon."

"Yes, that's what I said."

Embarrassed, I said impulsively, "I wish I could see you," then realized my mistake. Now Mother would cry. I hated it when she cried. Something went mushy inside me as if a rib were dissolving, little pieces of bone going soggy and wet so that I drooped down deeper into myself.

Monday evening was overcast, the air brisk with the first hints of fall. The gray sky, darkening around the fringes, promised rain, so I hurried on to class, stuffing my hands in my pockets because I didn't own gloves. Dr. McKune lectured as if we were all English majors, ready to write a thesis on one of the many "conceits" of modernism. He gave no notice of me, and this so dampened my spirits that I peeled a hangnail until it bled, but by the end of class my natural enthusiasm won out and I listened eagerly as if my very life depended on it. In Soldier Creek the point of an education was to sound smart, to impress with big words like expiate and anomaly, but at Trinity, the idea seemed to be to turn all thoughts on their heads. Could I do that? Could I—

"Miss Soldier."

I was so involved in my reverie, his voice startled me. "What? . . . I mean, Sir?"

"Could you stay for a moment after class?" He was so perfectly elegant in gray flannels and a crisp white shirt that I felt frumpy and leaden in my schoolgirl clothes. A pleated wool skirt and blue sweater. But I was excited too because "it" had happened. He knew my name.

After the other students had filed out of the room, Professor McKune lifted his gray-templed head and said softly, "Sit down, Miss Soldier. I promise not to keep you too long," and then he gazed at me in studied silence as if seeing me clearly, fingering the hidden impulses of my brain. I returned his gaze as fixedly as I could. I didn't intend to be undone.

"Miss Soldier, tell me about your high school."

This surprised me. What did my high school have to do with my paper?

"Well, it was quite small, only eighty in my graduating class in Moss Point, Alabama. Actually, there were that many only because it was a consolidated school with many feeder schools, you know, smaller schools who sent students there in ninth grade."

"And you wrote papers in this school, I presume."

I blushed. "No, not really the kind of papers we do here. But we did book reports, and I was editor of the newspaper."

"I see." He looked down at the papers before him, silent, intent, as if making a decision.

What, I wondered, did he see?

Then from the stack of papers, he pulled out one and looked at me with a narrowed gaze. "Miss Soldier, your paper...well, I'm afraid it reflects some lack of preparation. I suspected as much. You see, it's not quite an essay yet. It's more a collection of personal opinions and musings, rather unfocused and disorganized, but"—and he paused and smiled gently at me—"with some potential insight that might be developed with work. It will require a more forceful argument in the next draft and further explicated examples from the text. There's no need to do pirouettes on the page, you see. Leave that to the poets. You should simply try to make your meaning clear."

I stared at the holes in his nostrils. I was no longer a body but a small pebble that had rolled to a stop at the edge of the abyss. My mind felt needle sharp in the center but fuzzy around the edges. The needle sharp part was trying to intensify the fuzzy edges, to muster a protective front against his words—*reflects your lack of preparation, not quite an essay yet*. Instead, the fuzziness took over, making my mind a soft, vulnerable thing. I nodded.

"Instead of giving you a grade on this," he continued more softly now, "I want you to look over my comments and rewrite the essay for Friday. It's important, you see, that you understand the form, that you determine a focus and maintain it throughout rather than present a rambling structure."

The gray light of evening was lost in the darkness; stars sprinkled the sky. I moved automatically, the paper clutched in my hand as if glued to my palms. As I walked through the empty dark, my hopes and dreams seemed suddenly vague and tarnished. What was it anyway that I'd wanted to be? Something marvelous. But what was that? What exactly was marvelous? I stared up at the sky. It was just a word. Nothing but a word. And now I didn't trust words. I didn't know how to use them. Professor McKune had said as much.

I didn't remember the bus ride back to the other side of campus or acknowledge the dorm assistant's message written on a white index card: CALL YOUR MOTHER. What I saw was my closet at Soldier Creek with its stacks of paperback thrillers. "My sweeties." I wanted more than anything to step inside that closet, to pick up *Brazen Love* and slam shut the door.

That night I didn't sleep. I couldn't. Instead, I remembered a morning years ago when Jit and Daddy zoomed away in the boat while Mother and I slept. Only I wasn't asleep. I woke in the silvery light of early morning, a time when the mist hovered over the creek, a wet chill pressed into the air. I didn't know what woke me, maybe the sound of a paddle in the water or a gull cawing in the sky, searching that ghostly surface for food. I only know that I lifted the curtains from my window and was surprised to see Jit and Daddy in the boat casting off, both of them facing away from me, toward the creek. I jumped out of bed and ran down the stairs and out onto the bluff, yelling, "Don't leave me!" But they had already moved to the center of the creek and didn't turn around. Maybe they didn't hear me. Maybe they were too far away, the motor already churning up white foam beneath the boat. The reasons didn't matter. I stood there and cried, feeling more bereft than I ever had before, believing they would never come back, that they'd left me permanently, intending to exclude me. When I couldn't see them anymore, I went back to the house and moped around, refusing to tell Mother what was wrong, refusing her comfort. I knew that Mother would humor me, would do anything I wanted to do, but suddenly it seemed to me her compliance was just another sign I'd been sacrificed. Of course when Jit came back I was secretly relieved though I ignored her, refusing majestically to play with her, making her tag along behind me just to be near me. I refused to give her ice cream. I refused to give her her toothbrush. I refused, at one point, to even look at her. It was only when she cried out in forlornness that my heart bloomed with relief. See? I wanted to say. See the shape of my revenge? But what could I do now when the perpetrator wasn't Daddy and Jit but mean old Professor McKune?

14

The next morning I took one look at my desk, the paper dropped dead center, and I walked out of the room. For the first time I left campus, moving haphazardly away from all the tended lawns and well-handled books. I wasn't conscious of where I was walking, but simply stared down at my tennis shoes and kept going. When I glanced up, I saw that I'd wandered into one of the poorer sections of town where women sat on porch steps and children splashed rocks in puddles, the kids' clothes thick with dirt, their faces heated in play. As I walked past, they turned, sullen and still, staring at me. One young mother sat bundled in a man's heavy sweater that covered everything but her fingers, which were snapping beans.

I walked for hours, going up side streets, staring at the cracks in the sidewalk, at houses stacked so close together they looked like building blocks. Between them, there was no breathing room, just worn paths kids must have made scuttling through them to play. No men. Only women and children. Relieved to be anonymous, I sat down on a scruffy park bench, paint peeling from wind and rain, and wrote furiously in my notebook: *I hate Professor McKune. I hate his rich, dramatic voice. I hate his vocabulary. I hate his tongue, his nose, his eyes that snap you to attention. I hate his*— When I looked up from my notes, a little girl had materialized, a pint-sized kid with dirt in her hair and dried blood on her lips. I didn't know where the girl had come from. One moment I'd been alone writing, and the next moment this kid was beside me, a weed clutched between her dirty hands. Her face was pale as if she'd spent most of her life indoors, though from the scratches on her arms and the blood on her lip, she must have tangled with something. Her dark eyes stared at my pencil; then, in a quick maneuver, she grabbed it and held it in her hands with the weed. Almost as suddenly, she ran.

"Hey," I called, but she'd turned the corner of a building and was out of sight. I closed my eyes, pulled back into my own odd mood. How could I be so excited one moment, so despondent the next? I couldn't say a word to Mother and Jit about this part of me as if it was a secret, something they'd never understand. I'd thought college would be like climbing a ladder, seeing clearly the rungs to follow, one leading to the next. But what if it wasn't that way at all? What if, even as I climbed, I slipped, not quite knowing how to hold on?

A hand tickled me. I jumped, almost knocking over the little girl.

"Now where did you come back from?"

The little girl tried to smile, but before she could manage it, tears rolled from her eyes and she held up her hand. A wood shaving was stuck into the fleshy part of her palm. I could see she'd been digging at it, the skin red and scratched around the splinter.

"We need tweezers to get this out," I said, wondering where I'd ever find a pair of tweezers in this neighborhood. I looked around me at the stooped houses, the trash blowing in the wind. Then I remembered the woman snapping beans. "Com'on, let's see if we can get you fixed up," and the little girl followed along beside me, just as Jit had done as a kid, holding her injured palm out in front.

"Lord, Gwenie, how you do fix you'self," the woman said when we came to her porch, Gwenie already holding out her hand. "Always inta something." I was relieved that the woman recognized the child.

"Does she live around here, ma'am?"

"Up the corner," the woman said, nodding her head to the right.

"Well, maybe I should just take her home." The woman gave me such a look of scorn I wondered what I'd said wrong. "Do you know her parents?"

"Parents," the woman frowned. "Who said nothing about parents?"

"But I thought you said she lived up there. I thought—"

"She's been placed there. Them people take in children for the state, and it's a good sight better than the county jail, what with hoodlums and all."

I looked at Gwenie. "You mean she was at the county jail? Why would anyone leave a child there?" The questions spilled over into each other. "What about her parents?"

"They done died or run off or something, and she was put there for a few days 'til she went wild and broke her arm. Then they give her to the Williams."

"Well, maybe I should take her on to the Williams after you get the splinter—"

"It ain't a good place in the daytime," the woman said, looking suddenly suspicious. "You ain't with the welfare, is you?"

"Oh no, I'm a student. I was just sitting down at the park—"

"Well, old man Williams is outta work, and he can be real mean when a kid do the kinda upsetting most kids do. It's better she stay out on the streets."

When I looked down at the little girl, she was smiling up at me, holding out half of the broken pencil. She had said nothing but had waited patiently for my help. "Thank you," I said, taking the eraser end. "You keep the point." And then I was backing out of there, something in the child's face reminding me of Jit, the way Jit looked at me, so hopeful, so expectant, waiting for me to solve whatever had gone wrong. That trusting face hid all the distrust in the world, a face I wasn't ready to see. "Well, I have to get back. I have to write—"

The little girl waved. And as suddenly she was Jit, Jit who believed in me, Jit who trusted me, who didn't know all of the story. I stopped as suddenly as I'd moved, an invisible wall rising before me. Last week Professor McKune had asked, "How does one enter the intellectual life, the creative life instead of the acquisitive life?" He'd asked this as if we'd know the former was a *better life*, the life we should strive for, the life we must lead others toward. When I was writing down notes in class, I nodded my head in agreement, of course, of course, but as I stared at the run-down houses and weedy dirt yards with broken fences and crumbling steps, I thought about how different it was when you were on the bottom, when the better life was shoes and pencils and schools, when the better life let you gaze serenely at the evening sky.

I glanced back at the little girl, and without another word, I started running, following the street to the corner, then slowing down to catch my breath, then running again.

When I got back to the dorm, I opened the window, letting the cool air flood the room, then pulled out my paper with Professor McKune's scrawl of comments. I read them carefully, following their logic: You have astutely asserted Lily's function as the surrogate daughter of Mrs. Ramsey, but you have not clarified specifically the different set of values Lily adheres to. Now I went back through the book, making notes, marking passages, highlighting words. With a new surge of energy, I began to write: *What Lily Briscoe asserts is the need for creative autonomy as more fundamental than the solace of relationship.* I stared at that sentence, and I knew I'd understood something essential and difficult, something I too would need to know.

15

A night in late November. When I looked out the library window, I saw tiny flakes floating and swirling like dust in the dark. Snow! I'd never seen snow before, and I rushed outside, leaving my books and papers spread out on the table so I could scoop up handfuls and toss it in the air. I twirled, dancing, spinning, letting the snow frost my hair, my coat, the tops of my shoes, the little space between my socks and my pants. As I spun, all the old worry loosened as if a weight were being lifted from my shoulders and I could move freely, as light as a cinder caught by the wind. A feeling of cleanness swept through me. I lifted my face to the snow and let it fall on my eyelids, my lips, on the very tip of my chin.

Within two hours the snow had melted, leaving nothing but a blanket of ice and a softness to the air. But the next morning I woke early, the sky barely flush with light. I dressed in warm clothes—my old pea coat and a wool scarf—and rushed out of the dorm before anyone else had stirred. I stared at the branches glazed with ice, icicles dripping from bare, hungry limbs. The world looked brand new, not bleak or crazy as it often did in the cold gray mornings, but bursting with life. I felt a bubble of happiness float up inside me, and I walked slowly, oblivious to everything but this feeling. I had a key to the scholarship room at West Annex, a reading room reserved for scholarship students and research fellows teaching at the college. The old wing chairs were worn but deep-seated and comfy, and the room was crowded with floor lamps and end tables full of nicks and scars. You could drop your books on the floor, throw your feet on a table, and start reading history or literature. Or you could plunk down, close your eyes, and sleep the sleep of the blessed. No one would bother you until the troops came in at 8:00, and then there would be coffee, even doughnuts if Mrs. Pritchett stopped by Krispy Kreme on her way to work. As I walked toward West Annex, I was thinking about the paper I'd rewrite on Virginia Woolf—theories of identity this time—and didn't notice anyone behind me until I stopped to pick up a sheet of ice, holding it like a prism. I was so immersed

in my thoughts I didn't hear them at first, until a peel of laughter startled
me, and I turned to see two guys in turtleneck sweaters and jeans, no socks
on their feet as if they were immune to the cold. One, a blonde of medium
height, was talking, his hands agitated, darting about as he talked. The
dark one looked straight ahead, his face impassive but thoughtful, hands
scrunched deep inside his jeans pockets. Damn! I'd wanted the morning
to myself. The six-thirty chimes hadn't even rung. Almost in unison, they
turned toward me, their faces as surprised as my own.

I hurried on, hunching down into the collar of my coat like a turtle
half in its shell, but even though I walked quickly past them toward the
Annex, I couldn't help overhearing their talk.

"Quit bird-dogging that girl, Teddy," the dark one laughed, his voice
cocky, full of muscle. He leaned intimately toward the blonde guy, though
he was loud enough for me to hear.

"Shut up, Jer."

"Shit, man, she's got skinny legs. Skinny legs means you know what—"

"*Shut-up!*" The blonde guy sounded so embarrassed I almost stopped
to get a good look, but had a better idea. I turned quickly and chucked my
piece of ice at their feet. But my aim was bad, and the ice went skittering
through the air and hit the blonde guy on the knee, though I'd been aiming
for the other one. I stopped, watching the blonde guy's stunned, almost
injured look, his clear blue eyes suddenly wary, studying me. He looked so
surprised, I laughed. And then the dark-haired guy did too. "Hey, Teddy
bear. She got you. She really got you!" And he did a little jig right there on
the icy ground.

"I was aiming at you," I said, looking at the pale pink-gray of his
sleeve. Where had I seen that before? Then I turned quickly and began
walking, but not before I heard him mutter, "Bitch!"

As I neared the Annex, thrilled as always to see the worn brick facade
and the stone steps leading up to solid oak double doors, I told myself
to forget about them. Creeps! You couldn't escape them even early in the
morning. They were probably private school boys, full of themselves. But
I was so relieved to be in love with Trinity College again, to have righted
the balance, I didn't want to burst my bubble. In minutes I'd be deep into
rereading *The Waves*, listening to Bernard and Rhoda and Louis, trying to
see clearly this time how each identity was created from the inside out. Or
was it the outside in?

As I started up the steps the blonde guy rushed past, then backed
up, his breathing fast and nasal as if he had allergies. His hair—blonde
corkscrews curling wildly around his face—gave him a mad scientist look.

At least, he was alone; I'd have had to abuse the other one, and I wasn't in the mood.

"Don't mind Jer," he said, giving me a quick, apprehensive look from the step below. I was halfway up the eight steps and paused at the sound of his voice. "He's a real hick. He thinks insults are the sweetest kind of flattery."

I remained silent, waiting, my bubble of happiness beginning to dissolve.

"Mind if I walk to the door with you?"

"It's just four more steps."

He grinned, showing brilliant white teeth, and he was transformed from a mad scientist to a college boy. "We could walk back four, make it eight."

"You're crazy." But I smiled. The bubble wobbled, expanded. I would still have my day.

He must have taken my smile for encouragement. "I'm Teddy," he continued, "but I guess you heard that. Jer's not exactly quiet. He's a real trigger mouth. Teddy Ashirsch. New York City, thank-you-very-much."

By now I was at the top of the steps and anxious to get inside. "Well, I guess you have to defend your friend," I said, opening the door.

"Now, wait a minute. You've got it all wrong." He came three steps up, almost lunging toward me. "Hey, aren't you in my chem class?"

"No," I said. I moved inside the door, feeling its weight against my hip.

"Wait," he called, leaping the next few steps.

But I needed to be alone and let the door click shut. Inside the heat hissed in the radiators. I needed coffee and silence. I needed the emptiness of this room that smelled of mildew and old magazines. I needed to read. Still, I could hear him talking through the door, so I turned and waved, thinking of that crazy chapter "Circe" in *Ulysses* where fantasy and reality change places, where nothing makes sense. In my mind, it was the dark guy who beckoned, the dark guy who put his hand to the door, but I turned quickly and walked farther down the hall.

When Teddy Ashirsch called three nights later, asking me to meet him for pizza at the Roundhouse, I said only one word. "Can't." It shot out like a bullet though I hadn't meant to sound so determined, so resolved to be difficult. I simply wasn't attracted to him, and Professor McKune had assigned another paper while I was still in the middle of my rewrite. Each night I embedded myself in the library, going to the same carrel, making notes from *The Waves*, believing myself now the master of tranquility and order. And the fact of the matter was, Teddy Ashirsch was neither dark nor intriguing, and I knew it would be a mess.

"What do you mean can't? That word's not in my vocabulary."

"I'm sorry, but I have a class. It doesn't get out until late and then I have work to do. I'm on scholarship so I can't afford to goof off."

"You've gotta eat, don't you? I'm on scholarship too, but I still eat."

And suddenly I remembered how he looked through the glass door of the Annex, like a wired cocker spaniel left alone in the cold. I thought of the frost breaking all around me and the warm sun shooting straight to my heart. I thought of Beth who had recently deserted me for a pre-law student obsessed with terrorists. I thought of those nights I'd spent in the library, my head bent intently over my books, and as quickly as that, I broke my promise. "OK, but only for supper. I can't stay out late." I told him to pick me up outside the Annex.

"Absolutely," he said. "I'll be there with roses in my arms."

The next evening I waited outside the Annex, watching ice crystals forming on the ground. There were so many shades of white in ice: gray-white, blue-white, pinkish-white, sparkling white. I'd never seen so many colors, and as suddenly, I saw straight through the ice to the creek. I saw all the colors of the sand: blue and green and lavender, pink and ochre, everything alive, even the colors wiggling into each other, and despite myself, I thought about Soldier Creek. I'd gotten a strange letter from Jit, one that said almost nothing but seemed to be trying to tell me about her life with Mother. She said that she and Mother watched the news together every night and after that, she went up to her room. *It just seems better that way. Too much silence can make your ears hurt and up in my room I open the windows and the outside world comes in.*

When she wasn't in her room, I could imagine Jit sitting on the pier, staring at the still, gray water, depressed, eerily quiet while Mother, working in her garden, ignored her. I could feel the rough wet boards of the pier, the thick, humid air, the way the horizon seemed to merge with the creek so there was nothing but gray matter, nothing to hold on to. And in that moment I hated Mother, hated her big puffy silences, her creepy withdrawals, the way she acted as if no one was there. The only way to get her out of these moods was to tease her, make her go to the store for some brownie mix and ice cream, gently bring her back to the world. But Jit didn't know how to do that. She'd do the very worst thing, become just as formal as Mother, both of them staring into middle distance and pursing their lips. I wanted to shake Mother. Shake her good. Get a grip. Look what you're doing. Poor Jit. How was she ever going to make it? I pressed my hands hard against my head, gripping my skull. *No, don't think about them.* But even as I said those words, I saw them whole, then broken, and the worry started up again, but this time I wanted to yank Jit up and say, "Get busy. Don't just brood."

"You waiting for someone?" I looked up, embarrassed, as if I'd been caught dreaming about something obscene. It was Dr. McKune, bundled up in a tweed wool coat and gray fedora, a wine cashmere scarf tucked around his neck.

"Yes."

"Well, it's twenty after nine. I wouldn't wait much longer. You can catch the 9:30 bus, you know."

It was the kindest thing Dr. McKune had said to me, and I felt both immensely grateful and resentful that he saw me standing here waiting, vulnerable and alone. Twenty after nine. As if a knife had been plunged into me, I knew that Teddy wasn't coming. And I had one of those moments, a sudden, intense feeling of embarrassment as if my socks were dripping with pee or my hair wired straight up from my head, and everyone could see all the hunger inside, a big slippery tongue poking out of me.

After I watched him walk through the trees to his car, then saw his Volvo pulling away from the curve, I began the long walk back to Cole Dorm. Fuck the bus! Fuck them all! Teddy Aschirsh hadn't come, *he didn't come, he didn't come*, but I was suddenly too depressed to hate him properly and wanted only to squirrel myself away in my room and eat chocolate chip cookies. When I got to the dorm, the girl at the desk handed me a note. Mother, I thought and folded it inside my pocket unread. I walked quickly to my room, closed the door and stood silently in the dark staring out at the silvery sea of icy ground, wondering why I felt so lost, so defeated. I crawled in bed, curling my knees up close to my stomach, arms drawn in to my chest. I lay very still. All evening Professor McKune had lectured about the modernist conflict between ideology, style, and personal history. In his early years, he told us, Yeats had defined himself politically and stylistically as a symbolist, but later he wrote that all his poems—all—had been made from the "rag and bone shop of the heart." Yeat's heart, Professor McKune had said, was his hydraulic, doling out the measurement of truth. "He wrote everything out of personal history. Everything. The heart would not be fooled." I turned over on my back and stared at the ceiling. Couldn't you ever be free of it? Of personal history? I pulled the covers over my head and prayed only to forget Soldier Creek.

When I got up, it was Sunday. I'd slept through Saturday, Saturday night, a fuzzy trip to the bathroom sometime early this morning. Now I heard the chapel bells ringing their sad, insistent wail, calling the faithful to penance.

I leaned against the window, making spots of fog with my breath. I glanced at the big red brick buildings across the quad; they reminded me suddenly of a fortress with locked towers and hidden rooms, but I shook that thought loose, picked at a recent scab on my knee. Then the bells went again: ding, dong, ding. And sadder, ding, dong...dong. I pressed my face against the window so I could see the early risers moving across campus, girls in dark coats and floppy hats, hair streaming out in subdued waves. When they talked, their voices were full of money. It was money not smarts, after all, that gave them such carefree confidence, a sense of floating through life as if all they had to do was stretch out their pale arms to soar. I looked up at the graying sky, like a sheet of lint pulled out of the dryer. Thick. Opaque. I thought of the sky at Soldier Creek, stormy and dark. That was the way I liked it best. A sudden squall coming up, the air electric, ruffles of white-capped waves rushing toward the pier. Suddenly guilty, I reached inside my jeans lying on the floor for the folded note I'd put there Friday night. Mother. But when I opened it, it wasn't a message from Mother at all, but from Teddy Ashirsch.

> *Amanda,*
> *If there is fate, then I must be fated to lose you already.*
> *Lucky for me I've been an optimistic sort for some time. I was*
> *on the way back to my dorm Friday when I slid on the ice and*
> *twisted my ankle. It hurts like hell, but I'm hobbling over*
> *to your dorm, courtesy of the Health Department's crutches to*
> *deliver this before I settle in for some heat. I'll call.*

Then in a scrawl below:

> *Sorry, I missed you. I tried to get to your dorm before you*
> *left for class.*

Despite myself, I smiled. He hadn't stood me up after all! I knew he was surely trouble, but right now, I needed a distraction.

16

Icy ground cracked beneath my feet. A gusty wind stung the backs of my knees. But it felt wonderful! I loved its harshness and ran exuberantly through the colonnade of leafless oaks. When I reached Kellum Hall, I'd have the RA page Teddy, then we'd sit by the fire, Teddy playing invalid to my Florence Nightingale. After that, I promised myself, I'd come back to the dorm and write my paper.

The wood framing around the doors was oak, a well-polished, dark-stained oak, much nicer, much subtler than the white-washed walls of the girls' scholarship dorm. The lounge was fitted with slightly shabby wing chairs perched beside a fireplace where a fire roared behind the brass andirons. Desk lamps lit the room with deep maroon sofas and study tables. It wasn't elegant, but I could see that it might once have been. I was leaning over the desk, checking out the dusty books grouped there—Simone Weil, André Breton, Willa Cather—when Teddy limped into view, his left foot taped above a dirty blue bedroom slipper. He leaned on crutches, and I saw that his body was slight, more wiry than I'd remembered. He wasn't tall, maybe 5'10" with that bush of blonde kinky hair and piercing blue eyes. I'd forgotten his eyes.

As he settled in one of the wing chairs, he looked at me, resting his injured foot on an upholstered stool. I sat down on the sofa beside him, telling him I was sorry about his foot, but he smiled and said it was predictable. "I was trying to read while I walked. Bad habit of mine. Reading about Mother Jones and the UMW strikes in West Virginia, and before I'd even gotten to the good part, I was on my ass."

When I looked blankly at him—I'd never heard of Mother Jones and knew nothing about strikes, though my own grandfather had supposedly tried to bust the unions in Alabama—he leaned forward, rubbing the wood on his crutch in an unconscious, automatic way. "I guess I'm garden-variety radical," he said. "You see, my grandparents came from Poland and Germany and went through pogroms and raids and every kind of hardship because they were Jewish, so it's just natural that everybody in my family looks at what the government does with a heap of skepticism. My parents hate the Vietnam War." He gave me a sympathetic look, but I had no idea why he was telling me this.

"Mine don't even know there's a war going on." I smiled into his pleasant, attentive face. "The war outside the house, that is."

"You're kidding?" He leaned forward. "Why not? I thought—"

"Don't ask. I don't think you want to know."

"Sure I do." He placed one hand on the couch near my knee.

The intensity of his eyes disturbed me. What I'd planned was a mild, frivolous flirtation, not some discussion about the war. "It's not that important," I said, looking away from him. "We live in a rural area. We have other things to worry about." Immediately I saw Mother and Jit silent in front of the TV, awkward and tense, their lives folded inward like dying plants.

"Rural America. That's where they get most of the meat for the army," he said.

"The what?"

"The guys, you know, from hick towns in the South and Midwest, and from the East Coast inner cities."

But I didn't know anything about the army or the positions of the country regarding Vietnam. I didn't know much more than the first two chapters of my history book about government or radicals. *I'm trying to get an education, I wanted to say, not get politicized.*

"Well, I want to know everything." He leaned forward again as if he might consume me, his blue eyes boring into mine. "Go on, tell me about them."

"No," I said. "Let's hear about you first. Tell me about—" I was about to say "your foot," but he interrupted, settling back in the chair.

"Nothing but political resisters in my family. Hard hats, Wobblies, socialists, a coupla Commies, but I think old McCarthy put the squeeze on them. They don't spout about it anymore, none of that 'everything for everybody' stuff. They're liberal but not involved. Then, of course, there's this disease in my generation of affection for the South. An unpopular disease, according to my mother. *What? You have to reverse Quentin Compson's role, going down there instead of to Harvard like a good Jewish boy?"* She thinks I've come down here to get myself confused. 'Messed up,' is the way she puts it." He laughed, then talked about Faulkner, about the Bundrens and the Compsons and Old Ben and Ikkemotubbe and even Sam Fathers. I heard the names, then the knowing behind the names, and my mind curled back into itself, became small and still while my heart pumped out its anxious blood. I worried, but I was excited too. I wanted to say, "Yes, yes, I know about old Ikkemotubbe. Let me tell you what I think about him." Instead I nodded, waited, marked yet another group of books I needed to read. And to my surprise, I thought about the creek. I suddenly wanted to tell him how the light at dusk looked heavy and golden as if you were seeing it through a film of gauze, how the water sometimes went dead still as if it were held under glass. But then he leaned forward, this time so close I could feel his breath on my knee. "I'm going out with you, you know, despite your wimp of a past. Now, what about you?"

I laughed. His teasing was preposterous, and yet I was beginning to be entertained. My mood lightened. Northern men were different. "I grew up in Alabama," I said, "but leave my past out of it. It's innocent. It's just a stinky old past like everyone else's."

"Jesus!" Teddy exploded. "Alabama! That means George Wallace!"

I nodded, smiling. "That's right. And Hugo Black and Rosa Parks and Bull Connor and Zelda Fitzgerald—"

"Did you know my parents won't even say Wallace's name in our house? They say, 'that man who ran his wife for governor.' Alabama! Just my luck." He readjusted his foot on the pillow, his gaze still burning into me as if he were trying to stare the Alabama out.

I studied the fire where a log burned crisply. Alabama!

Teddy said low, leaning nearer. "Fuck George Wallace."

His boldness surprised me, and despite myself I smiled. I had expected . . . what? A subdued, quiet man. He reminded me of a colt whinnying in the cool autumn air.

"George Wallace came out of nowhere," I said, wondering why I was defending the man. "He did what he could, what was pragmatic, given his background."

"Listen," his voice was breathless now. "I don't give a shit about George Wallace or Bull Connor or any of those bastards." He lowered his head so that I could smell the salty odor of his breath. He smelled like peanuts. Pretzels. Potato chips. He moved even closer, so close I was afraid he was going to touch my hair.

"Good," I said, pulling back, "because I'm not going back to Alabama. I'm going—" but I was interrupted by a figure behind us, a voice I recognized, deep and mocking.

"You don't waste any time do you, Red?"

It was Teddy's friend, the dark-haired guy who'd called me a bitch the other day. Immediately, I stiffened, readying for battle. Yet I couldn't help staring at him, at his high slanted cheekbones, his mussed dark hair and heavy brows. He was all aloofness and beauty in an old jeans jacket, the pockets ripped off. Taller and thinner than Teddy, his dark hair rippled against his wrinkled collar, a shock against lily-white skin. His eyes were deep-set, furious but with a coolness that reminded me of a Doberman pinscher's.

"Jer!" Pleasure beamed across Teddy's face, and in that one moment I saw how much he admired this friend. "Sit down, old buddy. This is Amanda Soldier, who, if you remember, is an early riser." Then he turned to me, and with mock seriousness, said, "Amanda, Jeremy Barnes, radical thinker and general fuck-up. Can't get himself out of his room. Listens to damn swamp tunes all day long, then hauls himself up for his literature class."

Jeremy Barnes. Barnes. The word stuck in my throat. The gray-pink sweater. I had it! Professor's McKune's genius! I didn't dare look at him, for he had written a paper that Professor McKune openly admired in class, a paper on *Ulysses*, that unbearable book. A book no one in her right mind could understand. Even the CliffsNotes had been impossible, futile. But Professor McKune had called his essay both original and cohesive. Cohesive! That nasty word. As Professor McKune had read, the actual beauty of the words pressed hard against me, and I felt the first prick of jealousy. I thought of the long nights I'd spent rewriting my papers, crumpling up failed pages, looking up footnotes in a stupid handbook, while Jeremy Barnes listened to music, or so Teddy had said. I could see him sprawled on the bed, no, no, Teddy would sprawl, but this one would lie flat on his back, arms behind his head, staring at the ceiling. Then oddly, the fury began to calm me, singing inside me like the buzz of a florescent light. "So nice to meet a genius," I said, holding out my hand as blood rushed to my face. I felt giddy, the slumbering competitive drive waking up, a hammer beating inside my skull. "I bet you've got some great idea to tell us, something to change the course of our day." I knew I sounded absurd, but I couldn't help myself. I was rattled.

"Of course," he said, seeming pleased with himself. He slouched against Teddy's chair, his hand affectionately touching Teddy's shoulder, dribbling with his fingers. "Love what you love totally," he murmured, grinning. "That's my motto."

Teddy laughed.

"That's ridiculous!" The smugness between the two of them sickened me. I laughed nervously, frightened that I might never love anything at all. "That has nothing to do with our messy, little complicated lives. You're talking about—"

"Passion," he said simply. And his face became grave and thoughtful, more beautiful than it had been in motion.

The simplicity of his reply startled me. "But passion is complicated—"

"Not really," he said. "It's intuitive, primary, even irrational."

And immediately I thought of Jit who knew what she loved and loved it despite everything else. "But that leaves out so much of the world," I began.

"Not really," he repeated. The grin was back. A grin that said he liked to play this game.

"You're just being a romantic," I said. "Love isn't simple. Honesty either. You've left no room for ambivalence, the most natural response in everything."

Jeremy smiled, a mild, soft smile, his eyes deepening. "Then," he said, his voice lower and calmer, the sarcastic edge totally gone. "I want to see you. That's honest. Will you have dinner with me tonight while my friend Teddy gets his rest?"

Teddy's face tightened; his nostrils quivered as he looked not at me or Jeremy but at his foot wrapped in its bulky bandage. "Cut it out, Jer," he said, his voice curt now as if he were hacking out the words.

"It's a fair question," Jeremy went on, puckish again. Yet I noticed a vein throbbing in his temple. What game were they playing? "She should give a fair answer."

I turned away from them, looking at the wind gusting through the trees. Leaves blew past the window. Gold and red and burgundy. Like the late sun on the water at Soldier Creek. Like my old shoes. Poor old shoes. Suddenly I felt tired. My shoulders slumped beneath my sweater, and I watched a leaf dangle like a charm from a branch, then disappear out of sight. A genius, Professor McKune had said. But I...I was something too. *I saw myself running down to the pier in my bunny slippers, the ears flapping on the pine needles as I ran to see the rainbow that curved from the water into the sky. I screamed back to Mother, "Look! Look!" and I believed it was mine, had appeared just for me.* "No, I don't think so," I said turning back to them.

"Then tell me why. Honestly, of course." The smirk was back. Mr. Ulysses. Mr. God's Gift. Mr. Genius Himself.

"Because I want to sleep," I said. And for a moment I closed my eyes. I did want to sleep, to sleep and sleep and sleep.

But when I opened them again, Jeremy was smiling. He bent over Teddy and mussed his hair, whispering in his ear. Teddy's face loosened as Jeremy waved good-bye.

Why, he was a tease, a consummate snob.

"Did you mean that?" Teddy asked, interrupting my thoughts.

"What?"

"About Jer?"

"Of course. He was only teasing you, Teddy." I laughed, it was so obvious.

Teddy grinned. "You don't understand Jer. He meant it. He doesn't say anything he doesn't mean."

"Don't you see what he was doing?"

"Sure, he was trying to steal my girl."

17

In no time I found myself seeing Teddy on a regular basis, meeting him on Friday nights outside the West Annex, going to the Sweet Shop on Sunday morning for coffee and donuts, studying across from each other at the library and taking breaks together in the basement where we ate powdered donuts and chocolate chip cookies and hot cocoa out of the vending machines. Each Friday he insisted on carrying my books as we ran—both of us starving—to the Rathskeller for beer and ribs, baked beans and cole slaw, our week's culinary treat. Teddy ate fast, shoving gobs of bread into his mouth, then tackling the ribs as if he hadn't eaten in a week; despite his wiry frame, he always seemed to be starving, and once he'd had his fill, he sat back, sipping beer and telling stories about his parents and German Jewish grandparents who'd lived with his parents since his birth. He was remarkably enthusiastic about life, something I couldn't fathom, a human being without some deep, disfiguring neurosis.

"Too much Freud," Teddy teased me when I mocked his optimism. "You just think it's cool to be worried. You'd like to think the world's more complex than it is."

"It is," I said, feigning shock. "There aren't just gods and monsters, Teddy. It's not that simple. There are all the smaller, meaner devils as well. Greed and lust and anxiety and insomnia."

"I'm not saying *that*." He gave me a mock scornful look. "I'm just saying you don't have to stay in that big gray area of confusion all the time. Com'on, where would romance be, where would creativity be, where would genius live if we worried all the time?"

"You're just afraid of the bad stuff," I bantered, smiling at him, "terrified of the bogeyman. But let me tell you, when you trip, you'll fall off a mountain."

"God, you're so optimistic." He leaned across the table and squeezed my arm. "And that's what I love about you. My little fatalist."

For a moment I felt heartened. It was so easy to talk to Teddy, so easy to tell him the embarrassing, exhilarating moments of my life. Sometimes after a beer, I told him little bits and pieces about Soldier Creek, like seeing the grizzled, toothless shrimpers who docked at Josie's One-Stop to get beer and supplies, and the summer crowd of fisherman from northern Georgia, all decked out in L.L.Bean with coolers full of Heineken. I avoided references to Mother and Jit, and never once mentioned Daddy.

But of course, Teddy, noticed this. And I could feel him zeroing in, looking at me with sly curiosity as if my past were a white road curling endlessly away. "What's your family like?" he asked one night after we'd finished our ribs and were both hunched over the table rehashing our week.

I blew the foam off of my beer, then glanced around at the noisy crowd in the back booth toasting each other. "Oh, normal, frustrated, dependent. They hate Cinderella and adore Little Red Riding Hood." I moved the glass toward my face, knowing I couldn't explain the world of Mother and Jit, the world of an isolated rural life complicated by an obsessive mother and a confused sister. Soldier Creek was where I was from. Not where I was going. I took another sip of beer.

When I was alone, I dissected Teddy's character: he was terribly needy, which should have bothered me, but oddly it didn't because he seemed to require only my company to make him happy. And besides, he was smart. He knew a lot about the world, things I had no inkling of. Often while we sat at the Rathskeller, he tried to explain quantum physics, the Copenhagen interpretation, the Heisenberg uncertainty principle, making hasty diagrams on napkins and walking me through conceptual hoops. No one had ever talked this way to me before; no one had assumed that I would be interested in everything. In many ways, Teddy was the antidote to my continued embarrassment in Professor McKune's class, that place where inadequacy shook its painful stick in my face. Teddy talked about labor history and was full of stories about the "oddballs" in his life. Including his best friend, Jeremy Barnes. Though I pretended disinterest, a shadow of uneasiness fluttered inside me. I imagined Jeremy tripping me in the halls of grammar school, then snickering at my clumsiness as he flirted with my best friend. He brought up all my dreams of desire and retribution. But of course, it was deeper than that. I wanted something from him, a signal that I was desirable, interesting. When Teddy talked about him, I got sweaty under the arms, poked my tongue around in my mouth, sat on my hands. But Teddy never saw Jeremy as a threat. Jeremy, he explained, took the dog by the tail. If he wanted something, he took it. If that something resisted, he either dropped it and came back later with a new strategy or got into a fight over it.

"Sounds pretty neanderthal to me."

"Not at all. And he's charismatic," Teddy argued. "Haven't you noticed that certain people do get what they want because people just naturally give it to them?"

Though I hated to admit it, I agreed. And perhaps this is what frightened me the most: the idea that there were charmed people, the ones who didn't have to ask. Or beg. Or work very hard. I didn't like thinking of Jeremy as one of them; it endowed him with too much power. "He doesn't sound very modern," I said, unwilling to give him credit.

"Modern?" Teddy laughed at the thought. "I never said he was modern. He doesn't even want to be. He likes to think of himself as a throwback, a neo-absurdist. Should have lived in the nineteenth century. But he knows what he wants, and in a funny way he reads himself pretty well."

I squinched up my face.

"Listen, he's a goddamn bird dog from Mississippi. Stays on point. The bird dog, he says, is his model."

"Mississippi? He's from Mississippi?"

"Sure."

I laughed. "That's worse than Alabama."

"Oh, they're about neck and neck, I'd say," Teddy teased, kissing the palms of my hands.

I'd begun to think of Teddy as manageable, someone who would give me up as a quest and settle for friendship, and yet one night in late fall things changed. At the Rathskeller, he ate quickly, silently, watching me from behind his fork as if I might slip away, vanish in thin air. When I told him about Professor McKune giving me a B- for a change, he only nodded. Ordinarily, he would have been exuberant. Once outside in the frosty air, we walked more leisurely toward my dorm. Yet when we stopped to say goodnight, he leaned over and kissed me hard, not letting me go as he usually did. I heard laughter behind me, the sounds of students teasing before the front door.

"Well," I said, pushing him back, my fingers flat against his chest. It wasn't the first time he'd kissed me or even the first time his hands had wandered down the front of my dress, but tonight he was persistent.

"Come back here." He dragged me toward him.

"Ted-dy."

But he was insistent. "Listen," he whispered, "You've got to let me. I can't stand it. I love you." His hands touched the base of my neck, stroking it, running his fingers through my hair. I closed my eyes, yielding, and he kissed me again, long and slow. "Please," he whispered, but already I felt myself stiffening as if I had been a limp string pulled into a taut, thin thread. I wasn't in love with him. I couldn't pretend.

"I can't." I pulled away again. "There are things you don't understand about me. I can't throw off my clothes just like that," though alone in my room, I thought that was exactly what I could do. "I don't believe in all this free love stuff." I looked away from him toward the corner of the building where the spotlight shone brightly, like a halo of liquid warmth. The night air was brisk, invigorating.

But he turned my face toward him so that I had to look into his eyes. I hadn't thought of Teddy as terribly perceptive about me, but now he was looking right through me, as if he could see clearly into my brain where the synapses sparked. "What is it?" he whispered, "What is it that holds you so tight in Soldier's Creek?"

"It's just Soldier Creek. No apostrophe s."

But he wasn't buying my deflection. "Well?"

"Please, it's too complicated to explain, and I don't know if I can even explain it to myself. Even if I could, I'm not sure I'd want to."

"Try me."

"I can't. Not now, Teddy."

He loosened his hand from around my waist, and I felt my body as an infinitesimal molecule in the universe. I was nothing, dissolving into invisibility. A girl from nowhere fading out of existence. I needed Soldier Creek, but I couldn't tell Teddy how this dependence enraged me and how the rage motivated me, how Soldier Creek was and always would be the impetus for everything inside me. I couldn't tell Teddy because I didn't want to admit it so clearly to myself. "I'm hungry," I said instead. "I want something disgustingly sweet."

"Substitution." But he smiled. He had patience. I had to give him that. We went to Swabb's and ordered the biggest hot fudge sundaes on the menu.

It was late afternoon the following week when Jit called the dorm, barely whispering into the phone. "Talk louder," I kept saying. "I can't hear you," and then she mumbled something else.

"What?" I said. "What is it?"

"I hate that *sweater*," she finally said. She sounded incensed.

"What sweater?" I allowed a beat of silence. "What are you talking about?"

"That blue sweater, the one you left behind. You gave it to me, remember?" Her voice was louder now, and I listened for sounds in the background, but heard only somebody singing on the radio. "It's too tight," she said, "but I didn't know."

"Oh, that sweater." I remembered it now. It wasn't a great sweater, but the color was a deep blue, like the color of the creek on early summer mornings when the sun was just beginning to rise. "You're just chicken," I teased.

"I'm not. You can't say that," she whispered fiercely, and then I heard the sound of footsteps, the clatter of something, maybe a pot dropped on the counter, and suddenly the phone went dead.

When I tried to call back, the line was busy. I called again after supper, but it was still tied up. When had Mother and Jit become such talkers?

While I waited to call again, I sat at my desk, working through the last chapters of *Ulysses*. It was just a big, crazy, jumbled-up story that I couldn't unravel, even with Professor McKune's expert help. When Teddy called, begging me to take a break with him at the Rathskeller, I quickly wrapped myself up in a woolen scarf and jacket and was out the door, both Jit and *Ulysses* forgotten.

I felt coddled by the cold, the icy wind nipping at my sleeves, the hem of my pants leg, the collar of my jacket, all buffered from the cold with gloves, socks, wool scarves, leggings. Winter hung in the air, frost coated the trees, tightening into icicles. The ground was slick across sidewalks, but I liked to see the steam rising from cars and buildings, from my own breath. As we walked slowly back toward my dorm, arm in arm, I swore I could smell into the heart of winter. "It's so clean," I whispered, feeling the tingle inside my nostrils as I breathed. It was never this clean in Soldier Creek, the air thick with moisture and heat, bugs and sweat.

But then Teddy pulled me beneath a tree, its limbs spiraling out like Kali's arms, leaves piled around its trunk. I didn't resist, but cuddled with him, seeking more warmth in the cold. "It's so beautiful," I said. "Isn't it beautiful?"

"You're beautiful."

"Hush." I closed my eyes, smelling the fullness of winter air, its dry crispness.

"Well, you are—"

"Hush now." I patted his shoulder. A sister's touch.

But he wouldn't stop. "Everything about you is beautiful. Your skin, your eyes, oh, baby, you don't even see your own eyes." And then his hands were reaching beneath my coat, up through the layers of sweater, feeling the bareness of my breasts.

"No, Teddy, please."

For a little while we struggled with each other, and I didn't know when I started crying and stopped resisting until he stopped too and held me close.

"You have to tell me," he whispered, his hands now on the outside of my jacket, stroking my back. "You have to tell me what holds you down so tight."

A week's worth of tension burst inside me, my mind cluttered with how persistent they were, always pulling on me, depending on me, hurrying me. In my darkest moments I worried that I'd never have a life without Mother in one corner of my mind and Jit in another, both of them wanting me to fix things, to make everything okay. My fingers crushed leaves, the wet smell of decay clinging to them as I tried to explain this to Teddy.

"And your father?"

"Daddy just wants someone to watch him sink. He's lost. And I just want to get away. I thought I'd be able to do it here. But I can't. Not yet."

Before I could stop him, he held me closer, kissing my neck, his lips soft as apricots. "My poor baby," he said. "Just stay with me." But his words only made me sadder; all he'd be doing was hanging on me too.

I'd planted the seed of my past, and now he couldn't give it up. Every few days he asked about my family: what they looked like, why my father had left, how they lived in such an isolated community with nothing but gossip and fish and half-crazed townspeople to interfere. But what I remember most about that period was the day Teddy brought a banana back to our table, peeled it whole, and began to eat. As I watched the way the banana slid around in his mouth, gooshy bits of it on his teeth before his tongue slurped them away, I felt such sudden revulsion I had to look away. I hated the way he took in everything I told him as if he were figuring me out by some grand design, some chemical formula that wasn't me at all, but only his idea of me. I looked beyond him in the distance to young men and women strolling across campus, sliding on the ice, pulling their coats tighter around their necks as they laughed into their collars. "Teddy, stop this."

"What?"

"Stop trying to figure me out. And stop eating that banana. It looks disgusting."

Though he frowned, he remained silent, the banana peel folded neatly on his knee.

"No matter which way you figure it, you'll be wrong. Just be with me."

"Okay, but I can't help wanting to know . . . well, everything."

"Please," I turned away from him, the old mean pain beginning to throb in my head. "It doesn't work that way."

18

Late at night I didn't think about Teddy. In that dreamy interlude between sleepiness and sleep, the dark one reached across my bed, touching the warmth of my skin while I nestled my face closer into the cool pillow, exhilaration rushing up my spine. As I imagined Jeremy moving closer, his face no longer mocking and arrogant but with eyes locked to mine, I let my fingers move against my skin, a tingling hum spreading straight up my thighs, then exploding in a new delicious warmth. Evil. It's gotta be evil if it feels so good. But I drifted into sleep.

Awake, I was ashamed of myself. Each morning I rushed into the showers, letting the hot water pound the night's fantasies from my body. School. You're here to go to school! You're here to read Joyce and Stein and Woolf and Eliot. I didn't want to admit that around Jeremy I became jangly, as if my body were separate metal parts, held together by rusty screws and wires, a nervous Tin Man. Yet at night in my fantasies, he touched what needed to be touched, and I relaxed, a wild energy feeding between us like an electric charge. This was what I missed with Teddy. He didn't read my body, didn't make my skin dissolve, didn't make my breasts ache, didn't knot my stomach, whereas Jeremy slid down my bones like a slick drop of sweat.

In high school, I had teased and bullied the boys, beaten them on chemistry tests and English exams, and I assumed there was something wrong with me since no one bothered to ask me out. Even my friend Marla cooed and squealed when Jason Wiggins noticed her in the hallway and tried to steal her geometry book, but no one tried to flirt with me. Oh, they teased me, hid my lab equipment, put toothpaste in my pencil box, but they did it just to set me off. They liked to watch me explode and retaliate. We played a game of war, little strategies to see who could hack it, who could retaliate the quickest, who could stand patient and attentive before Mrs. Gladstone while zeroing in on a neighbor with a pair of tweezers. But no one tried to cop a feel, no one tried to pull my panties off in the backseat of a car. No one treated me like a body, like a juicy, panting hunk of flesh. Only once did that happen, and it was so weird, I tried not to think about it.

I'd gone over to Marla's house to help her study for our chemistry final. We'd only worked for thirty minutes when Jason called and Marla nodded me out of the room. Dismissed, I went wandering through her house until I found a set of bookcases in the laundry room. It was a neat little room, small and compact, thick with the smell of soap. The light was dim, and I stood on tiptoe trying to read the titles of a group of books. Mostly they were romance novels and mystery books, but I was no snob. I read whatever was available, so I pulled one out and leaned over the dryer to read the first chapter when out of the darkness a voice said, "Hey there."

Surprised, I closed the book and turned toward the doorway.

He was short, dark with the scruffy beginning of a beard. He stood framed in the doorway, but then quickly stepped into the laundry room, letting the door close behind him. I saw then he was older, with faint wrinkles around his eyes. "What are you doing?" he asked, blithely, authoritatively, as if this were his house. I didn't recognize him. I knew Marla's parents were at a meeting and her little brother at a friend's house, but this man came out of nowhere.

"Reading," I said, opening the book again. I made my face bland, blank.

He moved closer until he stood right beside me, his trouser legs touching mine. As if interested in my book, he leaned toward it, an Agatha Christi mystery, and before I knew what was happening, he slipped his arm around me and, quick as lightning, squeezed hard at my breast, saying, "Mysteries . . . want to find the bad guy, do you?" then squeezed again and winked as if we'd both agreed on something funny. Everything he did was so unexpected, I stood paralyzed, but attentive as if I were looking at this scene from the wrong end of a telescope. His hand slid down to my waist, his fingers plying my butt, little taps and pinches. "Not always who you think it is, is it?" he asked, his eyes dark and impertinent, a little smile playing across his face. "The bad guy isn't always so bad, uh?" He cupped my behind. Who knows what might have occurred if Marla hadn't shouted for me, her querulous voice interrupting his offensive. "Aman-da," she yelled. "Where are you? I've got things to tell!" And then she opened the door (by this time he'd moved a polite distance away) and said, "Jeez, Uncle Frank, I didn't know you were here. Did you just get in? Do you want some lasagna? Do you know anything about chemistry?"

"Sure thing," he said, looking at me, widening his eyes.

On the way home I was sure that Uncle Frank had seen something nasty in me, something awful I hadn't yet unleashed but was holding back, rolled up in a tight spring of tension. Otherwise, why had he acted that way? And why had I stood mute and will-less, letting him touch me as if he'd had every right? This was the part of me that Jeremy spoke to in my night dreams, the secret, depraved part of me, awakened with every movement of his tongue. He was trying to force something new out of me, something that might be uncontrollable. I turned the hot water hotter and tried to think of Mother and Jit, but part of the wonder I felt was that they were completely blotted out.

In Dr. McKune's class, Jeremy sat in the back row, nearest the door. Many days he was as silent as the rest of us while Dr. McKune lectured on the emergence of the imagists. And yet once I knew he was there, he was like a ticking bomb behind me, and I tensed, waiting for him to say something outrageous. "The imagists are too restrictive," he began. "Too careful. Stingy, almost . . . with their finely chiseled prose. They don't inspire revolt, and they're too tame in their rebellions. It isn't until the late modernists that revolt really starts cooking."

Dr. McKune looked interested rather than piqued that Jeremy Barnes had raised his hand and interrupted his lecture. He pulled off his glasses and nodded sagely, then argued the opposite: "Imagism in itself is a revolt against pompous abstractions and romantic idealism, Mr. Barnes. You have to look at it in context. It's because of a desire to be more organic that the imagists have succeeded, a desire to get to the visceral level of things. This in itself is a revolt. An aesthetic and philosophical revolt."

But Jeremy did not back down. "I can see that, Professor McKune, but at the same time the 'thing itself'—the objects, the words, the places they describe—are such elite objects, such ancient words, something only the upper class could be familiar with, that it makes me suspicious. Who can make sense of Eliot's work without a classical education? Who knows that much about high church religion except Episcopalians? Their poetic fidelity to 'things' doesn't include the many ordinary and extraordinary things that a kid from Mississippi or Michigan might identify with."

"But Eliot isn't really an imagist, Mr. Barnes," Professor McKune retorted, and then he put his glasses back on and resumed his lecture, asking us to pay particular attention to the ending of "The Waste Land."

Each time Jeremy spoke, I felt both exhilarated and diminished. I longed to answer him, to argue with him, but I hadn't decided what I thought about the imagists. My critical apparatus was bound up with appreciation—everything I read I swallowed whole, slick and fast as if it were so much candy—and it bothered me that Jeremy could make discriminations when I couldn't.

When Teddy called that night, I stood firm, canceling our Saturday date. "I can't go. I have to study." I twisted the cord around my arm and read the next assignment in my notebook.

Teddy suggested a study date. "You know, load up on coffee like we—"

"No, I mean *really* study."

He seemed genuinely puzzled by this sudden defiance, but I didn't explain; when I thought of him, I saw him eating that banana.

And yet when I hung up, I didn't go to my desk with its stack of books and articles ready to be read, but yanked on my coat and went walking. I had to beat the tension out of me before I could settle down and sit at my desk. I walked a mile in darkness, then stood perfectly still, staring at the distant stars.

The next Friday night when I came out of Professor McKune's class, I was certain Teddy would be waiting on the steps, anxious to talk; he'd called every day, and even on the phone I imagined him smacking on a banana, the gooey bits stuck between his teeth. I didn't so much hate that he ate bananas as that he was oblivious to the fact that it bothered me. To avoid him, I left by the back entrance then hid behind the bushes like some kid playing hide and seek from the class bully. When I was certain he wasn't there, I climbed out, feeling foolish but safe and suddenly adventurous. I breathed easily now, swinging my arms in the cold, sweet air as if I'd evaded capture. Alone, I walked toward the bus stop, humming to myself. Yet when I reached the first crossover, someone stepped out of the darkness into my path.

Startled, I jumped back. My knees shook. My toes tightened inside my shoes as adrenalin raced through my body, the anxiety I'd kept knotted up flooding through my nerves. "Jesus, you scared me," I blurted, staring into the shadows as Jeremy Barnes' eyes stared back into mine.

"I'm—" he started, but his voice caught and died. "I'm sorry. I didn't mean—"

"You scared me," I repeated, and then we looked at each other and laughed.

"Just thought I'd take a walk with you," and now he smiled that reckless, crooked smile as if it were entirely natural that he should wait in the shadows for me to come walking by.

"Well, it's not funny," I said, but my voice showed no displeasure. We stood staring at each other as the wind rustled the dry branches of the maple trees and clouds moved in flurries across the slice of moon. The air was brisk, clean, a smell of winter in the sky. He straightened his shoulders now, and from him came the scent of soap and toothpaste. "You weren't in class," I said. He took long strides, and I found myself speeding up.

"I couldn't tonight." He hesitated. "I mean, I wasn't ready—"

That hint of uncertainty made me relax. My arms loosened. I slowed down. I had been prepared tonight, had understood exactly what Professor McKune presented. The extra studying was taking hold like new cells growing in my body. Now I turned back to the street. "I've got to catch the bus." I began walking faster, but Jeremy fell in step with me, not talking as I'd expected, but as silent as the night. His arm brushed mine, and I shifted my books, embarrassed at the pleasure. My mind bubbled with questions. Why was he here? What did he want with me? Was he trying out some gamble I couldn't imagine, trying to bait Teddy? I sneaked a look at him. His mouth, a thin slash, his cheekbones, angled steel. Those goddamn beautiful bones.

When we arrived at the bus stop, he paused, and instinctively I did too, listening to the wind rise in the trees. There was a shiver of branches, the hiss of twigs beating against the bark. Dried leaves swirled around us, scattering across the path. Jeremy glanced up, then looked at me with an intensity I hadn't seen before. "What is it about you . . . I mean, what do you believe in?" he asked in a soft, low voice, one I had to lean into.

"Hot fudge sundaes," I said quickly, but his face darkened; disappointment rippled across the surface. I was too embarrassed to go on.

He held me with his eyes. You could swim to China in those eyes. You could lose your whole scary self. "Does this . . ." he held out his arms to the campus, the night, the immutable, mysterious night, "does it mean anything to you?"

No one had ever asked me such a thing—if the world meant something to me—and self-conscious, I stepped too long off the curb, going down on one knee, then catching myself before he could offer his help. He seemed to sense that his help would not be welcomed, and he waited until I'd righted myself. When the bus came, the wide doors wheezed open, and I turned quickly to him. "Yes." Then I stumbled up into the warmth of the bus.

But I didn't think about the world. I thought about *him*. A goddamn bird dog from Mississippi. I kissed the spot where his arm had touched even as I saw him in some beat-up country store expertly rolling tobacco or behind the butcher counter in a bloody white apron cutting up slabs of beef. Then my mind switched, and he stood before a lectern, smelling of wood and air and leather and talking easily about Joyce and Eliot and Yeats. I idled upstairs as if in a slumber, practically immune to the noise. Music and talk whirled around me, the eerie combination of guitars and giggles and the rustle of pages, but I closed my door and sat on my bed, staring out the window at the blackness of the trees against the black velvet sky. Goose bumps crawled up my flesh. A silly grin crept across my face. "Don't be stupid." But the smile remained. I lay back, lifting one leg, admiring it, then the other. I stroked the calf of my left leg, feeling the prickly hairs I'd forgotten to shave. "Stupid!" I whispered, shivering with the first thrill of anticipation.

"I'm not going to the library tonight, Teddy," I said the next day. "I've already told you, I'm not doing anything."

"Well, come have a hamburger anyway," he coaxed. "Since when did you start turning down food?"

"Ted-dy—"

"Listen, it's one of those nights. It's a real New York night, don't you see, crisp and bright, and I'm hungry, hungry, hungry."

"I thought you had a big chemistry test. A big chemistry test. You want to go to medical school, don't you? You want to be the certified Dr. Ashirsch, remember, with the stethoscope and the white coat and the degree certificate framed on the wall."

A sigh. "All right, all right, you win. I have a goddamned big test and I'll study. But I won't like it, and I won't take this crap next week." He hung up.

I held the phone, a crazy smile on my face. I'd made him mad, and it felt good. Almost clean. When the phone rang again, I was still standing there, smiling.

"But I still love you." Then the phone clicked dead.

I stared out the window where a lavender light slowly faded from the sky. Night would come, the smell of smoke from chimneys perfuming the air, the clicking of the holly leaves scratching against brick walls, the sound of drawers slamming shut. The lost and forlorn closeness of winter wrapped me in its warmth, and I had a sudden swift ache for Jit. Her innocent face. The way she wandered in and out of a room, almost noiselessly, waiting for me to look up from my book. If only she'd come now through the door, I'd grab her, pull her out into the air, the two of us rushing across the lawn just for the thrill of it, stopping only to gawk at some couple pressed together, kissing. In a seizure of loneliness, I grabbed my pea coat and hurried outside. I had no idea where I was going, nowhere really to go. Though I'd promised myself I'd study, I felt nostalgic, restless, anxious to connect. I could walk to the library and find Teddy, but that seemed too much like defeat. I wandered instead not toward the main library, but toward the reading room in Roberts Hall on the other side of campus because it was a long walk and the air was brisk and clean. As if drawn by an invisible cord, I pushed through the front doors, dragging my feet on the smooth wooden floors until I reached the reading room, small, intimate, and cozy, with comfortable sofas and easy chairs.

I sat down on one of the cushiony sofas, stared at the soft globed lights, but the pulse of my body wouldn't allow for comfort. I opened my book, dug my elbows into the pillows. I bounced my leg against the floor as I tried to read. "Stupid," I hissed, then jumped up and ran down the steps, nervous and excited and oblivious to everything but the cool, clean air. Turning the corner, I almost collided with someone going in the opposite direction. "Oh, watch it—"

Jeremy Barnes turned to face me. "I'm sorry." He looked surprised, uneasy, his breath smoking the air. His jacket, I noticed for the first time, looked old, tattered.

We stood silently staring at each other, amazed that we would meet in this unlikely place. Stupid, I kept thinking. But my heart beat wildly, all my restless anxiety lingering there.

"Are you walking back this way?" he asked finally, gesturing toward the dorms.

I nodded, and he asked if I'd wait for him to turn in a book. Then we began walking together in uncomfortable silence. An owl hooted somewhere in the woods. A cat appeared from behind a building, stealthily stalking prey, its yellow eyes glittering greedily in the dark. I wanted to pick it up, to have something to touch. Instead, I listened to my shoes clattering on the sidewalk, and as suddenly I laughed, feeling the old pull of the world. The wonderful world! Why not laugh at the ridiculousness of it all? And to my surprise, Jeremy smiled at me then, an easy, boyish smile, and I laughed again for the sheer pleasure of the night. Other couples walked by, holding hands, some nodding to him. "Hey, Jer! What's up, Jer?" I had no idea he was known on campus. As we came near to one of the men's dorms, he said, "If you're not too tired, I mean, do you want to hear some blues like Charley Patton? Maybe a little Robert Johnson?"

"Well," I hesitated. "I have to study." I looked up at the entrance to his dorm. It was also Teddy's dorm.

"Teddy's out. He's studying at the chem library for that big test. We could just play a couple of records, but if you don't want—"

It was, of course, his sudden relinquishment that made me decide. I didn't answer, but we kept walking silently in the direction of his dorm, the air fresh against my body, the night black in between the lights. The smell of logs burning in fireplaces was faint even here, and I looked up to see smoke rising from the chimney of his dorm. Inside the dorm, no one passed us as we entered the lounge. I stood by the fireplace, warming my hands, waiting for him to get the records from his room just as I'd waited for Teddy many nights. This is betrayal, I thought, pure and simple—deceit, lies, dishonesty—but I'd only listen to a record or two, then go back to my room where I'd open my notebook and begin my last paper for Professor McKune, "An Anatomy of Marriage in Modernist Fiction: Leopold and Molly Bloom." I wasn't sure I believed in marriage, only the wedding of anatomies, which could, at most, be temporary.

When Jeremy reappeared, he held a stack of records in his hands. He motioned toward the music room, adjacent to the lounge, and I followed him breathlessly inside. The room held two blue velvet couches, thready on the arms with wear, but large and comfortable looking. Bookshelves stacked with books framed one wall, a round table with uncomfortable chairs and a stereo completed the decor. This was really just a listening room. Other rooms had pianos and brocaded couches and Oriental rugs.

"I have to close the door," Jeremy said, his back to me. "House rules when you're playing records."

Immediately, he put on an old blues song, the record scratchy at first before the music jumped out. He sat at the opposite end of the couch from me, seemingly lost in the music, his eyes closed, his head moving gently to the beat while I waited, feeling awkward and abandoned and alone. I settled back, listening to the gravelly voice, the heated-up beat, the sudden twang. Then the slow, sultry pull of a saxophone. Swamp grass and dirt roads. Honky-tonks and heroin. I thought of black men in the thirties and forties wandering the back roads of Georgia, Alabama, Mississippi, those red clay hills, the dust as thick as cloth. I closed my eyes, but felt so self-conscious I opened them again. I didn't know where to put my mind until I saw a sheet of paper stuck between the albums stacked in front of me. Impulsively, I pulled it out. A scrawl of red ink over the draft of a paper. I looked closer. I recognized that scrawl. Professor McKune's brutal red pen. After glancing at Jeremy's closed eyes, seeing the pulse jumping beneath the closed lids, I began to read; it was something about the Eucharist in *Ulysses*, but it wasn't the paper Professor McKune had read to us in class, the paper he'd praised.

When the record ended, Jeremy opened his eyes, staring at me.

"I'm sorry," I said, lifting the paper, "I'm being nosy. I found this in between the records and couldn't help but notice Dr. McKune's red marks."

"Ah, those masterful jabs at my intelligence?"

I smiled. It was nice to hear someone else complain about Dr. McKune, and I longed for more. In one fluid motion, Jeremy got up and put another record on, then stood beside me, leaning over. I was aware of his body next to mine; he smelled like a wool blanket, one that had been left in mountain air. "But this wasn't the paper he read in class, was it? I mean, how many did you do?"

His leg pushed closer to mine as he leaned toward the paper as if he meant to read it too. He stared at it playfully, tapped it with a prodding finger. "I started this one on the Eucharist mockery, but when I showed it to Professor McKune, he said"—he pointed to the scrawl of red writing at the top—"that it had been written only about fifty thousand times." Then Jeremy dropped down beside me, his knee grazing mine.

I expected him to defend himself, but when I glanced toward him, he was staring at me, not the paper. And then he was so close I could feel his breath. Startled, I shifted my gaze back to his paper. "And so you just had this other, this brilliant idea about time, just like that?"

As I spoke, I could feel his lips on my hair, near my ear, moving to my neck. My stomach tightened, then released with a flood of excitement as his lips made contact with my neck. "No," he whispered at my lips. I wanted to lean back, like a sacrifice, to let everything go limp, *who cared?*, but I willed myself to look at the paper, at the red slashing marks.

"What do you mean?" I whispered.

He put his hand on my cheek and pulled it around toward him as if my head were on a spindle. My thoughts dissolved into bubbles that would float up to the ceiling and dissolve. He kissed my cheek, inching toward my lips. I opened my mouth to speak.

"I met with him and he suggested"—he nipped at the corner of my mouth—"that I write on the collapse of time." He whispered it, and then his lips were on mine, and I fell into a slippery warmth, my body leaning toward him, giving into the heat, a liquid delirium. I suppose it happened quickly, but in my mind it was a slow crossing, a slipping of boundaries as if we were crawling across a bridge together over high water, thrilled and terrified of the danger. My mind dimmed to a low purr while my body floated toward pleasure, a new country, one I'd had no inkling of. His face so close to mine, I could smell his hair, a mix of winter and wool and shampoo, but in that instant he touched my thigh and an electric charge shot through me and I closed my eyes, leaning into him. I don't know how we slid down into the sofa, how I went from being beside him to being under him, still kissing, my mind slapping at thoughts like waves at a shore, running forward, then retreating.

"Then it wasn't your idea?" I whispered, feeling his hand moving from my neck down my arm, across the terrain of my sweater.

"No," he whispered in my ear, a sound of endearment. "I don't have any ideas."

Nina Simone sang in the background, slow and sultry. And then again the pressure of his hand crawling up my thigh, a stroke that released a pleasure so deep I floated, like a buoy on an open sea. And yet beneath the pleasure there was a tiny yank of fear. Subterranean thoughts were flowing, thoughts I had no control over. *Dr. McKune had conferred with him before the paper was turned in.* His hand rubbed my thigh, soft, slow strokes. I surfaced, oozed into a puddle. *I had never thought of speaking with Dr. McKune about my paper before it was due. Had he asked for an appointment? Was that what you did?* As he moved against me, I could feel his erection beneath the cloth of his trousers, and to my surprise, my body began slipping away from me as if I'd lost all control, easing into position while my mind thought, *I'm out of the loop, I've always been out of the loop but I didn't even know until now that there was a loop to be out of.* And then something new and definite rattled my consciousness. *If I'm out of the loop, I'll have to figure it out on my own.* I felt again the insistence of his hands moving up my thighs, but now alongside desire there was something else: dread.

"No," I said as if coming up for air. There was something besides pleasure I needed to understand.

"I've wanted this," he whispered, his voice silk. He looked at me with pleading eyes.

"Please, no—" I wanted to say that this was too fast, but his hand shushed me, placed so gently over my lips while his fingers did miraculous things, soothing my will. For a moment my mind went blank, beautifully blank, everything blurring and fading as his fingers lifted the edge of my panties, and there was only softness, wetness. Somewhere in the outer world I heard him unzipping his pants. Maybe it was that sound—jerky, slightly grating—that brought me back to my old life as if Professor McKune were standing behind us, talking intently to Jeremy, ignoring me. With that image my body surged back to me with all of its heaviness, a flood of infinite weight. "No," I said, louder. I pushed against his hand. "No, I don't want—"

"But you do." His eyes velvet. "We both do."

I could see my thighs exposed on the worn blue couch. They looked too white, too pale to be so ludicrously exposed. "No," I whispered as if I'd lost the ability to speak. "Not now . . . no, you don't under—"

"Yes, I do," he said. "It's okay." And he stroked my arm, soothing me, his eyes dark shards gone heavy-lidded. "Teddy's out for the night."

Perhaps it was the mention of Teddy that finally awakened me. I stiffened. I didn't want to be soothed. I was beginning to see something clearly, a dividing line that kept me outside, a dividing line I'd have to cross alone. I'd had no trouble corralling Mother and Jit to follow my agenda, but they were docile, easily persuaded, while this was something else. "No," I said more emphatically. And when he looked at me now there was something else in his eyes besides lust, something of the old Jeremy, crafty and mocking, and I shuddered, feeling a deep remorse, a fear I had never known. He wanted power over me. He thought it was possible to hold me down, to make me do what he wanted, and as if reading my mind, he pushed down hard against my body, holding me still. "Don't," he whispered, his knees burrowing into my legs. "I told you I've waited a long time."

But now I was pushing against him too. I tried to get my knee up to his groin, but he caught it, shoved it back beneath his legs. *Too late*, my mind said. His body tensed over me, quivering with strength as if adrenalin had suddenly surged through him. Though I pushed harder against him, tightening my body, he didn't stop. He held me down. I felt his penis against my leg, hard, insistent, pushing against me, into me, pushing . . . a sudden pain. "No." I tried to bite at his tongue, but he covered my mouth with his hand. He seemed oblivious to me as if he was traveling alone, and then I saw the clean sweep of his cheek, its soft smoothness, a plane of evenness. On impulse, I snatched free my hand and scratched hard, a quick, tense motion that made him cry out.

"Aaaaaaahhhh!" He reared up, mouth quivering, a blush spreading across his marked face. "Goddamn you!"

I felt the sting of his hand on my cheek, the shock of a slap. But he was up and off of me, putting himself back inside his trousers, unlocking the door—which I hadn't known was locked—tearing out of the room and knocking over a stack of record jackets, which fell in a heap to the floor.

Then I was alone, the needle of the stereo going round and round and round, the hissing rhythm of a scratch.

"Jer? You in there, Jer? The RA said—"

Teddy opened the door and stared blankly at me. I stared blankly back, my skirt wrinkled up around my thighs, my arms at my side, irrelevant, useless. I didn't say anything. Instead, I plucked at my skirt, trying to pull it down, but my hands were clumsily fisted. Finally I just flipped it, but the material caught on itself and stood up like a ruffle. Only then did I start to cry, staring not at Teddy, but at the cracked plaster of the ceiling, the lines converging like a map of divided rivers. "You sons of bitches." But it wasn't just Jeremy and Teddy I meant; Dr. McKune flashed in my mind. And Daddy—why had he never called me here at Trinity?

Teddy lifted the needle from the record and suddenly there was silence. "Baby," he said as if he'd just found me in the hospital. "What are you doing here?"

I tried to move, but my legs were as limp as seaweed floating in the current.

Teddy looked at me again, his face darkening as he noticed the record covers. "Goddamn him! Jesus H. Christ, I'll kill—"

"Please." I closed my eyes.

"How could you? What kind of joke is this—" He started to scold, his voice injured, hurt, excited, but my stomach was rising to my throat. I was going to be sick.

"Get me out of here," I whispered, clutching my stomach. "Please."

Quickly, Teddy helped me on with my coat, and together we walked out into the night, Teddy holding me against him, tugging me along because my legs were wobbly, my stomach cramped. We looked as if we were cuddling when we passed a group of men coming back from the library.

"Lo, Ted."

"Hey, Ross."

"Study group at midnight. You in?"

"Not tonight, Ross."

We didn't speak as we walked out the door, out under the trees, but as I began to breathe in the night air, my stomach revolted and I ran to the bushes and heaved. Then we walked in silence, Teddy's arms around me as if I might fall. I smelled the sweat of exertion on him as if we'd just climbed a steep cliff. For a long time there were only the mingled smells of tobacco and smoke in the wind, the hollow sound of our footsteps on the sidewalk. When I remembered my books at the foot of the sofa, I started crying again.

Teddy held me tighter. "Bastard," he said. I knew his anger would come around to me, but right now I didn't care.

"My books, Teddy."

"Where?"

I pointed back at his dorm.

"Let me take you somewhere. You want to go to—"

"Take me to the Pancake House." Let me just go somewhere bright and busy where they have a bathroom.

The Pancake House, across the street from campus, glowed with bright, willful light. At the sight of other people, I felt sick again and rushed to the bathroom, throwing open the stall door and lurching inside, unable to throw up, but bending over, gagging. Outside, Teddy had gotten me a booth, put a menu in my hand and sat down beside me, not touching me, for which I was thankful. "Just sit here. Promise me you'll just sit here until I get back."

I nodded. While I waited, I ordered coffee, but when it came I couldn't drink it. Instead, I let the steam bathe my face. When Teddy walked in with my books under his arms, I was already up and moving. "Let's get out of here."

He followed, then led me down a familiar path to the chem lab. We sneaked in, not turning on any lights, but smelling the strong stink of formaldehyde. "Lie down," he said, after he'd sat down on the floor and spread his jacket over his lap.

"I can take care of myself." I pulled away from him. "Nobody needs to help me. Don't you start helping me."

"For Christ's sake, just let me. Something's happened to you."

"No." I sat up. I wanted to leave.

"It's because of your mother, isn't it? You think you can't ever show any feelings. Your mother just drained you dry. Well, he hurt you. You're gonna have to feel something."

"Shut up about my mother."

"That does it every time, doesn't it?"

"You sons of bitches."

"You're just screwed up. It's not me."

And then I felt the wet on my face, but I didn't want to cry. Tonight, I wanted only to curl up in my bed and eat Milk Duds, let the sugar settle my stomach. I didn't need anybody pulling more out of me. "Just leave me alone." I got up and walked out of the chem lab, waiting to see if he would follow. When I knew I was alone, I walked fast, hurrying until I was in my room, where I crawled into bed naked, facing the window where I could see the moon.

When I came down the next morning, Teddy was waiting in the lounge. His red sweater had large holes in the elbows and his jeans drooped in the butt. He looked like a blonde Bob Dylan, scruffy, tired.

"Amanda, let me do something."

"No please. Just leave me alone." I started away from him toward the door.

"I can't. I can't leave you alone. I have to do something."

I walked back to him and held his face between my hands. His face was soft as a baby's. "Teddy, nothing happened," I said. "Nothing I can't take care of." For a moment, I thought I could make him understand that it wasn't Jeremy, that it was all of them, all of the world outside Soldier Creek that suddenly seemed beyond my reach. It was the world I thought I could tackle, the only way I could survive. "Please, don't do anything. It's not as simple as you think. All I want to do is to be alone. I need to be alone."

"I love you," he said. "You don't know what that's like. I have to *do* something."

A day went by. A week. I began to work. From noon until 6:00 I stayed at

the library, time magically suspended. As I walked home, I took out my
Milk Duds, watching the sky flushed with light as I sucked on chocolate and
avoided patches of ice. I shunned conversation, only nodding and smiling
occasionally. Once in my room, I curled in my bed, the sheets pulled up
around my shoulders. I looked out the window at the trees, the branches
bare, like scarecrow arms angled toward the sky. I saw the yard at Soldier
Creek, the dark green vines crawling over the house, wrapping it up like a
vise. And I smiled to myself. I was safe. I would be home soon. I opened
another box of Milk Duds and began to eat.

From six in the morning until noon I studied nineteenth-century
American history, learning how the slave rhythms influenced the first
assembly line, the songs of the cotton fields determining the rhythms of
American industry. For six hours, cogs of noise and song replaced sleep. At
noon, I went to the library. I wrote Mother, letters crammed full of gossip,
juicy comments about teachers, the waking prattle of former days. Now I
felt completely free to embellish my life.

Each night when I returned from the library, I found a note from
Teddy. Without reading it, I threw it out the window into the bushes below.
There must have been twenty or thirty notes hidden by the hedge.

I wouldn't have bothered about Teddy—his notes were so regular they
were easy to ignore—if I hadn't been walking by the chemistry building
one day and heard a bunch of students talking about the chemistry test,
what a burn it had been. It was almost exam time, the last flurry of pre-
exam tests. I saw the grades posted, and out of curiosity, I edged forward
to look for Teddy's name. Dr. Ashirsch. He had to do well in chemistry or
they'd yank the white coat from his hands before he even got the feel of it.

When I looked at the space beside his name, there was no grade at
all, only an I for incomplete. I had to push in closer to see, my shoulders
rubbing against others. "Didn't Teddy Ashirsch take this test?" I asked one
of the students nearby.

"Absent," he said. "He never showed."

It was unlike Teddy to miss an exam. And it worried me. I rushed down
the steps, moving toward his dorm. Behind a desk, a tall, skinny guy sat
reading *Being and Nothingness*, his ascetic face lowered to the book. He didn't
look up when I walked to the window, so I tapped the bell on the desk.

"Yes?" he asked irritably.

"I'm looking for Teddy Ashirsch. He lives in this dorm. He didn't
show up for his chem test, and I just want to make sure he's not sick."

"Blonde guy. Kinda skinny?"

"Yes."

"He went home."

"All the way to—"

The guy looked down at a roster in front of him. "Says right here, he went home to Soldier Creek, Alabama. Didn't even know he was a southerner."

JIT SOLDIER

19

One Saturday morning in early December a boy named Teddy Ashirsch came for a visit. When he called at 9:00 that morning from a nearby town, saying he was a friend of Amanda's from Trinity College, Mother immediately invited him to Soldier Creek. To Mother he was already a revered human being simply because he went to Trinity College. Neither Daddy nor Mother had gone to college, and to them it was like a foreign country, a hallowed place associated with dignity and learning. Both Mother and I pictured the smooth-cheeked boys we'd seen in Amanda's catalogues and the Kennedy brothers with their smart, clipped speech and their tough, outdoor good looks.

When Mr. Feely's taxi arrived, Mother and I stood side by side at the kitchen window where we'd have a good view of this new distinguished person. As Teddy Ashirsch stepped out of the cab I was shocked to see he wasn't tall and dark as I'd expected, but wiry and thin, with curly blonde hair that shot out wildly in every direction, his skin as white as a bar of soap.

"Goodness," Mother whispered as he stood beside the taxi. A frown creased her forehead and she gripped the windowsill for support. This boy named Teddy paused in absolute stillness, staring at the house as if he'd never seen a house before, then he whirled around toward the woods which were still thick with foliage, the trees and bushes so dense they formed a boundary of green against the oyster shell drive. When his gaze shifted back to the house, I wondered if he saw the mildew creeping up the side wall toward the bathroom window or the crooked doors, their frames warped by humidity.

Even as I thought this, he jerked himself up straighter, and I noticed his rumpled wine corduroy jacket and pale bell-bottomed blue jeans, the knees bagged out, one pocket ripped off. He looked awful. Forget the Kennedys!

Mother's face sagged then took on a look of earnest duty. "Well," she said, then she opened the door and went out to him, smiling her sweet southern smile. She introduced herself, held out her hand, pulling him secretly into our orbit. Then she leaned into the cab and said brightly, "Mr. Feely, you don't know how happy I am today. You've just brought me one of Amanda's friends, and that's the second best thing to bringing Amanda herself."

It was one of those December days we sometimes get at Soldier Creek when the weather doubles back to summer, the air thick with humidity, heat lifting from the ground and lingering listlessly in the trees. It was the kind of heat that made you sweat, and though Mother and I wore light cotton dresses, Teddy in his sweater and corduroy coat looked hot and damp. He looked plain weird. As Mr. Feely put the old cab into reverse, turning around almost at our feet and heading out the creek road at top speed, I saw Teddy glance at the taxi as if he were abandoned, as if we were two women aiming at him with a squirrel gun. His eyes blinked rapidly, and I realized he was nervous, skittish, about to jump out of his skin.

For a moment no one moved, then Mother said lightly, "Is this your first visit to the Alabama coast?" On the surface she seemed relaxed, confident and gracious, but I knew she was worried, hungry for news of Amanda.

"Yes." He bobbed his head. I saw a package of peanuts bunched in his shirt pocket. And then he smiled. A splash of white, even teeth. With the smile, something loosened, opened in him so that suddenly he looked attractive, eager, a little boy who wanted so much to please.

"Well, do come inside where it's cooler and have something to eat."

At the table, Mother stood over Teddy, a plate of hot biscuits in her hands. She had just poured Teddy a glass of sherry, placed the one cut-glass stem beside his plate (Daddy had broken all the wine glasses long ago). After he took a biscuit, Mother didn't move until he took another. Although the outer crust had browned too much, the insides looked perfect, soft and swimming with butter. There was also crisp bacon; apple butter and scuppernong jelly; an omelet with mushrooms, red peppers, and onions; a bowl of strawberries and fresh cream. For a moment I felt happy for Mother that everything had turned out so well, that we were all sitting at the table with a white linen tablecloth and linen napkins—things we rarely used—and that this boy, Teddy, who seemed such a contradiction to our expectations, was so enthusiastically finishing most of the biscuits, as if he hadn't had a decent meal in weeks, though he hadn't touched the sherry. That is, until Mother raised her glass in a toast. "To Amanda," she said, and he had no choice but to touch his glass to hers.

"How is she?" Mother asked shyly, her hand automatically going toward his arm. "I worry about her so," her hand hovered, then lowered, not touching him, but coming very close. "She never had much, you see, and now she's in the middle of, well . . . everything, isn't she?"

Teddy took another sip of the sherry, then his mouth tightened. "Yes," he said in a sudden gush of enthusiasm. "I think she's going to make the dean's list."

"Well, that's wonderful," Mother leaned forward, her face flushed as if accepting the compliment for herself. "I know she writes about people I've never heard of, people she tells me are famous, but I can't keep track of them." Mother laughed and poured him another glass of sherry which he drank quickly this time, loosening a little, his Adam's apple bobbing. Although Mother hated drinking, she considered sherry refined, genteel, the drink that proper ladies in the South presented to their guests at bridge parties and socials and family reunions, and more than anything Mother wanted to do things right, to be considered a lady. She sipped at hers, then got up to pour them both fresh-brewed coffee.

I drank neither. But I couldn't keep my eyes off Teddy. He had brought no bags, no books, and I wondered why exactly he had come to Alabama.

"Have you come down here on some business for school, Mr. . . . Teddy?" Mother curled her finger through her coffee cup, asking the question that buzzed through my mind.

"No, not school. It's really just a study I'm doing, a kind of personal study." He glanced down for a moment, self-conscious, wiping his mouth with the linen napkin.

"Oh." Mother looked perplexed and slightly disappointed.

"Well, you see," he smiled, looking again boyish and unassuming, "I've always had a keen interest in southern culture because of my interest in southern writers. My family are great readers, and I've liked Faulkner and Wolfe and McCullers ever since I was a kid, and even Tate's 'Ode to the Confederate Dead' though I'm a Yankee, you know. Southern writers are just . . . so tragic, so undeniably honest, yet with that elegiac tone . . . so it was just natural . . ." He nodded as if this explained everything, why he'd stopped in this small Alabama town to visit the home of Amanda Soldier.

Mother leaned forward again. "Why you must tell us about them, about these famous writers," she said, and I saw his eyes widen in surprise, though he recovered quickly and began to explain why he was interested in Faulkner, how a writer from Oxford, Mississippi, could examine his culture while still being a part of it, a man who never really fit in temperament or style, but felt compelled to stay and tell the morality of the very place that had rebuked him. Teddy was giving Mother a lecture on the writers in my literature book, and I began to feel a little bit better about him. He reminded me of Mr. Hesse, obsessed and bewildered and happy to talk.

During a lull in their conversation, I asked if he'd like to see the creek.

"Sure," he said, and I could tell by the way he hesitated that Amanda hadn't said much about the creek, at least not in the way I would have.

I smiled and led the way down the path to the pier, dawdling only to check the crab traps, pushing at the two crabs that clawed at the wire.

When Teddy took off his coat, I saw the bones of his shoulders pressing through his sweater. Suddenly, he looked like a waif, uncertain of his way. I could see there was something odd about him, something obsessive as if he were on a mission, maybe to reform us or to tell us bad news. "Your mother's terribly excited, isn't she?"

I nodded, wondering if he knew how much of our lives depended on Amanda. "Sure, because Amanda's so far away. And she's smart."

"She's smart all right," he murmured, "*some* of the time."

"What do you mean?"

"Oh, you know, she's not smart about *everything.*"

"I thought she was," I said gazing out at the water, thinking how Amanda was always making a string of essential, unassailable judgments. Since I'd depended on those judgments, I couldn't imagine her slipping. I stared at the waves lapping against the pilings, sending up shards of light, and for an instant I felt a peculiar satisfaction as if I were about to learn something new about Amanda.

"She's hooked in pretty deep here, isn't she?" Teddy glanced back at the house where I imagined Mother washing the dishes and singing because she was happy.

"She always says it's me who's stuck to this place." Like glue, you crazy idiot, was the way she put it. But then it dawned on me he didn't mean the creek. "Oh, you mean Mother?"

He nodded his head. "Yeah, I guess I do."

"If you want to talk with her, now would be a good time. She'll be up there fixing your dinner, if you're not careful. But it'll be pizza, so don't get excited."

"I like pizza," he grinned, and his smile was so infectious I found myself liking him despite my disappointment in his looks.

"Anyway, she's dying for news of Amanda."

The smile left his face. He pulled on his hair, a nervous gesture. "I guess she wants to know everything, doesn't she?"

"Sure." I felt a flutter of fear.

He leaned against one of the pilings of pier. "She isn't very happy right now," he said softly.

After he left, I sat on the end of the pier, dangling my feet just above the water, repeating that phrase . . . *Amanda not happy, Amanda not happy . . .* and then as if waking from a dream, I realized what that meant: Amanda had been keeping secrets too! I dropped the crab trap into the water and hurried up the bluff, slowing only when I reached the porch where I heard the murmur of voices in the living room. Head down, I crept inside, crawling onto the old couch on the porch where I could listen undetected.

"Well, I know she misses us, Mr....Teddy," Mother said, "but you must tell her to be strong. Tell her we depend on her strength." Mother laughed a small, lilting laugh, and I could imagine the brightness of her eyes. "More sherry?" she asked, and she felt for the handle of the pitcher.

"Oh, no ma'am."

"But you must be tired." She poured him another glassful. She had put the sherry in a cut glass crystal pitcher, something Daddy had given her years ago, one of the few things she'd salvaged from our childhood. It was the only "nice" piece of crystal she could show off, and she didn't want him to think we had nothing. Even if Amanda was on scholarship.

Teddy sipped gingerly, politely, and shook his head. "Fine, fine." His voice was clipped and tense.

"Does she seem extraordinarily homesick? I mean, do you notice anything that . . . well, that interferes with her classes?"

Teddy tugged on a curl of hair, twisting it unconsciously as if he didn't know how to answer such a thing. "Well . . ." he began.

"Oh, I know I'm being silly," Mother interrupted, smiling. "Amanda's never had a problem with adjustment. Why she went from elementary school to junior high as if it were as simple as throwing a stick. And in high school, she practically ran the place."

"Well, there is one thing—"

"Yes, she told me people bother her up there. Calling her every day, not letting her get her work done. I . . . well, I don't call her except on Sundays, though, oh, sometimes I fudge." Mother grinned like a schoolgirl, then looked shy, uncomfortable. "I can't help myself," she whispered, flirtatious, leaning nearer as if she were about to tell a secret. "But to tell you the truth, I don't think she minds."

They were silent for a moment, then Teddy straightened up, said quietly, "Mrs. Soldier, I think that Amanda needs to talk to you—"

"And I need to talk to her," Mother said. "I wasn't joking, you know, when I said that you were the next best thing to having her right here. I knew you'd bring me news. How is she, Teddy? Now I want the truth. Is she studying too much? Is she overworking?" Mother settled strands of hair that had come free from her combs. She wore her hair pulled back on each side with a tortoiseshell comb, and when she was nervous, she fiddled with the combs. "You know you can ruin a perfectly good brain by working it to death. My father did that. He had a really beautiful brain, he'd sit in his chair and talk about the world, how technology would kill us, drown us in its tedious repetition, and you just knew he was 'elevated,' but then he tried to outsmart everybody, to think about every possible angle and that was just too much and it destroyed him, killed him really and I worry—"

"No . . . no ma'am," Teddy said, tugging again on his hair, twisting it into a tight coil. It stood out like a corkscrew. "I didn't mean that."

"Oh," Mother said, and she visibly shrank, her face a sharp point of worry. Then she laughed her girlish laugh. "I guess you didn't. You certainly couldn't have known my father."

Teddy nodded, wiping his forehead with his hand.

"I just hope everything's going well," Mother said. "When we talk, she sounds so excited."

"I . . . I think I'll have some more of that sherry." Now he squirmed in the chair, pushing his hair back from his face, though it fell forward again across his forehead. "I guess I'm a little warmer than I thought." Beads of perspiration stood out above his lip.

When Mother left the room to get more sherry, he stood up, glancing around him, curious, almost furtive as he walked toward the mantel where there were pictures of Amanda and me. There was one of Amanda sitting in the car sticking out her big fat tongue at the world. Mother had wanted to throw the picture away, but Amanda wouldn't let her. "Oh, Mother, it's so me," she'd said, pleased with herself. Now Teddy held the picture and grinned at it as if he were seeing her too. The real Amanda: the clown, the tease, the comic. But when he looked up, Mother stood in the doorway frowning.

"It's a great picture. She's such a...well, a joker sometimes." He smiled.

Mother said nothing as she handed him the sherry. Although Mother depended on Amanda's joking, her teasing manner, in public she maintained that everything about Amanda was serious and ambitious.

"Well, tell me," Mother began, sitting down, spreading out her skirt so that she seemed like a woman in an antebellum drawing room, poised and perfect. Teddy sipped at the sherry, then took a full swallow, mumbling something I couldn't hear, so I crept closer, lifting myself up on the sofa so I could see them both clearly. I lost the beginning of his sentence when my shoe caught on the sofa and I had to be extra quiet getting it free.

"... you see, she's tied right here to this place," he said, "well, especially to you, Mrs. Soldier." He barely paused for that to sink in before he was off and running, drinking the sherry, swilling it now, and telling whatever it was he'd come down here to tell. "And of course, I'm sure it's wonderful"—he smiled—"but it's also like a knot inside her, Mrs. Soldier"—he twisted his hands together like a child making the church before the steeple—"and I believe she doesn't feel she has a right to love anybody else because to love anybody else would take love away from you, you see?" He gazed earnestly at Mother as if she were a student, one he was explaining the mysteries of the universe to. He told her he'd been studying psychology and literature and this, this thing in Amanda was pathological. He said that word slowly, "path-o-log-i-cal," as if Mother might not understand the meaning. "I know I have no right to ask, I mean, it's absurd for me to pressure . . . but you've got to help her, Mrs. Soldier. You're the only one who can. You've got to set her free."

Mother sat paralyzed, her face stricken as if she'd been slapped for no good reason, her hands clutching the cloth of her dress. Couldn't he see what he was doing? And why did he have to talk in that pleading voice, asking for Mother's sympathy? Then it dawned on me: why, he was in love with Amanda, crazy in love with her like a man baying at the moon. He was in some kind of love-dream, going faster and faster toward the bottom, almost drowning, then fighting his way back up to the surface. As he spoke, his voice pushed Mother further and further into that dream with him, a dream she didn't want any part of. Then I realized he was drunk; the sherry had slapped him into the dream and he didn't have the faintest idea what he was doing.

"I know I shouldn't say anything about this, Mrs. Soldier, because you don't really know me, but I love her," he burst out, "and I can't stand by and watch while she . . ." He stopped abruptly and burped a thin little burp. "Sorry," he apologized. Mother visibly tightened. He must have noticed this because for a moment he seemed to snap out of the dream; he looked utterly miserable, even disgusted with himself. Quickly, he wiped the sweat from his brow.

I stood completely still in the doorway as if I were a bird in a branch watching a worm on the ground. Neither of them noticed me. Neither of them shifted their eyes from the blackness they were staring into.

"She's really messed up," he said, suddenly angry as if he were no longer fending off panic. "I mean, she won't let anyone touch her. Touch her so she feels anything. She can't feel anything. Do you know what that means, Mrs. Soldier? She won't let herself feel anything . . . until—" he stopped, his hand automatically twisting his hair, "until, well, until . . . someone *made* her."

Now Mother's head jerked up, her eyes wide with fright, the whites flickering like a horse's seeing fire. But Teddy, looking suddenly exhausted and defeated, went on in his dogged way as if telling a story to himself, sitting limp and spent in the chair, his eyes focused on the rug, "After this boy did that, all she seemed to want to do was eat . . . gobbling down chocolate bars, clutching her books."

"What do you mean, until somebody *made* her?" Mother demanded.

"He was . . ." he sighed and whispered, "my best friend." He looked forlorn, despairing. "But I never thought he'd hurt anybody. I never thought he'd—" His eyes widened as if he were seeing something horrible. "But . . . and this is what I'm trying to understand . . . she didn't blame him. She blamed herself because if she'd been thinking about you she wouldn't have gone to that room in the first place. She wouldn't have—" He reached out as if to touch Mother.

Mother yelped, the scream low, so deep in her throat it was like the growl of a protective bitch dog. Only then did he seem to wake from his dream. He got up quickly. "No, you don't understand. I'm only trying to—"

"Get out," Mother said, standing.

Automatically, as if the hand were not his own, he reached out to touch her again.

"Get out before I call the police." And she drew her hand back as if she meant to strike him.

He didn't move. It was the first time he turned and saw me standing in the door, a look of helplessness on his face. He stood utterly still. Then he began moving, tangling in his own feet, finally picking himself up, opening the door, and rushing out into the light.

I ran out the porch door, around the house and into the woods.

I wonder now if things would have turned out differently if I'd just let him go, if I hadn't tried to interfere. But hadn't Amanda and I been brought up to save one another, to pull each other free of the muddle? At least, Amanda was meant to find the fire escape, the life preserver, but now for the first time I understood she needed my help.

I watched as Teddy ran down the drive, making quick glances behind him as if he expected Mother to rush at him with a broom. I moved alongside him in the woods, and when he slowed to a walk, I slowed. When I stepped on a branch and it snapped under my feet, he looked anxiously toward the woods, fear big in his eyes. Poor city boy. Poor Yankee fool.

At the curve of the drive, I stepped out in front of him, and he stopped, jolted, his eyes bugging out. I told him to keep walking, and we moved awkwardly in silence down the road. I hoped he'd start talking, would tell me the truth about Amanda so I wouldn't have to ask, but he looked too startled, too afraid to begin. "Why did you come here to tell us these lies?" I said finally.

"They aren't lies." He stared obstinately down at the oyster shell drive.

"I don't believe you."

"She's all confused," he said. "You've got to believe me."

"Confused about what?" I asked boldly, "I'll bet you're in love with Amanda and she isn't in love with you. Isn't that it?"

He sighed. "You've got to believe me. She's in bad shape. She's not going to classes . . . she's not . . . doing anything."

A flock of blackbirds shook a nearby tree as they fluttered wildly into the air in a thunder of black. They screeched as they rose, and Teddy shivered, his face going white as if he felt for the first time the shudder of fear. "But she knows what she feels about you?" I asked.

A blush crept up his neck, settling in his cheeks. He nodded, and I knew he was more trouble than I'd thought. "She won't even answer my notes." He sounded injured, insulted, but then desperation came back into his voice. As if sorry for admitting this, he looked past me toward the woods, his eyes wild now, like Mother's. "But that wasn't what I meant back there."

"What did that guy—"

"I don't know . . ." Embarrassed, he looked at his feet, at the dirty tennis shoes that must have once been white. I believed him. He didn't know. He'd come down here to scare us, but he didn't really know what had happened to Amanda. That would be for us to find out. Now all I had to do was get him to Josie's, back to town and away from here. Away from us.

20

What happened next seemed more nightmare than dream. Teddy did as I told him: went to Josie's, sat at the One-Stop like some kid half out of his wits, called Frank Feely's cab and rode the fifteen desperate miles back into town. Mother made frantic calls to Amanda's dorm, then paced back and forth between the kitchen and the den, picking up a glass, holding it up to the light as if looking for streaks or clouds of stain, then putting it back inside the cupboard without once touching it with a cloth. She wrote down every time she called Amanda: 6:15 . . . 6:40 . . . 7:20 . . . 7:45 . . . 8:50 . . . 9:20 . . . 9:40 . . . each time getting the same answer from the dorm counselor that Amanda was out and that a message would be left for her at the desk. "An urgent message," Mother finally said.

The next morning Mother seemed less frightened. The only ritual we faithfully followed was our 5:00 call to Amanda on Sunday afternoon, and to my surprise, Mother decided to put on a blue linen dress and drive the fifteen miles into town for church, where she prayed for continuity while I prayed for luck. All around me people seemed so normal—Mr. Hastings yawning during the doxology, Mrs. Childress shushing her children as the minister read from Ecclesiastes, Bobby Dobson wrapping a piece of gum around his middle finger—that I couldn't help wondering if we were the only people with problems. Josie said problems were as certain as loose teeth, and everyone had them eventually. But I wasn't so sure. Only as we sang "Holy, holy, holy, Lord God Almighty," our voices rising softly into the air, did I think of Amanda rushing home in two weeks, gathering us together, crowing over us, demanding something to eat. "Ice cream, chocolate sauce, bananas," she'd shout, and when I mentioned Teddy Ashrisch, she'd say, "Oh, please, a dramatic nuisance, don't even think about it!" Imagining this, a calm settled over me, and I looked fondly at the varnished pews, at the bound hymnals, at my feet planted solidly on the wooden floor while an ancient harmony swirled all around me. "Lord in his hea-vens . . ." There was no reason for these stirrings of alarm. Amanda

113

would call tonight and everything would be all right.

Driving back through town I saw the usual crowd of people waiting outside the Coffee Cup Café, women's hats lifting gently in the breeze, feathers ruffling from their brims, the men caught together in a knot, loosening ties, their necks as white and thin as veined stalks. I settled down in my seat, a little sleepy, thinking only about taking off my stockings and putting on a pair of pants when I got home. I glanced toward the park where the dogwood trees lifted their bare, graceful arms. Then I saw Teddy Ashirsch's blonde wiry hair spiraling above the collars of his dull wine jacket. Abruptly I sat up, knocking one knee against the dash.

Mother's eyes followed my gaze. "My God!" She gripped the steering wheel as if it were an anchor, her body stiffening.

"He must have missed yesterday's bus."

The light changed, and Mother pressed the accelerator so abruptly that we lurched forward, bumping over the railroad tracks, the tailpipe dragging. Neither of us spoke. I stared out the window at the soybean crops, wide fields of deep velvet green with spurts of yellow seeding through the land. A tractor sat idle in the fields. A harvester roared down a dirt drive. Chickens scattered. Dogs barked. On my left, Mr. Hendrie's barn. On my right, Miss Sootie's clothesline, empty of wash. Hay bales lay abandoned in the fields. It was only when we turned off the highway into the county road that led to Soldier Creek that Mother whispered, "If anyone should ever touch you—" She made a low sound, an angry sound that shivered under my skin.

"No," I said quietly, looking straight ahead, though what I saw was myself running frantically through the woods, creeping into the house, a streak of dirt traveling up my leg.

"But if they should, if anyone ever—"

"I don't let them," I said quickly, planting my gaze on the flat plane of the road, staring at the way the tar bubbled and broke at the edge. "Even at the dance—" I braved a look at Mother who was still bent intently over the wheel. I saw her eyes narrow, her face contract as if caught by a nagging pain.

"That's right. Don't . . . don't do anything to provoke them." Then she looked directly at me. "You shouldn't have worn that blue sweater. It was too tight. You're bustier than Amanda, and I want you to get rid of it."

I saw the sweater lying in the dirt in the Parker's drive, but still I nodded, a familiar constriction in my throat.

We turned into the stand of pines, and I could smell the water, a damp, brackish smell that entered my nose, my throat . . . the smell of home. Oyster shells crackled beneath the tires, and for a moment, I shut my eyes, hearing Mother's sigh and the odd rush of wind that rose from the water.

When we stopped at the house, Mother straightened and looked anxiously at me. "You bring it to me. I want to get rid of that sweater."

Surely I'd find the sweater lying in the dirt or picked up by the wind, dragged and flung into a bush behind the old Parker place. I imagined it stiff, crusted with dirt, knotted with briars. I waited until Mother had undressed, had tried to call Amanda again. When she lay down in her room, biding her time until the clock inched its way to 5:00, I crept down the stairs and out through the woods, pushing my way through bushes and scrub-brush, thinking of how I'd clean it. I'd drop it in the creek, rinse it out, and hang it to dry outside my window. Or maybe I'd wash it in Josie's sink. But when I reached the clearing of the old driveway, I saw nothing blue at all. Red dirt had been gorged out by a year of rain, and I could still make out the tire tracks that were surely Johnny Turner's. But no sweater. I combed the bushes, pushed aside branches, dug with my foot into the weeds. I stepped up on the wrecked porch of the old Parker place, prodding the cracks, the secret passages of rot that could only be worked with a kitchen spoon. Then I walked back out toward the road, my eye anxious for any scrap of blue. When I'd reached the highway, stood by the old tires now full of weeds, and heard the cars hurtling over the hill, whizzing toward town, I made a second fateful decision. I would go find Teddy. I'd make sure he left. It was the least I could do for Mother and for myself.

He hadn't moved from the park bench. I spotted him immediately—his jacket still flapped in the wind while he stared straight ahead. His eyes had a stunned frozen glare, and he slumped as if he were either too tired or too crazy to move on. I'd hitchhiked into town with four women, crouched in the backseat with two grandmothers on their way to a church picnic, plastic containers full of Jello salad in their laps. "Jesus is our savior," one of the women said pointedly to me, her eyes flat gray like the eyes of a fish. "He saved everybody, but if he'd been a woman he could have saved himself too." Uncertain, I nodded and to my surprise they laughed, whether at me or at each other I couldn't tell.

I slipped onto the opposite side of the bench from Teddy, sitting down quietly so as not to scare him. He looked at me in baffled surprise. "She doesn't understand," he began, as if we were in the middle of a conversation.

"Who?"

"Amanda."

"What doesn't she understand?"

"That . . . that I can help her."

"You missed the bus," I said, staring at my feet. I'd forgotten to put on socks, and there was a tiny hole in my tennis shoe so that dirt settled between my toes. "If you want to help her you'll go back to North Carolina."

He nodded as if I'd only said good morning, then turned insistently to me, holding out his hand, which was pale and trembling. "I'm more worried now than I ever was before. I can't get my thoughts together."

And then I understood. "You have a hangover. A sherry hangover. It's the worst kind my daddy says. There's no cure except time."

"God, is that what this is?" His face was glazed and sweaty, blanching white as if he might vomit. "I couldn't move last night." Then he straightened, swallowed. "I've never felt like this before."

Now we both sat slumped on the bench. I worried about my sweater. Had Johnny Turner picked it up? Had someone else found it? But I knew that my search was futile, hopeless. There seemed no escape for me, no place to land. A sudden wind brushed against me, a coldness quenching the warmth of the sun. I stared blankly at Teddy's blue-jeaned knee, at the flat weave of the cloth, like a worn but predictable map, until a new idea heated up inside, startling me to attention. *I'll go with him. I'll go up to North Carolina and see about Amanda myself.* I wouldn't worry about the sweater. I'd do what Amanda would do if our lives were reversed. I'd march myself up to North Carolina and see for myself that she was all right. "How much money do you have?" I asked. I'd never been this bold before, but I'd never had such a clear purpose. "I'm going with you on the 5:30 bus, but I don't have any money."

Mechanically, he put his hand in his pocket and pulled out wads of bills mixed with notes, receipts, gum wrappers, old theater tickets, and together we began separating the money from the trash, letting the trash drift to the ground, both of us so caught up in the counting we didn't notice the man coming toward us.

Officer Budd's shoes shone like brass as he wedged one foot between us on the bench. I jerked upright. Teddy looked confused, exhaustion etched like stupidity on his face. Officer Budd cleared his throat. "Listen, sonny, we've had some complaints about you sleeping in the park." Officer Budd glanced up at the sky as if the complaints might have been celestial, direct rumblings from God Almighty. "Complaints of a nature I'm not going to discuss in front of a lady, but I'll try to give you the picture." Officer Budd was a burly man, tall but husky, his shirt and trousers fitted tightly over his thick chest and legs. Now he leaned over us, his head tipped near Teddy's forehead. "Son, we don't want your kind down here. We don't need no radicals come to clean us up, no revolutionaries with a colored streak inside who think they can change the world 'cause they seen a movie about it once."

"Officer Budd," I began.

He straightened, clicking his tongue against his teeth. "You just wait a minute, young lady. I'm getting to you." And then he turned back to Teddy, again lowering his face so that it was level with his. "What I'm suggesting is this: git out of here, and if I see skid marks, I ain't complaining."

"Officer Budd—"

"Now, Miss, if you know a thing or two, you'll be getting on home and finishing up your homework like a good girl. That's what Sundays are for if I remember right. You hurry on now, and I'm gonna forget I'm seeing you hanging around with this type."

"But we haven't done anything, Officer Budd. We're just sitting here talking, counting—"

"You want me to call your mother, young lady?"

I didn't move. Only my knee twitched.

"I didn't think so."

I stood up. "I'm taking him to the bus station. That's why we're counting the money."

Officer Budd leaned over and flicked a blade of grass from his shoe. "Well, see that he gets on that bus and stays on."

I nodded, pulling Teddy up. "Com'on," I said. "That bus leaves at 5:30." It was almost 4:30.

The bus station was really just the Shell Service Station with three greasy chairs that looked as if they'd been hauled out of a wrecked automobile, the stitching loose, dirty foam stuffing coming out of the sides. Streaks of wax blurred the windows, and years of grime had been etched in the walls and floor. Ignoring the mechanic who sat at the desk, squinting suspiciously at us from beneath his baseball cap, Teddy said, "She didn't like me, did she? She thinks I told a lie."

I put my fingers to my lips. "Ssssshh." Teddy turned and nodded at the mechanic as if they'd been formally introduced, but the mechanic just shook his head in disgust.

"Mother's afraid you *did* tell the truth," I whispered, amazed that he could be so blind to what he'd done. He'd just talked to Mother about the two things that most frightened her: the terrible cost of Amanda's loyalty and the threats of men. All our lives Mother had warned us about sex, about the filth of the body, about what might happen if we let men take advantage of us, how we'd be lost and dirty forever. What we had, we understood, was each other, regardless of how recklessly we'd divided that up.

"Then she won't hate me."

"You scared her, don't you see? But that's not important. What's important is that we get back to Amanda."

When the mechanic left to work in the garage, I bought potato chips and a Milky Way out of the vending machine, the only two slots that worked. I had to get food in Teddy, but as soon as he ate, he went suddenly silent, sleepy, his head drooping against my shoulder, eyelids closing. I decided to count the money again, to make sure we had enough, before going back to that fly-specked vending machine. I wanted a Milky Way myself.

I'd finished with the bills and was counting the change, oblivious to the sounds of cars driving in for gas, honking, then speeding out again in a flurry of noise. Afternoon darkness closed over the shop, and I'd just lined up three quarters on one knee when I was yanked up, and the bills and coins went flying from my lap, scattering and rolling across the floor. Tiny bits of fuzz flew before my eyes. A fluff of pink. Mother stood speechless before me, her face a blur as she slapped Amanda's bunny slipper softly against my face.

I didn't move. I couldn't.

"She wanted *you*," Mother whispered. "She asked to speak to you. But you weren't there, so she hung up." Mother gripped me, my body limp, pliant, still caught by surprise, the bunny slipper tight in her other hand as she pulled me outside into the harsh angry light, her fingers pinching my arm so hard I could feel the sharpness of her nails digging into my skin. She opened the passenger door and shoved me inside. I smelled the rancid fumes of gasoline mixed with something sickly sweet like peppermint. The engine rattled. Our tires squealed. I turned in time to see Teddy, standing paralyzed in the doorway, his face gleaming white, a Milky Way wrapper still held in his hand.

Amanda called. But I wasn't there.

As we sped down the highway, I tried to explain. "Mother," I whispered, my voice low, strangled for sound. I couldn't make the air push through my throat. "Mother," I whispered again, louder, but she turned quickly and said, "Shut up!" then pressed her foot hard on the accelerator, and we flew through the brightness, barely missing the lower branches of the oak tree on the corner of Mr. Bauer's yard, rising in a blur of motion over the railroad tracks. I watched in blank dread as the fields flew by, telephone poles streaking eerily toward a cloudless sky. I held myself rigid, every muscle tightened as if I expected again to be hit. Mother stared straight ahead, her body as tense as my own, her knuckles white. Neither of us spoke until we pulled into the driveway at Soldier Creek. Only then did she turn to me, her face pale and strained, her hands gripping the wheel. "Give me that sweater," she said, the coldness of ice in her voice. "It's not in the wash room. I searched all over." Then she tightened her hands on the wheel until the veins stood out. "You find it."

I knew this was irrational, crazy, that my sweater had nothing to do with our worries about Amanda. This wasn't a dream. And there was no chance of waking up, blotting it out, washing away the fear. I jumped out of the car and ran straight into the kitchen where the light was so bright I stopped by the kitchen table, gripping it as if it could steady me and make everything real. I glanced down quickly at the old, white painted table and stared at the scattered pieces of paper dropped there. At first, I wasn't quite sure what they were until I saw the dark center of one hungry eye, the swing of brown hair, and pushed up against that scrap was another: Amanda's long pointy tongue. The photograph. I tried to move, pushing one foot away from the table when the screen door swung open and Mother stood staring at me, something new in her eyes. In the brightness, her eyes shone and then darkened. "Get up to your room," she said, her words entering me like a knife.

But I couldn't move. Cold dread settled in my stomach. I gripped the table. And then as suddenly, I was running, flying up the stairs and into my room where drawers had been jarred open, clothes spilling out in a wild tangle of colors. There was my rose-colored dress, the one I wore to the airport with Amanda, now wadded up in a knot on the floor beside a swirl of underwear. Beside it there was a pile of gray dirt and twigs, swept up into a ridge of colorless chalk filled with flat fragments of white that looked familiar, recognizable . . . I glanced quickly to my windowsill where I kept the shells and sand dollars and pieces of driftwood, the little collection I'd scavenged from the Point. Gone. I imagined Mother's hand sweeping them brusquely to the floor, her feet stomping them, smashing them. Once I'd found a sea horse that had made its arduous journey from the Gulf of Mexico into Perdido Bay, burrowing into the sand, then being lifted by the tides into Soldier Creek. It lay now beside the rose-colored dress, broken neatly in half. Then I saw on the chair my blue bathing suit, the one with the frayed straps and threads unraveling like fringe. It was wound around the back of the chair, the body of it twisted like a rope. Twisted the way she would like to twist my body if she only dared, gripping me end to end, squeezing the life from me.

I unwound my suit, put my fingers to it, stroking it, leaving runs where my nails caught in the weave. I put my cheek to it, rubbing it. It smelled like the creek, like seaweed and sunlight and mildew, sharp and salty and damp. When I put my tongue to it, it tasted of salt. Everything I loved torn up. Even Amanda's picture, the one that pleased her, the joker, the teaser, Amanda taunting the world. But Mother didn't want either of us to be who we were.

I heard a footstep. I dropped the bathing suit and sat very still, waiting, both feet planted side by side on the floor.

I didn't move, not even a finger, though my mind raced backward, seeing again that warm December day when I was ten, the day Mother and Amanda had gone to Mr. Avery's to get holly for Christmas wreaths and I'd found Daddy at the pier, lying drunk and weepy in the boat. He'd just been banished to Perdido Bay, and he was angry, full of despair and self-pity. Though I tried to get him to come up to the house, to act normal, he only made funny noises, giggling and crying all at the same time until I couldn't stand it anymore, and I ran up the hill so fast I grew dizzy with speed, my feet slipping on the mossy path. I rushed through the back door, up the stairs and into my room, hearing the hum of the wasps before I saw them, the nest hanging just above my window, hornets buzzing like tiny, frantic swallows, fidgeting at the eaves. Even as I lifted the window and thrust out my hand, they swarmed on my fingers, my knuckles, the palms and pads of my hand. And I felt something pure and secret and horrible, my hand knocking at the scraggly nest while the stingers lodged deep into my skin. That's how Amanda found me. She pulled me away, wrestling me onto the bed, and only then did I start to cry, my hand swelling, needles of pain shooting like fire through my fist. That's when Amanda lay down beside me on the bed, her arms cradling me while she crooned, "Hush now, hush, it's all over. It's all right. I've got you." And for a moment I released myself, tucking myself into Amanda's warmth, closing my eyes and letting go. When I opened them again, I saw Mother standing in the doorway, her face lit with something awful as she watched her two girls bound together as one. It sent a shiver through me then because I didn't understand it. But now I knew. Though Mother didn't want me, she didn't want me to have Amanda either.

I was awakened from this reverie by the sound of her footsteps thumping up the stairs, the swish of her dress against wood. My feet went numb, my mouth dry. I hugged my arms to my chest, not knowing what to expect.

For a moment there was only silence on the other side of my door. Silence, then the sound of the wind shifting through the bare net of the trees. I stared at the door as if I could see through it, could make Mother keep walking toward her room. I wanted her there, secure in her room, door closed, lights out. I wanted the night over, daylight to come, Amanda to call. I knew she'd call us tomorrow. She'd have to. Amanda was as bound to us as we were to her. It was only a matter of time. Of waiting.

The rap of the hammer startled me. A pounding against my door. I jerked forward, and for a moment couldn't breathe. Then there was a pause. A long deadly silence. Frightened, I watched the door, heard the ticking of the clock beside my bed, the swish of pine needles against the roof as a squirrel sprinted from the limb of a tree outside my window. Outside, an animal screeched, a high wailing sound. Again, sharp, staccato strokes on wood and something being pushed with great effort against my door. And then I knew. Mother was locking me in . . . or forcing me to escape. I understood that punishment was indispensable, unavoidable. Damage had been done, and someone must pay.

Midnight. I stared at the sleek black strip of water out my window. It looked like a slice of tar rounded on the ends with a streak of gray jutting through where the point divided the creek from the bay. In the dark it looked solid enough to walk across; if only I could walk right out the back door, down the bluff and keep going until I was at Josie's One-Stop, until I was any other place in the world. When I heard Mother thumping downstairs, I went absolutely still. Her steps trolled back and forth beneath me, a dusting of cloth, her robe trailing the floor. Sometime past midnight I heard her come up the stairs and stop for a moment at the top as if she were listening for me, then close the door to her room. I didn't move. I clutched the rose dress. When a night breeze lifted the curtains, raising them slightly, I unrolled the dress and dropped it to the floor.

Birds cawed in the hovering blackness, then burst into the air. I heard a motor choke then catch, its throttle opening as it moved far out in the bay, heading for the gulf. Crickets chirped, and a lizard scurried up the window, then stopped midway, looking like a piece of black string. I breathed in the smell of the creek, then stared at the window. Climb out, I thought. That's what they'd do in the movies. It was an eighteen-foot drop, but without another thought, I tied my flowered sheets together—"baby sheets," Amanda called them—anchored them to the bedpost, threw my pillows out to break my fall, and climbed onto the roof. Before the fear took hold, I grabbed my handmade rope and slithered down, then, dangling at the end, let out my breath and jumped. One knee hit the pillows, but I didn't stop to worry about whether it hurt or not. I had to get to Amanda.

I slowed down only to catch my breath, to stay on the path through the woods. When I reached Daddy's cabin, I accidentally knocked over a chair near the door so that Daddy woke, groaning, sitting up halfway in bed, his hair wild, eyes widened in surprise. I patted his shoulder until he quieted, then he lay back down, drifting in and out of sleep. I tried to tell him about Teddy, about Mother, and then, giving up, I stood on a chair beside the refrigerator and reached for the jar with his dog track winnings. I could feel the wad of bills in my hand and something longer, stiffer, an envelope. Quickly I stuffed it all in my pocket.

Tears came as I went back to Daddy's bed to say good-bye. Gently, I pushed his mouth closed, but the next snore dropped it open again. He woke once and looked clearly at me. "Baby," he said in surprise, but then his eyelids fluttered and I was holding his hand, my throat shut as tight as a trap. I looked at the window, heard the flap-flap-flap of the frogs jumping at the screens and then falling with a plop back to the ground. I stared at the thick darkness, knowing I should go but holding on until his breathing was soft and regular. Finally I dropped his hand, tucked the sheet snug around him, and kissed him on the cheek. Daddy. Without looking back, I walked out into the night.

21

Only a smooth blackness blanketed the land until I pressed my nose against the glass and saw the massive stalks of trees and an occasional graveled road that cut like a dark finger through the fields. I eased back in my seat then, my feet tapping the floor, but as the darkness flew by I could see those trees only in my mind, the branches waving like arms in the wind. I tried to hold them there, humming a little. It seemed the right thing to do. That and keeping my purse hidden from the black man who sat across the aisle and watched me, a bag of unopened Cheetos in his lap. Already I could feel his gaze eating me up, licking across my body as if I had no resistance. As if I weren't real.

But I couldn't think about that. I turned back to the window, pretending I could see all those trees swaddled in heaps of Spanish moss; it hung tangled to the ground like the beards of old Chinese men. Damned stuff killed the trees, sucked out the life force just as men's eyes could suck it out of me if I wasn't careful. But I was going to be careful. "I shoulda worn a bra," I whispered, my breath making little round spots on the window. I touched a finger to one. It was moist. I tasted it, but it tasted like dust. Then I leaned my forehead against the window and closed my eyes. "I tried to find you, Amanda, but there wasn't a bus going to Atlanta or Birmingham till noon and I had to . . ." Cars whizzed by as the bus raced on down the highway, and I imagined I could hear the rhythm of their wheels. I closed my eyes and saw the night spooky dark, no wind in the trees.

When I opened them again, Mobile Bay lay before me, blacker than the earth, the water swelling beneath me, lost and running, running out to the sea just as I was running from Soldier Creek. I closed my eyes. Then the bus bumped across a bridge, and when I looked up, the sign said, WELCOME TO MISSISSIPPI.

"Wanna Cheeto?" The black hand reached across the aisle, startling me. He held the crumpled bag out toward me, the neck torn open. I looked up at him. I could have been looking at a statue, those eyes so closed against

123

me. I wanted to tell him that I was scared, that I'd been trying to get to my sister in North Carolina but the only bus I could get was headed for New Orleans; then as suddenly as he'd offered the Cheetos, he withdrew the bag and there was nothing but emptiness between us. I looked at the emptiness, wanted to drag it away like a big, gray sheet.

"Yes," I whispered, scooting over into the aisle seat. I could feel my body moving against the cracked upholstery as I wordlessly reached my hand toward the bag. I locked my eyes to his, but he didn't reopen or extend the bag, so I slowly slid back across and slumped in my seat.

The man turned and looked out his window.

I curled up my legs, drew my arms around my body, and stared out my window at the small frame houses with falling-down porches where poor people lived, houses butted up so close to the highway you could see figures moving inside. I wished suddenly I could talk to him. If I were Amanda, I'd already be deep in conversation, asking him first what he meant by offering me the Cheetos, then after his assurance that he'd meant no harm, I'd learn his entire life story, including whether or not he'd had a mystical experience involving God and if his family believed, as Amanda did, that the Civil Rights movement was still the most ethical method of integration, though not the most efficient.

I spit into my hands and rubbed them together, then put my hands up to my eyes which burned from the cigarette smoke floating forward from the rear of the bus. My legs were weak from running through the woods, and now they rubbed against the pine straw that stuck like glue to my plastic bag. To distract myself, I looked out at the fields, flatter and lower here. Ditches filled with swamp water gutted the land. Pines looked like stick men, skinny and tall against a black night sky. When birds burst suddenly apart from a telephone wire in a flutter of feathers, I remembered Teddy. She thinks every little bit of her is tied to you, Mrs. Soldier, he'd said, looking at Mother with his deep, pathetic eyes as if he could really help Amanda. Oh, poor Amanda. If only this bus were going toward North Carolina, I'd be with you in a little while. I'd run across campus, no matter how late it was, no matter how tired I was. I'd bring you anything you wanted, even that awful whipped cream you ate straight from the spray can. "Oh, baby," you whispered to me before you left for college, "look out for yourself. Don't let Mother gobble you up." But what if you were the one being gobbled?

I wrapped my arms around my knees as if I were another person hugging myself. I clawed my fingers into my back beneath my t shirt, wishing I could claw through my own skin until I felt the realness, the "something else" that made up myself. Then I'd have answers for Mother: Why can't you be like Amanda? Why can't you take some initiative instead of swimming all the time?

I looked over at the black man. What if he turned those smoking eyes dead on me and said, "Just what is it you're afraid of?"

That would do it. I'd put my nose against the glass, looking for water, for a bay or a creek or even a skinny slice of river so I could remember why I had to leave tonight.

A black arm shot across the aisle. "You alright?" he asked, his voice low and husky, thick with concern. I looked him full in the face and knew then I'd screamed it, screamed Mother. I heard the others behind me grumbling, and the bus driver turned around.

"Everything all right back there?"

"Yes, sir," the black man said with authority, his eyes looking straight at the bus driver. "Everything's fine back here."

I turned again toward the window, hoping I could sleep, but when I closed my eyes and tried to imagine emptiness, some wasteland of gray velvet that could swallow me up, I saw Daddy's face, puffy from drink, his eyes focused on the frogs that jumped against the screen door of his cabin. I heard the flap flap flap of them jumping at the mesh, then falling back to the ground. What would happen to him without me there to check on him, to bring him food and see that the money wasn't stolen from the jar? But then, I'd been the one to steal the money

"Bayou La Batre," the bus driver announced over the intercom, his voice gravelly, impatient. "Twenty five minutes, folks."

I went immediately into the bright, greasy restaurant with the Formica counter and red plastic stools, flies buzzing around the pie cases and lighting delicately on the plastic wrapped doughnuts. I felt glad for a change of scene. Even in this brightly lit place, I felt more alive, and when the waitress leaned toward me I ordered quickly. "Coffee, please."

The two men in combat boots and fatigues who'd gotten on at Spanish Fort sat to the left of me at a small table barely big enough for two. They seemed to dwarf the table, their legs out in the aisles, their boots booby trapping the space. Maybe they were on their way to Vietnam or maybe they'd just come back. At the far end of the counter, the black man sat hunched over his cup of coffee, dropping pennies onto the linoleum with absent minded repetition. A woman tried to calm a child, "You little sugar, you," she kept saying, "you little sugar, you," but still the child whined and tried to twist out of her grasp.

"Hey, sweetheart," a voice whispered at my neck. "Come on back here with us buddies. Sit with us." It was one of the two men in combat boots, but I didn't dare turn around to see which one it was. He must have leaned back in his seat because he whispered in that over-loud way, "I like 'em young and skinny. Ain't much got their feet wet."

"Hush, Tommy," the other said. "Don't start that crap here. We got a long ride tonight. Think of Loreen," he laughed, "whistling up your ass."

The first one laughed, too, but blew smoke toward the counter. "I can't think about her till I see her." He turned away from his buddy. "Hey, honey," he persisted, "have yourself a doughnut on big Tom now." I looked down at my coffee, black and greasy in the white cup. I motioned for the waitress, and she sighed as she came toward me. I put two sugars in my refill and stirred furiously.

"Hey, cheerleader." He was beside me now. I could feel him before he said a word, his body crowding up right next to me so I couldn't turn without touching him. "Where you going past your bedtime?" He tapped a finger on my cup, his nails clipped right to the skin. "You gonna need somebody to sit the night with, hold your hand when that old buzzared we got for a driver starts boozing and speeding. Takes curves like a surfer, know what I mean?"

I stared at the steam rising from the coffee. "There aren't any curves on this highway," I said, my voice barely a whisper.

"Well, ain't you *somethin'*! No curves." He turned to the other guy. "Hear that, Gus. No curves, she says. Sure there's curves, sweetheart. There's curves all right." He plucked at my sleeve. "There's curves all right." He leaned nearer, his breath warm against my ear. "That old driver makes them himself."

He sat down on the stool beside me and kept talking as though we were having a real conversation. I snuck a look at him. His chin crept into his neck without a definite division and there was a little space between his front teeth as if someone had pushed them apart with a toothpick. Otherwise, he looked forbidding; he was freckled with a bristly crew cut, his eyes like bullets. His body was as solid as a fireplug—thick shoulders and short, heavy arms. He picked up the sugar container and shook out a little pile in his palm, then thrust his head back and threw it in his mouth, dusting his hands over the counter. Then he ducked his head closer, his shoulder almost touching mine. "What do you say to us getting a little room when she sets down in New Orleans and you won't have to put up with any hustle from that old driver who's been eyeing you from the first minute you got on this bus. Whadayasay, little cheerleader? Whadayasay you shake your little pompoms and I'll clap all night."

I stared at the space between his eyes and something heavy clamped shut inside me.

"Well, don't go stubborn on me, now, I mean, you being such a pretty little thing and—"

I stood up quickly. "I've gotta go to the bathroom."

"Now, jus' wait a damn minute."

"Please," I turned away from him, but he blocked my path.

"Aw, com'on now. Let yourself have a little fun."

"Please." I tried to move in the other direction, but he caught the strap of my purse, jerking me back.

"LISTEN, I'M TALKING TO YOU." And he yanked me around.

I looked straight into his surly blue eyes. "If you'll excuse me," I said politely, "I'm with him." I motioned to the black man at the end of the counter.

His mouth hung open as if the spring inside had broken loose. "We ull, damn, Gawd damn! Suit yourself, girl," he said, "you give it away long enough, that's all that's left." And he dropped a cigarette butt on the floor beside my foot, not bothering even to stomp it out before he walked back to his seat.

I got back on the bus, and I never looked away from the darkness until daybreak when the old buzzard at the wheel started to sing, "If you can't git what you wannnnnt, then sometiiiiimmes, you git what you neeeeeeeed."

We were stuck in Slidell, Louisiana, waiting three hours for a new driver, the old one more than ready for a snooze. He must have started on a pint in Bayou La Batre and kept at it until he pulled into a local cafe for relief. Bus officials from New Orleans promised us a driver by morning, but it was midmorning before we boarded again, the day already tired. I tried to get a bus back to Atlanta, but they said I'd have to wait until New Orleans. "Get the express in New Orleans," the man at the counter said. And I meant to get off at New Orleans, but the two soldiers got off there, the one named Big Tom squeezing my leg as he went by, dribbling his fingers up my thigh, whispering, "I'm waiting for you!" and lightly cupping his crotch, so I stayed on, watching the countryside get flatter and flatter, water standing in puddles on the ground as the bus raced down the interstate. Everything suddenly looked soggy and hopeless, and I didn't know where I was going or why. My mind went skittering back to that sweater I'd lost the night Johnny Turner drove me home from the dance. I saw it flipping over and over as if it were alive and Johnny laughing and whistling while I ran through the bushes in my bra and skirt, the moths fluttering around my face. Could Mother have seen that? I lay my head back against the seat and tried to keep the horrible thoughts in the back of my mind until the most awful one jumped out in front: What if I can't find Amanda?

Houston, Texas. Through the windows I saw the thick foliage and the slick streets, people milling around as if all they had to do was wait for that first gush of oil. I decided to get off and call Amanda from here. I waited twenty minutes beside the phones, but each time a person hung up, another person rushed in front of me. My feet were lead weights. When I closed my eyes, I fell quickly to sleep, my hands going slack. Waking a minute later, my hands were empty. The plastic bag. But there it was beside me, dropped on its side. I knew I had to get some coffee in me, then find a place to sleep.

Damp air cloaked the city in a fog, and my hair was wet by the time I'd walked the block to the Red Rose Inn from the bus station. I never looked around to see who else got off the bus, though I saw the black man stride ahead of me into the station and disappear into the Lone Star Café. I expected he'd go on to the West Coast, maybe to San Francisco.

The Red Rose Inn, completely sheltered by banana leaves, looked soft, almost romantic beneath the dripping leaves, and I went toward it eagerly with the thin hope of sleep. Though weary from the bus ride, a new excitement nudged me forward. Perhaps it was just the feeling of this small success: finding a place to stop. As I got closer to the entrance, I saw the peeled paint scarring one wall, the insects creeping out of drain spouts, crawling into the night, but I shut my eyes. Surely the world outside Soldier Creek would be a healing hand I could hold

"Upstairs, 202," the man said. I didn't notice him until he spoke, for I was too intent on the way I wrote my name on the register. When I glanced up, I was surprised to see he was just a kid, hardly older than me, dressed in a snugly fitting cowboy shirt with fringe on the pockets and faded jeans pressed tight against his skinny body. He nodded at me and repeated "202" as he tapped the little bell on the desk, his wrist making a sharp, staccato movement. "Listen, I'll take 'em up, lady, compliments of the house."

"No, really," I said, but he'd already picked up my bag and headed through the door.

It was nice. He was just trying to be nice. You could always tell whether someone was pulling the wool over you if you looked them straight in the eyes. *It's the eyes, Daddy always said. Look deep into people's eyes and see them for who they are.* But I didn't have much time to think because he was talking, his voice galloping into the damp hall like a horse that couldn't stop.

"So, you've come to Texas," he said. "Get you some boots tomorrow.

A job the next day. Everybody comes here for that. People think this place is some new heaven, but this—" he turned to me, "is a rich folks' town. I guess that makes it heaven for them." I followed him up the steps to the second floor where the palm fronds touched the railing and drooped over into the walkway, tickling my elbow as I walked by. He saw me looking. "Rats live in those trees," he said pointing to the palms, then he put the bag down on the concrete slab walkway, took a key out of his pocket and opened the door with a flourish. He went quickly to the small bureau and flung open a few empty drawers as if showing me how clean they were. "Just put your things in here," he said. "They're all ready. Sanitized. Perfumed, just like new every day of every week. Fresh scent from the Rio Grande. Texas scent!"

I stood in the doorway, turning the knob round and round, hoping he wouldn't notice how nervous I was, hoping he'd keep talking, keep the sound going so I wouldn't think about that awful bus ride. I imagined him standing idly in the open doorway, rambling on in that friendly voice while I drifted off to sleep, everything soft beneath me, everything forgotten but the water, just me floating on the water . . . but I had to call Amanda.

When he turned on a lamp beside the bed, I saw the room wasn't much: a double bed against one wall and jalousie windows behind it where a little breeze flipped the curtains. For a moment I thought of the air outside, the warm, humid breeze blowing through my hair just like at home, softening my skin.

He jiggled his keys. "Good golly, you're nervous, aren't you? You're new and you're nervous. Everybody's like that. It's in the air here. Like money."

"Everybody's nervous?"

"Sure. People come down here expecting to relax, but everybody's nervous. See how they don't move quick? Not because they don't want to, but because they're waiting for something."

"What are they waiting for?"

"Don't know. Help, maybe." He looked down at his knees. "Listen, let me get you some ice and a Coke. Naw, don't worry," he said as I began to fumble in my purse. "It's on the house. The house is against nerves." He smiled at his little joke. I smiled too. Then he was back in a jiffy, setting down a full bucket of ice and opening two frosty Cokes which he set on the dresser. Sweat bubbled on their cold surfaces. I could already taste it, cool and sweet. I'd hardly had anything but coffee all day. In my mind we were sitting in a restaurant, a nice restaurant with linen napkins, talking about old times until he pulled a shiny flask from his back pocket and looked up at me with that half scared look on his face. He poured some in a glass, then poured Coke in. "Here, you take the first one. 'Cause you're tired," he said.

"Just plain Coke," I said, looking around the room for a phone, but there was nothing but an ashtray and a Bible on the bedside table. I hoped he'd go on talking.

As if he knew what I was thinking, he sat on top of the dresser and smiled. "Guess what I do?" he said, slouching against the wall, one foot still touching the floor. The sun shone through the window on his head, making his hair look like dandelion fluff when the breeze caught it.

"Well, I don't know," I said. "I mean, you could be anything." I sipped my drink. "You could be mayor of this town." It had jumped out. A flirty tone, but I didn't care. It felt so good to talk, as good as somebody rubbing my back. I loosened my hold on the doorknob and leaned up against the frame. I could stop now. I could call Amanda.

"Pardon me, ma'am," he tipped an imaginary hat, "but I mean what I am when I ain't in this here shithole." He looked at me expectantly, as though I would know just by looking at him. He held the Coke balanced on his palm, the ice in it rattling.

"I don't know," I said. I looked at him more keenly. Maybe he was a lifeguard or a baseball player.

"Com'on," he said. "Do I look like any thick wood to you? I'll help you." He straightened, put the Coke back on the dresser. "Clue number one. What's somebody who looks at the world and then puts what he sees down?"

"A writer."

He shook his head, the dandelion fluff moving every which way as he moved.

"A geologist. My daddy wanted to be a geologist once."

"Naw, an artist!" His eyes grew darker as he said the word. "See, look at my hands." He held them out to me, palms upward as if the very structure of his hands would validate his words. "I'm going to ask you one more thing, okay, and you answer it, okay?"

"Sure."

"Name one thing that's beautiful."

"I don't know anything beautiful except the creek back home."

"All riii ight," he said and kicked the bed, his face crimped with glee.

I moved a bit further into the room. How could he know about the creek, how it flowed through the Narrows into Crystal Lake, then eased past the point into the bay? How could he know that in moonlight, the saw grass turned luminous, fragile, like stalks of silk shimmering in the black water? How could he know that during a storm, the cypress trees creaked and swayed as lightning braided flashes of gold through the pines?

I stepped closer to the bed. Beyond me, the curtains swayed, blowing out like a skirt, then lay flat against the window. A daddy longlegs was squashed against the wall just below the curtain. "That's it, isn't it? I mean, pretty stuff is what's already here before it gets fiddled with."

"Yes." I felt warm for the first time, a current shifting directions inside me as the need for sleep pulled me down to the bed. *Call Amanda*, I thought, and I imagined Amanda with her head bent down over her books, her brain eating up the words, not concerned about Teddy or Mother or anybody, but only those words like boats taking her out to sea. Before I knew what I was doing, I was sitting on the bed, and it hit me: this was the way it would be, I would meet gentle people like this young man who would talk to me and make me feel at home. It wouldn't matter what we said. And I smiled until I felt the soft fuzz against my face, Mother's hands swinging Amanda's slipper, hitting me, hitting me. *"She wanted you. She asked to speak to you."* Then I had to get into the creek, into the cool darkness. "Maybe I'll have a little of that," I said to the boy, pointing to the flask. He grinned, pouring me a taste in the paper cup. The whiskey stung my throat, then spread in a warm, fuzzy way inside my chest, waltzing inside. I felt bigger, a giggle coming out. *Oops, there it went again.* I couldn't seem to stop them even with my hands over my mouth. My nose tingled as the giggles jumped out. I slid further back on the bed, the spread so worn I could feel the blanket, scratchy and harsh beneath it, but it didn't matter. The giggles kept jumping out. I touched a rough spot on the blanket as I rushed down the oyster shell drive beneath the canopy of trees, then fled down the path. I was almost in the creek. My body sank into the mattress as if I had made a clean dive, straight to the bottom. I let my shoes fall off. Underwater, it wasn't even a sound. I yawned, the alcohol racing through my blood while the giggles bunched up one on top of another, falling out in a rush as I stretched out, fluttering my hands just to keep me afloat. The boy talked on about painting old junk that he found, but what I saw was Daddy leaning out toward the water from the pier, looking down into the bottom of the creek. *Get back, Daddy*, I kept saying, putting my hand out to stop him. I swam toward him, but he stared at a mullet jumping.

I wanted to wrap up in the blankets and float toward the point, but I had to watch out for Daddy. When he leaned further toward the water, I reached out.

"You okay?" the boy asked. And then he was moving toward me, toward the bed.

"No." It was a whisper. "I didn't mean—" because I knew then that

I'd been reaching out to Daddy. When his hand touched my skin, I was up and running, slamming the bathroom door. "Com'on, now," he called as I sat with my back to the closed door. "Don't do that." Water dripped in the sink. Light bloomed through the tiny window, illuminating a patch of gray tile. Then I heard someone yell, "Red, hey, you, git back in this office or your butt's in the street."

Outside the little window, I saw the breeze whip the trees, the palm fronds beating against the wrought iron railings, and I thought of those rats running up and down in a frenzy of hunger. I sat very still and listened, but I heard nothing, only the wind. When I got up to look at my face in the mirror, my skin looked splotchy, my nose swollen and red, but it was my eyes that frightened me: they stared gravely back at me.

I reached up and placed my hands flat on the mirror, standing in the hot, sweating breeze, not knowing what to do, so I got in the shower and let the hot water strike me in a hard, clean spray like needles, cleansing two days of traveling. Then I packed quickly and walked out into the noon heat in the direction of the bus station, the air thick and warm, the city a fuzz of brightness. Once inside the station, I looked at the departure schedules on the wall until I found Pensacola, Florida. That would do fine. Pensacola was some twenty odd miles from Soldier Creek, Alabama, and I could easily get a bus from there. I felt a flush of happiness as if I'd finally touched the mesh of a safety net after falling for hours in empty air.

When I first saw the black man, I thought he must have hit me. My stomach caved in, and I bent over in pain, but my eyes couldn't leave him. He sat alone on the long row of fiberglass seats, a newspaper opened in his lap, and he looked at me with that same controlled stare. And yet what I saw were my own eyes as I'd seen them in the mirror: *No place to run, baby. You got to stay with it this time.*

A swelter of people suddenly grouped around me, bumping my legs, grabbing at things. "Jesus," an old woman said. "You get any, Beale?" I didn't know that I'd dropped the money, ten and twenty dollar bills fluttering all around me. People grabbed at them. The quarters and nickels and pennies didn't stop rolling. Then they were just standing there, holding the money, not offering it back until the black man said, "Give it back to her," and then they handed me the bills. When I raised my head again, he was gone.

I still had $215.00 left from the money I'd taken from Daddy's jar two nights ago. In the bathroom I splashed water on my face, and when I came out, I looked up at the board where the names of cities spread out like zones of terror: Albuquerque, Tucson, San Diego, Los Angeles, San Francisco. When my turn came, I asked where the next bus was headed. "Los Angeles," the lady said, hurrying me with her eyes. Los Angeles. The City of Angels. I remembered that Aunt Katy lived there. I felt as if a hand reached out to touch me, stroking my cheek, smoothing my brow. "Go," a voice whispered. Someone nudged me from behind. "One, please," I said, touching the envelope in my purse. For a single instant I believed I wasn't running anymore.

AMANDA SOLDIER

22

Two nights before exams I stuck a sign on my door: SICK! DON'T DISTURB
ME FOR ANYTHING! I pushed a chair up against the door, then lay
naked in bed and ate chocolate in the dark. Mars Bars, Snickers, Reese's
Cups, Milky Ways, Hershey's, Milk Duds. Even Tootsie Rolls. I lined them
up on my stomach like a little army in formation; when I finished one, I
dropped the wrapper beside my bed and started on the next one, inching
my way down my stomach as if I were at a smorgasbord. As I ate, my mind
went numb, as blank as a cleaned-out cupboard. When I got to the last
one, I ate it slowly, imagining that it was my last meal on earth: I stared up
at the white pitted ceiling, getting fuller and fuller, but somehow smaller
and smaller until I was about the size of one of those dots on the ceiling.
I listened to the wind beating the trees and looked out at the branches
whacking against the sides of the building and felt an astonishing rush of
pleasure. Then I remembered Teddy. At any moment, he'd be arriving in
Soldier Creek, ready to ruin my life, trying to convince Mother to be a free-
thinking parent. Sons of bitches! I jumped out of bed and got that extra
candy bar, the one I kept in reserve in my underwear drawer, then I pulled
the covers up to my chin.

The next day, while the other girls ate smothered pork chops, green
beans, and corn pudding for supper, I snuck out of the dorm, a scarf over
my head, a raincoat over my slip and ran to the corner store. Bending over
the racks of candy, I added a Nestlé Crunch bar and some chocolate mints
to the Almond Joy, PayDay, and Hershey's bar before I scrambled back to
my dorm, holding up a newspaper in case anybody tried to talk. Once in
my room, I lay back in bed, not touching the chocolate yet, but watching
the trees turn a mossy black, the sky as gray as an old wool blanket. When
it was completely dark, I began. Eeny meeny miny mo . . . Hershey's bar!
I wiped my hands on the sheets, leaving muddy streaks of chocolate, and

turned toward the window where tobacco odors from the factories blew through my room and the curtains waved like sails. I propped myself up on my bed in the dark, listening to the night sounds, the pipes thumping, the toilets flushing, someone's footsteps in the hall.

The next morning, I slept, curtains drawn, a pillow over my head. I knew I should be studying—I never could remember the date Chaucer was released from the rape charge, a fact my medieval literature teacher seemed obsessed with, or the underlying reasons the cotton mills had reduced wages during the 1940s—yet I couldn't let go. I kept at it. Two nights. Three nights. Four. On the fourth night, something lightened in me. I no longer felt myself spinning off into space. For a moment, I did worry about Teddy. I could imagine him striding into the house at Soldier Creek with his long, curly hair and his torn jeans for a showdown with Mother. Jesus! He didn't seem to see dangers right in front of his face; but instead of compassion, all I felt was contempt.

I tore off another wrapper. Even in the dark I could tell by smell: a Milky Way. I saw Mother take one look at Teddy and I knew who would win. Poor Teddy. Poor little Teddy! I gobbled up the rest of the Milky Way, stuffing it almost whole in my mouth, the chocolate thick against my gums, squished between my teeth. They used to tell us in grammar school that candy would rot our teeth. I'd see a kid eating a candy bar and just stand there waiting for his teeth to moss over and turn dirty black. And that's what I felt now: I was waiting for the rot, the decay, waiting for my mind to moss over, spotted with mildew until it turned dirty black. To stave it off, I painted my toenails Raspberry Delight, then reached over to my bedside table for the chocolate flavored Ex Lax that sat in a heap of peeled aluminum foil. Carefully, with my legs placed just so on a pillow so as not to mess up my toenail polish, I lined up the laxatives where the candy had been. A counterattack. First you go up, swelling out like a toad, and then poof! you go down. The chocolate-flavored Ex Lax tasted almost like candy, melting in my mouth, my tongue flicking to crevices between my teeth. Then I lay back on the pillow, ready for something new to happen.

Nothing did.

On the fifth day, I shifted my books, huddling them closer to my chest while I walked to class. When the storm came up, I moved underneath the bus shelter to keep what was left of me dry, my socks already wet, sloshing in my shoes. I had to take a test, and I was determined to show them. I felt queasy with fear because I hadn't studied, hadn't even opened a book, but quickly I ate a Baby Ruth, telling myself it didn't matter, that I could do it, and I licked my fingers while rain pelted the ground. Last night I'd retreated to the library with my books; I had to go somewhere Mother couldn't reach me, but when I came back from the library, notes were taped all over my door: CALL HOME. CALL YOUR MOTHER. SOUNDS URGENT. CALL ANY HOUR! I ripped them off, then lay on my bed and clinched my eyes shut tight as if they were fists. Very late, when the dorm became still with only the ruffling of pages of the late-night studiers, I took out my chocolate and began to eat.

Finishing my Baby Ruth, I walked out of the shelter into the soft Carolina rain, down the hill to Old Brick where I wrote the test very quickly, my hand skipping across the paper as if it had a life of its own: *The Agrarian Movement challenged the gospel of industrialism and materialism and asked that the nation reassess traditional values and sense of community. The Agrarians were particularly opposed to the industrial perception of the individual as a unit of production.* I had learned that much before my mind went dry and blank as an old bone. I couldn't remember anything more, and my argument went in circles, my points going nowhere. All my thoughts sat on the top of my brain as if they were items on a shelf while my mind continued its insistent argument: Call her and get it over with. No, let them sweat it out. A groan rose in my throat. That's stupid. They can't. You're only delaying the trouble.

The next day I stuffed clothes into a pillowcase, jamming them in tight so they'd fit in this duffel I bought from a Connecticut girl who'd finished with playing poor. On impulse, I ran to the phone and dialed the number, waiting impatiently for someone to answer. When Mother did, I said quickly, "Let me speak to Jit."

"Amanda? Is that you—"

"Please, Mother. Let me speak to Jit." I was crying by then, soft, throaty sobs I tried to cover up, to hide from Mother.

"Oh, darling," and then Mother began to cry.

"Mother—" I put the phone to my chest so I wouldn't have to listen to her misery, but it was then my stomach started its revolt as if a giant clamp of steel was squeezing out my intestines, and I bent over in pain as the clamp tightened its grip. Quickly, I jammed the phone back on the hook and raced to the bathroom.

I was sick, my stomach rumbling like an old dryer on the quits. When the diarrhea finally stopped, I crept back to my bed and lay curled in a ball, weak and frightened, uncertain what to do. Tomorrow was my final with Dr. McKune, and secretly I'd planned to pull myself together and study, but for the first time I wondered if I could. In my head, I heard Mother crying. "Don't," I said aloud. "Just don't." Before I could stop it, I heard her cooing, "Mama's little smart one," and I rolled over on my pillows, pushing my face deep into the wrinkled wad of cloth.

I must have slept all night for the morning light woke me, sprinkling me with all the old worries. I jumped up and ran to the showers, letting the hot water pelt my shoulders as I turned and turned, but still I could hear Mother weeping, her fear leaping through the spigot, draining over my head, dribbling down my back.

When I stepped out of the shower, Beth breezed in to wash her face. "Aren't you taking your lit final?" she asked, surprised at my wet hair, my naked body. And suddenly I knew I wasn't. I wasn't taking anything. Instead, I went back to bed, still damp, the sheets streaked like mud. I rolled over, forcing the pillow in my mouth and tried not to think about what was happening. "I'm sick," I said and pulled the covers up to my chin. "I just need a little rest."

The next day I felt stronger. The rain had stopped, the sky clearing. I thought about calling Mother, but when I did, the cramps grabbed me again and I rushed to the toilets, then collapsed into bed. Vaguely, I heard people coming in from tests, complaining about grades and test questions—"I can't believe he asked that," and "I should have known he'd focus on Dimmesdale"—but I couldn't move. I opened my eyes, saw the candy wrappers scattered around me. Then I went back to sleep, waking with the sun on my face. I yawned, stretched, before I remembered I'd been sick. My hair was clotted together in clumps. Well, I could wash it. I got up and put on a sweatshirt and jeans, but as I bent down to lace my shoe I saw a note on the floor: CALL YOUR MOTHER! That sent me to the Union, past the aisles of toothpaste and deodorants, tampons and shower caps to the tiny ten-cent packages of Milk Duds. I grabbed a handful, stuffing them in an inside pocket of my shirt before I picked up a *Vogue* and some trash, *The Last of the Love Slaves*, to read on the bus.

Past midnight, I went to a phone booth, the bus schedule clutched in one arm. It was a cold, damp night, the dark branches of trees curled toward me like claws. I shivered as I dialed Soldier Creek. "I'll be home Friday," I said after Mother answered the phone.

"Amanda? Is that you? Oh honey," and I could hear her crying into the phone.

A wave of nausea threw me into silence. "At two o'clock in Pensacola," I whispered before the cramps twisted my stomach into knots. "Mother," I said quickly, "I'm coming home. Don't cry now. Everything's okay. I promise."

As the bus sped through the frost-covered fields of Georgia, I thought about how I'd lie low, let Mother baby me, then dream up the energy to propel me out of Soldier Creek. I didn't let myself think about Trinity College. About failure. I couldn't. Instead, I thought about being *Mama's little smart one* until my mind eased out of its darkness. Only then could I return to the intellectual life. Only then could I demand attention. But that night when I arrived in Soldier Creek, anxious for comfort and relief, I discovered I wasn't the only disaster.

"What do you mean, Jit's gone?" I asked, coming into the kitchen, dog tired and sullen and needing to brush my teeth. Mother hugged me fiercely, then choked out words about Jit. "What are you talking about? Speak English," I said.

Mother's shoulders slumped and she looked beyond me, up the stairs as if there was something I needed to understand. I dropped my purse and raced up to the second floor, flinging open Jit's door to a feast of disorder. Jesus! Clothes were strewn everywhere. Not in piles or stacks, but on mirrors and lamps and chairs and all over the floor. Jit was prissy-neat, her clothes always in drawers, her shell collection arranged just so on her bureau, her prize display of sand dollars lined up on the windowsill.

When I saw the smashed pieces of shell, the fragments of sand dollars, some flattened to powder, my stomach turned. I knew then that Jit wasn't visiting Josie's or hiding out at Daddy's. Something had happened here, something scary, and everything else in my life took a backseat.

23

It seems odd to me now that Mother and I didn't talk much about Jit, didn't sit down and worry out what had happened, but each time I brought it up, Mother insisted everything fell apart because of "that boy from Trinity."

"But what did he do? I mean, why did Teddy upset Jit?"

"He upset both of us," Mother said. "He was rude and unkempt, and he kept saying we had to let you go...and that something bad had happened."

I ignored the last part of that sentence, telling Mother only that everything he said was an exaggeration. "But what did he say to Jit?"

We were sitting at the kitchen table, both of us tired and anxious, having gotten only a few hours sleep. Mother looked out the window at the leaves spread across the yard like a carpet of gold. "I don't know," she whispered. "I found them together at the bus station. I don't know what he said, but I made Jit come home."

"And then?"

She turned back to me, and now her gaze was full of love. "Why, we waited for you to call."

Alone in my room each night I told myself I'd figure out what happened. Mother cleaned up Jit's room, and I listened to the racket of bugs outside, the screech and whine of insects, and banged down my window, then sat thinking in the dark. I'd already called the local police and the state police to report Jit as missing, telling them that my mother, under the circumstances, was not well and they should speak with me. Even that word – missing-- gave me the creeps. But no matter how much I tried to piece together the little I knew, I had no idea why Jit had taken off. My little sister, I went to bed thinking. *Goddamn you!*

The only person I hadn't talked to was Daddy.

A light breeze whipped the smell of wild onions into the car as I drove down the Lillian highway toward Pirate's Cove, eight miles as the crow flies from Soldier Creek. On the winding road it seemed to take forever, the air mushy, thick with moisture though it was late December, the sun hidden in a blanket of white sky. My damp sweater stuck to me and seemed to pin me to the plastic coating of the front seat. But I had to see him and find out what he knew. Damn him for not having a telephone, not coming to see me. "Jesus, Daddy," I said aloud, but there was no one to hear but the cows grazing beneath the trees, their tails swishing in the fine gray mist. To soothe myself I drank a Coke and drove fast down the strip of black highway, the trees bending over the road, a canopy of blurred darkness. I rolled the windows down, felt a slice of breeze cool against my neck. For a moment I closed my eyes. Pleasure. Nothing else mattered.

I didn't really want to see him. Who was he to me but an unrepentant failure, a stranger who hid himself away like a hermit, never adventuring into my life? Not once did he write to me at Trinity College. Not once did he so much as send me a five-dollar bill. I doubt he even thought about me, and that made me blaze with resentment. And yet he might know something about Jit. He had to know something about Jit. She wouldn't leave without seeing him. She wouldn't leave Soldier Creek without saying good-bye.

I pulled into the sandy drive, the pampas grass yellowed and thick, blackberry vines woven like barbed wire around the trees. When I got out, I loosened my sweater and tossed my Coke bottle back into the car. I didn't see him at first. I went to the back of the cottage where mildew crept up the walls, then changed my mind and walked around to the side of the house. The sight of the water stopped me. It looked like a field of smoke, fog rising just above the surface of the cove, hovering there, a tapestry of dusky mauve. I took a deep breath. I'd forgotten that it was sometimes beautiful here. A fragile beauty dependent on the vagaries of weather, the bluish haze of the horizon. I stood quite still. Even the air felt lighter here, as if the trees held coolness in their branches, though there wasn't the slightest hint of a breeze.

Then I saw him. He darted forward, crawling, his head extended. He stopped abruptly, waiting, then crept carefully toward the crepe myrtle, pushing the bushes apart as if looking for something, his head now down, rump in the air. "Com'on," I heard him say. "Com'on now, Mister Lucky."

I didn't move. I stood frozen to the spot and watched until something inside me snapped, and I scurried back to the car, slammed the door hard and yelled, "Anybody home?" If I was going to see him, I didn't want it to be weird.

Minutes later he came around the side of the house, brushing grass off his knees. Pine needles were caught in his shoes. He rubbed at the dirt on his hands. I expected him to be embarrassed, guilty, but he looked preoccupied, almost contemplative. We stood staring at each other, neither of us speaking.

I hadn't seen him since August, and he looked older than I remembered, his cheeks gaunt, his clothes all grass stained, but there was still something gentlemanly about him. The least he could do was grow ugly.

"I came to find out about Jit," I said though I hadn't meant to be so abrupt. I thought that we'd hug, say hello, do a little of the father-daughter stuff.

"Well," he said. He didn't move an inch closer to me. He squinted beyond me at the house as if watching for something.

"She's been here, hasn't she?" Instinctively, I moved closer, smelling the ripe sweetness of the grass on him, the moldy taint of dirt. He only shrugged.

"Don't know." He was still squinting.

"What do you mean. If she came here—"

"I think so—" Now his eyes were etched to mine, eyes as blue as the bottom of the creek. "But . . . well . . . I musta been a little tight. I'd been asleep and she startled me. She talked, I think, but when I woke up she was gone. Maybe she even told me where she was going. I can't remember. But if she did, I probably told her to go. Find her own place in the world." He put his hands over his eyes as if suddenly he were tired. "Maybe I dreamed it all. I don't know."

"Damn you!" I punched a fist at the air. I wanted to hit him.

He turned quickly and started walking toward the water while I stared at the delicate shape of his head, his neck still clean and unlined rising from bony shoulders. "Wait," I yelled, but he kept walking. He looked broken, his back hunched, his head drooped low. "Daddy, please."

When he turned there were tears in his eyes.

"She's my sister," I said. "She's only sixteen years old. She's—"

"I don't think you'll find her unless she wants to be found." Then he turned again and walked toward the cabin, his eyes studying the ground.

"I hate you!"

But by then, he'd disappeared around the side of the house, and I was left with the creeping silence, the soft, fertile air.

"I hate you," I said to the water, the house, the quiet umbrella of trees. I wanted to scream. Instead I looked at my shoe, saw the ugly cracks in the leather, the fissures of wear, the frayed, withered laces. A lizard ran up to the edge of my shoe, stopped, then leapt onto the cracked dome as if it were a stone. I couldn't move my foot. I was trapped, mesmerized by its stillness. "I don't hate you," I whispered. "But I wish I did."

It was inevitable we'd hear all the rumors: a body found in the woods near

Atmore, face held together with rubber bands, feet twisted backward as if they were collapsible parts. "A female youth, approximately five feet, five inches in height," the six o'clock newscaster said while I held my breath, fingers digging scars into my thighs. But when the picture flashed onto the screen, it was a small blonde girl, smiling sunnily into the camera, her even front teeth pearl white against soft, pale lips. "Thank god!" I jumped up from my seat, then realized how awful that was and snapped off the TV.

That same afternoon, Flo Hinton called to say a child had just drowned in the Gulf of Mexico near Alabama Point. "But they don't know what age or sex, hon. If they knew, I'd be saying my prayers right now." As I hung up the phone, I imagined the lifeguard beating through high surf, seeing an arm, then losing it, a leg, an elbow, then nothing but the foam of the waves while the body twisted like a rag doll beneath the water, pulled by the current out to sea. Why can't Mrs. Hinton keep her big mouth shut? I thought, dialing Officer Budd.

"That drowning?" he asked, burping slightly into the phone. I could see him adjusting his glasses, staring out into the ticking brightness of the alley. "No, that wasn't your sister. Les' see now . . . it was a ten-year-old boy." I hung up fast and stormed out to the pier, my knees like jelly.

I slapped at a mosquito devouring my ankle, then ran back to the house, flipping on the TV. Mother sat at the table and turned pages of an old catalog with a wet finger as if new information might have sprouted on the page. I knew she was waiting for the pieces to fall into place, the puzzle to be complete so I could tell her what to do. Since I'd come home, she'd been unnaturally still, like the summer air before a storm. I told myself I should be glad, but I needed her panting and frantic; her craziness calmed me. Without it, I lit up like a fuse, and depression settled, like an old visitor, inside me.

When I heard the mailman opening up our rusty box, thrusting letters and bills into that dark hole, I rushed out, foolishly hoping there might be a letter from Jit. After shuffling through flyers and bills, looking for her familiar scrawl—there was nothing but the typed-up notices from the electric company and the telephone company and another I didn't recognize—I tore open an unfamiliar letter, staring at the typed words, PAST DUE: RENT FOR TWO MONTHS.

> *In the matter of rent, it is our policy to extend*
> *a grace period of one month, followed by eviction if*
> *the rent is not paid. You can see that I have been*

generous, considering your circumstances. I think you
understand the measure I must resort to if rent is not paid swiftly.
                    Mr. Turner

I crumpled the note into a ball, but kept it tight in my fist. Maybe we should all go on the road. Maybe we should all be lost. I kicked at the dirt, sending trails of dust into the bushes, and stared into the mute darkness of the woods. When I turned around, Mother stood at the door, looking wistfully at her garden as if planning a plantation. Of course, she must know about the overdue rent. But she'd said nothing. Not one word. "Guess what I've got?" I held up the letter.

"I don't want to know." Mother turned quickly back into the room, not closing the door.

"I'VE GOT," I yelled, "A DUE BILL FOR THE RENT."

"Your father owes me money," she said, staring just above my head. "He's been late before." Then she paused, looking at me. "But we'll need more."

I sat down on the grass, holding the bills away from me as if they were ropes that would bind me firmly in place. I had not told Mother that my grades were all Fs, that I had done the impossible thing: failed. I hadn't even said this aloud to myself, for I intended to go back, to make everything up. I believed I could simply walk into the dean's office in January and blame all of my failure on Jit. A lost sister. A runaway girl. What else could I do but skip out on exams?

But now the rope was tightening. Money. Mother. No sign of Jit.

Money. It would all be left up to me.

Before I left for my interview with Herb Lassiter, the inhalation therapist at South Baldwin Hospital, I looked at myself in the mirror. "Wish me luck," I whispered to my reflection, noting that at least I was clean. Spick-and-span, not a spot of dirt anywhere near me. Sterile, I thought. Antiseptic. And I did a little fishtail squirm for myself in the mirror and crossed my eyes. For some dumb reason, I felt good today, as if the ropes had loosened, giving me a little wiggle room. But when I looked at my watch and saw it was time to go, I pointed my finger at my image in the mirror. "You straighten up," I said. "In hospitals, people are brisk and efficient."

Herb Lassiter had bedroom eyes: dark, deep-set and fringed with black lashes, thick as any woman could hope for. With his dark hair (a little on the longish side for a small town hospital employee), he could have been a lounge act in St. Louis or Memphis. I could see his face hyped by stage lights and soft music while he held his hands open in welcome; I must have been dreaming this thought when he noticed me standing in the doorway and nodded me to a chair. I blinked back to reality, my application tight in my hand. Equipment was stacked up all around, boxing Herb in: cartons that said MED ARTS TUBING in blue graphics across the side and bottles of saline solution in cardboard boxes, collecting dust. He followed me with his eyes for a moment, then smiled a slow grin. "Clutter," he said. "This isn't a hospital, it's a storage unit."

I liked him immediately. "Then those aren't real people I saw in the rooms. Only spare parts, huh?"

He looked surprised for a moment and I wanted to kick myself, but then he laughed and looked sheepish. "We try not to let anyone know this. That Number One Secret," he said Charlie Chan fashion. At which he looked attentively down at my application, then up at my face. "So, you're a college girl."

"Yes."

"But you didn't go to 'Bama?"

"No." I thought this a curious line of questioning. Why should he care if I went to the University of Alabama or not? I wondered what it had to do with inhalation therapy. "I went to Trinity College in North Carolina."

"You got any other job prospects in this town?" His eyes suddenly looked hooded, concealing, though I had no idea what he meant to conceal.

"Well—" I began to get uneasy, "—they're looking for rate clerks at the telephone company."

"Geez!" He rolled his eyes. "Those squirrels! Okay, you don't have much hope in this town, but I'll see if I can work with you."

I looked at him with gratitude, though it wasn't one of my favorite expressions. "You mean—"

He held up his hands. "I'm not saying anything yet. I have to see. Close the door first."

I reached behind me to close it as he came out from behind his desk. Standing up, it was clear he'd spent a lot of time using elbow action on pitchers of beer; he had the beginning of a paunch. He came closer until he stood almost over me, breathing into my face. "Okay, now, do what I do. First, stand up. Yep, stand up. Breathe a little." I stood up beside him. "Get some air into those lungs. This is a lung test. This is inhalation. Air control and release. Now, bend down. Yep, bend down like you're gonna lift a big balloon. Okay, loosen your shoulders. The backs of your knees. That's it. You're feeling swell. You've got nothing to lose, everything to gain. There's a hot spot creeping up your neck, creeping down your spine, going right to the bottom of your toes. Now you're gonna take that hot spot up with you, you're gonna—" and he began to spin his hands between his knees in a rotary motion, bringing them spinning up to his waist as he growled, then changed to a cheer, "Rooooolllllll Tiiiiiiiiiiddde"—he jumped in the air—"Roooooooollllll!" He shot a fist toward the ceiling as he jumped. When he finished he looked exhausted. I sat back down in my chair, staring at him as if he'd gone off the beam. "Okay, now you do it."

"That?"

"All right. I'll do it with you. It's for the job." He winked at me. Then I was bent over like a broken corn stalk contemplating my feet, sucking in my wind, feeling the throb of my heart and the knotting of my fists as I copied his actions, circling my fists as I screamed, "Rooooooollll, Tiiiiiiiddde, rooooooooollll!" and threw my hands up in the air.

"You got the job," he said and went back behind his desk. "Can you start tomorrow?"

"Tomorrow . . . but I don't know anything about—"

He shifted through what must have been other applications. "Well, if you can't start tomorrow—" He looked significantly at me.

"Tomorrow is fine."

"Good. Now here," he reached in his desk drawer and brought out a few pamphlets, some photocopied sheets. "Read these tonight and come with me. I'm about to make rounds. Just do what I do. Don't let any of them spook you. People in pajamas think they have different rights, but you just tell them it's America in here too and you're not buying. Tell them Santa Claus closed up shop this year." He smiled. "They always try to get out of their treatments."

I followed Herb and his inhalation equipment around the hospital. It looked like a recycled ice cream machine. In each room, the women smiled sweetly at him, calling him, "Big Boy" and taking his hand, while the men kidded him about me, asking him if I was "new stuff to make the wife jealous."

"Listen," Herb told them, "she's tough as nails. Wouldn't touch her with a ten-foot pole. I like 'em soft, you know. This one, you gotta deal with." He winked at me. With each person, he was conscientious, watching them the full fifteen minutes to make sure they didn't fudge on the "breathing," but once outside the room, his shoulders drooped, his face went gray and tired. After an hour and a half we finished the rounds. Anxious and sweaty, I followed Herb to his office, but when we got to the door, he didn't invite me back inside. "Be here at three tomorrow," he said. "I'll leave some notes for you, telling you exactly what to do." He opened his door and disappeared. Training complete.

I started down the hall, but when I was halfway to the front door I stopped, realizing I didn't know the first thing about inhalation therapy and these pamphlets he'd given me were little better than advertising sheets for the products. I turned around. When I knocked on his door, I got no answer. I took a deep breath and turned the handle, opening it gently. Herb was sprawled across his desk, sound asleep. I stood looking at him, wondering what I should do when, without raising his head, he said, "I know you're looking for books on inhalation therapy, but there's nothing here. You'll just have to do what I tell you. Now I have to sleep. I've been doing two shifts for more than three months, and this is the only sleep I get." With that, he began to snore.

When I got home, Mother—who spent most of her days working in the garden—was asleep on the couch, a catalog folded neatly across her lap. Behind her, the TV picture scrolled, images flashing an instant before they seemed to disappear into the set. I didn't listen to the words as I twisted the vertical knob so that the picture stabilized into one of the many news programs that had suddenly become popular. I looked over at Mother. Her cheeks were sunken, her wrists thin, frail looking. Her knees poked up through her dress like knobby stumps. Ordinarily, I'd have yelled and jumped around, making a show about my new job, but when I watched Mother in sleep, so innocent looking, so detached from the world of Soldier Creek, I decided to leave her in peace. I wondered if she fled in her dreams back to her childhood, back to that haunted past where time never etched away at her fantasies. I didn't know what made me look up at the screen, but just as I did, a commentator said gravely, "They call it the moral sickness of our times," while behind him flashed scenes of hippies walking around a "crash pad" in the San Francisco Haight district, the kids' clothing outrageous, like something you'd imagine at a costume ball. One fair skinned woman wore a deep green sari and a pirate's hat, a red dot in the middle of her forehead. Another danced by in a white, flowing gown with an army fatigue jacket draped over her shoulders. Indian beads swirled across the screen.

Some young girl, who looked no more than fourteen, pushed her face toward the screen. "We're not like those other places. Those other places, some of those places are sick. They tie you up, put needles in your nipples. I don't need that stuff, I mean, I just went there to get free acid, but these people . . . these people are too weird. I mean—" but the camera flashed past her, roving through the rooms like a voyeur, past beds on the floor, beds in the hall, in the dining room, in the foyer, some no more than pallets or towels bunched together where young girls and boys lay together, their eyes glazed with drugs.

"Man, it's heaven," a boy's voice could be heard in the background. "There's every kind of girl you could want in here." As if the camera were looking for just such a symbol, a short, dark-haired girl in a torn pink slip wandered through the room, oblivious to the camera, her shrunken body with its small, knotty elbows and knees on display. Tears streamed unheeded down her face.

I ran out of the room, down the bluff, through the high weeds toward the creek, but that image of the girl staring at nothing, tears leaking from her eyes was stamped in my mind. Goddamn you, Jit! I picked up a pine cone and threw it toward the water as hard as I could, wishing I could find something heavier, something that might hurt me to lift. The pine cone barely made a splash in the creek before it bobbed happily to the surface. But in that instant of impact, I saw something red among the weeds, something that caught my eye because of its odd color. Everything here was a muted brown or blue. Even the insects were camouflaged. I walked toward it as if it were a clue, something left behind. I knelt down near the water's edge and pulled out the remains of one of my old red shoes. Well! But just as I lifted it toward my face, tiny frogs jumped out in an avalanche of motion, and I dropped the shoe and shrieked. Jesus God! I shivered involuntarily, then tried to breathe normally. I kicked the shoe to make sure there was nothing alive in it, then picked it up, shook it, dumping out dirt and water. My old red shoe.

In my room, I wiped the shoe off with a towel and set it on the windowsill to dry. It looked pathetic, like our family life: worn out, discarded but refusing to die. I lay back on my bed and closed my eyes. For a moment, I could see Jit sealed away in her room with Mother sealed away in hers while I was studying at Trinity. I imagined the hours ticking by, the minutes, the seconds, the feeling of claustrophobia stretching its dark wings over the silence of the house. Did Jit have friends? Did she see Daddy often? Did she and Mother ever talk about anything in their lives? I'd never asked. Only now, lying in my bed, staring at my old red shoe did I see how fully my life at Trinity had consumed me and how little I knew about my sister. At Trinity, it was Mother I worried about, Mother who seemed unstable and frightened. But Jit? I closed my eyes as if only there, in that dark absence could I find clues. Water. Sun. Solitude. A little room with sea shells. A bathing suit. But that could be anywhere, anywhere at all. Did Jit have money? Had she gotten money from Teddy? Mother had told me just enough about Teddy's visit for me to imagine how strained it was, but I still didn't understand why Jit would have gone to find him.

Of course, Officer Budd had given his version of the two of them in the park. But after that, I got confused. Mother had gone to get Jit and bring her back and had stayed up until midnight, waiting for me to call; when she went to bed, she made sure Jit was in her room. But that's the moment I kept returning to: Jit lying in bed, barely breathing while Mother paced the floor below. CALL YOUR MOTHER! Those notes littered my dorm floor. Now what I saw was Jit, her eyes socketed to the ceiling, strained for any signal from below, and I understood for the first time how useless it must have felt for her to stay.

"Get outta here, baby," I used to say. "Fly to the moon."

And Jit had opened her window and taken flight.

That night I couldn't sleep. Discouraged, I got up from bed and stared out at the creek, the water as still and smooth as glass. It looked like a dark walkway, a ghostly passage. As I stood there, I knew there was some element missing, something I hadn't yet done. I went into Jit's room and picked up her blue bathing suit. It hung over a chair. Quietly, with only the sound of my breath and the creaking of the stairs, I made my way down to the pier, walking carefully, slowly, as if everything were part of a ritual only I could perform. I tied Jit's bathing suit to one of the pilings and watched as it fluttered in the early morning breeze. All travelers need a beacon, a talisman to beam them luck; maybe everybody wants a protector, someone to look out for them and wish them well. I stared out across the emptiness of the creek, toward Josie's point and beyond that to the Gulf of Mexico where whitecaps ruffled the surface and the sun was nudging its round head above the horizon. "Be safe, baby," I whispered. "You take care of yourself."

JIT SOLDIER

24

Stepping off the bus in Los Angeles at 4:00 in the morning, I stumbled beneath bright, freakish lights. I hadn't washed my face or brushed my teeth in two days. The blouse I wore smelled like cigarettes, sweat, and fear, the collar stained with a blob of gravy. Too exhausted to be wary, I went straight to the restroom, wanting only to clean up before I got something to eat and copied out all the numbers in the phone book for Katy Harper.

I splashed hot water on my face, not daring to look in the mirror until I felt the warmth flood back into my body and my skin prickle with surprise. Then I brushed my teeth mechanically, changed into a white t-shirt and brought out the scrap of paper I'd taken from Daddy's jar: a folded envelope with Katy's name and part of an address printed beneath it. Only then did I wonder how I'd find a woman I hadn't seen for six years from a little scrap of paper.

That thought sent me to the pay phones where I found a thick, tattered phone book and, to my surprise, two pages of K. Harpers with middle initials from A to S. As I began to copy down the numbers, I saw once again those yellow ringlets, heard that low, silvery laugh.

I was ten. All morning Amanda and I watched Mother rush around the kitchen, basting the turkey, stirring cream sauces we'd never heard the names of before: velouté, hollandaise, Mornay, words so exotic, so ridiculous, they flattened to mush on our tongues. When Mother stopped suddenly in her frenzy of cooking, stunned perhaps at the number of pots and bowls crowded around her, she turned to us in annoyance as we sneaked fingers in the meringue and the pumpkin pies. "Just look at yourselves!" she said. "You look like ragamuffins. You're not even dressed," and she marched us to our room and shut the door.

Inside our room, Amanda looked at her skinny body in the mirror and said breathlessly, "Now, I know I have fine proportions, a real natural poetic line from the shoulders on down, but you can't touch me, you hear. I'm waiting for luuuve." She said this in a low, dramatic voice that made me laugh. "I'm going to be beautiful." She stared at the dust motes floating in the light. "Beautiful and worshipped and lazy. I'm not ever going to lift a finger." At that moment we heard a car engine sputtering in the drive, and Amanda threw on her clothes and rushed out the door before I even had my sash tied.

When Uncle Buddy—short and dark—opened Aunt Katy's car door and she stretched out to stand beside him, I saw she was a full head taller than he was, her bright green flowered dress a hot house around her body. She shook her head, fluffing her blonde curls, and smoothed the dimpled cloth of her skirt.

To Amanda and me, Buddy and Katy looked like movie stars, and we rushed out toward them, then stood awkward and uncertain a foot away.

Katy reached out to us immediately, squeezing our arms while looking around her at the swags of moss that hung from the trees and the old scuppernong orchard that bordered the jungle of pines. "Lord, this is such a pretty place, Buddy. Just like in a magazine." And I was drawn to her as if she were a new exotic bird, one who might sing for me a secret, silvery song. I sat beside her when Daddy served drinks, and Mother, nervous and jumpy as a cornered cat, wandered around the room touching the epergne she'd ordered from New York and the candlesticks we'd never used, not even once. Mother hadn't seen her brother in several years, and we were all waiting for something to happen; it was like waiting for a wobbling china dish to fall from the edge of a table and shatter into a million pieces. When Daddy suggested he show Katy the creek, I followed behind them, knowing in my heart that pleasure is always stolen. Katy, already talking, reached out and took my hand in hers.

"You see, my daddy was a chicken farmer," she was saying as we wandered down the bluff to the pier, Katy making little exclamations of delight as we went, "and when I was a little girl I had to wear chicken sack dresses that my mama made. After I married Buddy, I swore I'd never look at another chicken if I could help it. When I go to the grocery store now, I simply turn my head away from all those packaged chicken parts because I know what would happen if I looked. I'd start screaming." She smiled, then looked out over the water and said almost wistfully. "Now that I'm married to Buddy Harper, I can buy real lean ground beef. Twenty percent fat." Then she laughed and swung my arm in an arc as if nothing bad could ever touch her again. Holding her hand, I felt safe.

But in the afternoon things began to go all wrong. After dinner Daddy insisted he row Katy and Buddy across Crystal Lake to the island where the herons nested. Mother was furious. She hated the water, but hated more that Buddy had gone off with Daddy and that there would most certainly be drinking in that boat. For an hour, she stood in the kitchen and washed each dish by hand, insisting that no one help her. And yet when Buddy, slightly drunk, fell in the creek and we had to drag him shivering and moaning up to the house, it wasn't Daddy Mother turned on, but Katy.

"You should know better! He's frail. He's never had good health—"

While Mother railed at her, Katy sat very still, her cheap dress, wet from holding up Buddy, now wrinkling tightly against her full body. She shivered, her head bowed, but didn't say a word. Once Mother left, I brought Katy a blanket from my room, wrapping it around her, tucking it in at the knees. "Here," I said, trying to think of soothing things, baby aspirin, a damp cloth, a glass of hot milk.

"What happened?" Katy asked suddenly, still looking at the door where Mother had exited. "Why is she so mad?"

I didn't know what to tell her about Mother; it seemed disloyal to criticize your own family. "She hasn't seen him in more than three years," I mumbled, looking beyond Katy to the creek, which had become gray and still. I couldn't say that Buddy had left home for the army and come back with Katy, a woman with no background, nothing but dirt and chickens.

"She doesn't like me. She thinks I'm not good enough—"

Don't be silly, I wanted to say, but my tongue hid like a piece of old flannel in my mouth, thick and dry. All I could do was pat the blanket, little pats of comfort.

"Come hug Katy," she whispered. "Katy would just love a little girl like you."

I put my cheek against her cheek. It felt cool and smooth, and for a moment I lay against that warm body, cuddled against her soft curves. I felt her tears running freely between our pressed skins. But it was then she pulled away and looked intently at me, her eyes dark velvet, thick with emotion. "Look at me worrying only about myself," she said, wiping her eyes. Then she cradled my face in her hands. "Oh, honey, you're living in a minefield." She brought my hand to her cheek. "You will have to be strong, little one. You will have to love yourself." Then she placed her hands on my back and began tracing stars across my spine, whispering to me the new constellations—Zolanda and Lotilla and Cassandra della Maria—as if they were love calls, a secret language between the two of us.

After Houston, I'd let myself pretend that Katy knew I was on my way, that a psychic message had traveled on an invisible track right to Katy's doorstep. I imagined her in a lilac sprigged dress waiting at the door, a smile on her lips, tomato soup already warmed on the stove, a place set with silverware and iced tea. But now, looking at all those names in the phone book, I felt a moment of helplessness, my stomach turning over like a fish in deep water. I didn't really know Aunt Katy. Didn't know anything about her except what I'd seen as a girl. And why hadn't I called Amanda in Phoenix? But when I remembered getting off the bus in Phoenix, I knew that had been impossible. It had taken only one minute for the man in the fringed shirt to spot me, to touch my elbow with that friendly familiarity, his gaze scanning me like radar so that I pulled the window shade down behind my eyes, then scurried past him into the restroom and sat beneath a paper towel dispenser until the next bus was called.

I tried the first ten numbers. Three were answered by Spanish speaking maids who couldn't seem to understand what I said. "Harper residence, Harper residence," they repeated as if I were deaf. Katrina Harper, Katherine Harper, and Karol Sue Stansbury Harper all swore they'd never heard of a Katy. The next five weren't home. Then two men answered and immediately hung up. As I crossed out these numbers, feeling numbed and confused, I heard from behind me the tinkling of chimes. When I turned, young men in golden robes, with shaved heads, moved toward me in a wall of sound, ringing cymbals and chanting a strange, monotone song. They moved in slow motion, like honeyed clouds drifting across the sky, coming toward me, then enveloping me, the cymbals throbbing, closing off the air. Without thinking, I dropped the piece of paper with all the Harper names and numbers and darted across the station to the door marked WOMEN.

I sat on a chair inside the restroom, an old plastic coated chair with a split seam down the middle that made crease marks on my arms and the backs of my thighs. I felt drowsy, suddenly very tired. An hour later, I wasn't sure what had awakened me until I heard a quiet but insistent voice. "Well, do you want to?"

I jerked up, clutching my purse and bag to my chest before I saw the girl squatting on the floor, the hood of a faded red parka almost covering her elfin face. Her eyes were bright green, the color of new summer leaves, her lips a sallow pink.

"I was saying like we could split it three ways," she said, her hand moving the metal tag nervously up and down on her front zipper as her eyes circled the room. "I mean, nothing's happening here. It's deadsville, a bunch of crackers and weasels, but if we head south . . ."

I stared rudely at the girl, unaware of the meaning of her words.

"Christ!" she muttered, yanking the zipper close to her throat. "You got the only chair. I can't sleep here no more. I gotta get to the beach."

And then it dawned on me what she must have asked. "Are there places to stay at the beach? Are there phones?" I asked hopefully. It hadn't occurred to me until now that I could leave the bus station before I'd found Katy; for two days the bus station with its pay phones had been my umbilical cord, still attaching me to the possibility of Soldier Creek.

"Sure," she said, letting strands of her hair slip from behind her parka, long pale blonde silky strands. "We just gotta get a cab. My friend's out there hustling up money."

Still I waited, uncertain.

"Com'on to the beach," she said. "It's where the scene is. Not downtown."

Water. I could feel it tugging at my calves, swishing around my ankles, rushing up to my knees. For the first time in a week, I knew what I wanted. "Okay," I said, and she made a little yippee sound, telling me her name was Molly and then running to get her friend so the three of us could share a cab to the beach.

"The Pacific Ocean!" Molly shouted. I'd been staring at the squat little bungalows alongside the road, surprised at the bright colors, the turquoises and yellows and muddy oranges, so different from the white houses in Soldier Creek. Now I turned and saw that wall of blue and felt the tug of water like invisible fingers drumming against my throat. "Okay girls," the driver said, turning to us.

I got out quickly. I heard Molly calling me, yelling, "You've got to pay your share," but I didn't turn around. Instead, I ran. The sand buzzed with heat. Water glistened, shards flung into the air. "Diamonds," I whispered, as waves crashed against the shore, spray spilling across my feet, splashing my ankles. I breathed it in as I ran, not thinking, not feeling, forgetting all about the bag in my hands, everything erased except water and sky and air. Somewhere behind me, I could hear Molly calling, shrill, empty sounds that lingered in the air—"come baaaaaaccck"—but there was no me anymore, only a girl running into the water, letting it splash against her jeans as she twirled.

25

They continued to yell at me, but I pushed away from them, running down the beach, pretending to be alone. It was a tactic I'd learned from Amanda, and I kept running past sunbathers sleeping in the hot sun, the sea breeze drying the cuffs of my jeans, my mind anxious, but less frightened than the day before. I knew I had to get away from them, and after fifteen minutes, I glanced back to see that Molly was nowhere in sight. Hungry suddenly, I turned from the water and walked down the beach toward a restaurant with tables in a courtyard covered by bright yellow umbrellas, where people were talking and eating and listening to a soft music that I'd later learn was reggae. It took me a few minutes to get up the nerve to plow through those outdoor tables to the inside section where I found a phone between the men's and women's restrooms. Patiently, I again copied down the numbers for K. Harper, Robert Harper, and R. Harper, and with renewed hope, I began dialing, only to hear the same voices, the Spanish and black voices of men and women confusing everything I said.

"You finished?" a man behind me asked.

I nodded, aware suddenly of my dark hair matted from the wind, my shirt wrinkled and stained. My dishevelment seemed to represent my state of mind, and I turned quickly back to the courtyard, letting a waitress seat me at a little table that faced the water. For the first time I realized I'd have to find a room for the night, would have to sleep alone in a strange city. Bereft, I picked up a newspaper and pretended to read while the waitress brought me a croissant and a pat of butter and a steaming cup of coffee.

"May I borrow this chair?" It was a man's voice, thick and heavy, yet so low I barely heard the words. When I lowered the paper, a black man stood before me, a bag of Cheetos in his hand. Surprised, I let the paper fall into my lap, its weight knocking over my glass of water, a puddle racing across the cloth, then dripping onto the floor. He wore a white sports shirt and khaki pants, his feet in marachi sandals, his big toe sliding over the side of the thongs. Nodding, he sat down without speaking and ordered coffee when the waitress reappeared. I waited for him to speak, but he only pulled out a notebook and began writing as if he were sitting at the table alone. I had never sat with a black man before, having lived all my life in segregated Alabama, in Soldier Creek where there were hardly enough people to claim a community. The only thing that distinguished us was the annual Mullet Festival at the Lillian Community Center and the Stamp Collectors Society that met once a year. There were no black people at either. When the waitress brought me a second croissant, I ate slowly, waiting for something inside our silence to spill into speech.

For what seemed like hours I struggled between hesitation and determination, then finally I blurted, "I don't know your name."

When he glanced up, his eyes were dark, the lids hooded, his glance incisive, and then a mask seemed to fall in place. "What do you want it to be?"

I clamped my knees tight together and looked at my empty plate, the crumbs flaky and dry, the coffee cup empty. "What do you mean?"

"I thought we were deciding on my name." He sounded perfectly serious, but I knew he was playing a joke on me, a joke I didn't understand.

"But don't you have a name?" I looked at him now with suspicion and irritation. "A name you grew up with, a name that people call you and that you answer to?"

"Yes," he said, rather gravely, his face impassive, the mask still in place. "Call me Jones if you want."

"And you?" he asked, lifting his chin. "What do you call yourself?"

I told him my name—Jit—but at the sound of it, I saw again the familiar worn spot on the pier where I jumped into the water.

"Yes," he said, and there was something tender in his voice, a softness that made me wonder if he too were remembering another time, another place, maybe the mist rising from the rivers, or the white sheet of steam drifting south from the town's factory. Embarrassed, I picked up the paper, pretending to look at the want ads, though I read the same ad for a jewelry store clerk four times. Finally I put the paper down and turned toward the ocean, the old sadness creeping back in.

"May I see that?" he asked, motioning to the paper.

The paper was my protection, but of course, I handed it over to him.

"Are you going to be needing this?" He touched the paper.

"Yes," I said and in that moment it occurred to me that I would need more money, that $215 would not get me very far. SALES, DISPLAY CASE JEWELRY, MINIMUM WAGE WITH BENEFITS, APPLY AT BULLOCKS, WESTWOOD STORE, the ad said.

"I suppose you're looking for a job."

I nodded, though I hadn't until this moment thought about anything other than finding Aunt Katy and calling Amanda.

"What do you do, if you don't mind my asking?"

I thought of the creek, of the cool, wet water. "Swim."

He looked at me curiously, as if perplexed. "What does that mean?"

"I don't know," I whispered. And with the sound of my voice I felt again a rush of fear, a palpable thing like a bee buzzing beneath a sheath of organdy, buzzing frantically, then finding a hole from which it could explode into the air . . . and then I was up and running, dodging tables and people until I was in one of the tiny, claustrophobic stalls in the bathroom where I sat down and furiously wept. *It means I can't do anything else*, I thought, wringing and twisting a wad of toilet paper between my hands. I pressed my knees tight together until I felt physical pain, realizing the moment my knees locked that I'd left my purse and bag under the table. Aunt Katy's envelope with my money was in that purse, my only link to help. But then my knees went limp and I dropped the wadded-up toilet paper to the floor because I knew that I wouldn't find Aunt Katy. I'd believed that rescue would have to happen, but now as a whiteness closed over my mind, I saw that this had been merely a soft voice in the middle of a nightmare, a lullaby sung just before the storm. Now I would have to find a place where I could sit and think. Think about what to do. I wasn't even sure what I wanted to tell Amanda anymore, except to say I was sorry, sorry I hadn't been able to get to North Carolina, sorry it had gone all wrong, that Teddy had frightened us, that Mother didn't love me. I looked up at the door of the stall, at the scribbling of initials and dirty words, and I knew that somehow I would have to take care of myself.

When I returned, Mr. Jones, was still sitting at the table, his face as solemn as ever. But when I looked at him, he winced, and in that one moment I knew that he was frightened too. I said nothing. I sat down, relieved that my purse and bag were where I'd left them. I dumped two packets of sugar into my glass of water, an old habit from childhood, and I drank it quickly.

"Swimming," he mumbled as if talking to himself. "That's a funny occupation. But it just so happens I know a guy around here who employs women to swim around in a tank. The tank's behind a bar, one of those new kind of bars that have big windows where customers can watch the women in the tank while they drink. It's not quite antiseptic, but almost." He paused, frowning, then sighing. "His name's Earl Ray, and he likes for the women to kick a lot and wear bright colored suits." Mr. Jones spoke precisely as though English were not his native language, but as I listened to him, his face began to relax. "It's not a job that pays much, but it requires swimming only."

He wrote an address and phone number on a piece of paper and tore it out. He placed it beside the Cheetos. "Tell him you know Born Jones," he said softly, his voice husky now as if he'd saved it for just this line. He stood up, the frieze dropping from his face as he touched my arm. I looked up quickly.

"I'm sorry if I frightened you," he said. Then he walked away from the table and out of the courtyard into the midday sun.

26

Each morning there was that smell: shrimp shells rotting beneath the piers, floating in little pink clusters from boats out in the bay. I tightened my nose against it, then gave up and turned over, pulling the covers over my head. Always there was this stupid smell, this stupid heat. Heat lay across everything: it mildewed walls, rusted drainpipes and gutters, even ate at the screens almost as fast as the bugs could smash against them, splattering into a soft, moist ooze. With the covers over my head, I breathed in the smell of shrimp. "Shit!" Then I remembered: I had to get to work at the hospital.

I'd been at South Central Hospital for eleven weeks, and though neither Mother nor I mentioned it, Trinity College was receding, vanishing as quietly as a lily pad washed out to sea. At the beginning of January, I'd had letters from the dean and the admissions department about my scholarship. When I explained the context of our family problems, I expected a curt good-bye, but to my surprise, the director of admissions called personally to say that if I wrote a report explaining the details of my situation, the scholarship might be held until next semester. There was no absolute guarantee, and of course, I'd have to come back in the spring and retake my fall exams. I dutifully agreed to do this, but the forms still sat on my bedroom table, unopened, not responded to, as abstract to me as my old life. Could I go back? Suddenly I didn't know. All I could do was brood on the startling fact that Jit had done what I'd been unable to do: gotten free of Soldier Creek.

"Shirley, if I have to help one more old man suck on a nozzle and pee in a bottle, I'm going to lose all enthusiasm for the male sex."

"Why, honey, don't be a fool now. What do you think men are once you take away their money?" Shirley laughed her big hearty laugh, her bosoms shaking like huge grapefruits underneath her uniform as she pulled back wisps of hair and caught them with a bobby pin. "You get one to pee without spraying and that's progress!" Shirley was one of the night nurses on the three to eleven shift at South Central Hospital (South Central Borrow and Loan, Shirley called it: "We borrow your body, then loan it back"). I liked her humor immediately.

"You start thinking of men as some salvation, honey, and you'd do better giving all your money to Jesus," Shirley said watching me pout. "Men are just folks too. Lord, are they folks! My Hal, bless his heart, can't figure out what the trouble is with women these days. 'Women want to wear the pants all of a sudden,' he says to me the other morning. 'No, shug,' I told him. 'They just want to get credit for being the pants half the time. They don't want anything more than recognition for what they've been doing all along, which is taking care of the whole damn world.' 'Cept with Hal', I don't cuss. He was raised Baptist and I respect that."

I laughed with Shirley and sat down in the extra chair in the nurses' station before making my rounds. I usually tried to get ten minutes of straight talk before the buzzers started going and everybody scattered. After I left the nurses' station, I poured distilled water into the machine, checked all the equipment, then got out the night's charts.

"Mrs. Longinivic," I said, touching my first patient's shoulder gently. "Come on now. Wake up for me. This is important for you to get well. The doctor has ordered it, and he wants you to have it so you'll feel better once you leave here."

Mrs. Longinivic snapped out a curse. Cancer had eaten through almost every organ in her body. What was there really to prolong, I wondered. But they didn't pay me to think. I stared at the curved back, the most natural rejection of humankind and considered letting the old woman sleep. Then I thought of Herb saying, "Make sure you get them late at night. That's important." And I touched the sheet.

Sometimes when I left the hospital, I stopped at Willie Joe's Texaco station just on the outskirts of town and washed my hands. I washed them again and again, trying to free myself of the smell of the hospital, of illness and dying. Always I brought my wet hands to my face and smelled my own life again, inhaling fully and deeply. And then very quickly I turned off the light and went back into the darkness.

When they brought Mr. Turner to South Central Hospital, I wasn't on duty, but by the time I arrived, gossip about him had spread through the wards quicker than air through the vents. "Ambulance came and unloaded that man," Shirley said when I stopped by her desk. "Pale as a ghost he was, hon. Then you should have seen the family getting out of that gray Cadillac, walking through here just as rude as you please as if they owned the hospital and everybody in it. 'Where's the doctor? Where's the head nurse?' Not a one of them so much as thanked anybody. I told the wife, I said, 'You can't talk to the doctor yet, not till after he's finished examining.' She didn't even look at me. 'Get him,' she said as if I were one of her servants."

"How bad is he?"

"Pretty bad, I hear. Dr. Worth's got him set up for all kinds of specialists, but he's set up for surgery first. You'll have to go in and give him his treatments after surgery, doll."

"That's fine. In here, he's just another patient."

"Now that son'll be around here all the time," Shirley said. "They stick together like pack rats, that family. You get one, you get the whole mess of them." She pretended to spit. "That boy! Lord, I guess they've had him in a half a dozen schools trying to get him educated. Looks like if you had that much money, you could afford enough tutors to get somebody through anything, doesn't it? Maybe he can finish at one of them though, maybe in physical education. If I remember right, he is big."

"You're talking about Johnny? Johnny Turner?" I'd forgotten all about him, though saying his name brought back a clear image of acute arrested development. "Testosterone Turner I used to call him," I giggled. But he'd graduated a year before me, and I knew he couldn't have gone to that many schools.

"You bad girl," Shirley said, but she laughed too, the frown erased from her face. "Was he really that bad?"

"Let's just say his anatomy claimed most of his affection."

"Maybe that's better than just loving money."

"He's not lacking either."

You're going to have to clean out his tracheotomy tube," Ida Gaines, the head nurse, said to me the next day. Ida Gaines' gaunt face was tight, the lines around her mouth deepened by fatigue and worry. "If there was anybody else, I wouldn't suggest you, my dear, but Herb can't come back. He's got sick little ones, and you can't expect him to just walk off because of this." She stopped talking abruptly and picked up the chart. "Look here, I'm going to show you and Shirley how to do this, so watch close. Herb did it this morning, and he assured me that you—" she stopped, looking at my face, "that you'd do fine."

Ida Gaines pulled back the curtain revealing the emaciated face and bloated belly of Mr. Turner. He looked like something beached, a body dragged up onto the bed. The tube in his throat protruded, bubbling as he breathed, the IVs in his lifeless arms like wires holding him steady, as if he were a marionette who had no life of his own. I had to turn away to catch my breath; even with all the antiseptics in the room, he smelled like vomit. "See here," Mrs. Gaines said, noticing my squeamishness.

"I'm fine," I said, looking into the closed purple lids of Mr. Turner.

"Mr. Turner," Mrs. Gaines said firmly. "Mr. Turner, it's time for me to clean you up, suction out your tube."

Mr. Turner's eyelids flickered briefly, the fear darting up, then drifting away, forgotten. He closed his eyes, sinking back into some eternal slumber. Mrs. Gaines put on gloves, then took the package, ripping open the fresh suction, holding it like a carpenter picking up a familiar tool as she bent over Mr. Turner's tracheotomy with a keen eye. Mucus and phlegm raced up the tube and Mrs. Gaines nodded, satisfied. She looked at the suction as if it were a miracle device, something she'd want for her own kitchen.

I thought that everything would stay the same when I did the suction, but the first time I leaned over him with the suction in my hand, his eyes flashed open and his entire face seemed to resist the phlegm being pulled up the tube. "It hurts them," Mrs. Gaines said matter-of-factly as she watched. "But the main thing is to be steady and to keep an eye on his face, make sure he's not choking," she continued. "Some of them fight it so you have to say calming words to them. It's almost done now, Mr. Turner. This will make you breathe easier. Now, now, Mr. Turner, just relax." I pulled the suction out and Mr. Turner visibly slumped further into the bed, his face grayer, more distorted than before. Mrs. Gaines nodded approval. "Afterwards, you can increase the Valium for a half hour, get him back to sleep good."

As we walked out of ICU, Mrs. Gaines put her hand on my shoulder. "I'll be watching you tonight, then I'll ask Shirley to be watching you. At the end of the week, you should be able to do it on your own."

"Yes," I said. "I'm sure I will."

As she walked away, I shot her the bird. I was suddenly very tired of orders, of veiled threats and competence tests. For a moment I imagined the ease of hiding behind someone else.

"She'll watch every move you make," Shirley said. "One week with her and you can go straight into the Marines."

I patted Shirley's arm. "Don't worry. I can do it." *I'll think about snow in North Carolina, snow coming up that little tube, me sucking it up into myself so I can feel it against the heat, against the boredom of this place.*

In the middle of the night Mother came into my room, her hair loose down her back, her eyes painfully wide. "Amanda. Wake up, honey. I had such a scare."

I pulled the sheet from my legs and sat up, pushing hair from my eyes. "What is it, Mother? What's wrong?"

Mother didn't move or speak. The dream still held her as if she were under a cloud.

"Come sit down here, Mother, and tell me." I patted the bed, smoothing out the sheet which was cool now in the night. A moist wind blew outside, leaving the next morning's dew on the ground. "Just relax now. It's over. You can tell me."

Mother sat on the bed, her hands between her knees. "I dreamed . . . why we were turned out of here, darling, the two of us just walking down the road like orphans wandering in a place I'd never seen before. It was lush and green. Oh, darling, with flowers, yet we couldn't touch them. Then, as if I'd known it all along, I knew Jit had come back. She'd come back here, don't you see, but we'd already gone. We were walking down this graveled road I'd never seen before, and I was so scared." She buried her face in her hands. "So scared."

I smoothed her hair, caressing her head in gentle strokes. "It's just a dream, Mother. It's not real at all. We're still here. We'll always be here."

"It seemed so real." Mother moved closer to me, huddling against me. "Well, that's why they call them nightmares," I said, trying to laugh, "because they scare the bejesus out of you. Listen, we won't leave here. And she'll come back. That's the part of the dream that you can believe. She'll come back. Jit can't leave here either."

Mother put her arm on my leg, hugging me.

"Rub my neck, darling. I think I can sleep now if you'll just rub my neck here."

After Mother left, I lay awake a long time, knowing full well that something had been exchanged between us, something lost on my part, gained on Mother's.

"Goddamn mother-fucking-son-of-a-bitch!" I jerked at the broken tube, then dropped it to the floor.

"Who're you talking to?" I didn't see Johnny Turner until he spoke. He stood almost directly behind me, not near his father's bed, but slouched against the wall, his thumbs in his jeans as if he were still in the school yard, that smug look of appraisal on his face as if I were something up for sale. Jesus, as if he'd ever change, I thought. Give him a funeral, he'll be looking for something to hump.

"I'm talking to your father. Who else do you see in this bed? The tube is bent. It could hurt him and I'm just glad I found it."

Johnny looked up at the ceiling as if this required serious contemplation. "I won't tell on you," he said, tapping his foot now too.

"Beg your pardon?"

"I mean I won't tell my mother what you said because she'd say something to the head nurse about it."

I started to reply, but just then the old man gurgled to life and I picked up the suction tube. "All right, Mr. Turner. I'm going to fix you up now. We'll get that old phlegm out and you can sleep like a baby tonight." His eyes stared up at me with that paralyzed amazement of the sick and dying, as if each time he awoke he wasn't sure that what was happening was actually happening to him. I stroked his arm, smoothing the covers around him. I'd learned the words of the other nurses, not so much individual words as tones, rhythms, syllables meant to soothe hysteria, to cajole patients into permanent acceptance of our tending so that we could get on with it. My attention now diverted by Mr. Turner, I worked out the phlegm, twisting the suction slightly, being careful not to hurt him, though his eyes stared up at me, veiled in pain and confusion. I forgot that Johnny stood behind me as I finished the suctioning and withdrew the tube. Then Johnny made a sound, the sound of heaving, and I heard his footsteps as he left the room.

A few moments later when I came out into the hall, he slouched against the wall, pulling on each knuckle so that crack-pause-crack filled the silence. I intended to walk around him—hadn't I done my duty, talked with him even if in a rather obnoxious fashion?—but as I came abreast of him, he grabbed my arm.

"Listen," he said, "could we—"

Expecting some idiotic proposition, I pulled away, startled. "Don't touch me!"

Johnny became silent. "Never mind," he said, looking down the corridor as if even with his adolescent slouch he expected nothing from the night.

"What is it?" I asked, moving a little closer. There was no one near enough to hear us, and oddly, now that he'd refused to continue, I was curious. Johnny Turner never struck me as a guy with something on his mind, but I had a vague, disquieting fear that sometimes I misread people. Now Johnny Turner dropped his head, the kind of gesture imitative of profound misery. Yet immediately, I became suspicious again. "If it's about your dad," I said carefully, "you know, I'm not really the one to ask. He seems to be coming along. His color is partially back and the nurses don't hover so much around him as they did that first week, but you could talk to Shirley if you're really—"

He looked at me with such profound astonishment, I stopped talking. What had I done? Then I understood what any normal person would have understood: he couldn't talk about his father's illness, and here I was blabbing on about it. "I'm sorry," I said, and then started down the hall to the little office I used, intending to put Johnny Turner behind me and forgive myself for my bad manners. I had to make rounds in ten minutes, and I needed to check the equipment and grab a cup of coffee.

I poured a cup of coffee at the nurses' station, then checked the saline supply. As I pulled out a new pair of rubber gloves, Johnny appeared at my door, his face in that same rapt astonishment in which I'd left him. I was about to apologize again when he said abruptly, "I'm failing English."

"I'm sorry," I said, hoping he understood I meant it to be inclusive.

"I'm . . . I may not pass," he started again, looking keenly at me now.

I placed the charts on the table. "English is hard for some people," I said stupidly, not wanting to make another gaffe. "But it's really a matter of interpretation. Sometimes it just takes a while to find the right slant."

"But I have to pass it." He still had not moved from the door.

Then it dawned on me. "You mean, it's not . . . you're not worried about your father?"

"English," he grunted. There flashed for a second the old taunting smile on his face, but he caught it, squelched it. He stared at the gray walls, his eyes serious.

I gathered the extra bottles of saline solution, tucked them on the trays beneath the cart.

"Look, I am sorry you're failing English, but I have to make my last rounds. If I wait too late they're hard to wake up."

"Oh," he said, stepping aside.

I'd just gotten the cart out the door and started down the hall when he blurted, "Look, I know you don't like me, but I'm not asking you to like me. I don't care about that, just . . . help me pass English."

"What?"

"I could get drafted," he said, "because I'm failing English."

I stopped. "You want—"

He smiled, nodding at me. "I'll pay you."

Those magic words.

"Just help me pass English. I need a tutor. I need—"

"Seven dollars an hour," I said. "I can't do it for less." It was a gamble. I only made $5 an hour at the hospital.

"Hired." He grinned suddenly, then he stuck his hand out. "Hired by unanimous vote."

So it began. Once again I was stuck with a country boy, but this time his paws held a pencil and a book. I tutored Johnny Turner in the empty cafeteria of the hospital one hour each night after I finished my shift, from 11:00 until midnight. It was an unorthodox hour, not of my own choosing, but his schedule turned out to be even more inflexible than my own. It gave me a new perspective on him, on that cocky dance he did in front of any female, strutting out his stuff as if he were the last hunk on earth. He didn't have time to do much talking. He was too busy. Each morning he drove to Mobile to college, attended classes, drove home, went to work at his father's bank until 5:00, took his mother to see his father from 5:00 to 6:00, ate supper, went back to the bank to oversee the books, brought his mother back to the hospital between 9:00 and 10:00 and was supposed to study after that. "The main verbs in my life," he said that first night when we sat across from each other in the empty cafeteria, "are fetch and take." I laughed, but he meant it. He'd said it as solemnly as a schoolchild, a kind of apology, I understood later, because by the time he got to me there wasn't much left of him to tutor. "You need an IV of coffee," I said. "Wait a sec."

He looked nervous until I put the coffee, three packs of sugar and a cold doughnut before him. "It's just a substitute—the doctors' pick me up, but it'll have to do." He drank the coffee while I watched and nodded my chin when he seemed to lag. When he finished the cup, he offered up his first paper.

After reading it, I realized I could spend an entire year on punctuation and grammar alone, but I didn't. Johnny Turner needed a broader scope. This was a literature class, and so we started with the assigned short stories of Faulkner, O'Connor, and Welty. When I read Flannery O'Connor's "Everything That Rises Must Converge" out loud, he laughed every time Julian deliberately frustrated his mother. I always stopped when he laughed. "Write down why you're laughing at this particular point, Johnny." I continued to read to him and ask questions when he didn't have a specific assignment; when he had some physical or emotional response, I made him explain why he had the response in writing, what he felt when he laughed, even if he just shook his head.

Literary therapy, I called it. Or I might have called it that, had it not led to a conversion I was slow to understand. It started one night after his father had become visibly better. The old man had improved so much that he could talk to us now, small sentences, sometimes just words, a single word— "Nurse!" or "Urinal!"—but the family, Johnny said, had become less cautious, less tense. "They're not so dinged out about the fucker," was the way he put it. Wives of business associates now brought flowers and little bits of bank gossip when they came. They stopped tiptoeing around him, crying into handkerchiefs. The trach tube had been removed, the scar healing.

Johnny was more nervous now that his father's health was improving, and yet I continued to discuss the use of active verbs and concrete detail as if nothing had changed. We worked well together until the week before the final exam when suddenly Johnny seemed to forget everything we'd discussed, digging in his heels like a frustrated two-year-old. I couldn't believe it. I'd never watched someone actively regress, his mind closed down, all the doors shut. "What's the matter? Com'on, talk about the significance of the hat in 'Everything That Rises Must Converge.' We've discussed this, Johnny. You've written an essay on it." But he shook his head.

"I can't do it."

"Sure you can. You did it last week as a matter of fact."

Johnny drummed his fingers on the table, and then he jerked up as if something inside him had snapped. "He's always on me. 'Do better, jump higher, hit harder, run faster. Think, think, think.' Like this: 'snap, snap, snap,' right up in my face, and then I can't think." He looked at me, blushing, the pulse throbbing in his temple, a streak of red blooming across his face. "I go into a test and all I see is him snapping those fingers at me. 'You missed that pass. Absolutely beautiful pass, like a comet coming right at you, practically going to hit you if you didn't move out of the way, but what do you do? You look away. If you were in war, boy, you'd be dead. Kaput. Lights out.' Then before I know it, the professor's taking up the test."

"Why does he do that?" I had the inclination to take his hand but resisted. The room was close and hot, and I was afraid Johnny might misinterpret the gesture.

"Wha'cha mean?" Johnny had this way of suddenly slipping into the vernacular of a backwoods cracker, lopping off syllables to accommodate his mood. At first I thought he did it to attract attention, but now I knew he wasn't trying to attract attention. He was worried. Even his tongue became sloppy when anxiety fueled him.

"I mean what does he get out of badgering you? Does it make him feel bigger or what?"

"Why would he need to feel bigger? He owns the whole damn town." He put his face flat down on the cafeteria table. "He calls me goofball. 'Hey, did you get goofball his milk,' he asks my mom. Or, 'Did ya take your vitamins, Mr. McGoof?'"

"So what do you do?"

"I tell him to knock it off, particularly with Mom." He raised his head, his eyes bloodshot and blinking as if he weren't quite awake yet. "But all he does is say," he leaned over and whispered, "'maybe you need a little pussy, son, to stir up your blood, improve the concentration, huh?'"

"He says that to you?"

"Yeah. They all say it, all those old codgers. They don't know nothing. They're not even acting on hormones anymore. They're just trying to impress the rest of the old farts. 'Scuse me."

"It's okay. I know a few old farts myself." And yet it bothered me to hear about such people. "What was your dad's childhood like?"

"I don't know. Average, I guess."

"I mean, was he on the football team or very popular or—"

"Just average. He always says the best years were when he was a Boy Scout."

"But that's it. He's so typical it's pathetic. He's just trying to live it all over through you, to be spectacular through you. That way it's a lot less work. I mean, he doesn't have to catch the ball. You do. But if you do there's that vicarious family pride, this sense of accomplishment he can take credit for. Don't you see, Johnny, he wants you to do it for him as if you were him, so he doesn't have to do it himself."

"Nah. He just don't like me."

"Doesn't." It was automatic.

"What?"

"Nothing." I curled up in my chair, thinking. "You're being unfair to yourself. You're letting him get the better of you." I thought about how my history professor had said that each generation has to hope that the next generation will do better, be smarter, have more guts and energy and ideas because otherwise, what would be the point? And I told Johnny that. "Families have to have some reason for being besides accident. Progress is a good enough reason for most people, so they grab onto it, hold it so tight they squeeze the life out of you. Progress in the bloodline, you know. Cleaning up the blood. It's why people like to marry upward, I guess. It's not just the money. They figure they can refine the rough edges through the next generation, perfect the story." I knew I should stop but I'd had too much coffee. "Don't you see, you aren't disappointing your father because it's not you he's seeing, but himself. It's what he wants to be."

"You're crazy, you know." But he smiled.

I pushed Johnny's books across the table. "If you could be anywhere right now, where would you be?"

"Riding out to the West Coast, to San Francisco maybe, in a convertible. I'd stop right by the ocean and just lean back between the ocean and the sky."

"Listen, when you take that test, think about that moment. Really, just put yourself there and if your daddy and his goofballs start haunting you, go right back to that sun and sky."

"Okay, Teach." He grinned at me then and suddenly looked embarrassed. "I always thought you were stuck-up, that you didn't think about anybody except the others sitting in front of the class, but you're not like that at all." He lifted his cup of coffee. There were only dregs settled in the bottom. "Thank you." He barely whispered it as he put the cup to his lips and drank.

I nodded. We really understood each other. Johnny Turner and me. It made me sort of giddy.

Johnny Turner. So, the tadpole became a frog, and the frog jumped on a lily pad and croaked his heart out, his eyeballs bulging, his heart a tenor sax. All for the dying bullfrog. Funny how it cycled on and on like a top set in motion. Fathers crush sons who grow up wanting to crush fathers but end up crushing their own sons. You smash him, Johnny. You're gonna show him, or I'm no lonely white girl.

Poor Johnny. Thinking of him, I eased out of the parking lot and onto the highway in darkness, patches of fog rolling in from the coast. I drove slowly out of town, creeping along because there were only occasional farmhouses lighting my way. When I turned the lights on bright, I saw, right in front of me, a cow standing smack in the middle of the road. Jesus! I slammed on my brakes and stopped in front of it, its tail swishing against the bumper. It stared patiently at the car. I sat waiting for it to move, but it only turned slowly.

It had Mother's face, placid but with that hysterical edge to the eyes, the whites so white there was almost no color at all. As if I were moving in tune with the fog, I eased out of the car, not even bothering to move the car off the highway. Beyond me, the trees loomed in shadowy mist. I could hear the slow drip of water as it condensed on the leaves.

"Shoo!" I screamed. "Get away! Shoo!"

But the cow only turned its eyes toward me, flicking its tail, hitting a headlight. It didn't move an inch.

I reached inside the car and turned out the lights. "Shoo now! Shoo!"

The cow remained stationery as I climbed on top of the hood, tempting fate. Some nights cars rushed down the highway from Pensacola to Mobile, cars that never stopped for anything, the drivers humming or cursing as they sped along through the countryside. Now I sat cross-legged, looking at the animal as clouds of fog drifted toward us; my hair lay damp on my neck as I watched the cow's nostrils dilate and contract. It snorted, its breath hot and moist on my legs.

As my eyes became accustomed to the dark, I saw the cow more clearly, the large, languid eyes, the short, stiff, one directional hairs. "We're not so different, huh? You're wedged in between my car and the whole damn world and can't move, can you?" I stared at my pale knees in the moonlight, felt the hardness of my bones, and thought how I wasn't much different from Johnny Turner. Both of us indentured to a demanding parent, both of us lost to the world of dreams. I'd always thought I was better than people like Johnny, that anyone with gumption could get out of here, but now . . . I wasn't so sure.

The cow mooed suddenly, a sound so plaintive, so primal, that without any warning, I began to cry. I was crying for all of us: myself, Jit, Mother, Daddy, even Johnny Turner. I never thought much about Daddy, had seen little of him except for that one trip to his cabin to ask about Jit. I still resented the fact that he never made enough money to take care of us. And he lost Soldier Creek. I could never forgive him for that.

The cow mooed again, turning its head toward me, almost putting it in my lap; I reached out and stroked its wet coat, its body shivering until I lowered my face to its neck and began whispering into its ear. It didn't move, so slowly I got off the car and gently talked the cow toward the side of the road. I couldn't see where it had broken out of the fence, but I couldn't worry about that. I had to move my car. I had to protect myself.

A week passed without any sign of Johnny Turner until the day his father was released from the hospital. Even Mr. Turner's disposition seemed to improve as he teased the nurses about not getting his bacon and biscuits with his grits. "Shame on you," they said. "You can't swallow bacon. You try to sneak one little thing in your mouth that's thicker then grits, you aren't going to own the bank anymore." They laughed with him, friendlier than anyone had ever dared be. Mr. Turner in recovery was almost human.

I worried about Johnny the few minutes I worried about anything beyond myself, but I assumed he was studying for the final, going over the notes we'd made. We'd finished up the last paper on a Wednesday, and he'd written several practice exams with questions I furnished. I hadn't known about his father's release, which was given before my shift, yet as I passed his room, an orderly was helping Mr. Turner into a wheelchair, his fresh blue pajamas so new the folded wrinkles were still creased in them. Mr. Turner smiled as I passed. I stopped in the doorway and was surprised to see Johnny slouching against the wall while Mrs. Turner patted the pajamas smooth in the suitcase.

"Moving out, Mr. Turner?"

"Yes, dahling." He called all women dahling while in the hospital, even old grandmothers.

"Going home to some real food, huh?" It was a constant joke around the hospital that you'd probably survive if the food didn't kill you. I looked quickly toward Johnny to catch his eye, but his eyes wandered, bored, distracted around the room, as if he didn't know me. "Well, hello, Johnny," I said finally, trying for the old camaraderie.

He merely nodded at me, looking past my shoulder. Not even one stupid word. So he was more cowed by his father than I'd assumed. As if reading my mind, he went quickly to the back of the wheelchair and steered the old man out of the room and into the hall.

"We're not running a race for Godsakes," I heard his father bark as Johnny wheeled him around a corner.

Something funny was going on. But I couldn't think about it now. I had my patients to attend. I might not have known so soon if I hadn't idly mentioned it to Shirley later in the shift when I took a break and sat with her at the nurses' station. Shirley knew I'd been tutoring Johnny, but I never told Shirley that he'd actually confided in me or that he had such a fear of taking tests.

"Honey, I don't know why it is with your brain you're always the last to know things. Gossip passes through this hospital like fire on a grease track. That boy got thrown out of school again."

"What?" Surely, it was a mistake. Hadn't I seen all of his themes, his returned papers with the grades solidly marked in red? He wasn't a brilliant student, but he'd worked hard this spring and had brought his English grade from an F to a B. "I just don't believe that, Shirley."

Shirley shuffled papers before me on her desk, not noticing my concern. "Sure, he was caught cheating on his final, had things written down all over the place just like he wanted to be caught."

I sat down, dumbfounded. Sons of bitches!

"Now I guess he'll have to go in the army. Probably already got his draft notice."

"What do you mean?" I asked.

"Why, honey, they're calling boys up for Vietnam."

JIT SOLDIER

27

I stood in the cool darkness of the bar, my eyes focused on a big glass window set into one wall. Without the underwater lights, the glass looked fuzzy, more like a delicate frieze painted on the backside of the glass. Then a figure dove through the blueness, a body too large for life—an Amazon who swirled and kicked, strands of silky hair floating past her face. I took a step closer. The girl opened her eyes and stared back at me.

"You waiting for somebody?" The man behind the bar turned from wiping glasses, his face so blank I could have thrown a penny at it and he wouldn't have blinked.

"I have an appointment with Mr. Earl Ray." I glanced at the window just in time to see the exact curve of the girl's breasts beneath her suit as she arched backward and somersaulted in a rush of bubbles.

"Pretty slick, huh?" the bartender said, nodding in admiration. "It magnifies so big you can almost watch them breathe.

Just then a tall man with a blonde ponytail emerged from an inner office and paused near the bar. Everything about him suggested perfection, from his smoothly pressed beige linen pants to the silver pen he held in his hand. "Jit," he said simply, then turned back to the office, not waiting for any response.

"So you know Mr. Jones," he began, seating himself behind a big desk where he immediately rearranged a group of papers, not looking at me, though I had the feeling he was watching me closely in his peripheral vision. "So what do you know about our friend, Mr. Jones?"

"He was traveling on the same bus as I was from Alabama," I said, then wondered if I'd given away too much.

"Yes, I see." His face and voice remained bland, neutral, as he bounced the tip of his pen against his index finger. "What does he look like these days, if you don't mind my asking?"

I didn't know what to say. I could say he was big. I could say he was
black. "He looks like . . . he doesn't dress funny if that's what you mean. He
wore blue jeans and sneakers on the bus."

"I see." He seemed to be waiting for more.

"I don't know how to describe him. His eyes . . . his eyes are like
smoke, they watch you and then they glaze over, and then they watch you
again—"

"Yes," he smiled, pleased, and leaned toward me as though confirming
what I'd said. "Why don't you get suited up and let's just try a few things in
the pool before we open."

My hair, soft as seaweed, flowed around my head, swirling in chlorine; the
water, cold and dark like the water at the bottom of the creek, pushed itself
against me until I didn't know where I was, where I wanted to be. I kicked
to the bottom of the pool, seeing again the cracked plaster in the small
hotel I'd stayed in last night, a room near the beach that cost me twenty
dollars, leaving three fifties in my wallet. I remembered Josie grabbing my
hand once when I stole a Hershey bar from the One-Stop. "But I want it,"
I'd said. "Well, you have to work for it. You have to work for everything in
this world. Ain't nothing free. Not even freedom's free. You sweep out this
back porch and then you can have it." Remembering this, I felt comforted.
If this was work, then I could work, and I pushed to the top, breathed
deeply, then glided into flip after flip after flip.

Earl Ray gave me thirty dollars and an aqua bikini that fit tight over
my breasts, the bikini bottom riding high over my hips so that part of my
buttocks hung out. "The butt tease," Amanda would have called it, but at
least I was swimming.

I didn't know that Mr. Jones was often there when I swam at night, swam
until I was exhausted, the only thing that brought me sleep. I didn't know
until much later when even exhaustion wasn't enough and I lay awake until
the early sounds of morning—cars starting, children crying—soothed me
into oblivion. If I could have seen through the glass, I might have noticed
him, sitting alone, dressed like the others in rolled white pants or chinos,
wrinkled shirts and canvas deck shoes—the clothes of afternoon sailors
and afternoon drinkers. Several times I went into the club before I swam
to get a Coke or peanuts for later; the men inside all looked alike, too
old to do much damage. The other girls laughed at them. Over the hill,
they said. Can't get it up anymore but still trying to butter some itty bitty
piece of bread. I didn't know that Mr. Jones came to this bar to sketch the

girls as they drifted past the window or breast-stroked toward it, quick line drawings, curves and slashes, like something I'd see years later in prints by Matisse. I might never have known about any of it if I hadn't gotten a cramp in my leg one Tuesday night and had to stop swimming. The cramp tightened like a fist in my calf, and I floated to the surface, pulled myself up on the side of the pool, and massaged my leg for five minutes. The cramp began to ease and I stood up, breathing deeply, shaking my leg, getting ready to dive back into the pool when I was yanked aside and then pulled out into the parking lot to face Earl Ray.

His face was white with anger while I stood absolutely still, chloroformed with fear. "But I got a cramp, Mr. Ray," I began. "You said—"

"I said if you have another girl in there with you, but you were alone, missy. You were prima donna tonight. For twenty minutes I couldn't replace you. Lisa with the flu and Rachel on her way in. Now I made this clear to you—" He dragged on a cigarette, blowing smoke toward the palmetto fronds where it hung in a dense, threatening cloud. "How do you plan to make up for this?" He reached a hand out toward my shoulder, but instead of touching me, he pulled a leaf from a palmetto tree and began to crush it. I backed away from him, my wet hair dripping down my neck. If he touched me, I'd leave in three seconds. I could feel one drop running down my back, following the bumpy ridge of my spine. It was almost to my waist when Mr. Jones stepped out from the darkness and pinned Earl Ray's arm behind him.

"Professor," he said, squeezing Mr. Ray's arm.

Earl Ray didn't move a muscle, but I could see something in him relax. He laughed, grunting a little. "You old swamp coon. Lemme go before I bust your ass, send it flying back home where they eat meat like yours for snacks."

"Just what I need to hear, Professor." He released Earl Ray and they embraced, patting each other on the back.

"Jesus Christ, what are you doing in this neck of the woods? I thought you couldn't cram this place down your throat with a pistol pointed to your head."

"I'm corruptible," Born Jones said. "I love hating. Gets my blood going."

Earl Ray smiled. They'd forgotten about me, and I stepped further back, nearer the bushes, not moving, barely breathing, only waiting for a chance to escape. "Come on inside, let's put two on the table," Earl Ray said.

"No more tonight, Professor. I've put too many there already. I'm just checking on how you treat the help here. A little freelance spying. Make sure you run a clean ship and all." They both turned to me. "He doing all right by you?" Born Jones asked.

Before I could answer, Earl Ray pointed a finger at him. "You did send her. I didn't believe it. I didn't know that a fool like you would ever find me."

Born Jones pointed to his head. "Memory."

"Well, why not bring that memory back here tomorrow, name the time."

"Noon."

"Jesus Christ," Earl Ray said. "Don't sneak up on me like that." And he clapped him on the shoulder before he left.

When I tried to thank Mr. Jones, he acted as though I were the one to thank.

"Let me get you a cup of coffee," he said. "That's the least I can do."

I didn't really want to have coffee with him, but he'd done me a favor, so I changed quickly and walked with him to a nearby café, more dark bungalow than anything else, with red leather booths and a bar with padded swivel stools. Mr. Jones slung himself into a booth, rubbed his eyes as if he were fatigued. "Earl Ray, he treating you all right?"

I nodded. "I guess . . . I mean, he likes the way I swim."

Mr. Jones lit a cigarette, the smoke drifting in a swirl above our heads. "Tell me about swimming," he said, his eyes looking at me curiously.

But for me, there was nothing to tell.

"Why swimming?" He looked intently at me, his eyes a liquid black, blacker than his skin, eyes like ink spills, like the dark side of the moon.

I shifted away from him, staring out the window where a sprinkling of stars interrupted the sky. "Because . . . well, because I don't drown," I said.

Suddenly his face relaxed. He leaned toward me, smiling. "Yes," he said. And still smiling, "I'd like to sketch you. Is that something you'd let me do?"

28

While we swam—two girls breast-stroking around the perimeter of the pool and two others swan-diving toward the window, flutter-kicking and somersaulting until we all met in the middle, forming a circle—Earl Ray stood in the bar, watching, giving orders to the waitresses and to his assistant, Mr. Jimmy. Vivian did a kind of strip-tease beneath the water, dressed in a red chiffon dress, with long white gloves and silver high heels. She stripped down to her bikini and then circled the pool holding onto her tiny silver purse. Each week we also swam laps for two hours, just to keep our strokes even and our breathing in good form. After practicing we wrapped in towels, drinking Cokes and eating Cracker Jacks, gossiping among ourselves. I didn't know about the other girls, but I felt something I'd never felt before. I was doing my job and I was good at it.

At times like this, I thought about Aunt Katy, trying to imagine how she'd look now, six years since I'd seen her in Soldier Creek: would she wear striped denim bell-bottoms and embroidered peasant blouses or something more conventional like a tailored pantsuit? For a moment, I imagined her face painted like a butterfly, velvety wings spreading across each cheek, a mandala blooming from the center of her forehead. I'd seen someone like that last week, a woman picking up avocados in the supermarket, her face so theatrical, I followed her into the next aisle. But maybe Aunt Katy wore only t-strapped sun dresses and sandals like the women in Alabama, women who got freckles on their shoulders instead of an all-over tan, women who were slightly embarrassed by their bodies and slouched beneath their clothes. Or maybe she was like any other housewife outside California, grocery shopping and cooking and taking care of the house, so busy she didn't pay that much attention to what she wore.

I was daydreaming when I felt Earl Ray's touch on my shoulder. I stood up straighter, staring blankly at nothing. "Get her another aqua suit, Mr. Jimmy. This one's getting . . . loose."

And then it was time to swim for the customers. After that, it was back to my creepy little room.

The phone's loud ring startled me. I must have been sleeping because I sat upright, glancing at the clock. 6:00 a.m. No one from work called this early. "Hello," I said cautiously, then listened to what sounded like heavy breathing. I was about to hang up when a voice said, "I'm sorry to call you so early. I've been up all night, working."

The voice seemed slower, thicker than I remembered. "Who is this?"

"Mr. Jones. Born Jones." He sounded weary, a solemn weight to his voice. "I meant to call sooner, last week, but I worked extra hours for a printer."

He'd said he wanted to make sketches of me, but when I didn't hear from him, I assumed he'd forgotten. I'd been sad that he never called; I'd begun to think of him as a good omen, a person who had twice saved me and was destined to bring me luck.

"I didn't forget," he said quickly as if reading my mind. "Can you come tomorrow night, straight from the club?"

I knew I should be frightened, but I was too lonely to resist. "It's awfully late," I said. I would swim until 10:00, then need to clean up.

"Come with your hair wet," he said, ignoring my remark. "I'll make dinner, a good southern meal, and then we can start."

It sounded magical: eat dinner with someone other than the girls who swam for Earl Ray, the kind of cheap meals we got at the Hungry Hobo or a hamburger at one of the quick stops not far from the bar. There was silence on the line as if Mr. Jones was waiting for me to speak while I, uncertain and anxious, was waiting for him to convince me to come. "I'm a little afraid about going downtown," I finally said. "And I need to find my aunt."

"Does your aunt live here in Los Angeles?"

I saw Aunt Katy's hair brushing the grass as she leaned back in her lawn chair, a Pepsi in her hand. I told him what I knew about Aunt Katy, about the letter with the partial address, the street name blurred except for the first two letters.

"Okay," he said matter-of-factly. "I'll help you find her. But not tomorrow. Tomorrow I sketch and feed you, and the next day we look for your aunt. How does that sound?"

For the first time, I felt a singing in my chest. If I could find Aunt Katy, then I might reconnect. I might find my way home.

29

The next night I smelled sulfur in the air, the stink of rotten eggs bursting from the sea, blown about by a humid wind. It moved inland, wind gusting the awnings on the restaurants, pulling the putrid smell with it as I stood outside the club in jeans and a t-shirt, my hair still wet, already curling around my neck. When the taxi came, I got in quickly, the cab stale and moldy with the stink of old cigarettes, the man grizzled-looking, greasy, a sleepy grin on his face. As we moved down Wilshire, I watched the bright lights of the hotels, the movie marquees, the striding pedestrians moving in and out of bars and restaurants with gilded ease. We drove through residential areas where bougainvillea bloomed behind wrought iron gates, bright reds and purples splashing over pointed fence-lines onto the sidewalk, then into the heart of downtown L.A., the clot of night traffic surging to some unknown rhythm. I kept my eyes pasted to the windows, watching the people cluster on street corners, women in tight-fitting dresses stopping cars, talking, laughing, cursing. A couple of boys beat on the cab's hood, and the cabby growled. Abruptly the scenery changed: the streets, which had been crowded and bright, suddenly lost color and brightness as if the blood supply had been cut off. There were dimly lit, dilapidated buildings, their screens torn loose, paint peeled away from the doors. Garbage cluttered the alleys. As we passed one building, a long, low scream escaped from a high window. When the cab stopped before an old brick building with a metal fire escape out front, I understood fear. A bare light bulb shone above the door, the windows papered over from the inside. The cabby shut off the meter and opened the back door, still without a word.

"You're supposed to wait until I get inside," I said. The man looked skeptically at me, wiping his nose on his sleeve, as if I'd asked him to carry me to the door. For the first time I wondered if this was a hoax, something to trap me, but then I remembered Mr. Jones' voice when he said, "I'll help you find your aunt," and I stepped out onto the curb.

"Lady, I'm not going nowhere until that guy pays me," the cabby said suddenly. "You can count on that."

When I rang the bell, nothing happened, but I turned the knob, and the door opened easily. Light spilled across half the room. On the opposite wall I could see canvasses stacked up, some turned toward me, others turned away so that only their naked cross frames were visible. I scanned the room for Born Jones, for any sign of human habitation, but I saw nothing but a blue shirt hanging over a chair, heard nothing but the drip of a faucet and the scurrying of something inside the walls. "Hello," I called out. I felt foolish. "Is anybody here?"

Think of Aunt Katy, this is all for Aunt Katy, but in a little secret room of my mind, I knew it was a mistake. Aunt Katy seemed further away than ever.

The room was bare except for a sink, a counter with a hot plate at one end, a coffee pot and boxes of food at the other. An old enamel kitchen table, two chairs, and a radio were the only other items I could recognize. A pipe ran down the far wall, a tentacle of steel that divided the room. In the dim light, the ugly walls glistened, sweating inside from the heat. My eyes followed the water stains until quite suddenly, by accident, I saw him lying on the couch with his back toward me, his body pulled in, legs and arms bent toward the middle as if protecting himself from approach. When I leaned over him, he opened one eye, looked at me and closed it again. He didn't move.

Then abruptly he jackknifed into a sitting position. "I'm sorry," he said, his eyes blinking rapidly. In seconds he looked fully alert, yet the intensity of his face frightened me. His sunken eyes were deep black. He wore old jeans, a loose t-shirt, both splattered with paint. He ran a hand over the back of his head, not scratching it but checking for something. Then he reached for his cap, an old cloth hat that lay on the floor, and put it on. "I've been up a long time," he said, stretching out one leg. "I thought I'd just doze a bit until right before you got here." He slid his feet to the floor. "Do you want coffee?"

I'd imagined fried chicken or something breakfasty like sausage and eggs, with fluffy biscuits and jelly, maybe even hash browns, but I nodded yes to the coffee. "The cabby's waiting outside."

He rose in one motion, walking in his sock feet to the door, his back broader than I'd remembered. Standing, he looked bunched up, his pants leg crawling up his thigh, his socks mismatched. This, for some reason, made me less frightened. I knew I should mention Aunt Katy, ask how we'd find her, what plans he might have, but I stood silent, watching him move toward the door.

"I didn't think you'd come," he said simply, smiling as he came back inside. His face changed when he smiled, became less fierce, though not quite tender. What he said surprised me. I'd have come even if it was only to tell him I'd decided not to come. Those were the rules of Soldier Creek.

"But you did," he said as he began to make the coffee, opening up a brown paper bag and taking out filters. He set out two white cups from the counter, putting them on the table while he got sugar from the cupboard, cream from a tiny refrigerator that was barely bigger than a bread box. I knew now that he'd forgotten about dinner, just as he'd forgotten to be awake when I came.

Though my stomach knotted, I drank the coffee, hoping it would fill me up, dumping in oodles of sugar and most of the cream. When he went into a small room and closed the door—a bathroom, I assumed, because I heard running water—I let my eyes wander to the drawings tacked up on the walls: in one, a woman's strong, bare legs emerged from the top of the paper and angled to the right where a burst of bubbles crowded out all form, everything shaded, shimmery as if seen from underwater; in another an old man's hand, the knuckles like bruised bumps, gripped what looked like a skeletal ladder; in a third, the beginning of a face, the eyes spread wide, pupils dilated, the nose a slash, hooked at the end.

When he came back, he poured himself another cup of coffee and picked up a sketch pad, watching me. My stomach rumbled with hunger. The coffee made me jittery and restless, and I didn't want to sit here in silence. But he said nothing, just sat quietly, watching me. I thought of Aunt Katy, imagining her body receding over the waves of the ocean, rising and falling, floating toward infinity. I was alone. "I've got to find my aunt," I said simply.

"Who?"

"My Aunt Katy. Remember I told you about her last night. I came here—" I felt the air drain out of the room as if by a siphon, leaving me nauseated. "You promised, remember?"

He looked at me with a face full of pain. "No, I'm sorry to say I don't."

A sadness like the depth of the ocean weighted me. I couldn't move. There was no reason to move. The bed covers that once must have covered him had fallen to the floor, the table wobbled as a car rumbled past. Amanda had once told me that I needed too much, that it made me selfish and dependent. "Baby," she used to say, "What is it you want?" We both knew I wanted to see the world from protective covering, from beneath the surface of the water. But I was on land now. I was *here*. Here.

When I looked up, he was sketching me, his face so locked into mine, it was like looking into a mirror. I felt dizzy with pain and loneliness, the old sadness unfurling. I remembered floating in the creek. I remembered how the water would hold me up even though my weight was heavier. I saw myself being borne across the creek by the movement of the waves while all I did was lie peacefully on the surface. I don't know how long I sat there while he drew. I only knew, in that moment, that I'd decided not to drown.

When he called the next week, I was dressing for work. "I owe you dinner," he said. "Then let's go find your aunt. What do you say to that?"

I looked around at my room, at the shells that lined the windowsill, the simple bed, the cardboard box with my three changes of clothes, and for the first time in days, I felt an unspeakable joy. "Yes," I said. "Yes."

We met in a little restaurant off Wilshire in Santa Monica, a place with ferns and white tablecloths and tanned couples with the easy laughter of money. I saw the white napkins, the violets and sprigs of lily on the table and breathed a sigh of relief. This meant he was serious. I was also hungry. I'd been eating only the cheapest of food: hot dogs, oatmeal, crackers, sometimes a slice of cheese. I sat down at that beautiful table and told him about Aunt Katy, about her marvelous hair and her voice that was as soft and fluid as honey. I didn't mention my own family.

"You came here to find this lady?" He held Aunt Katy's letter with the numbers and the first letters of the address but no street name. Just Los Angeles printed on the envelope. I didn't answer. "Well, you want to find her. That's all that matters." He looked at the letter. "Do you mind if I read it. It might have some clue that could give us a start."

I nodded, and he began to read. "Okay, this mentions Inglewood here, a store I know there. It's a black district now, and she's probably moved on, but let's go check. She may have gotten stuck there."

His matter-of-fact mention of race surprised me. I'd never talked with a black man before, much less eaten dinner with one, but he smiled tentatively at me and ordered grilled flounder for both of us. He offered to go alone, to start the search, but I was too anxious, too unsure of what might happen if I let the opportunity slip by. He might go to sleep again. He might forget. He might not call me back.

We ate our salads and then busied ourselves with huge plates of flounder. Mr. Jones insisted I get a big meal, "to make up for the one I missed," he said, and smiled.

After lunch, we rode silently together on the bus. I sat by the window, staring out at two girls who looked like grown-up women in their slinky clothes, their high-heeled boots, their hair hanging down to their waists, swinging languidly as they walked. I saw an old man with a young woman and her child, a couple of bums sitting on the sidewalks with their bottles, young kids who looked no older than eight. Scorched sidewalks beneath squat, one-story buildings, bowling alleys, machine shops, and motels gave way to cracked concrete with stores bunched up against one another, junky signs littering the windows, loot crammed on trays outside the doors. As we traveled further southeast, the doors and windows were all barred, the pedestrians Asian and black and Hispanic, the races so mixed I couldn't tell what origin many people were.

"We're getting near," Born Jones said, following my eyes.

We got off at a corner, in front of a little market where several Mexican men squatted together like hens roosting. There was the smell of spilled gasoline, of old food rotting inside the trash bins overflowing with refuse, paper wadded up with an oily residue that smelled like sewage mixed with a sickeningly sweet odor of cheap perfume. I watched a black man come out of the store carrying a loaf of bread and walk nonchalantly by the Mexicans who only huddled closer, tightening in a knot.

Born Jones talked a minute with the man carrying the loaf of bread, then came back to me. "Okay, this fellow says a white woman used to live on Bodega. Let's see if the number fits."

We set off walking toward Bodega, a narrow, bumpy street with small, frumpy houses in shades of pink and pale green, the paint peeling from the porches, the yards patchy with dirt and weeds. Children's bicycles and broken machinery parts were scattered beneath the trees, car parts dropped beside driveways, puddles of oil mixing with the dirt. The sight of these houses didn't lighten my heart. Poor Aunt Katy. I thought of all the sweet bungalows I'd imagined, the ones with shutters and bougainvillea and trim, green lawns. We walked until we found a house whose numbers fit the numbers on the letter. I felt suddenly tense and nervous, wondering what would be behind the door. Would Aunt Katy be old and ugly? Dull and tired? Overworked and unfriendly? Would she even remember me, want to see me again? The house must have at one time been pink, though now it was a streaky white, a board in one window where the glass had once been. It looked dead, defeated.

The house, upon inspection, was empty. There were no curtains in the windows, so we peeked inside at the bare room, at the doorless entryways where we could see into other rooms, the refrigerator unplugged and pulled away from the wall, a skirt of rust at the bottom, roaches scurrying undisturbed across the counter.

I felt my breath tighten inside. I let it go, surprised that I was so relieved that Aunt Katy didn't live here. But where?

"Let's ask around," Born Jones said, guessing my thoughts.

Next door, a black woman shuffled to the screen, not opening the door. "What you want?" she asked, her voice crisp, irritable, a small child held against her hip.

Born Jones asked about the white woman, gave her name.

Waiting, my heart muscle contracted, a tiny seed lodged somewhere in my chest.

"I don't know nothing about that woman."

"But you know her?"

"I seen her."

I breathed out, my breath pulsing in the hot, dry air.

"Do you know when she moved out?"

"Been gone a month. And I be glad too. They was too noisy."

So Aunt Katy had lived here. I turned back to the house and sighed. She'd watched the roaches crawl up that counter, had probably battled them with sprays and cleansers, had crushed them between her fingers with a paper towel, then dropped them down the toilet. I hoped the back window at least showed something besides these dirt yards.

"Do you have any idea who might know where she went?" Born Jones asked.

"Nah, but you can ask up at the market. Them people might know."

Born Jones thanked her and we left, walking fast now back up the pitiful street. I felt the stares of people hidden behind window curtains and screens. Stares of scrutiny, even malice. I looked straight ahead, my brain empty as if all the blood had drained to my feet. "Let me handle this," he said. "All they're gonna do is stare at you."

The market was tiny, jammed with canned goods and refrigerated food, full of unfamiliar smells. Jars of strange floating objects stood on the counter along with beef jerky and chewing tobacco. "There was a white lady used to live in this neighborhood," Born Jones said to the cashier as he paid for the bottle of pop. "Lived down on Bodega Street. I've got a delivery to make to her, and now I find out she's done moved from here. You happen to know where she's at now?"

The cashier nodded, took a toothpick out of her mouth. "No white lady."

But Born Jones didn't move from the counter. A young kid behind him, his hair pulled back into a nappy ponytail slapped his tennis shoe. "That blonde woman you talking about, Mister. Got real pretty hair and a little boy?"

"Yeah, I reckon that's the one."

"I seen her."

"Where, sonny?"

The boy put his hands on a candy bar, held it out to Born Jones to pay for, trying to hide his smile. "She used to work at a day care center out past the arena, sometimes used to walk there and I'd walk with her."

"Around the arena, huh?" Born Jones watched the kid tear off the wrapper. He took one half of the candy bar in his mouth.

"Yeah, it was a real crappy place."

I shivered when he said that and turned my face to the heads of wilted lettuce lined up on the shelves. They looked old and dead, and I wondered why any store in California didn't have fresh produce. Then Born Jones nudged me and said, "Let's go."

At the day care center a bunch of squalling kids met us at the door. A black woman in a white uniform stood stolidly at the stove, ignoring the children. "Y'all kids come on back in here now. Ain't I fixed you food to keep you quiet? Come eat y'all food."

When the woman saw Born Jones and me, she looked suspicious. "What you want? I can't be spending time talking to a lot of government people. I'm short of help today."

When we convinced her we were only looking for a white lady, she just turned her head away. "I'm busy." But then I asked about Aunt Katy, explaining that I was looking for my aunt. "Well, she ain't showed today, sugar. Don't know why. Usually she's regular as clockwork, and these kids wild as Indians. Need to put them in a dark room and tie them together." She looked back at her boiling pot. "I hadn't even had a chance to call her. Been one disaster after another."

"How is she?" I couldn't keep from asking.

The woman stared at me. "Why, she's like everybody else, honey. She's keeping on."

30

When Aunt Katy opened the door, I couldn't move fast enough. "I'm Jit,"
I said. "Jit from Soldier Creek." I didn't wait to see if she recognized me,
but rushed heedlessly toward her, and all I can remember is Aunt Katy
hugging me, drawing my thin shoulders into her chest, patting my hair, and
mumbling, "Goodness gracious. I can't believe it. Look at you!" I closed
my eyes, letting her draw me in out of my aloneness, not breathing, not
thinking, but smelling the scent of detergent and eucalyptus on her clothes
and hearing that musical voice whisper, "Oh, goodness. I can't believe—"

For a single instant I was hopeful and relieved. It was only when I
came up for air that I noticed the putty-colored walls, the shabby sofa
with a rip in one cushion, a lamp shade torn beyond repair, then the little
attempts she'd made to brighten things up: plump pillows in blues and
purples, a braided rug, some childish drawings framed in dark red frames,
the curtains as white as new, soft snow. The rest was just California ugly:
high, narrow windows, square boxy rooms, low ceilings, linoleum floors.
But it didn't matter. She was still Aunt Katy, that head of fluffy blonde
curls, a smile to break my heart.

While we hugged, Born Jones stood outside on the steps, looking at
the street as if he were about to walk away. But then Aunt Katy said to him,
"Have you ever seen anything so purty? Look at this one."

He smiled, a slight movement of his mouth, not quite a grin.

"Come on in now and let me ask you one thousand questions. Both of
you. We've got to have coffee. And you're lucky. I've got real cream today.
I've been treating myself." Then she looked wistful, embarrassed, holding
out her hand. "I'm Katy Harper," she said to Mr. Jones. "I almost forgot to
introduce myself. I'm so keyed up."

And he nodded and took her hand. "Born Jones."

"Well, I'm pleased. Plenty pleased. Come on in now and just move
against the mess." She put her arms around me and swung us through the
door into the kitchen. I could see there was an awful lot of mess, not only

184

boxes of toys littering the floor, but dishes and pots and pans cluttering the counter. A bathrobe lay in a puddle on the floor, an apple core wedged up near the refrigerator. There were stacks of coupons littering the table. But Aunt Katy seemed not to notice. She scooped the coffee from the can and plugged in her little coffeemaker.

"Now, start at the beginning," she said, whirling around, catching hold of my hand. "How did you get here?"

I held up her letter, the one I'd found in Daddy's cabin, then we told her about going to the old house on Bodega and from there to the day care center.

She touched her head nervously. "Yes, I didn't make it in today. I was feeling low." She looked suddenly nervous and tired, and her eyes drifted away from us, staring out the window as if she saw something disturbing there. But then she turned back, smiled her sweet smile and laughed a low, thrilling laugh. I saw that there was something different in her, her youthful buoyancy pulled down by trouble. "Now you've come to take me out of my black clouds." She leaned over and picked up the robe from the floor. It was red plaid, and I could see it was a kid's robe with black stallions galloping across the hem. Aunt Katy's mood seemed to slip as she folded the robe in her arms; she looked distracted, uncertain. "Buddy left me. I don't know if anybody told you. He left me and Henley, that's my little boy. Henley's all I've got now, and some days I can't seem to keep up with things. He's not a mean child, but he don't like those days. And I don't like those days—"

"But them days do come," Born Jones said suddenly. "Come and blow your heart away." He'd picked up the vernacular like it was a long-lost friend. "Trying to miss them days is like asking a tornado, 'Please, sir, would you go round this house?'"

Aunt Katy laughed, relieved. "It sure is." His words seemed to lighten her. And he smiled, tipping his hat. She poured coffee for us, and we all talked in bits and pieces about how long I'd been in Los Angeles and how I'd met Born Jones. We told her about the bus ride, about the restaurant, about my job with Earl Ray. I didn't mention Mother or Amanda or Soldier Creek.

"Well, you two are just lucky for each other," she said. "Where are you from, Mr. Jones? I've been here long enough to know that nobody's from this place."

Born Jones kept smiling, nodding his head. "You're right about that one. I'm here from Baltimore, I guess you could say, though I don't always claim it. Grew up near Savannah."

"Lord, that's in our neck of the woods."

"It sure ain't mine." He continued to smile. "At least not my people's."

"I guess not."

"But I've been other places. I got hauled off to Vietnam."

I looked at him curiously, realizing I had no idea of his history. We knew nothing about each other and yet we'd come on this strange, lonely journey.

After he finished his coffee, Born Jones picked up his old seriousness as if it'd never left him, put it on like a hat and tried to leave, but Aunt Katy didn't let it stand in her way. She insisted he come back to dinner again and made him name the night. "Then you can meet Henley," she said, as if that were the only purpose in her life. "I'll bake you a cake too. I don't bake much anymore, but I bet you like cake. You look like a cake man."

"Angel food with a little ice cream would do it," he said.

"It's my pleasure."

After Born Jones left, she grabbed me and hugged me all over again as if we were just finding each other. She blew her nose, then laughed at herself. "Come sit on this old couch and tell me everything. Start from the beginning."

It was the first time I'd tried to put my story into words, to string it out like a line of clothes ready to dry. I told everything I could remember, starting with Amanda leaving for college and my speech for Toby Reznick to Teddy's odd visit to Soldier Creek. I got to the part about the two of us at the bus station, waiting for the bus to North Carolina, the bus I never got on, and suddenly I couldn't continue.

"Oh, honey, what's got you so down?" she asked, grabbing my hand again.

And then it all tumbled out, how miserable and shameful I was, how I'd left Amanda, how I'd meant to go to her and help her, but had run away instead. "I just left her," I finished.

"Yes, I guess you did do that, but you didn't know what else to do, did you? We all do things that way, honey. We try as best we can to save ourselves."

"But she wouldn't have left me."

"Maybe not," Aunt Katy said. I noticed that she looked very serious when she talked, her eyes seeking mine as if she were trying to find words in my eyes. "But she's got her own bundle of things she gets confused about. Everyone does."

Still I hung my head. "I can't even call her. I pick up the phone to call Soldier Creek and before I finish dialing, I start to cry." I believed that if our roles were reversed, Amanda would race across the country if nothing else just to tell me she was sorry. True, she'd probably leave again, spin around in her tracks, but she would at least have tried to connect. As she was probably doing right now. For the first time, I imagined Amanda putting up signs and pictures, calling agencies and bus stations, trying to find out where I was. Now that I felt a little safer, I realized that Amanda was probably worried sick about me. And despite myself, I felt a deep throb of pleasure.

Aunt Katy stood up and went to the window, looking out into the yard where the fierce sun had dried the grass to a dull yellow-green, the weeds so wild they crowded out the flowers. "You were drowning, and you just did what all of us do. You have to save yourself before you can save anybody else. That's what they tell you on airplanes even. 'Put your own oxygen mask on first before you try to help your child.' That's what you did."

Saving Amanda. I hadn't thought of doing more than comforting Amanda, lying on her bed and letting her tell me how shitty the world was, how ridiculous everyone in it. "But I feel so bad," I said. It came out a sob.

Aunt Katy knelt down beside my knees. "Oh honey, don't you see? You learned that. You learned to feel bad about things. Somehow you thought you had to feel bad when you did something only for yourself, and that's what you've done, don't you see? But you've got to stop feeling guilty and look at the whole thing. You've got to decide what to do next. About school and how you want to live and—" She stopped and I could see some old sorrow had climbed back inside her, nesting in her heart. She shook suddenly as if shaking it loose. Very quietly she asked, "Have you let your folks know where you are?"

I shook my head.

"Well, you ought to do that now. They'll worry too—"

"I can't call. I tried. I just freeze up."

"Well, maybe you should write them a letter then. I'll help you. We'll do it after Henley comes home from school, then send it air mail."

But before I could meet Henley, I had to be back at work. I was scheduled to swim at 4:00. Of course, Aunt Katy wouldn't let me leave until I'd promised to come back the next night for dinner. "And you'll spend the night," she said. "We'll stay up late and gab and write that letter. And then you'll feel much better."

Henley was the most beautiful child I had ever seen. He looked like Mother with that sculpted Harper face, but with a mop of soft blonde curls, a little darker than Aunt Katy's. And yet the minute I came into the room, Henley zoomed around me with a plastic airplane in his hand, not slowing down to be introduced or hugged. He raced around the table, climbed up on the chairs, then jumped to the floor, his mouth buzzing as if it were the motor of a plane. "Now, Henley," she said, catching his arm firmly, trying to focus his attention, but he wiggled out of her grasp. Twenty minutes later he was still streaking through the rooms. I couldn't get his attention enough to say hello. Neither could Aunt Katy. When she looked at me, her face sagged and she grimaced, then she stood very still and said calmly, "Com'on, Henley, you need to run outdoors." As she opened the door, he rushed into the yard, his hand still held aloft with its plane, his mouth still making that drumming motor sound.

Aunt Katy fiddled with the curtain, watching him, then she turned back to me. "I've got to tell you about Henley." She seemed older suddenly as if what she had to tell me aged her, her shoulders slumping, shadows deepening beneath her eyes. Her skin looked pale and tight. She went to the kitchen to make tea, then brought us two cups and a bowl of little sugars. She sat down across from me and stirred sugar into her tea. "Henley, he has what they call hyperactivity," she said with an odd little smile. "Some days, like today, he can't seem to sit still. It's like he's got a hive of bees in his brain and they're all sending him in different directions at once. When something new happens, he's a little beside himself. He has to stay on a schedule, one he understands, or he just gets out of control. That's what I've learned finally," she said, stirring a sugar into her tea. "To keep him on a schedule and a special diet. Now when he was a baby, just walking and running into things . . . everything, I should say . . . I thought he was just trying to get my attention, and I just about ate that child up. I gave him every bit of attention I could. But it made Buddy mad. He'd see me and Henley together and something in it rubbed him wrong. If he came home and Henley was running around crazy, Buddy would wear him out. Of course, I tried to stop him, but he had something else in mind. Buddy did. Buddy never wanted another soul to be near me even if he didn't want me himself. He was crazy that way." She stopped here and looked up at me, her face tight with sadness. "And here come Henley, and he needed me in a special way. Well, for a long time I thought Henley was just reacting to Buddy and not something wrong in himself. I just tried to keep the two of them apart and protect Henley when I could, thinking that things would get better when Henley was a little older and could throw a baseball around with his dad. But Henley kept getting worse and worse. Tantrums. Upsets. And something I couldn't understand, but I guess it was a kind of depression. If I took him with me to the day care center, he'd run into the other kids, throw his food on the floor, then sit in a corner and not speak, just tearing paper apart. After Buddy left me, they told me at kindergarten that there was something wrong with his brain, something he didn't have no control over, and I felt ashamed. See, I'd thought it was because of

Buddy's jealousy, because I brought out something in Buddy that a woman had no right to, and Henley was the result. Then I find out it's not that way, that there's something physically wrong with Henley, something he can't help. Only waiting this long, things have set in and he's got used to certain ways. So we're trying to change them." Her voice sounded weary, tired. She turned and held me with her eyes. "But it takes a while to change. It's not an overnight reality." She paused. "He can't help it," she repeated, looking down at her knees.

I squeezed her hands and nodded.

"I got so worried I wrote your daddy once. I just had to write somebody and get it off my mind, what was happening with Henley. I don't know why I did it. It just seemed like he might understand what it was like to feel you're going under." She looked out the windows where Henley was playing. I could see him running in circles, zigzagging his plane in the air, dipping and swerving. "And he said what I needed to hear. Said I had to hold on and go slow. He said I couldn't move a mountain overnight, but I could bit by bit change that mountain into a small hill."

Then Aunt Katy smiled a shy smile and touched my arm. "It's been hard," she said. "But we're taking down that mountain."

When Born Jones came in the door, Henley had slowed down, the plane dropped by the doorstep, his interest now in his fingers. He stopped crossing his fingers for a minute and pointed one in a gun at Born Jones. "Nigger," he said. "Mama, he's a nigger."

Before Aunt Katy could scold him, Born Jones said, "That's right and you're a honky."

That made Henley laugh. He said, "Honky," over and over, totally pleased with the word. He'd sneak up and whisper it under his breath as if he'd just made it up.

Aunt Katy seemed nervous and flustered now. She tried to get Henley to calm down, to apologize without making a scene, and Henley finally sat at his place rattling the silverware and punching holes through his napkin. He said, "I'm sorry," and dropped his napkin to the floor.

"I hope y'all like this food," Aunt Katy said. "Me and Henley are used to it, but then we had a little trouble getting used to it. Henley can't eat anything with chemicals in it or any sugar, so we just don't ever fix them."

Though the meal was plain: pork chops, green peas, broccoli, and bread and butter, we all ate our fill. I sat next to Aunt Katy, and every now and then she would just reach out and squeeze my arm. Henley wiggled in his chair, but otherwise was quite pleasant, talking and bothering Born Jones over words he'd just learned. "Bozo," he said over and over. "Beebop," Born Jones answered. "Crazy," Henley said. "Clementine," Born Jones replied. They went down the alphabet like that, and it made Henley happy as if he'd just found his first playmate. Aunt Katy said they'd have to make Born Jones an honorary uncle if he didn't watch out. And all went well until she brought out the angel food cake.

"Ta-daaaa," she said, balancing the plate on her palm. It was a high, full cake, the kind I hadn't eaten in years. She set it before Born Jones with a knife. "Take as much as you want while I get the ice cream."

After Born Jones had cut three pieces and put them on a plate, Henley jumped up from the table and ran screaming into the other room. His screams were terrified, furious. It sounded as if a world war had broken out. A real temper tantrum. From where I sat I could see Henley grabbing onto Aunt Katy's ankles, scratching at her legs. She stood very still and said, "Stop that," firmly and yet without defiance until Henley lay in a puddle on the floor. Finally, she brought him into the room again, the ice cream in one hand, Henley's hand in the other. He pulled on her arm, trying to drag her away, but she pretended as if nothing were happening. When she put the ice cream down in front of the cake, Henley looked at the cake then glared belligerently at Born Jones and said with a stuck-out lip. "You're a nigger."

"Henley, stop that," she warned him, her mouth tight. "Stop acting like a brat. You're a big boy now."

But Born Jones just looked eye to eye with Henley, then stood up, picking up his plate of cake with the mound of ice cream Aunt Katy had dished out. He walked very sedately into the kitchen and turned on the water, then dumped the cake into the drain. He came back for the other two pieces and did the same. Henley quit crying and rubbed at his eyes.

"There now. What are you having for dessert, Henley?" Born Jones asked.

Henley looked at his mother.

"Raspberry Jello."

"Well, I think a pile of Jello would be just fine."

That night after Born Jones left, I wrote a letter to Daddy, telling him where I was and how I'd found Aunt Katy. Next I tried to write one to Amanda, but I couldn't find the words to say what I meant, how I'd ended up here, in a place I never meant to be. Aunt Katy read the letter to Daddy and smiled at me. "It'll set everyone at ease to know you're with family." Then she blinked. "Your daddy, I mean." In the letter, I asked Daddy to get in touch with Amanda. I knew this wasn't right, it wasn't what I wanted, but I could only get out one line to Amanda: "I don't know when I'll come home."

Aunt Katy tried to calm me, telling me to just let things come in their own good time. I was so relieved at her reassurance, I hugged her tight, afraid to let go. "Remember that night you rubbed stars across my spine?"

"Yes." She sat beside me in a yellow nightgown that had once been frilly and pretty but was now shabby and faded, the lace frayed and unraveling across her shoulder.

"Well, I was in love with you that night. I pretended you were my mother."

"Maybe I'm one of them," she said. In the low light, she looked as soft as tissue paper, just the way she'd looked years ago in Soldier Creek.

"I hope so." I sighed, exhausted, closing my eyes. I slept that night without seeing the creek opening up over my head or dreaming that I was floating out into the ocean. The only voices I heard were the voices of stars rushing into the sky, stars with all their secrets ready to spill.

AMANDA SOLDIER

31

As I stood in the equipment room checking out bottles of saline, a horrible thought struck me: this is my life—taking care of business and trying to find my lost sister while everything else slides quickly into the dust. I leaned back against the tanks of oxygen into that cool metallic darkness, closing my eyes and swearing softly. After the fiasco with Johnny Turner I'd sealed myself off for weeks, but now the old longings were leaking through, flooding my brain. How could I get out of here? How could I escape?

It was only 3:00 in the afternoon, the beginning of my shift. Automatically, I marked off another bottle of saline, but instead of going to my office to check my treatment schedule, I turned off the light and slid down to a sitting position, my knees drawn up to my chin. A new sadness filled me, solidified like dirt in my chest. I couldn't believe this was my life: I woke every morning to bills and problems, went to work where I coddled and rankled patients, came home and died. This was shit. Goddamn shit!

Fifteen minutes later, I was still sitting there—legs splayed out, arms limp beside me—when I heard a knock, then Shirley's whisper. "Amanda." Her voice was soft, secretive. "Amanda," she said a little louder. She knew I was hiding and wanted to spare me any trouble with Ida Gaines who was probably on her high horse again, checking up on me. "Open up, hon," Shirley pleaded. Perhaps Mrs. Longinivic's buzzer had gone off or Dr. Dickson had called in an immediate inhalation treatment; still I stayed quiet, my breath soft, my muscles as stiff and tight as a bow. Only when I heard Shirley's footsteps retreating did I breathe easily again.

Fifteen minutes later another voice, male and authoritarian called out my name. "Amanda." Still I didn't open the door, didn't speak, but waited, resigned to discovery. "Amanda, can you come out here a minute?" The voice was softer now, and I recognized it immediately as Mr. Kirk's, the hospital administrator. Big Daddy Kirk with his bony white features, his weak choirboy chin, the dark strands of hair covering a pale pink bald spot.

"I'd rather not," I said, just loud enough to be heard. I suspected he meant to fire me, not because of anything I'd done, but because a certified inhalation therapist had just moved into town. Since that was the case, why not have another hour alone. In the dark.

"Please, Amanda." His voice was oddly pleading. "I...there's something I must tell you."

"It's okay, Mr. Kirk. I know this is hard on both of us." I didn't want him to feel bad about letting me go. At least I hadn't killed anybody. I didn't have that on my conscience. Just this measly hour of gripping the saline and oxygen bottles, breathing in this cool, dark air.

"Please, I must ask—" He sounded desperate now; he was probably afraid I'd gone bonkers, flipped my wig. Well, I hadn't. The rest of the world was taking care of that.

I opened the door just enough to see the pointed toe of his white buck shoe thrust toward me.

"Amanda," he began again, his deep voice pinching the air. "Listen, I'm sorry I have to tell you this, but . . . well . . . this is hard to say so I'm just going to say it straight." He paused, sighed, then said bluntly, "They found your father, that is, well, drowned in the creek this afternoon."

I didn't go directly home. Instead, I took a right turn to Perdido Bay where the hot, parched fields on either side of the road looked starved and dying. It hadn't rained in weeks, and the heat covered the fields like a closed tent. Sweat started at my forehead, moving in rivulets down my body until I was wet clear through, my clothes soaking the seat. Puddles formed around me. Don't breathe, I kept thinking. Don't breathe. Even the air can hurt you. I sat slippery in the seat, driving fast while telephone wires hummed overhead and birds cawed, tired and hungry, the road a hot skillet, dark and shiny. Faster and faster I drove, the needle sliding to seventy, until I saw a silent sweep of blue: Perdido Bay. I had barely stopped the car before I was out and running toward the water. "Who do you think you are?" I screamed. "Just who do you think you are to get yourself drowned?" I ran straight into the water, my legs moving so fast it took the mucky bottom of silt and seaweed to stop them. Then I sank down to my knees, suddenly stilled, finished. It didn't matter anymore. It didn't matter if I cried. It didn't matter if I won or lost because my daddy was dead, and now I'd never get to know who he was.

An hour later I was still floating, the water ballooning out the blouse of my uniform, filling the pockets and sleeves, the cuffs of my pants. I let my legs sink straight into the sand, water cradling my shoulders. Strangely, I felt at peace as minnows swam in parabolas under my arm and the tide crested at my chin. *Well, Daddy, so that was it. Kinda tired of the whole business.* I felt I understood. I was tired too. Absolutely worn out. *There wasn't much going for you, but dammit, why couldn't you have waited till I found Jit?* And I knew then I would have to step up the pace, look harder, longer. *My sister. Come home, please. Come home.*

I closed my eyes and breathed in the cool dankness of the water before I dragged myself up, my clothes sticking to my side, my tennis shoes thick with silt. Pine needles crackled beneath my feet. A bird whistled in a tree overhead. "Bye, Daddy," I whispered, watching as it flew away. And then suddenly I was trembling, unable to stop, my body empty, a frazzle of nerves. I stood on the shore dripping and shaking until everything in me seemed to go back into the water. I don't know how long I stood there, but when I looked up again, a full orange sun was sinking, slipping past the horizon.

32

When I drove up to the house, Mother was standing outside in the yard, hanging sheets on the line, sheets that had once been white, but were now the grayed out color of lint. The breeze lifted the sheets, blowing them back against her, almost enclosing her.

Silently, I got out of the car and walked toward the clothesline. Coming up behind her, I put my arms around Mother, squeezing her close. I could feel the bones of her shoulder blades protruding through her dress. When had she gotten so thin? "Let's leave these sheets for a minute, Mother—"

"The birds—" she protested.

"Screw the birds!"

"Amanda, I wish you wouldn't . . ." But now she stopped and looked at me suspiciously. "What are you doing home at this hour? You didn't . . . they didn't—"

"No, no, they didn't fire me." I was facing the creek, the white finger of the point cutting through it neatly, almost bisecting the creek and the bay. Looking back at Mother, I wondered for the first time if she had ever loved Daddy or if it had been something else—sex or escape—or if people even knew whether they loved one another.

"What?" Mother asked. "Why are you looking—"

I touched the air between us, feeling it slip through my fingers like silk. "Mother, they found Daddy in the creek this afternoon."

Mother's face cracked like a delicate plate, then froze in horror. She looked not at me, but back at a sheet that had fallen and puddled on the ground.

"I'm sorry, Mama." Tears welled in my eyes but didn't spill. "I'm so sorry."

Mother walked away from me, back to the sheet. She picked it up, grabbing it in her hands, rolling the cloth around and around into a jumbled knot. "I'll have to rewash it," she said, clutching it to her chest. "I'll have to—" and then she stopped, her face crumbling. She dropped the sheet and looked away from me, digging her fingernails into her palms.

"Officer Budd found him this afternoon," I said, picking up the sheet. I folded it into thirds, smoothing the cloth, flicking off little pieces of grass. "He must have swum too far out . . ." but I didn't go on. There was no need to make excuses for him. "I just wish Jit . . ." but I couldn't finish that either. "I've got to eat something," I said simply. And I strode into the house, leaving Mother alone with the news.

That night as I sat in front of the TV watching the lurid colors fuzz and blur, Mother put on her green robe, the soft one that swagged across the front and made her look young again. It must have been a trick of the light, but when she stood by the window, she could have been a young girl, all her hopes bound up in the future.

"Let me brush your hair," I said. I felt a softness toward her that I hadn't felt in a long time, maybe since I was a little girl. After all, we were the ones who were left. Mother and me. And tonight I was content to stare at the TV screen, to brush Mother's hair, to fall fast asleep.

"All right," Mother said, handing me her dark purple brush. Though her hair had lost some of its elasticity, it was still thick and shiny, and as I began to brush, a smile touched her lips. "Tell me about him, Mother. Tell me about Daddy."

I thought I'd have to beg, but she started talking as if the story were on the tip of her tongue. "When I first met him he brought me flowers, big bunches of petunias and daisies, but I was so embarrassed, I wouldn't even look at him. I was shelling peas, and I just went on shelling them as if he weren't there. I had a whole bushel to finish, and I kept at it as if the flowers were for someone else. He'd come to inspect the building we were living in. He worked for the city of Birmingham, and every year there had to be an inspection of the housing projects, someone coming around to poke their nose in your kitchen and your bedrooms. The next day he came back with those flowers, but the entire time he was there, he never let go of the flowers. I guess he left with them too, but I knew he'd meant them for me."

"Did you like him?"

"Oh, I don't know. I didn't even think about liking him. I had a lot to worry about just taking care of Papa. He'd gotten difficult, and he had no one else but me to take care of him. Buddy had gone away, enlisted in the Navy."

I pulled the brush through her long mahogany hair, keeping the brush close to the scalp but moving it through the long strands. Mother, I knew, needed prodding. She tended to stay on the same track, only stiffly turning her wheels. "Did you know other men besides Daddy?"

"Only Mr. Papagouli." As she said this name, she blushed. "He was there when your daddy came by the third time to check on the doors."

"Well?" I brightened, always ready for a story. "Who was Mr. Papagouli?"

But Mother refused to go on until I put my hands in her scalp and began rubbing, massaging, scratching out that story.

"What I remember is a summer day when Mr. Papagouli was visiting, a day Papa decided there was nothing to do but have ice cream because it was so hot." Mother leaned her head further back, almost resting it in my hands. I imagined the thick heat of Birmingham, working men in their undershirts, wet handkerchiefs draped around their necks. The women would be stuck with scooped necked blouses and pedal pushers, their hair pinned up in braids or buns, a fan in their hands. "I was sent across the street for ice cream," Mother continued, "but I was glad to be out of that stuffy room where Papa didn't like to have the curtains open, to let in much light. It took me longer than usual, the line full of people dying for anything cool, and when I got back, your daddy was there, sitting beside Mr. Papagouli and Papa. It surprised me. He had such a funny look on his face as if he didn't know where he was. He said he'd come to fix that door my father had complained about, a door that stuck, but he didn't move. He never fixed it." She turned to look at me. "Never. Isn't that just like him? He left in a hurry too—he almost ran out, but as he left, he said the funniest thing. 'I hope you enjoy New York.'"

I told him I only saw New York in pictures. He looked surprised and said maybe I'd see the real thing soon enough.

Well, I had no idea what he meant, but when I came back inside, I caught Mr. Papagouli's eye and he winked at me. And the thing is, I did go to New York with Mr. Papagouli the very next week." She paused. "He had been my music teacher when I was young, but . . . oooh, he turned out to be such a horrible man. Of course, I didn't know that yet. I wanted so much to see the big city, the lights and the people from everywhere in the world. I'd never been farther than Atlanta, you see. I thought he just wanted to show me off, to make people think he was a young man again, but it was something else. I didn't understand it at first. I don't mean he touched me. Nothing like that. We had separate rooms at a big hotel, the Algonquin, but I was so green, I depended on Mr. Papagouli to instruct me and protect me. I didn't know what to order at restaurants, and no one could understand my accent. They just looked at me as if I were a foreigner. Once he left me in a restaurant to get a newspaper, and while he was gone a dwarf tried to sit with me, saying dirty things to me, things I didn't really understand though I knew from his voice that they were vile, filthy. I sat there like a wooden statue. I didn't know what else to do, but when Mr. Papagouli saw me, he couldn't quit laughing. I was too embarrassed to be angry. It was little things like that."

I put my hands to Mother's forehead and began to massage in circles. I'd never known she'd been to New York. She always acted as if the entire circle of her world surrounded Birmingham, Alabama. "What else?" I asked. "I mean did you go to the opera? Did you get mad at Mr. Papagouli or what?"

"Oh, yes, we went to the opera once." Her voice lowered almost to a whisper, but I continued to work, pushing my fingers into the roots of her hair. I'd heard this was almost as good as hypnosis. "I don't remember much about it. Funny, I was so excited to go. My stomach actually fluttered when the curtains first opened and I saw the costumes and heard the music. I was paralyzed. I couldn't even think. Then something happened . . . I . . . . I clapped before anyone else had started, before the singers had finished. It probably wasn't much of anything, but it started Mr. Papagouli off. He laughed so hard he was leaning in my lap, and from then on he laughed at everything I did until I was afraid to go out of my room. Actually afraid. I even refused to go to another concert with him, so he went alone and brought people back to our rooms, people who were gaudy and horrible, theater people who cursed and drank and made lewd gestures. I was so miserable, I sold my train ticket and took the bus back to Birmingham the next day. When I got home, I called your father and asked him to fix our front door. He seemed so innocent then. After Mr. Papagouli. He came right over with his tools and left them sitting on the kitchen table while I made him a cup of coffee. I even tried to tell him I loved flowers. I said, 'I love pink tulips, and dark red ones even better.' He looked so pleased. He said he knew a place I could grow all the flowers I wanted." She bowed her head, her voice barely a whisper. "He meant here. Soldier Creek."

"Well, he was right about the flowers," I said, stroking Mother's scalp. The TV was turned down low and the night sounds of crickets pulled us closer.

"Yes," she said. "But it was so different . . . so difficult."

And then she looked at me, her face shining, not with tears but with the relief of confession. "You understand, don't you?"

I nodded. I thought of how Daddy had lost everything he'd ever wanted, lost it because he couldn't settle for the simple thing. One step at a time. With him, it was always the next big idea. And when he failed, there was another one on the horizon. It was funny, but I did understand Mother's side of it. She needed someone to cling to and my father couldn't be that person. I was.

"The funny thing was, your daddy kept coming around. About every week he'd show up with something. A tulip. A piece of pecan pie for Papa.

One time he brought me a little jewelry box, with velvet pouches inside. It was never much. But something. And he'd sit with me and have a cup of coffee. Or he'd ask me to walk with him to the park. I was always surprised to see him, and then, as suddenly, he quit coming. I don't know if we'd have gotten together if he hadn't simply stopped showing up. I noticed him then. I noticed his absence. And I realized I missed him. I missed the little things. The coffee in the kitchen. The way he drank cup after cup. How much he liked to talk. I'd become used to having him there, to his voice and his interest in the little things in my life. When he came back about eight months later, he was tan and glowing. He wore a new suit and a white shirt. He looked so handsome. I'd never even noticed that he was handsome until that day. And he was different. Something had happened to him, something that gave him confidence. Of course, later I found out he'd been working at Soldier Creek. Building this house. I guess it all makes sense now, how we started courting, how it was inevitable that he'd want to bring me here."

I stopped brushing. I put the brush down on the floor. At the beginning, I believed, she loved him.

When I called the funeral home the next morning to make arrangements, I pretended I was someone else, someone frozen and cold, a man from northernmost Canada who sold furs and skins, someone who saw death all year round. If I let myself think about Daddy, my chest tightened and my breath caught in the hollows of my throat.

"You have my deepest sympathy, Miss Soldier," Mr. Patterson began in his unctuous funeral director's voice. "You father was a treasured member of our community."

I tightened my grip on the phone. The man from Canada would be used to such garbage in matters of bargaining, would know it was the way of the world. I waited.

"I'm sure you'll wish to do him proud," Mr. Patterson continued, "and I'm here at your service. Whatever is your wish, I can promise to follow it to the letter."

"My wish," I said quickly before I lost my nerve, "is to give him a decent and dignified burial. I'm not trying to make any converts. He was no saint."

"Yes, yes." Mr. Patterson's voice was hushed, reverent. "No saint, but a fine man."

I sighed. Canada was getting further and further from my mind. I tried to summon up a cold wind, a sharp, relentless gale whipping leaves in the air, ice crystals forming on my brow. "Mr. Patterson, I need to know how much it'll cost to give my father a decent burial. You see, he only had the plot."

"Oh, my," Mr. Patterson said.

I wanted to erase his voice, but I had to know the cost. "Yes, so you see—"

"Miss Soldier, if you'll just trust me, now is not the time to talk about prices, about payments and balances, about what is owed and what due. Now is the time for the release of the spirit, for what will best prepare him for his solo journey to the next—"

"The price, Mr. Patterson."

"Very well. One minute please."

I stared out the window at the creek, which shimmered in the distance, the point as white as a snow peak flattened to the land. The sky was threaded with white. Wisps of cotton. I tapped my pencil on my shoe. Hurry, hurry.

"Miss Soldier," there was a pause and I could hear scribbling, "there is a base fee of $900 plus $100 extra if you want satin lining on the top. It's padded, of course. There are extras for the number of chairs, for the—"

"I'll take the base fee, Mr. Patterson. There's no need for extra chairs or refreshments. Now, please, since you're being so helpful, can you tell me who I should see about a monument?"

"Call Miller Brothers. Ask for George Santee."

The plainest marker I could get from Miller Brothers had a base price of $350. It astounded me. I remembered reading how Eugene Gant's father had brought up all those little Gants by making markers; only now did I realize this could be a lucrative profession. I could not explain to myself why the marker was important. A month ago, I'd have scoffed at such efforts to make a show, to assert that the Soldier family could take care of its own with a nice funeral. But something new had emerged. Sympathy. And with it, guilt.

Out the back window, I saw the sheets whipping in the breeze, mother sitting in a chair, only her profile visible. When I went to her, she said, "Thank you, darling. I don't know how you talk to people like that."

"I need to talk to you about money."

Mother looked at me with an expression of such pain I knew it would be difficult.

"I may need to borrow money. I just wanted you to know."

But she wasn't really listening. She got up and told me where the account books were, and then she began taking the sheets off the line.

33

The next day I drove the fifteen miles into Moss Point as if under a spell. The morning had gone soft and soupy, the air like a veil. There would be fog later, clouds floating low above the fields so that all sense of direction was erased and you were lost and alone. But at the moment I was oblivious to weather and scenery. All I could see before me was Mr. Turner with a tube in his throat looking up meekly while I suctioned out the phlegm.

"I'd like to see Mr. Turner, please," I said politely to his secretary.

While I waited, I pressed the pleats of my skirt flat with my hand and ran my fingers through my hair. I'd only glanced in the mirror before I left the house, and suddenly in this world of polish and order, I felt shabby and unkempt. I pulled at a loose thread, wound it around my finger and yanked. It occurred to me that Jit would be an asset today. There was something yearning in her face, something soft and uncertain that made you want to help her. Though using weakness was deplorable, today I saw its advantage, and in the current state of my life, I was not above strategy.

"He'll see you now," the secretary said. She looked sweet and pink, hardly critical, and yet I read a dismissive gesture in her quick appraisal as if she could see the outcome of my plea.

Mr. Turner didn't stand when I entered, and this worried me, made me feel at a disadvantage. He was a small man, and after his illness he seemed to have withered. As I stood before his desk, he squinted at me as if gaining recognition, then leaned forward to take both of my hands in his. "I'm sorry, my dear, about your poor father. A terrible accident. Terrible." I was glad for the lie and nodded. "Please give my regards to your lovely mother."

"Yes, thank you, Mr. Turner, I will." I tried to relax, but my smile remained stiff and formal as if I were posing for a photograph. "And how are you feeling?" I asked. "You look so well no one but us hospital personnel would know you'd ever darkened our door." My god, was I going to be this corny? I straightened my shoulders and sat erect.

"I'm fine." He frowned at the mention of illness. "Now what can I do for you, Amanda?"

It was the only time he'd called me by my first name, and I wondered if that were a positive or negative sign; every nuance today seemed weighted with meaning, every glance worthy of interpretation. I took a deep breath. "I'm here on behalf of my family, Mr. Turner. As you know, my mother and father were estranged, separated legally though never divorced, and my mother received half of my father's paycheck for support. Now after the . . . the accident, well, I want to give my father a decent burial. It's important to my family. We've had a lot of tragedy as you probably know, with my sister leaving Soldier Creek. My mother has worried a lot. She's not a strong woman emotionally, and I want to make things as easy as I can for her. I work at the hospital full-time now, the three to eleven shift, and I can double up on weekends so there'll be a regular cash flow, but most of all I need to know about the house, Mr. Turner. We need to keep renting the house, it was in Daddy's name, you know. Now I want to change it into mine." I took a deep breath. I didn't mention that the account book showed us in the hole. "I want also to apply for a loan, Mr. Turner, to bury my father and to—"

The change in his face stopped me. His eyes went so steely gray behind his glasses, the acid in my stomach surged, a splash of hot liquid bile.

"Miss Soldier," he said, becoming formal. "You of all people have my sympathy. You're a smart girl, a strong girl, and personally I admire what you're trying to do, but this is a business, you see, a business that's responsible to the community for using its money. What, may I ask, could I consider as collateral?"

"My youth," I said, staring hard at him.

He returned the look as if we were two warriors deciding on the fate of a brave loser. He sighed and reached inside his desk, pulling out a leather-bound book. "Let me advance you a personal loan, from me to you for your father's—"

I stood up. "I don't ask for personal favors."

"But my dear girl—"

"What about the house? I need to know about the house." I was leaning toward him and could feel the heat of my own body swelling around me like a fire igniting from rubbed sticks. "If you're going to boot us out now that he's not around to help with the rent, I want to know that too."

He drew back, his cool eyes steady, unblinking. For the first time I saw that he was an average man, a man who had learned cunning and expediency to shore up his physical inadequacies. "The house will be good through this year's lease. I can't promise anything more."

"Eight months then. You're giving me eight months."

"I don't have definite plans. I'm just saying I don't know."

"When will you know?" I felt bold, aggressive, as if suddenly I had the advantage.

"Well, I can't say. I'm—"

"Thank you for your time."

"Please—"

But I left without shaking his hand, my own hand trembling as I walked out the front door of the bank. And yet despite everything, I felt a ridiculous exhilaration, as if only this white anger could cleanse me while any hope of mercy withered like a dying weed. Now I knew where I stood. I knew where the world stood: on the side of the privileged, the moneyed, the successful. How could I ever have forgotten that the human heart is exempt from business? Business isn't personal.

I went immediately back to the hospital. I couldn't face Mother. Not yet. What I needed was a long look at those guys in pajamas who could barely breathe. Always it was the dark side of things that rallied my resilience. Jesus and the Virgin Mary never did a thing to raise my hopes, but give me a man struggling with emphysema, and I began to think myself blessed.

As I walked past Shirley at the nurse's station, she called to me. "Nadine's already taken your shift."

"Where is she? I need to do this one, Shirley." I turned, knowing Shirley would understand.

"She's in with Mr. Butterworth. You just tell her you're doing Jerkowitz and Mueller and she can come on back here and help me with these charts. Then let her do the 7:30 run."

"Thanks, Shirley." I rushed back to the nurse's station and kissed her on the face, lips to lips. "You're becoming a mind reader.'

"Lord, that was always called a bully where I come from."

"Well, I'm classing you up."

"Come here and say goodbye before you leave. They're things—"

I nodded and walked down the hall to Mr. Jerkowitz's room.

"Mr. Jerkowitz, you ready to see movie stars?" I pulled the machine up beside his bed and gave him the nozzle. He was lying flat on his back when I came into the room, and as soon as I raised the top of his bed so he could sit up, he started wheezing. I plumped the pillows behind him and tried to ease him back. His pajamas were all askew, buttoned wrong so that his pale, white, bloated stomach peeked through the faded cotton. "Easy now, Mr. J. You don't want to get excited too soon. I haven't even gone into my Bette Davis routine."

Mr. Jerkowitz smiled. He couldn't do much more than smile these days, but he had the sweetest smile, showing his four teeth when I told him about movie stars.

After I'd finished with fifteen patients, my problems were reduced to the size of rocks in my pockets. Oh, they were still there, certain to inflate again, but for a short while I was a freer person, and by the time I got back to Shirley, I was almost pleasant. Shirley was bent over her desk, matching charts and medication when I sat down beside her.

Not even looking up, she stopped, turned and hugged me. "Hey, girl."

"I'm all right," I said. "Just things, you know. They won't take care of themselves."

Shirley nodded. "We want to do something for your daddy, but we wanted to ask you first. Instead of flowers we thought you might like a donation—"

"To a runaway house," I said. "If you want to do anything, I think that's what he'd want. He'd want something for Jit. Not for himself."

"Done." And Shirley picked up a pile of charts.

"Shirley, what do you think of a very small, very plain headstone?"

"Doesn't bother me."

"I know. It's just—"

"Seems like not enough to you." Shirley patted my hand. Shirley was the only woman I could bear doling out this kind of sympathy.

"What do you think about no headstone at all?"

"Well, to be honest, I like to see a little mention myself, but if it'll put you in debt . . ."

"See, you're doing it again, reading my mind."

"Well, we're all in debt, every last one of us that walks this hall. Even the doctors. They're just in bigger debt."

"You trying to make me feel like I'm joining a club?"

"You could think of it like that."

On the way home, I stopped and bought a half gallon of chocolate chip ice cream. I'd become addicted to it in the last two days, consuming more ice cream than I had in weeks. I hadn't settled any of the questions from this morning that floated in my brain like air bubbles ready to burst, but as I sat at the kitchen table eating ice cream, the telephone rang. I let it ring once to finish my spoonful. Just my luck, it'd be Flo Hinton crying about Daddy.

But it wasn't. It was Josie.

"I want to do something for him," she said without introduction. Just one flat sentence. I hadn't talked to Josie since I'd left for North Carolina, and I didn't feel like renewing the acquaintance. She had too many opinions I didn't like, and besides, she'd slept with my father. "Amanda, I'd like to contribute to his headstone," she went on. "He was important to me. He gave me a chance when nobody else would, and I'll always be indebted to him for that."

"Maybe that wasn't all you were indebted to him for." Even as I said this, I knew it was hateful, my own spite blowing back in my face, but I couldn't stop myself.

"I see you can still be mean. But your meanness can't hurt me. I'm only doing you a courtesy by calling you to tell you I'm giving a gift, not to you, not to your family, but to him."

"We don't accept."

The phone clicked sharp in my ear.

"Who was it?" Mother asked. She was still wearing her robe, I noticed.

"Josie. She wanted to save us about $100, but I turned her down. She wanted to help buy the headstone."

"There's nothing she can give us that we need."

"That's what I said."

But after I finished my ice cream, one of my little bubbles burst. Why couldn't Josie have given a donation anonymously and let us use it as we saw fit? Why did she have to call and announce it?

As I lay in bed that night, sweat trickled down the front of my nightgown. I sat up and bunched the fabric tight, wiping at my neck, then letting it fall loosely around me. When I heard a squeak in the floor, I was surprised to see Mother in the doorway, a flashlight in her hand.

"What is it?" I asked, still irritable from the heat.

Mother edged toward my bed. "I can't sleep," she said. "Can I sleep in here?" She eased back the sheet even before I had time to say it wasn't a good idea. As she settled in, I got up and sat by the window, moody and distracted. The sky was dark, but I could see lights bobbing far out in the bay, shrimp boats or maybe even a yacht drifting up from the Caribbean. The leaves of the trees rustled against the screen, a breeze, and I lifted my hair up off my neck, closing my eyes. I felt restless. More than anything, I wanted to be alone.

But Mother wanted to talk. "I've been thinking about something that happened a long time ago." Her voice came soft and clear out of the darkness. I didn't open my eyes. I leaned my head against the wall, listening, thankful for the pressure of hard wood on my skull. "You were almost two," she continued, "when Papa, your granddaddy, got very ill in Birmingham."

She paused and I waited, thinking that she wanted to go down memory lane, some old story about her father. I'd heard all those boring tales . . . what a struggle they'd had in Birmingham after her mother died and he had to do the tending. I opened my eyes and said as gently as I could, "Mother, I know how hard it was. But it's late. Tomorrow will be difficult."

"No," she said. "You don't understand. It's about Jit . . . I've never told this, never—"

"About Jit?" I sat up, staring at her, my heart racing. Mother went quiet. "Tell me," I said, but now she just stared at her hands. My body felt damp, my mind swollen with fatigue, but I knew I had to woo her back. "Your father was ill and—"

"I took you with me to Birmingham," she started again, her voice very low, but I didn't dare stop her. "I planned to nurse him, you see, restore his health, giving him his medicine and his bath and even the bedpan several times a day. Papa always needed me," she said, pulling at the sheet, then letting it go. "But he was very sick." He was too far gone, she learned from the doctors, and after three painful weeks he died in his sleep.

"The very next day I called your father. I wanted him to come up for the funeral, to pay his respects. I wanted it to be nice. We'd been apart for several months because of his drinking, but he promised"—she looked at me, her eyes anxious—"that he wouldn't drink. He said he'd fix the steps that were rotting from termites and replace the torn screen in the kitchen door." Her lips parted, almost a smile. "He used to do things like that. Even said he'd rake the leaves and save the pine straw for my flower beds."

I sat very still in the darkness, wondering what secrets she had to tell, what new bogeymen would ambush us from this night.

"But when he arrived, I didn't know if I was glad or not. I didn't feel anything. All I could think about was how Papa had looked so confused and frightened that last week as if he didn't understand that he was dying. Oh, honey, if you could have seen him when I was a little girl—he was dark-haired and handsome, with flashing blue eyes. Everybody noticed him." I had a brief vision of mother's adoring gaze, carrying with it the pride of ownership. I knew well its effect. "But when he was sick, he was all swollen." Mother sighed as if she were seeing him again, a handsome man gone suddenly grotesque. "It was the medicines. They changed him. And then, right before he died, he became . . . well, strange. He started pushing me away, pulling his hands away from mine, fussing at his bed covers. He acted as if he didn't know me, his own daughter, and something else—" She paused. I could hear her breathing. "He never again called me by my name," she whispered. "He never said Maggie."

As the leaves fluttered in the trees and the heat lifted from the room, I sat very still, the night air brushing against my cheek. I knew Mother needed to tell it from the beginning, but I wanted her to hurry. I wanted to know what this had to do with Jit. *Com'on, I don't care about that old man!* Later I'd understand that all of it was necessary. Every little bit. I'd replay what she'd said again and again, sentence by sentence, thinking that maybe this was the missing piece, the link that made all our losses fit together. And so I listened as Mother droned on, talking about the funeral where only a few lonely old men showed up at the grave, men who had played poker with her father in the winter afternoons, and where my father stood beside her in his double-breasted suit while the sky clouded over, heavy with rain.

"After the funeral, your father and I sat in the living room," she continued. "I was exhausted but keyed up too, and we just sat listening to the rain and watching the sky full of lightning and thunder. I could see the rain sweeping against the windowpanes, making that swish-swish sound. I don't remember even speaking after we'd put you to bed.

"Your father was quiet too. He knew what this meant, Papa dying. And he surprised me. He waited on me, offering to get me coffee and brandy from the kitchen. I heard him filling the coffeepot, the water coming on, the opening of cabinets. I didn't know why I said yes to brandy. But I didn't care. I didn't care what happened. Let it all come apart, I said to myself. And when your father brought out a little tray—it looked so pretty with small white cups he'd found in the kitchen—I drank first a sip of coffee and then a sip of brandy. He was watching me, but I was watching him too, waiting to see if he poured himself a drink.

"But he didn't. When I got too quiet, he said, 'Maggie,' holding the glass to my lips, and before I could stop myself, I drank again. I liked it. And that surprised me. It tasted sweet. But with each sip I kept seeing that confused look on Papa's face. 'This will make you forget,' your father said. 'It will help you sleep.' But I didn't want to forget. Papa was dead."

To my surprise, Mother got up from the bed and walked to the window, pressing her head against the screen. There was almost no breeze now, no sound except the occasional splash of a fish in the creek, the scramble of some small animal rooting in the bushes. "I have to keep going," she said. "I have to tell this part." She didn't look at me.

And for a moment I didn't look at her. I stared out at the creek's black stillness. I wanted to say Stop, enough, I'm too tired. "Go on," I said.

"There was something that frightened me, a secret I've been afraid to tell." She looked straight at me now, a look of surprising clarity as she told about how the afternoon before he died, her papa had rallied, his eyes lit up at each little thing she did, bathing his face, giving him a drink of water, and especially as she leaned over him to take away the linen napkin she'd spread across his chest. "And that's when . . . he touched me," she said, glancing away. "His hand . . . it surprised me, suddenly strong as he stroked my breast, just a finger really . . . but I kept telling myself he's sick he's sick he's sick. I couldn't help remembering that when I was a little girl he'd had terrible nightmares. So bad, they woke me up. I'd lie in my bed, trying to decide what to do. Then I'd creep across the hallway, listening to him shouting words I couldn't understand, though he was still asleep. So I'd lie down beside him and hold him. 'It's okay, Papa. It's okay.'"

Mother turned from the window. She wasn't looking at me, only staring into the darkness, her voice lower but quicker as if she wasn't even talking to me anymore. "Just a bad dream, but I'm here, Papa. Your little Maggie."

She began pacing back and forth, a few steps toward the bed, then turning back a few steps to the window. "The night of his funeral, I kept drinking the brandy while your father watched. I don't think I'd ever been drunk before, but I kept sipping. It made me feel relaxed and all stirred up at the same time as if I were there in that living room but also in a dream. And then we were dancing, your father and I, waltzing together around the room. Your father must have pushed back the table. I don't remember. But I could see the rain sliding down the windows. I watched as the ceiling swirled, and I remembered how when I was a little girl Papa used to let me stand on his feet and waltz me around. Around and around like a princess. I'd felt so grown-up. I'd loved it, and it always made Papa laugh. I started to laugh, just thinking about it. And now your father laughed too. I stepped up on his shoes, and he liked that. He twirled me around and he told me he loved me. He barely whispered it. I felt reckless. Maybe it was the liquor in my blood, but I didn't care what we did that night, even knocking over a chair and giggling and pushing against the table, but then something happened to me, happened as if I were in a dream, something I could never—" She bit her lip, frowning, her gaze drifting as if she were seeing it again, as if she were that young woman full of loss and death, twirling around the room with my father, circling and laughing, losing herself in a labyrinth. "I lay down with him. I smelled the rain on his skin, in his hair. I closed my eyes and lay down, clutching him, holding on tight, thinking that he'd saved me, his little Maggie, pulled me away from those creepy miners. And then he was reaching for me after one of those awful nightmares, stroking my cheek, putting one finger, just one finger in my soft place because he said it soothed him . . . and he was calling out to me, 'Maggie!' because he loved me. I was so happy. I'd never felt so connected, so curious, something greedy in me wanting . . . until I heard you crying. I heard just that sound. 'Maaaaamaaaa,' you called out. 'Maaaamaaaa.' And that's when I saw where I was, your father on top of me and he wouldn't stop . . . he held me, whispering, pleading, the two of us in Papa's bed, on his sheets, in his room." Mother was crying now, both hands covering her face as I heard something splash in the creek. "Nine months . . . I couldn't bear to look at her. My punishment. She should never have been born."

For the first time in my life I didn't know what to say. Mother stood motionless, silently crying, her head bowed, her hands clasped. My mind felt heavy and thick, as if it was struggling with a clumsy weight, as if there wasn't enough oxygen for me to breathe. I bent over, crouched. I didn't want to look at her. What? She couldn't possibly believe, but she did . . . in her mind she wasn't making love to my father, but to—oh, I hated him— that old fart, that hustler, that bastard Papa!

"But it wasn't Jit's fault," I finally cried out. "She couldn't help . . . she has no idea. Mother, all her life . . . what was wrong."

"I know." It was barely a whisper. Now she began to weep in earnest, racking sobs that shook her body. "It's all my fault. That's what I wanted to tell you. It's all my fault."

After Mother finally slept, curled up in a corner of my bed, I lay awake, unable to sleep. Finally I got up and went out onto the porch to stare at the moon. It was barely a sliver, a razored slice, shadowed with haze. But what I thought about was Daddy rushing into the creek with Jit bouncing on his shoulders, her giggles floating out into the air. Of course they would be together. Bound to each other from the start. Was that how families survived? Always divided, picking up the pieces? Holding onto whatever they could find?

I went back inside and lay down on the sofa, waiting for sleep to find me. Tomorrow I would ask more questions, dig deeper, find new answers. Tomorrow, after I buried my father.

34

As the sun heated up the sky, sweat leaked between my breasts, down my spine, behind my knees. At the graveyard, I tried to think cooling thoughts: water swirling in a glass, ice cubes brushing against my lips, my tongue, and then dissolving down my throat, but by the end of the service I could have wadded up my dress, squeezed it out and watered the garden. Then a cloud covered the sun and the wet chilled my back. I shivered. It was the closest I could come to genuine emotion. I was too tired to feel much of anything, so I stared at the flag irises and arum lilies, flowers from Mother's garden, and I didn't think much about the casket being lowered into the ground or the preacher's words of soothing comfort. Beside me, Mother stood in her old black dress, and with her clean hair and powder she looked young and healthy while my father had looked gray and shrunken when I stared at him in his casket at the mortuary. I'd asked for a closed casket. I couldn't stand everybody mooning over dead people, satisfying their last curiosity, giving their last wishes. He'd drowned, for god's sake.

After the service, Shirley squeezed my hand. I was grateful that she held it a minute in silence. From where we stood I could see Josie clearly at the edge of the group, never quite joining in. I tried to catch her eye to telegraph my apology, but she never looked my way.

Some of the older men and women from the small Episcopal church came up to offer their sympathy. "Our prayers are with you, darling," they said, and, "He's in the glorious hereafter, honey . . . with the peacemaker." Shut up! I thought, my hand limp inside some man's palsied grip, a man who obviously hadn't shaved in weeks from the nicks on his throat. I couldn't move my lips—the lipstick seemed to coat them together like one formed piece—so I kept quiet. And yet once it was over, I knew I couldn't sit around the house with Mother, both of us skittish, too hot to put on clothes, wandering around in our slips, sweating, exhausted, with nothing in the world to do but eat. I made some excuse about returning the silver platters to Shirley and headed out to Perdido Bay. I could see rain in the sky, dark clouds moving fast toward the east. A storm suited my mood. Rainy days had always been my favorites, perfect reasons to shut myself away with a novel and some goodies to eat. Only today, I didn't know what I'd do. I only knew I needed to be there. Daddy's cabin.

I drove fast. I had to get past those endless cornfields with the crows flying through like an enemy force. When a hint of water broke through the trees at the horizon, I slowed, turning toward the cabin just as the gray, slanting rain hit the bay, obliterating the horizon line. Just as the storm moved in, I jumped out of the car and ran for the door, letting myself in with the key Daddy kept under the mat. I didn't know why I was here. I remembered suddenly how Daddy had crawled around the yard that day, how he'd refused to be embarrassed about the way he lived his life. It bothered me still.

Once inside, I slid into his bed and closed my eyes; when I woke, I heard the fast staccato of rain on the roof. I drifted lazily for a moment, forgetting why I was here, taking pleasure in the sharp clatter of the rain. I never wanted to move, only to stretch and realign myself in sleep. Then I remembered and sat bolt upright. It was late. I'd left Mother. Hastily, I went through Daddy's books, putting the ones I wanted in a pile on the table. When I opened the closet for a bag, bottles fell out, rolling everywhere on the floor. But I didn't try to pick them up. I only grabbed the books and ran, my head ducked against the rain. At the end of the drive, I automatically stopped, pulling out the rest of the mail. I hadn't thought to notify the post office, and of course, I'd have his bills to pay. I drove on. I didn't want to look at the bills, but when I stopped at the intersection to the highway, I saw a pale yellow envelope with a bird stamped on the front. I'd recognize that scrawl anywhere. Jesus! I ripped it open.

Dear Daddy,

I'm in California. In Los Angeles, and it's so big it scares me.
I'm here with Aunt Katy now so I feel better. She says "hello."
Daddy, I didn't mean to come here. I just sort of ended up here.
I was really trying to go to North Carolina to help Amanda but
things didn't work out that way. I know what I did was wrong, but I
didn't see any other way. I hope everybody will forgive me, but I
sort of doubt they will. I tried to call and let them know where I
was, but when I tried, I just froze. Please let Amanda know I'm
okay and that I'll be getting in touch with her, though I don't know
when I'll come home. I don't know what I'm going to do yet, but I

guess go back to school. Aunt Katy says I should. She's working
at a day care center and has her little boy, Henley, with her. Buddy
left her last year.

I'm sorry I took some money out of your jar. I didn't know what
else to do. Write and let me know if things are okay in Soldier Creek. I
miss you.

Love,
JIT

I held the letter to my chest, trembling. Jit was okay. She was safe. Relief
flooded through me, a flutter of lightness as if a weight had been lifted,
months of worry dropped to the ground, but no sooner did I relax than I
wanted to slap her face. How dare she do this to me! How dare she wait five
months before letting me know! Oh, it was just like Jit. Not to know what to
do. Not to call. Not to write. While her own father had drowned. Of course
she couldn't have known this, but I held it against her still.

Starving suddenly, I stopped at a little store on the way to Soldier
Creek and bought another half gallon of chocolate chip ice cream. When I
came through the kitchen door, Mother sat at the table in her bathrobe, her
hair loosened from its combs.

In silence I got out two bowls and heaped ice cream into each, then
sliced cake from the Tupperware containers on the counter. "I think I know
where Jit is."

Mother's head jerked up.

"I found a letter in Daddy's mailbox today. From her." I pulled the envelope
out of my purse.

Mother held the letter to her chest, not reading it immediately. Only
after I nodded did she begin to read. When she finished, there were tears in
her eyes. "She's safe," she said. "Thank God."

The muscle around my heart tightened; a dark chill crawled up my spine.
"You were worried about her, Mother? You were really worried about Jit?"

But Mother didn't seem to be listening to me. She looked out the
window. "I'll plant some new flowers," she said. "I'll try to make it better."

"I'll have to tell her. I mean, she doesn't know about Daddy."

Mother nodded, still looking out the window.

But when we finally got the number for Katy Harper from long
distance and dialed, there was no answer. Disappointed, I cursed the phone.
Mother's eyelids drooped.

"Go on to bed. I'll call you when I get her."

After Mother went upstairs, I sat for a long time looking at the phone and at the letter in my lap. I couldn't help but think of myself as some huge, rotting carcass whose stench fouled the air. I imagined everyone staring at me, but moving on, believing that I could handle it. Whatever it was. Just your basic rotting. Your basic falling apart.

Hours later I went into the kitchen and turned on the lights. We'd forgotten to put the ice cream back in the freezer, and it had melted into a soupy mess. I stuck my finger into the carton and licked, tasting milk and sugar as if the ingredients were separating. Then I got a spoon and dipped in, not thinking until the clock struck 9:00 p.m. Then I poured the rest of the ice cream down the drain.

At 9:15, I dialed and put the phone to my ear.

PART II

JIT SOLDIER

35

I'd just taken a bite of my hamburger when the call came. It was a night I was free from swimming at Earl Ray's, and I'd practically moved in with Aunt Katy, helping her with Henley, cutting up his hamburger into bite-size pieces and fixing the mashed potatoes the way he likes them, smooth as Dream Whip with a pat of butter melting in the center. When the phone rang, Henley put his thumb in the mashed potatoes, a big grin stirring his face.

"Oh, for goodness sakes," Aunt Katy said, giving him one of her exasperated looks as she removed his hand and wiped it off. "Now Henley, we don't do that to our food."

When the phone rang a second time, I swallowed and jumped up from the table. "I'll get it," I said, fishing a little piece of hamburger from between my teeth. I breathed into the phone.

"Guess who just found you?" Amanda's voice was a shock, like a voice in a dream from which I'd awakened, but so much softer than I remembered, as if the edge had been beaten out.

"You," I said, not bothering to say hello. My breath tunneled inward, caught in a secret corner of my throat. I'd been waiting five months for this moment, planning for just how it would be, how I'd feel, but now that it was here, I was too surprised to feel a thing. Instead I stared out the window at a white California sun.

"No thanks to you," Amanda flared, and I could feel her anger as if she were right next to me in the room. But then the phone went quiet, and in that space I imagined something new, something hidden.

"I'm . . . I'm here with Aunt Katy," I said, sitting down on the couch, pulling the phone cord so it didn't twist into a knot.

"I know," she said. "I'm calling you, remember?"

"Did Daddy tell you? Did he let you know I was all right?" I sank back on the couch, then hunched forward, my mind both tense and numb as if a big funnel was sucking out the inside of my thoughts. I saw the letter I finally wrote Daddy two weeks ago, telling him why I'd run away from Soldier Creek and where I'd ended up.

"Well," Amanda paused, and I could imagine her narrowing her eyes, fixing them in a snake-eyed stare. She'd be sitting on the wooden stool in our Alabama kitchen, the lights off, the fan whirring in the window, clouds of mosquitoes clotting the screens. I heard her breath ease out fast as if she'd been holding it in, then she was quiet, waiting.

"Well, what?" My own voice was charged with fear. I stared at the sun as it began to melt into the horizon, a flood of colors splashed against the blue California sky. Behind me, Henley slurped his milk and Aunt Katy said, "Hush, hush now," and wiped his mouth when he tried to protest.

"Jit," Amanda's voice went soft, edgeless, blurred into something like relief. I knew then it was trouble.

I felt myself slipping into the couch, then slipping further, into the floor of the earth. "What? What is it?"

"I don't know how to tell you," Amanda said. "I don't know . . ." Then she was silent, still, the air knotted with tension. "Jit," she whispered. "Daddy drowned."

The bus to Soldier Creek quivered and groaned like an old general grunting toward his grave. It stank of something awful like spoiled bologna or heat-ruined ham, but when I looked around at the dozing passengers, wondering who held the stink in their laps, all I saw was how easily they slept—knees open, hands limp, eyes twitching with the spasms of dreams. Sleep. I couldn't. Ever since I'd left Aunt Katy and Henley in California, flew across country, then got on the Greyhound in Mobile, I couldn't quit thinking that word: drowned. I closed my eyes, tried to shut it out, and when I opened them again, I saw my first glimpse of water. Just little patches. Like islands in the land. Then a wide stretch, a giant ribbon of blue. My heart beat faster. I leaned closer as though I could breathe in its moisture through closed glass, suck it into my throat and make the words come easier. *Soldier Creek. Soldier Creek. Soldier Creek.*

I heard the hoarse, ragged barks of dogs, then saw two of them—tails wagging, mouths open—leaping at the bus as the driver stopped with a screech of brakes to let me off at the road to Soldier Creek.

"Here you are, Miss," he said. People muttered in their sleep and changed their positions as the door creaked open. I hauled my bag from beneath the seat and stepped out into hot, moist air, the two dogs panting beside me, quivering in the heat. As the bus thundered on down the road, I shooed the dogs away and walked mechanically about fifty yards on the crushed oyster shell path until the creek road split in a V, one leg leading to the house—to Amanda and Mother—the other right around the creek to Josie's One-Stop. I wavered for a second, the wet air slapping my face, the sand warm on my feet, then with a pinch of guilt, I started down the road to the One-Stop. Josie will calm me down.

When I rounded the bend, there was the One-Stop, freshly painted a shiny gray with a porch that slanted downhill, the boards warped by humidity. I peered through the screen where I saw Josie sitting at the counter, drinking a Mountain Dew and reading the newspaper. I forgot it was Sunday. Her long face looked gnarled like a piece of stripped pine, a fisherman's tan starting at her shirt-sleeves and the top of her thighs.

"Hello," I said, stepping inside, standing before Josie in a dress I'd borrowed from Aunt Katy, a red cotton shirtwaist with the thinnest strip of belt, buttons the size of fifty-cent pieces. Josie looked up suspiciously from her newspaper. "Three packs Chiclets, one pack sugarless, any flavor," I said nervously, laying a dollar on the counter. The place was dark and cool like the inside of a cave. A ceiling fan whirred, its motor humming.

"Jesus-God," Josie smiled, "am I looking at the real thing or is the world just filling up with no-nonsense people?" Then she was up in a bound, her arms around me, one hand pinching my leg. "Where you been? I was worried and then some." She held me real close.

"California," I managed to get out.

"Loonies and fruitcakes." Josie shook her head, releasing me, but never taking her eyes off me as if I might vanish in thin air.

"I thought I'd fit in."

"Shame on you."

My eyes were more adjusted now and I could see the strings of lures over my head, the fishing rods propped up against the wall, nets piled up on shelves, oars and life jackets spilling out of the corner, corks packed in buckets. I thought of Daddy picking up a can of worms, pretending to toss it to me, knowing I'd race him to the creek. Once out on the pier we'd forget all about the worms and dangle our feet in the water, making waves. "This is ours," he'd say, pointing to the water. "The Soldiers of Soldier Creek."

Now I leaned toward Josie. "Did you see him before—" I whispered, holding my breath, not knowing what I wanted to hear.

"Nope. You don't get around Amanda."

I felt a tightening behind my knees. Amanda. "Well, I've gotta see—"

Josie nodded, locked the cash register and picked up her keys. "Let's go. I've been going by the cemetery every day since the funeral. Can't seem to say good-bye, can't seem—" but then she stopped, looked embarrassed, and said softly. "Course you want to pay your respects." And she stepped out of her moccasins and put on a pair of red sneakers, the laces gone. The shoes made me smile. Her feet looked like a teenager's feet. And for the first time since I'd left California, I felt a hint of relief. I was sixteen and I was here. With Josie. At the creek. Maybe it would all work out. Just me and Amanda and Mother. As if no one had ever left. As if trouble had walked further on down the road. But when I climbed into Josie's truck and looked across the creek at the bluff, the house just visible behind the maples and pines, the white porch jutting out, the hard slant of slate roof, a stab of fear pierced my heart, followed by a sharp pain that rose in me like a tide. Already I could feel their pressure, like a foot against my chest, Amanda demanding, "Why'd you do it, run away like that?" while Mother stood beside her, remote, uninvolved, an invisible fence rising between us.

Josie rolled down her window and cool air brushed against me, lifting my hair from my neck. I closed my eyes, thought of Aunt Katy and Henley sitting in the kitchen eating popcorn, and I said what Aunt Katy told me to say, "I'll be all right, everything will be all right." As Josie drove down the narrow creek road I remembered the names of every branch and vine that hung over the front windshield, wisteria, oak, honeysuckle, pine. I'd only been gone five months, but it felt like five years. The air was gentle, soft as an old blanket. As we passed from the tangled brush and brambles of the land around the creek to stark, flat potato fields, the earth was churned up with harvesting, combines and tractors in the fields, then after a sudden sharp curve, we pulled up into the grass behind St. Paul's Episcopal Church, a one-room white clapboard chapel with green shutters on the windows and wisteria vines climbing up the steeple. The grass had been mowed, the windows washed, the bushes trimmed, but I was looking beyond to the scattering of markers spread out like lost buoys at sea. A stand of trees, pines beside a few straggling oaks, their trunks thick as barrels, held the far corner.

Josie jumped out of the truck and started walking. Then I saw it, the freshly dug dirt, the edges of the grass still separate from the rest. I walked slowly, frightened. A small white cross marked the spot, and wilting flowers—roses and daffodils and even orchids—spilled out like a carpet over the top. There was my daddy. Dead. Drowned in the creek while I was lost in Los Angeles.

I knelt down and closed my eyes, trying to find him, trying to explain why I had to leave Soldier Creek. Because of Mother. Because of Amanda. And then something darker rippled across my mind. Because of me. I saw Daddy as I'd seen him the night I left, drunk and sleepy, sitting up in his bed facing the water, watching the tree frogs jumping at the screen door, but that wasn't what I wanted to remember. It was the other daddy, confident and sure, the one who let me ride like a surfer on his back as he swam from the pier to the island then back to the pier, the one who knew the creek like the back of his hand. *There's the sandbar,* he'd say. *Can't catch any bass on a sandbar. Watch out for the narrows. Lots of moccasins nest there in early spring.* But I kept getting them all tangled up and he was drunk and sleepy in the water, not bothering to flutter kick, to cup the fingers of his hand, but lying inert in a dead man's float. I got up quickly. "I don't want to be here anymore."

"All right," Josie said matter-of-factly. She rubbed her tennis shoes in the grass, cleaning them, then rattled her keys until she found the right one.

When we came to the V in the road, Josie slowed down and looked significantly at me, but I touched her arm and she drove on, neither of us speaking until we were back at the One-Stop. As I climbed out of the truck, I stared at the clean sweep of water, the sun falling in slow motion toward the horizon, a fiery ball about to be swallowed up by this floating cloud of land. *You can do it,* he said, when I wanted to learn to swim. *Let the water hold you up.*

"I've got to get into the creek, Josie."

"Fine by me."

At the store Josie went inside, shuffling her feet and talking to her dogs while I stood on the porch undressing. Josie handed me an old bathing suit that drooped and sagged all over, but at least covered me up. Though the late May heat lingered in the trees, goose bumps suddenly spread up my body, etching the underside of my arms. I took off at a run, the water so shallow I had to wade quickly to my thighs. Then I plunged in, the coolness shocking me until I went under. Coming up, treading water, I listened to the birds in the trees, a woodpecker not far off in the woods hammering at a maple, seagulls running in flurries near the shore, squawking when they landed. I lay on my back and remembered Daddy telling me, *Let the water do the work, baby.* I could feel his hand under my spine, supporting me, and I felt happy seeing him in his swim trunks, his white teeth gleaming, the hair on his chest bleached a silvery blonde. Then, as suddenly, the sun went behind a cloud and the water chilled. I knew it was time.

Josie handed me a towel and I dried off quickly, putting on my clothes.

"You want a ride?" she asked while I toweled my hair and combed it with my fingers. It was short because of my job at Earl Ray's and dried quickly.

"No, I'll walk."

"You've talked with Amanda?"

I nodded. "Some."

"Well, that's good. Then you already know she's mad as hell."

As I walked the creek road, dodging branches of pyracantha, skirting lizards that darted across the path, I thought that Amanda had always been mad as hell. I quickened my pace, catching hold of bushes, leaves, dragging them along with me. Pussy willows grew just beyond my reach. Kudzu climbed up the body of a pine, cloaking it in a wall of green. When I saw the old scuppernong orchard that bordered our yard, I felt the pull of my sister. I walked even faster, coming into the yard so suddenly I was startled to see Mother and Amanda outside, Mother raking pine needles and Amanda standing beside her, holding a big, black lawn bag. They looked, for a moment, so domestic, so natural, I stopped dead still. Amanda had her back to me, her long dark hair in a loose ponytail so that I could see the pale whiteness of her neck as she bent forward, arms holding open the bag. Mother was lifting a pile of pine needles into the bag, but when she saw me, she gasped, spilling the needles all over the ground.

Amanda turned with an impatient slap of the bag, her face open, then clouded. "You've been swimming!" These were Amanda's first words when she saw me standing in the driveway in my bright red dress. Instead of nodding I touched the damp curls crawling up my neck, but by then Amanda had her arms around me, hugging me, making me melt into the heat that is Amanda. Away from her, I forgot the sheer presence of her, how she could swallow up the air. I breathed deeply, then went slack and easy in her arms, not so much hugging as being hugged.

"Goddamn you," she whispered, pulling my hair so hard I winced. Then she hugged me harder as if she meant to crush something right there between us, kill it or keep it, I couldn't tell which. But when she pulled away, I saw something different in her face, a determination that hadn't been there before. I thought immediately of Teddy, poor Teddy, and then of that other boy who'd hurt her at Trinity College. I tried to touch her arm, but she shifted and my fingers caressed only air.

"I missed you," I blurted, surprised at myself.

But Amanda had already pulled away. She put both hands on her hips, "We've been waiting for you. I'm starving and you've been swimming!"

Then Mother, hovering like a black shadow, moved forward. She came between us, almost touching my shoulder, but I stepped back, out of her reach.

"Let's go in, girls," she said as if we had been dawdling outside on an ordinary day.

The house looked more run-down than ever, paint peeling from the doors, vines crawling up past the second story windows, twisting into the eaves of the roof. The back screen door was unhinged at the top, tilting away from the frame, the mesh bowed, torn at the edge. There were no lights on in the kitchen, and I saw the room as I often saw it at dusk, a trickle of light streaming through the window, shadowing the buckled linoleum floor. Our old oak table was pushed against the opposite window, a jelly jar full of drooping wild flowers dead center. A burst of snapdragons graced the sink. Mother. All along the counter there were mounds of food wrapped in crushed aluminum foil, sour cream pound cakes, casseroles of peas and pimento, jars of pickles and jam, Tupperware containers of chocolate chip cookies. Thursday's wake. *Daddy's food*, I thought, and walked straight through the kitchen to the living room where the windows opened onto the creek.

"I've gotta eat," Amanda said, somewhere behind me, and I couldn't help smiling. Amanda was always hungry. And suddenly I was too. I'd forgotten about lunch and had no thought about food or hunger on the bus. Tonight I hoped we'd be filled only with appetite, no scenes, no questions, no dark secrets to crack open and reveal. I wanted to sink into this place like sliding into sleep. "I'll get the chicken," Amanda said. "You get the tea."

The table was set with silverware and china, three places like it used to be before Amanda left for college. Mother brought out a platter heaped with cornbread sliced into squares and a bowl of green beans someone had left, the bacon swimming in juice on the top. She looked directly at me, a mute, unreadable gaze, but I turned quickly and stared at the beans. We both looked at the food until Amanda waltzed in with the chicken.

I sat at the place where I always sat, the chair that faced the windows; Amanda sat across from me and Mother at the head of the table. It seemed almost natural, as if nothing at all had happened, until that moment after we'd unfolded our napkins, after we'd served the food and nobody knew what to say or do; we were so anxious and frightened we pretended the business of food was all that mattered. I ladled green beans and summer squash onto my plate and ducked my head down, eating fast, suddenly famished, when Amanda clattered her fork and knife. "Jesus, I can't stand this. Come on, let's just say it. We're a mess." She laughed and put a hunk of cornbread in her mouth. Mother and I both looked up, silent, watching. I spread butter onto the crusty edge of my bread. "No, I mean it. Say it," Amanda said, and there was a new hardness in her voice. She glared at both of us, and for the first time I noticed that Mother looked frightened, her lips pressed together, the veins pulsing in her temples. She opened her mouth as if to speak, then shut it again. I watched all of this as if I were outside the window peeking in. I couldn't feel my body, couldn't claim the weight of arms or thighs. But my face felt pressed close to cold glass.

"Say it," Amanda repeated, her lips tight, her eyes pinned not to me but to Mother.

"Amanda, I don't—" Mother looked startled, uncertain as if awakened from a bad dream.

"Say it," Amanda whispered, still staring at us, but now there were tears filling her eyes.

"Hey," I said, leaning toward her. I never knew how to comfort Amanda. Upset, she seemed more distant than ever. Unreachable. A shield placed between her feelings and mine. "We know we're a mess."

Mother nodded.

Amanda looked from me to Mother, and then she smiled. "Good, then we're in agreement. Just like a democracy." And she reached for the platter of fried chicken, selected the largest breast and slid it onto her plate.

For a moment I didn't eat. I didn't quite know what had happened, why Amanda was so insistent and what that meant, but inside my head those words kept rotating, *we're a mess, a mess, a mess.*

Night fell across the sky like a blanket. The stars reared up and sparkled as if they'd just been turned on. Below, the creek glowed in the moonlight. It looked like satin, a smooth ride out to nowhere. It was so calm that anything seemed possible, a walk on water, a dive from the sky. When I was little I used to sit on the pier with Daddy, just the two of us, silent, serious, staring at the creek. I would hold his hand while we swung our feet in the water. Always I could feel things moving beneath the water, could feel the heat of Daddy's hand, a warmth bursting through my blood.

Now I walked out onto our big screened-in porch, not turning on the overhead light, but staring at Josie's spotlight across the point. It shone like a beacon, fierce and determined. Mother was washing dishes. Amanda had gone into the kitchen to get ice cream for one of the many desserts still on the counter, and I didn't hear her come back out. Bugs buzzed and thumped in the darkness beyond the screen, and always there was the sound of waves beating against the old pier. The point looked like a dark finger extending into the shivery shimmer of the creek, and I remembered feeding Dodo, how she glided down to the pier with a hard flap of her wings and stood erect, waiting for me to bring the bucket of eels.

"It's beautiful sometimes," Amanda said, moving beside me in the darkness, breathing in my hair. We stood together in silence, Amanda slumping slightly, a bowl of vanilla ice cream and a chocolate brownie in her hands.

"It's the only thing I've ever wanted," I said. Even seeing the Pacific Ocean didn't hold a candle to Soldier Creek.

"Yeah, I know." She shifted toward me, and I felt the closeness of her skin.

"I missed it." For a moment it was as if I'd never left, as if Amanda and I had been staring out this window forever, two girls out in nowhere, holding on to thin air. "I mean—"

"Well, take a long look," she interrupted, gesturing with her hand at the creek. "Because the Soldiers of Soldier Creek are coming to an end."

I could feel my breath become shallow in my throat. "Amanda, quit that. We've always lived here."

"Past perfect tense. Exactly my point." Amanda held up her spoon, and now I saw the hardness come back into her eyes.

"But Mr. Turner's always let us—"

"Mr. Turner!" she snorted, plunging her spoon into the bowl. "Money's the only thing that Mr. Turner wants. Rent money. And more of it."

"But we once owned it...it's been our arrangement. Daddy always said—"

Amanda was quiet, but I could feel her staring at me, judging me, and even in the dark I blushed. "Jit," she said gently, wearily, and touched the tender flesh of my arm. "Open your eyes, baby. We haven't got any money. Mr. Turner's throwing us out. We've got till the new year."

I didn't move. I couldn't. Daddy dead. The creek gone. A fish jumped somewhere out in the bay and we both heard the splash.

"Welcome home," Amanda said. Then she lifted her spoon to her mouth and turned abruptly, leaving me alone on the porch.

36

I woke to the sound of someone moving through my room. It was early morning. I could tell by the bluish cast to the light, the way the air hung heavy with moisture like syrup sliding down the lip of a cup. I knew, of course, it was Amanda, and when I turned my head slightly I saw her standing at the window, a mug of coffee in one hand. She wasn't looking at me, but out at the creek.

I closed my eyes, thinking of all the things we didn't talk about last night, not just Daddy's death, but the stuff about us: why I ran away and what really happened to her at Trinity College. Instead, Amanda fussed about how Josie's dogs were running wild around Soldier Creek, "digging up old, smelly garbage, shitting on the piers," and the cottonmouth she'd seen coiled in the Spanish moss near the old swing. Now I wanted to ask bluntly, *What about us? What happened to you? Don't you want to know what happened to me?* But I couldn't. Instead, I felt the pressure of our silence settle behind my eyes, and when I opened them again, Amanda was staring at me, so I said the only thing I could, "Who found Daddy?"

Amanda took a sip of coffee and pushed a strand of wispy hair away from her face. She looked tired, dark circles shadowing her eyes. "Officer Budd," she said, then added defiantly, "the same cop who was trying to find you." Her face flushed with anger, and then she went silent, still. "It's kind of creepy," she said finally. "Officer Budd found him washed up on the other side of the point. Not far from Josie's."

"What about right before?" I asked quickly. "I mean, did you see him this spring, did he say anything? Was he unhappy?"

Amanda turned away from the window, and in the morning light I saw that she was thinner than before though her stomach pooched out in its familiar soft curve.

"I saw him once," she said, and hearing that I pushed myself out of bed and sat cross-legged, my arms loose in my lap.

"Tell me." I straightened up. "Please."

"Well." Amanda sat down on the windowsill, her shoulders slumped, the coffee cup balanced in her lap. She closed her eyes as if deciding what to tell me and then opened them to gaze at me as she described the day in December she'd driven out to Perdido Bay, hoping she could bully Daddy into remembering whether he saw me the night I left. She told me how she'd watched him crawling on the ground as if he were hunting something in the bushes and how she'd rushed back to the car and yelled, "Anybody home?" so he'd stand up.

When she said that I untangled myself and swung my feet to the floor. I needed that support, the cool floor, a slight breeze as Amanda stood up and moved away from the window, turning away from me. Behind her the light was changing, sunlight flickering through the mist, shimmering on the tops of the waves. I wanted to jump up and close Amanda's mouth and simultaneously make her go on talking, telling me everything that Daddy had said.

But when she turned back, her face looked pinched, bitter. "He was goddamned drunk when you left and he admitted it. And I bet he was goddamned drunk when he drowned." She lifted her coffee cup to her mouth, taking a long swallow as she stared at me. "I guess that made it easier."

After Amanda left, I stood up then sat right back down. It shocked me that she believed Daddy had committed suicide, a thought I couldn't fix in my mind. Daddy in the creek was as natural as Mother in the garden.

I got up quickly, wanting a shower, but once in the bathroom, I couldn't quit thinking about Daddy, and I sat on the closed lid of the toilet, a towel in my hands. He'd drowned all right, but not intentionally. He wouldn't do that to me.

"Aren't you gonna take a shower?" Amanda asked moments later, standing in the doorway, licking brown sugar from her fingers.

"No . . . I want to go to Daddy's grave," I said. "I'll just wash my face."

Amanda leaned up against the doorframe, rubbing one foot against her calf. "Okay, I'll go with you. I haven't gone back since the funeral. Cemeteries give me the creeps."

As Amanda drove down the familiar driveway, I watched the sparrows dart from the trees. For a moment we fell back into the contentment of each other's company, our minds left to roam in our private thoughts. Maybe I would feel something this time. Maybe if I got real quiet I'd know how he died, could see what led him to the water. And it would lead me there too. Open me. Shock me. Drop the weight from my tongue. Then I could talk to him, talk to him the way I did as a girl. I didn't dare mention to Amanda that I'd been here with Josie, that I'd smoothed the dirt around the edges of his grave, seen the white cross, the lilies, the drooping roses. Instead, I let Amanda lead the way to the grave beneath the glade of trees. It looked less pathetic today because someone had put fresh flowers there. Josie.

I reached down and picked up one of the flowers. An iris, its center as velvet black as midnight. I closed my eyes, smelled it, but what came to me was Daddy, newly dead, lying stiff in his grave, wanting to sit up and talk, to tell me something he'd forgotten, something important that I needed to know. *What? What is it?* I stared at the grave, waiting to feel something, anything. Anger. Grief. Even resentment. I put my hand in the dirt. I leaned closer. I'd have keened if I could, bent my face to the earth. But it didn't seem real.

Amanda sat down beside me, cross-legged, leaning forward on her knees. She looked pensive, thoughtful, all the anger washed out of her face. "I used to wonder if they ever loved each other," she said. "What do you think? Did they?" She looked at me with such gravity, I sat up.

"I don't know," I said. "I think he loved her . . . but not in a way that she could love him back." What I meant to say is that he wanted to rip her away from her past so she'd have nothing but him. One Soldier. One man to lean on. "I don't think she loved him at all."

Amanda picked up a flower and began tearing away at the petals, dropping them on the grave. "Mother hated it here. He dragged her down here from Birmingham, where she'd had friends and music. She used to play the piano, you know. She even played when we were little girls, 'Adagio in A Major' and 'Malegueña' and some Chopin, but she came down here where there's nothing but roaches and heat and snakes and no one to talk to, nothing to do but listen to the water lapping against the pier. She stopped playing. She didn't make friends. God, who knows what hell she went through."

I tightened my knees against each other, hugging myself. *Mother.*

What flashed before me was Mother's face the night she brought me home from the bus station. In the glare of lights, her face was the paleness of ice, but with two flames of color blooming in her cheeks. The tendons on her neck stood out. Her eyes were fists. I couldn't look at them. Instead, I looked away, out into darkness as we drove toward Soldier Creek. And yet there was another moment, one I'd tried to forget: it was the moment we came into the house, me rushing ahead of her through the kitchen door as if I'd convinced myself I could find that blue sweater. I pushed through the kitchen and stopped, but something made me turn around. When I did, Mother was staring at me, her face feverish, strident with excitement, her gaze triumphant, gloating, as if finally she had won.

When I looked up again, Amanda was watching me, scrutinizing my face.

But I wasn't ready to talk about Mother. I shifted my gaze, staring at the grave. It frightened me that my feelings might be so transparent. A year ago Amanda could have made me blurt out my thoughts, but since then I'd learned to take on a little protective coloring. "What happened with Mr. Turner?" I asked quickly. "With the house, I mean."

Amanda looked beyond me, out over the cemetery. The light was high and bright and a ridge of clouds threaded the horizon. Just above the steeple the sun peeked out, as plump and yellow as an egg yolk. "Mr. Turner," she snorted, then leaned back on her heels, putting her arms around her knees. "That old bastard!" She made a face and I laughed, but she didn't smile. Instead, she did something unusual. She scooted closer to me, putting her arm around me, the way we'd sat together as girls out in the yard when we were hatching an idea. We were both sweating a little, and I felt the wetness move from her skin to mine, from mine back to hers until we were almost stuck together. She was quiet, and I wanted then to comfort her, but all I could do was let her hold me. I felt myself go very still, very quiet, imagining our thoughts cross-pollinating so that we knew all there was to know. If we can be this still, I thought, then everything might be all right. It was the stillness I craved.

"After Daddy died, I went to Mr. Turner's office to see about the house and to ask for a loan." Amanda sighed, then straightened, stiffening her back. "But he looked dead at me and said he'd give us till the first of the year. Said he didn't know what he'd be doing with the house, it had to be inspected, and depending on the reports either refurbished or torn down. The old buzzard."

Torn down. I saw yellow bulldozers, the roof fallen in, windows shattered, the porch flattened, screens slashed. I stood up, a blaze kindling in my head. "No! He can't."

Amanda didn't answer me. She looked benignly at me as if I were just coming round. "Yeah, Jit, he can. That's what I've been talking about. He and Daddy didn't have a legal agreement, just a gentleman's agreement between two hard-headed men." Then she stood up too. "Let's get outta here," she said and started walking toward the car as if nothing much had happened. "I need some aspirin or Darvon. Let's go into town, stop at Beemis Drugs and get a Coke float."

As Amanda drove, I watched the blackbirds line up on the telephone wires. They sat like spectators watching the traffic go by. I never saw birds in Los Angeles except for occasional gulls over the ocean and the pigeons in the park. In Los Angeles there was only sky and ocean and cars. Everything was paved over, sealed up, so that even a little patch of grass seemed precious, remarkable. When we took Henley to the park, Aunt Katy and I sat on the swings, brushing our feet against the hard-packed dirt, staring at the occasional bougainvillea blooming near the slides, the palms ruffling above our heads. Now driving by the fields I'd passed so many times on my way to and from school, I studied the still, endless crops, the ditches full of kudzu that grew so fast it circled trees and bushes, making monstrous shapes. Here, there was space. Flowers bloomed out of coffee cans, bloomed in front yards while the back yards were oceans of grass. I let myself breathe.

When I looked over at Amanda, she seemed to have left all our troubles at the cemetery. She chewed on a wisp of hair that had blown into her face, but her eyes were clear and bright. Maybe she really could pretend that everything was fine, I thought, as we moved into the outskirts of Moss Point, past Tiny Tim's Laundry and Slade's Fish Shack, past the trailer park where the colored people lived in what used to be Mr. Crowley's cornfield. Florence Endry still had underwear hanging out on her line, big panties billowing in the breeze, advertising themselves, just as I remembered them. The Clarks still had a mailbox with the Virgin Mary on top, blessing the bills and flyers coming in and going out. For the first time I noticed how small Moss Point was, how dilapidated the stores looked with their faded signs and crumbling facades. Sweety Pies, then Jerkowitz Hardware, the public library, Sugar Shack, and Mr. Bill's Dollar Store on the left. Only Beemis Drugstore looked fit, the front recently painted, the clear glass sparkling in the sun. Amanda parked in the shade, and when we walked in, it was surprisingly cool. Fans whirred on the ceilings and the air-conditioner was going full-blast. Amanda went immediately to the counter and slumped against it, chatting with Mr. Beemis while I waited beside her, looking at the ointments and creams for wrinkles and acne. I thought of walking down Sepulveda Boulevard in L.A., hearing only the noise of cars, the squeal of brakes and people cussing. Even the telephone wires trembled with tension. Here it was quiet.

"I need another prescription, Mr. B. Can't get rid of these headaches."

"You might try a rest," Mr. B said, smiling at her. "Like they say, sleep's the best medicine, but while you're waiting I 'spect you can have a few more Darvon."

Amanda smiled. "My drug of choice."

Amanda, I could see, was playing her friendly-girl card. She'd always gotten her way with doctors and pharmacists and shopkeepers because she talked to them as if she had no doubt they wanted to hear what she had to say.

"Be right with you, Mr. Turner."

Neither of us heard the door open, but we turned simultaneously as if on cue. And to my surprise, Johnny Turner followed his father, his sunburned face paling with surprise at the sight of us. I hadn't seen him since the night of the dance, and now he stared boldly at me, his eyes as dark as midnight. I felt again that little jump in my stomach. I blushed and looked at his father before turning to Amanda. To my surprise, Amanda wasn't staring at Mr. Turner, but at Johnny. It was such an obvious stare it unnerved me.

"I'm sorry about your father," Mr. Turner looked sternly at me as if I were responsible, the troublemaker who'd run off the face of the earth. Then he nudged his son. "Don't you have any manners, boy?"

There was a sudden pause, and I heard Mr. Beemis rattling the pills out of one bottle and into another, then setting them on the counter. Johnny turned and looked at the dead space between Amanda and me. "Sorry about your dad," he said, his voice so low it was almost a whisper. He looked cowed, beaten as he spoke, but then he jerked his head up defiantly, and to my surprise, heat rose in my stomach at the sight of his clenched jaw. Amanda gave me a tight stare, her eyes narrowing. I wondered if Mother had told her about the sweater, about the dance, but then all thought vanished. Amanda turned to Mr. Beemis, picked up the pills, and strode past Mr. Turner and Johnny as if she'd never seen them before.

I remembered almost nothing of the drive back to Soldier Creek. I had what I call one of my shutdowns where everything goes very far away, all sound extinguished, all sights blurred, my thinking numbed. I concentrated instead on a flickering of light on the windshield, a diamond of color like a brilliant gem that beamed out its radiance into that tiny spot. And yet even in a shutdown I was aware of Amanda as if we were linked in the very pumping of our blood. I heard her breathe, then turned and saw her lips parted, her back teeth clenched. Though I couldn't feel it, I knew I was trembling, the muscles shivering beneath my skin. And what I felt was fear, a fear so deep I couldn't let it out into the light.

As we turned into the drive at Soldier Creek, I saw a hawk split the air, its flight determined, arrogant, as if it owned the sky. The next thing I saw was a blue truck parked in our yard, its hood nosing Mother's forsythia bushes, the bed full of tarps and tools.

"One of Turner's men," Amanda muttered and lunged out of the car. I didn't move. I couldn't. A terrible loneliness seized me, slipping over me, and I looked up into the sky for the sight of the hawk.

The man stood in the living room, a notebook bulging from his khaki pants, his head tilted sideways, circles of sweat etching the underarms of his shirt.

"I have a notice right here," he said, and brought a paper from another pocket. "A notice to inspect this house. It's to be vacated in six months, and Mr. Turner, being the owner, has to inspect for damage and repair."

Mother lurked behind Amanda, her face polite, withdrawn as if she'd ceased to interact with the world, was merely at its mercy.

The man glanced briefly at Mother and pitched his next sentence to her. "Mrs. Soldier, I won't be bothering you except to make the inspection. I've just gotta look at that furnace and your plumbing, check the gutters and the roof. You might hear me squeaking over your heads when I check the roof, but I promise I won't fall through." And then he made the mistake of smiling.

"No," Amanda said. She didn't raise her voice. She looked at the man and said it again. "No." He didn't seem to hear, and so Amanda stepped forward. "Go back and tell Mr. Turner that he has no right to inspect our house unless he has an appointment to do so. Tell him that we are still legal tenants and we don't allow anyone poking around without our permission. Tell him I said so—that's Amanda Soldier, write that down, A-M-A-N-D-A—and if he wants to push us around, he'll have to go through me."

The man opened his mouth to speak, but Amanda took a step forward; she was so near she could have touched his sleeve. As she pointed her finger at the door, the man's mouth clenched shut. I could tell he wasn't used to being ordered around by a woman. But he must have seen there was nothing else to do, so he closed his notebook and tromped out without a word. As I heard his truck cough to a start, Amanda faced the window, watching, her back rigid, her shoulders tense. She looked like a solid muscle of steel. But when the truck moved away, Amanda turned toward us, and to my surprise, she was laughing.

37

Darkness. I sat up in bed, frightened, my senses not yet gathered into consciousness. A lizard darted across my sheets and scurried into the curtain, the fold of the curtain a shadow drifting across the floor. And then I remembered where I was. Soldier Creek. Home. I had been here two days.

Without thinking, I got up and walked out of my room, tiptoeing through the hall to Amanda's room. When I opened the door, I saw her sleeping on her back, one arm dangling off the bed, dark swirls of hair stuck to her cheeks and forehead as if she'd just walked out of the rain. She blew out soft bubbles like a frog.

At supper we had both been quiet. Amanda read a magazine. I'd eaten quickly, then snuck down to the pier, sitting on the warm, rough boards, the bench at my back. Now I moved quietly to the window, looking out at the creek, the moon half full beneath a scruff of clouds, the sky velvet black, a haze of stars. Sometimes in the stillness, I thought I could hear the crabs scuttling inside their wire nets, claws snapping, probing as they fought for territory, wrestling for advantage. I shivered with something old, scrubby, raw. My heart beat faster. I belonged here. Not Amanda. Me.

"What are you doing?"

I jumped, surprised by her voice. When I turned, she had raised up on one arm, squinting at me. "Nothing," I said, but I sounded guilty. "I just woke up. I can't sleep."

"Me neither." She laughed, then lay back down, her face turned toward me, watching me. "Let's both get up and eat some of those no-good crabs. I'm hungry."

"Amanda! You can't be."

"I am and proud of it." She sat up, straightening her t-shirt and putting on some flip-flops. "Besides boiled crabs aren't fattening. They're all protein." When she got up from bed, I could see the crazy tussle of her sheets as if there had been a struggle going on.

"Com'on," she whispered. "Let's go down to the pier."

I nodded, following silently past Mother's room, barely breathing, then down the stairs. In the kitchen I found a flashlight in the pantry, a deep enamel pot, and a pair of tongs. Gathering up the utensils in the dark, I felt the first kink of excitement as if what we'd waited for was finally here, the two of us together, alone, at the creek. "Hurry," Amanda called, and together we started down the path, walking slowly, lightly through patches of fog. The ground wavered in and out of sight. Amanda groped for my hand, and we scrambled through the darkness, bracing each other over the roots, stopping to find our footing on the path. At the pier, the water looked black, a smooth, flat blanket. A resting place. I knelt down to check the nets, the boards cool and rough beneath my knees. As I pulled a trap up, crabs thrust their claws out the sides, pinching at the air. Their claws made sharp, clacking sounds like empty beads knocking against each other. Like teeth clacking inside a noisy mouth.

Amanda straddled the bench of the pier. She leaned down on her elbows, staring dreamily at the water as if lost in deep thought.

"Okay, how many do you want?"

"Whhh-at?" She drawled, smiling.

I dangled the crab trap, water dripping from the mesh. "Remember?" A claw swam out, pinchers snapping toward my hand, but when I shook the net, it retreated. "Don't you want to eat these?"

"Oh, I don't know," she said. "I hate to look at their eyes. Such beady little eyes." And then she turned her face toward me. I was surprised at her sudden alertness, the way she stared at me as if she'd been thinking about me for hours. "You know, when I first got home from Trinity I thought I could find you. I thought I was the only one who could. I used to come out to the pier at night and stand in the quiet. It was cool then and I'd stand out here shivering, but I refused to leave. I just had this feeling." She paused. "I believed you were waiting for me, and you'd know when I got home. Sometimes I'd say that: *I'm here. I'm home now. You can come back.* I made myself believe you'd know, but . . ." Amanda's voice wavered. "I couldn't find you."

We were both silent. The night swooped back in. Cicadas trilled in the dark, and something fluttered soft against my cheek. For a moment I wanted to tell her everything that had happened here at Soldier Creek, how frightened I was. "I'm sorry," I began. "I didn't mean—" but then I saw her face crease into a familiar scowl and my words choked inside.

"You could have left a few clues, you know." Her voice was low, intense, a knife blade of anger. "I mean, just to help me out a little."

Inside the trap, the crabs thrashed, climbing over each other, their shells clacking like the lids of a pot. I breathed shallow breaths while near the pier a fish jumped. "I didn't plan it, Amanda." I saw myself hiding in bus station bathrooms, my t-shirt stained and smelly, my hair dirty, matted to my head. And before that, Teddy, wild-eyed and in love with Amanda. "You don't know what it was like when Teddy was here. I tried to make Mother see he didn't mean what he said, didn't mean to upset her—" I glanced toward the house, seized with the memory of Mother's face blanched, then flushed with fury. "He didn't know what he was doing, but it was awful."

Amanda followed my gaze toward the house. It looked like a pale white box floating on the crest of a hill, sealed and silent. "Why didn't you call me? I told you to call—"

"You weren't answering the phone, remember?"

Amanda winced, her face miserable as if the misery lived just beneath the press of her skin. "You think it's my fault, don't you?" She looked at me now as if she were unscrewing all her thoughts, examining them in a dark airless room with quiet, ruthless scrutiny, and I saw for the first time how frightened she was. I closed my eyes, smelling the wet seaweedy smell of the fog. I shook my head. But what I thought surprised me: I didn't want to see Amanda afraid.

"No . . . no, I don't . . ." In my mind it was a hopeless knot. "I don't know. Maybe it's no one's fault."

Then to my surprise, Amanda laughed a silvery laugh that splashed out into the air. "Teddy. Let's blame it on Teddy." A pause. "And Mother. The Big Bad Mother Bear."

But I didn't laugh. Instead, I set the trap down on the pier and tried to grab one of the scuttling crabs with my tongs as if we were still in the business of food. I knew I should tell her, start from the beginning, start with Mr. Hesse and the terrible mess I'd made. I'd tell her how I disgraced myself, became frightened and weird, and in trying to make everything better made everything so much worse. As I wrestled with the crab, letting it escape when the tongs slipped, then feeling its hard shell trapped beneath the metal clamps, I told myself to quiet down, to tell it straight, no drama, no hysterics. "Amanda, you don't know what happened here—"

"No, it's you who doesn't know."

"What? What do you mean?"

"I'm talking about what's happening to us now, what will happen to us. Daddy wanted to keep Soldier Creek. He never really thought we'd lose it."

When I turned, she was staring out across the creek toward Josie's. She could have been alone, her body in complete stillness, relaxed, her t-shirt bloused over her stomach, over the top of her legs. And for a moment she looked certain, determined. Her old hopeful self. "He thought he could give it to us," I said, turning again to the crabs. "But that wasn't what happened." Now I flipped on the flashlight, shining it into the net. Stunned by the light, the crabs crowded on one side of the trap, claws open, ready to snap. I clamped one tight with the tongs, lifting it high into the air. "Look at this!" Its claws opened and closed frantically in the air. I didn't want to discuss Daddy. I hadn't been able to talk to him since I'd come back, couldn't touch his life. Amanda slumped into silence, and I too felt quiet, suddenly tired.

"Amanda, I need to—"

"We could still try to get it," Amanda interrupted, sitting up.

Ignoring her, I held the crab over the pot, picked up the lid with my free hand and dropped the crab inside, closing the lid quickly. I could hear the two crabs scrambling, fighting. "Don't be silly," I wasn't looking at her. I didn't believe in false dreams anymore. "Listen, Amanda—"

"*You* could."

"Yeah, right. I guess I'll walk up to Mr. Turner and ask for a loan tomorrow." I expected Amanda to laugh, but when I looked up, she was studying me.

"I mean it." Now a nerve pricked in my neck. My hand tightened on the tongs.

"How?" I was serious now too. I needed to know the direction of her thoughts as if this was the trouble I'd been expecting.

"Johnny Turner."

I dropped the pot and crabs scattered, scuttling back into the water.

Amanda leaned toward me, her eyes wide with meaning. "I saw him looking at you today."

The lid wobbled across the dock toward the water where it sank with barely a splash. "Don't be silly."

"I think you could if you wanted to."

"What are you talking about? I don't understand . . . Johnny Turner's—"

"He's confused," she said. "And that's why he needs someone . . . someone with some influence. He's more vulnerable than you think . . . look, he's likely to get drafted to Vietnam—"

"No," I whispered, not because of Johnny Turner, but because I saw where Amanda was heading, but it was too stupid. It didn't make sense. I sat down on the pier, leaning back on my hands, frowning in the dark. "That's crazy. You can't possibly mean—"

"Yes, don't you see?" Now she was standing up, excited, and her voice had that manic edge that frightened me a little. "It does make sense. You love it here." I looked at her as if she were crazy. What could she be thinking? That I marry Johnny Turner? I was only sixteen years old. But of course, Amanda wasn't thinking about me. She was jumping through magical hoops, doing her own bright calculations. "Don't you see, we've both got to act, we've got to do something or we'll . . . we'll drown."

"But Amanda—" I started to say it won't work, but in seconds she was up from the bench, standing over me, her voice feverish, excited.

"You could do this," she said, and she leaned toward me. "I'd do it myself—"

"No," I whispered. "It's too crazy."

"Yes." She actually stamped her foot.

"No," I said again. I felt myself struggling against her, and I realized, to my surprise, that I'd been struggling against Amanda all my life.

"For god's sake, don't be such a little fool. We don't have a choice anymore. You don't get something for nothing."

Maybe it was that word nothing that made my stomach clench. I thought of Mr. Hesse glancing at me, distracted, unseeing. I heard Daddy calling drunkenly, "There goes Swifty!" when I needed to talk. And to my surprise I felt the first shock of fury. Hot. Dense. An electric charge racing through my body, lodging in my chest. "No," I said again. "You're crazy. You're—" I wanted to say, *trying to punish me.*

Before I could finish, Amanda grabbed my shoulders and yanked me up, her fingers tightening around my flesh, the nails digging into the skin. "You little fool," she whispered, "you little fool." She was hissing now, and I knew then that she blamed me, blamed me for everything that had happened, for the mess we were in. My head swayed backward, and I felt myself going slack, a rag doll, a limp, dirty cloth. *My fault. My fault. My fault.* There was no way to say it wasn't my fault. I left. I ran away. I saw the highway leaping toward me, my face pressed close against the window of the bus, the air ruffling my sleeve, rushing up the inside of my arm. I was dizzy with fear and anger, dirty and tired, clutching my purse that held all the money I'd taken from Daddy. But from somewhere wedged in the crowded corners of my mind Aunt Katy said softly, "Oh, honey, look at you." And as suddenly I was pushing back, my hands taking hold of Amanda's shoulders as if my fingers were steel. "No," I said. "No." Now I was shaking her just as she was shaking me. It wasn't my fault. This was what we'd been building toward: this fight, this tug-of-war for our lives. It didn't really matter about Johnny Turner. He was simply the excuse, the pawn, the dividing line. This was what we'd been waiting for: who would make a decision about our lives.

To my surprise, Amanda gave me one final shove, pushing me off-balance so that I stumbled backward, grabbing onto a piling, my shoulder hitting the wood, my fingers tracking splinters while she ran down the length of the pier. I watched as she raced up the path, groping and stumbling, a blur of soft, pale white. She was running. Back to the house. Back to Mother.

I didn't move. I felt the boards beneath my feet, listened to the crabs scuttling in their trap, and then I walked down the pier and away from the house toward the woods. My clothes caught on branches and briars; pine needles crackled beneath my feet. But I made myself walk slowly until I was in the middle of the woods. I stopped. You have to pay with your whole damn life. That's what Amanda meant. Then I began to walk again, slowly, and then faster, faster, gathering speed until I was gasping for breath.

I came out at the clearing, five miles from the house. And there it was. Daddy's shack. The old fishing cabin he'd been living in for six years. It looked dilapidated in the graying darkness, vines grown wild over the side windows, the roof tilting down, the steps leaning deep into the ground. The whole thing had settled unevenly and looked like it might pitch itself into the bay. I stood in the doorway, peering in through the window, staring at his bed now neatly made, a stack of books on one table, but I didn't want to go inside. Not yet. I saw an old canvas chair on the lawn facing the bay, and I went toward it and sat.

Before me, Perdido Bay was a moving darkness, a slippery rug of water rippling in the breeze. Pine trees grew right near the shore, banking the cove, protecting it from sight. I could imagine him sitting here, hiding, feeling safe. *And he lay me on my back in the water and I squealed. There,* he said softly, putting his hands under my body to anchor me. *Now just let the water hold you up, baby. Let yourself float. Just like some old barge going home. Taking a load home, baby. Back to Soldier Creek.*

Daddy.

I did come back, Daddy. I did.

38

Early dawn. I was surprised to see light fingering through inky darkness. A milky haze. I'd been sitting in Daddy's canvas chair, but now I walked to his cabin, hesitating only a minute before I plunged inside. Even in the dusky light I saw that the table and counters had been cleared of debris. No fish bones or wax paper. No onions dried to a seedy yellow. No wadded-up dollar bills or empty whiskey bottles. The only noise was the faucet dripping—plink, plink, plink. I crossed to it and, with a single movement, turned it off. The sink was spotless, shiny, the handles polished to a slippery glare. There was nothing out of order, nothing but a single leaf blown in from the roof. "What am I supposed to do, Daddy?" I asked, but of course, there was no answer. I turned in a complete circle. Nothing of him here.

I heard the rat-tat-tat of a woodpecker, hammering at his job, turning night into day. I walked out of the cabin, watching the fog sweep across the grass, wetting it like a carpet. Light haloed the trees, pale and amber. But when I looked at the horizon I saw a narrow wedge of blue, the way the creek looked from far away.

Then I knew.

I saw him walking toward the water, his feet in old tennis shoes sinking into the marsh, his eyes never leaving the creek. And I saw myself, a little girl in the middle of the creek, learning to float, my arms splayed out, crucifix-fashion, until I began to sink. I went under, then bobbed back up. Under and up. Under and up. "Hold on now, honey," he yelled, and hearing him, I turned toward shore, waving, smiling, knowing he was coming to help me. He waded through the shallows until water splashed his knees, his waist, his hairy chest, his shoulders, his neck, the tip of his chin. Then he was swimming with long, smooth strides, but as I watched I saw that the water began to tire him, to slow him though he pushed on, each stroke short and labored and cramped. He strained forward. He was barely moving. He wasn't going to make it.

Tears fell into my hands, trickled to the ground. He didn't mean to.

He didn't mean to let go, to stop swimming, but he was too tired, too wasted. There was no ground to hold him up. Nothing but creek water. How surprised he must have been to find himself stranded by water.

"It's okay," I whispered. "Don't worry about me. I'll be okay." And for the first time I knew. I would be able to breathe again.

As I left Daddy's fishing shack, light spread through the treetops, golden streaks as if the sky had rubbed up against darkness. Birds sang their morning chatter. Insects buzzed, seeking blood. Walking through the woods, I imagined Amanda in the kitchen fixing coffee, making waffles, putting her finger in the syrup to get a sugar rush. I walked fast. Faster.

The house loomed out of the shadows. Two intertwined trees shaded the front yard, and when I entered the back door to the kitchen, I had to stop to let my eyes adjust. Sunlight shot through the kitchen window. The first thing I noticed was that all the food from Daddy's wake was gone. I imagined Amanda eating it, sitting up all night with a spoon in her hand, dipping into cartons and casseroles, not bothering to chew fully before she swallowed it down. She'd be both pleased and cranky, disgusted with herself. Then I saw a large trash bag on the kitchen floor, and I knew they'd simply thrown it away. I stood still a minute, listening to the quiet. It was as if the house was sleeping, and for a moment I thought of Amanda and Mother curled in their beds, caught in the darkness of dreams. Instinctively, I went into the living room, then out onto the porch to stare across the bluff to the creek, wondering as I stood there if I should wake them. A ripple of movement made me glance to my left, and to my surprise I saw Mother squatting in the garden, her hands in the dirt. Almost simultaneously, she looked up at me.

For so long I hadn't been able to think about Mother, that when she started toward me, I shrank. Then I remembered where I'd been and something new settled around me, a protective spirit, as if Daddy were hovering just above my shoulder. When Mother came through the porch door, she smiled an uneasy, self-conscious smile. "Come let me fix you breakfast," she said, and it was such a simple request, I nodded. Yes. I will let you fix me breakfast.

Except for the bag of trash, the entire kitchen was clean. Counters were bare, washed and wiped. Skillets were hung from a giant hook on the wall. The sink sparkled. The floor had been mopped. Did Mother do this? Did she do this for me?

I watched silently as she got out eggs and Canadian bacon, wheat bread and orange juice. She poured me a glass of juice, and when she handed it to me she said, "Amanda has gone to the hospital to cover someone's shift. She left before 6:30." And then she turned to whip up the eggs, to let the Canadian bacon hiss on the grill, to punch in the toast.

"We didn't know where you were," she said. "We were worried."

It was the plural that stopped me, made my mouth go dry. Would I ever believe that my mother worried about me?

"I was over at Daddy's cabin," I said. "Amanda and I had a fight."

"I know." Mother turned and faced me. "Amanda told me. She's terribly upset. She can't let go of what's happened for a second and can't quit pushing the rest of us right along with her. That's why she went to the hospital. I don't think she really had to cover for anyone at all."

I was surprised that Mother revealed this, that she wanted to tell me, but I was more surprised that I wanted her to continue, to tell me something I didn't already know. Instead, she put my eggs, bacon, and toast on a plate, and to my relief, I was suddenly hungry, scooping up the eggs with a scrap of toast, chewing bacon, drinking juice.

Mother sat across from me as if we'd done this all of our lives, though in reality, Mother never sat with me unless she was eating too. She did this only with Amanda so that Amanda could tease her into pleasure, catapult her into the world of outraged life. Now I found myself embarrassed, self-conscious. I couldn't chew my toast. It lodged between my back teeth, and when I tried to swallow, it got stuck. Quickly, I drank my juice, but with it some old bitterness caught beneath my tongue. I'd never admitted bitterness before, but here it was, resentment as strong as lye, a defiance I didn't even know I had. In the silence I heard the ticking of the clock, the flutter of leaves as birds scattered from the trees. When I glanced up, I saw Mother watching me. She flushed and picked up a napkin, twisted it into a knot. "That Mr. Hesse, that teacher of yours," she began, "he called here last month to see if we'd heard any news about you. He seemed terribly concerned. He said something had happened at school, something he'd never understood, and he apologized for not getting to the bottom of it."

I shifted in my seat, staring out the window at the magnolia tree, the leaves thick and waxy, as shiny as mirrors, one branch bent so low it almost embraced the straw-studded ground. I was oddly touched, could slip fast toward tears; instead, I held myself very still, thinking of how Mr. Hesse once said, "It will be a pleasure to get to know you." But he didn't get to know me. I couldn't let him. And he didn't push. That's what he was apologizing for.

"The entire class wrote you letters," Mother continued. "He wanted me to give them to you when you came back. He sent them to me, and he asked me to please call him if . . . well, when you returned." She paused and twisted the napkin tighter around her finger. "I haven't called him yet because I wanted to tell you first. I wanted you to know . . ." her voice faltered and she looked frightened, uncertain as if she didn't quite know what to say, ". . . that we were so worried." She rose in one motion, rose so quickly I was startled. I thought for a minute that she was going to hug me; instead, she reached out to touch my hand.

I don't know if I can make anyone understand this, if I can even understand it myself, but when she touched me, I bolted. Why couldn't she say, "I missed you." First person singular. Why couldn't she hug me? Was that so hard?

There was no place to go but to Josie's, and I took the path without looking back. Josie missed me; I knew she did. Her face lit up when she saw me and something in me relaxed, my tongue unleashed to talk. But now my stomach was knotted up, a tight little pocket.

When I arrived at the One-Stop, Josie was standing on her pier, checking her crab traps. As she pulled up a wiry cage, I saw two crabs scramble to the other side of the net, their claws clicking against the wire. "Hey, early birds," Josie said, thumping the net, "don't be so scared. I'm not hungry for you yet."

I sank back against one of the pilings and watched Josie lower the trap, then check another one. "Breakfast?" she asked, but I shook my head.

"Talk," I said, as if I could speak only in shorthand.

Without another word, Josie put her arm around my shoulder and steered me into the One-Stop where she shoved over a pile of newspapers, pulled out chairs for us, and opened a package of peanut butter crackers. She crunched on one, the flakes drifting to her lap as she sat across from me and moved the clutter—the fishing nets and folded paper bags—from beneath our feet. The One-Stop had never been a neat place.

When I told Josie about the fight with Amanda, about Mother's admission of worry, she listened with such focused attention it was as if I were the only person in the world. Quietly she munched on the crackers, listening, nodding her head.

"Let me tell you a story," she began. She lit a cigarette and then leaned back against the counter, one foot crossed over the other. "When I was a girl, I was scared to death of water." She shook her head. "I know, I know, you can't believe that because I always splash around here sopping wet half the time, one foot in the creek, the other in the sand. But that was a long time coming. When I was about ten years old, it was a different story. There was this crick in our community; that's what we called them in the mountains, a 'crick' instead of a creek, where everyone went swimming in water churned up with silt because of everybody kicking and splashing. Well, the way they taught you to swim was just to throw you in and that worked pretty well for most people because you'll do most anything to save your life. But when they threw me in, I almost choked to death. Breathed in the water and about drowned. It scared me so bad, I swore I'd never go back in that crick or in any other water, for that matter. And I kept that promise until I was fourteen. When I reached that age, I knew that there was something better than this pitiful town where we lived, and I wanted to see it. The only trip available to us was with the P.E. teacher who gave you extra points for sports activities and took you to a Girl Scout camp thirty miles away. Part of P.E. was swimming class. Miss Liebecker. Lord, she was as tough as a drill sergeant, but I made up my mind that I was going to pass that class and be one of the ones chosen to go to the city with her. The only way I could do that was to get in the water. And to get in the water I had to pretend I was somewhere else, doing something else, so I pretended I was climbing a mountain or swinging through the air and that everything depended on doing this task. I made myself heroic. I made myself act because there was something at the end that I wanted."

Josie stopped, drank her coffee, took a drag off her cigarette, pausing to look beyond me where the morning light spread its warm coat across her rickety porch. "Now you're probably wondering why I'm telling you this, but the thing is I realized that year that I had to fight for what I wanted, and the fight was going to have setbacks and rewards and I'd have to settle for both. Well, you've been fighting this past year. You're in the water, so to speak, but what is it you want?" She bent down to scratch her dog behind the ears, to nuzzle his face against her knee, then she looked intently at me. "You probably think I'm being mean to ask you such a thing when you've just come home under such awful circumstances. But I'm not trying to be hard on you. I'm just saying that underneath all of this trouble, you've got to quiet down and know what you want from Amanda, from your mother, and most of all, from yourself. That's the important part." She turned and poured the coffee down the drain. "You may not get what you want from anybody else, but you set yourself on a path. You make a claim. And start in a direction."

39

At 6:30 in the morning the air was cool, the sun just breaking through the pines, splashing the sky with golden light as I drove to the hospital. In the distance I heard a tractor chugging through Donnie Kaiser's fields, saw a flock of birds in scattered flight. There was Mr. Dawson in his khaki pants and undershirt walking his terrier, Buzz, letting Buzz nose into Mrs. Henry's flower beds. By breakfast she'd be spitting mad. I raced past fields and barns, then the potato sheds, deserted and abandoned, tin roofs splattered with rust. I bumped over railroad tracks beside the old library, then hung a right to the hospital. "Hey, I'm here to help," I announced, dropping my purse to the floor and putting on a white lab coat. "When you can't think, it's best to work."

"Or when you don't want to think," Shirley replied, rattling a chart.

"Mind reader," I made a face, ready to tease Shirley about her psychic skills, but just as I was beginning my pitch, there was a Code 9 and a furious eruption of activity. Doctors and nurses raced down the hall, followed by Herb Lassiter. It was Mrs. Longinovic in respiratory failure. I didn't answer to codes, but when Shirley rose to go, I followed, standing in the doorway watching as Dr. Barnett intubated while Herb hovered ready to bag Mrs. Longinovic, whose lips and nails had turned a dull, metallic blue. She looked pasty white. She looked . . . well, dead.

The heart monitor was hooked up, and they were sending epinephrine and atropine through the IV.

Though I'd always disliked this old woman, I held my breath, uncertain what to feel. I watched Mrs. Longinovic's body jolt forward with each shock, her white braids flying out, and to my surprise tears wet my eyes. But what I saw wasn't Mrs. Longinovic, but Jit as a little girl crying because Mother wouldn't hug her. Always I tried to shield her from Mother's defection, tried to surround her with reflections of the world. I sowed the air with words. Bluebird. Gull. Sparrow. Finch. Crow. Tulip. Daylily. Azalea. Rose.

Mulberry. Oak. I taught Jit the names of birds, the names of flowers, the names of trees, the names of emotions, leaving out only anger.

"Again," Dr. Barnett barked. And they went through a second set of shocks.

Shirley moved in closer, and I saw the way her uniform pulled tight over her hips so that the ridge of her underwear pushed through the cloth. I stared at the dark boats that were Dr. Barnett's black dress shoes, then Herb's old tennies sideswiped with mud. Three pairs of nurse's shoes. Then the curtain swayed in a sudden breeze, and I closed my eyes, seeing Jit last night with her arms clamped tight to mine, her face clenched in determined fury. How, I wondered, had she learned anger without me?

I was sitting at the nurse's station, drinking cold coffee when Shirley came out of the room, her face beaded with sweat. "Whew, that was a close one, but I think she's coming round." Shirley looked exhausted, drained; her glasses had fallen down on her nose, and she squinted through them, then pushed them back up on her face. "Honey, are you sure you want to be here with all this mess? Don't you want to go home and look after your sister?"

It was the first time anyone had mentioned Jit.

Shirley wiped her face with a Kleenex. "I guess you're wondering how I know she's here, but news like that spreads through the grapevine like wildfire. Lou Ann saw you two coming out of Beemis Drugs yesterday and told us last night that she was here. How is she, love?"

For the first time I glanced away from Shirley, embarrassed because I didn't know how to answer. How is Jit? I didn't know. Our time together had moved too fast, been poisoned by too much fear and sadness. I hadn't asked her what happened to her in her flight from Soldier Creek. How did she ever find Aunt Katy? Was that why she went to L.A.? Was she mistreated, abused, deprived? Was she hungry? Scared to death? I couldn't believe I hadn't sat her down and said, "Tell me everything. Start at the beginning and don't leave a thing out."

"I don't know, Shirley. It's all happened so fast. I don't know how she is."

As if it was the most natural thing in the world, Shirley took hold of my hand and squeezed it tight. "You will," she said. "It just takes time. Why don't you go on back home?"

But I wasn't ready to talk to Jit. "No," I said. "I need to work."

"Well, come along then. I guess you won't mind checking temps and emptying bedpans."

For hours I did exactly what Shirley said, fetching and carrying, changing beds, giving meds, emptying bedpans, anything to keep me busy. The work was soothing, like a sedative to a fevered brain. When Shirley had a break, she asked if I'd sit with Mrs. Longinovic, who was now in ICU. "So her daughter, Marilyn, can get something to eat, honey. She's been on her feet since 6:00 this morning, feeding chickens and scrubbing potatoes, then rushing here when all this trouble started."

Sitting beside Mrs. Longinovic, I watched as her mouth alternately clawed for breath and relaxed into soft release. A deep frown pierced her forehead as if breathing took concentration. While I watched the heart monitor, I thought about how she'd emigrated from Yugoslavia and worked the land with her husband and kids. I imagined she kept house, minded children, fed chickens, tended the garden, put up vegetables and fruit, working every day of her life. Was that a good life? A heroic life? Or was it bitter, fractious, a hardness that seeped into her blood?

Even as I thought this, a new idea pricked the back of my mind. What if I couldn't be heroic, the one who sacrificed herself for the good of all? Of course, even at Trinity College, I hadn't intended just to sacrifice myself but to rise swiftly with Mother and Jit in tow. But I'd failed and landed right back in the world of my childhood, a world of endless demands.

Now for a brief moment, I stood apart from both worlds. I placed my hand on Mrs. Longinovic's hands, feeling their coolness. What if there was no need to be a hero or a martyr? What if there was no reward for sacrifice at all? I began lightly massaging the old woman's fingers, the skin as dry and thin as wax paper. I'd never asked myself what I wanted to do separate from Mother and Jit, as if they were attached to my hip. "I'll do something marvelous!" floated through my mind, and I laughed now at the cruel irony.

When I followed the wiry veins in Mrs. Longinovic's arms, I saw how they wove together in intricate ways, circling the body, feeding it with blood. The blood fed the heart. The brain. The lungs. I thought about my own body, how anxiety pumped through me, startling me, urging me to act, to leave. I closed my eyes. Now that Jit was home I tried to imagine myself back at Trinity College, but where there should have been a girl moving her stuff into the scholarship dorm, nothing showed up on the radar screen. No figures. No books. Not even shadows. I opened my eyes and stared at Mrs. Longinovic's hand. I'd been silently rubbing it, giving warmth. As if the rubbing had loosened something in me, I wondered what would happen if I didn't go back to Trinity College. Were there other places to go?

I saw Mother and Jit sitting at our kitchen table, silent and awkward because so much had damaged us here. And it came to me as a surprise that I no longer had to fight for Soldier Creek, no longer had to keep us in this little town at the bottom of Alabama. Mother and Jit could move.

They could uproot. We'd all have to give up something. If we didn't, we'd pull each other apart.

My mind raced with ideas. Herb Lassiter had often talked about the people he knew at the University of Alabama. Mr. Kirk too. Maybe the two of them had contacts at the hospital in Tuscaloosa, jobs I could work while enrolled in classes. And Mr. Hesse. Mr. Ellis and Mrs. Bryant. They too had gone there. Possibilities stretched before me, the potential of another life, not the one I'd longed for at Trinity, but a possible life where I could get on with the business of learning. I could hear Dr. McKune talking about the intricate web beneath the fabric of life: "All those dark, serpentine networks and mysterious stories that feed from all directions into a bigger stream like the veins of the body feeding into the brain and heart and lungs. Without knowing about the smaller systems, the bigger ones are overwhelming, as autocratic as prideful kingdoms, endangered and untenable." That's what I wanted to learn: how it all fit together, how the pieces made up a whole and how the whole could be dismantled and changed, revised so that it was dynamic, alive, like looking at cells under a microscope.

I looked at Mrs. Longinovic. She seemed to be sleeping. Her hand, long-boned and frail, the nails bruise-colored, lay limply in mine. I placed her hand on the bedcovers, alongside her hip, the palm curving inward as if shielding her from harm. I sat watching her, a ridiculous grin on my face, until Shirley came in to relieve me.

"You all right, hon?" she asked, looking oddly at me because of my fat, happy smile. "Not everybody thinks this is the Apple Pie Wing."

"Shirley." I leaped up, grabbing her. "I've figured it out. I think I've found a way."

"Oh, hon," Shirley started, but we were interrupted by Mrs. Longinovic's daughter, Marilyn, opening the door, bringing her worried face into the room.

"Has something happened? Is she all right?"

"Yes," Shirley said. "She's sleeping. Amanda said she's been doing just fine."

Shirley walked me back to the station, her gaze as steady as her tread. "Now what are you talking about?" she asked. "I haven't seen anybody this high since those glue-sniffers came into the emergency room and tried to rearrange the furniture."

When I told Shirley what had happened, how Mr. Turner was throwing us out and there was nowhere for us to go, then my sudden brainstorm about the state university while watching Mrs. Longinovic, she smiled her most indulgent smile. "Why, I think Mrs. Longinovic deserves a little credit for that. Seeing someone at the end of something makes you wake right up, don't it? Myself, I'm going home now and make Hal a pile of pancakes. With as much butter and syrup as his heart desires."

"Shirley, don't start me thinking of food."

"Go home," she said, shooing me away. "Go home and talk to your family."

I nodded, but before I left, I typed notes to Herb Lassiter and Mr. Kirk, asking for their help. Though ashamed to admit it, I knew I could rely on the town's sympathy so soon after my father's death. And that was just how I said it, *"If you could find your way to help me during this crucial time in my family's life, I'd be most grateful."* I asked both of them for references to the hospital in Tuscaloosa and recommendations to the university.

For the first time in months I didn't hate the drive home, didn't hate the soybean fields, the pastures of clover, the hot, thick smell of manure. I smiled at the cows. "Howdy-do Mr. Brown Cow. Hello there, Miss Guernsey. Hey there, Miss Flop-Under-the-Tree." I saluted the barns, the weedy ditches, the paint-peeling fences, the long snake of blacktop that crept toward Perdido and Lillian. When I turned onto the Creek Road, I felt as if a burden had been lifted. I could see the three of us in a little white bungalow with dark green shutters, roses climbing a trellis around the front stoop, people strolling by on their way to class. Jit could go to high school, and surely Mother could find part-time work in a laundry or doing clothes for one of the sororities while I reclaimed myself in the library. For the first time since I'd left Trinity College, I wanted the straightforward life. To hell with Mr. Turner. To hell with Soldier Creek.

When I pulled into the drive, I barely noticed the house, the yard, the flowered sheets drying on the old string clothesline. What I saw in front of me were piles and piles of things to sort through—books and clothes and magazines and bills—what to keep and what to throw away for our move up north. Or maybe it was just that I needed something to do, something busy and productive and hopeful after all these months of disaster.

"Mother!" I shouted as I pushed open the kitchen door. I didn't know what I expected to find, but I was surprised to see Mother sitting in the living room, staring out at the creek. "Mother," I said softly, gliding toward her, touching her shoulder until she turned toward me. She looked grave, unsettled—that little twitch at her temple always trouble—but I wouldn't be slowed down, diverted by worry. "I've got to talk to you. I've got . . ." excitement chased away all doubt, and I shifted from foot to foot as if I had to pee. "Oh, Mother, I think, well, I think there might be a way . . . there might be a way for it to work out after all!" And then I couldn't stop myself.

I did a little twirl right there in the afternoon sun, my arms outstretched, a giggle in my throat. "Look at these books," and I began to pull books off the shelves, forgetting that I hadn't even told Mother the great plan I'd devised. *Ivanhoe. Little Women. Great Expectations. Jane Eyre. Frankenstein.* I stacked them together, but when I turned around Mother was still staring out at the creek.

"Mother." I knelt down beside her. I tried to be calm. "Mother, listen, you've always wanted so much for me. I know you have. And I've tried, I really tried to do well at Trinity . . . I mean, I was doing well, but I was also confused. I didn't know what a school like that would demand. I didn't quite know what to expect, and things got complicated in ways I couldn't have imagined, but now . . . well, being back here in Soldier Creek I realized I can't deny that other life. I have to have it. I can't ignore it and live here like a nobody. And I think there's a way." I saw her face pinch with fear, and I said quickly, "No, no, I don't mean going back to Trinity. My scholarship won't be available, and too much has happened to make me want that again. But there are other places." And despite myself I sensed the plea in my voice. "Places nearer to us where I might start again. Places we can all go. You and me and Jit. Because we do have to leave here. I can't fight Mr. Turner no matter how much I want to, I can't get the house back. I can't—" and I looked around at the row of windows settled unevenly in their frames, at the way the ceiling bowed in the middle, the flecked paint, the scuffed wooden floors. "But we could all be together somewhere else. We could start fresh. We could begin again." I paused. "You've always wanted to leave here, move back to northern Alabama. Well, that's where the university is, where I feel sure I could thrive."

"What about Jit?" Mother said, and I was surprised that this was the first thing she said.

"Well, she'll come with us. She'll need to finish high school, and we'll all be together, won't we?" I looked around. "Where is she? I've gotta talk to her. We had this silly fight."

Mother sighed. "She was here for breakfast, but she didn't stay." Again she looked troubled. She nibbled on her bottom lip. "I don't know where she went."

"She'll be back," I reassured her. "I know she will." And I thought about how much I had to tell Jit, how pleased she'd be that I'd figured it out. "Com'on, help me," I said because I didn't want to lose the enthusiasm of my mood, to be pulled down some bumpy side road of worry. "Let's go through these books and magazines and see what we'd take if we left."

Before Mother could refuse, I handed her a stack of magazines to sort, some so old and brown with age I imagined them sitting on the bookshelf through hurricanes and floods, growing spotted with mildew, damp with moisture. Mother, as I suspected, began dutifully looking through them, opening a page and getting lost in some old life, then putting each one in the trash pile. How easy this seemed. To pick up the pieces. To sort through the old life. To begin a new one. It all depended on a decision, a direction, a burst of hope. Almost immediately I saw myself sitting in my dorm room at Trinity, opening up another piece of chocolate. Already I could taste it in my mouth, feel the squish of it on the back of my tongue, the stickiness between my teeth. The floor was littered with wrappers, my bed messy with smears. What I'd felt then was the opposite of hope, two worlds crashing together, crushing me between their hungry jaws. Since I'd been home, I'd pushed that time to the back of my mind. But now it walked out into daylight. A flutter of fear pulsed through me. How frightened I'd been!

I must have paused in my sorting because when I looked up again, Mother was studying me, her eyes curious, filled with her old reckless love. It washed over me, thick and warm and sweet. I was like a swimmer being rescued, breath pumped into my lungs. I hadn't realized I'd missed it until now.

"We've got so much to do," I squealed, happiness bursting inside me as I leaned closer to her. "And I can start working weekends before we go. If not at the hospital, then at the nursing home. You just can't imagine what I can do with diapers!"

Despite herself, Mother laughed, relaxing. The lines around her mouth smoothed out.

"No charter-farter-starters for me. I go right for the poopers."

While we were laughing we heard the kitchen door swing open, the screen slam shut. We both glanced up as Jit appeared in the room, looking breathless and rushed. "Amanda—" she gushed. "I ran—" And then she bent over, breathing fast, trying to catch her breath.

"Hey, com'ere. We're going through all our things," I said, scooting over to make a spot for her. "Come sit down with us." But Jit didn't move. She just stared and breathed deeply.

"I ran all the way," she said finally. "I tried to catch up with you."

"Ran . . . from where?"

"I was coming from Josie's and saw you turning down the creek road." She stopped, leaning against the wall, still breathing in ragged gasps. "You didn't see me . . . but I just kept running. I kept shouting AMANDA! AMANDA! Because . . . there's so much we have to talk about, so much—"

"I know," I said, reaching out as if I could pull her to me. "You won't believe it, but I've figured out what we've got to do. It just came to me!

I was sitting with Mrs. Longinovic at the hospital, this old woman who's barely alive. I was watching her trying to breathe, and suddenly I saw it all. You and mother and me moving up to Tuscaloosa, to the university where I can work and finish college and you can finish high school and—"

"What are you talking about?" Jit's strangled voice cut through the air.

For a moment neither of us spoke. Silence sizzled between us, and I remembered the pressure of her fingers on my arm. Now Jit's face was as pale as the moon.

"I'm talking about the future," I said. "About what we can do."

Before I said another word Jit muttered, "What you can do." Then she wheeled around and was out the door before I could reply.

Mother and I didn't move. The air trembled with the force of Jit's leaving.

I jumped up. "Don't worry," I said quickly to Mother. "I'll talk to her."

Jit's feet were propped up on the first step of the ladder, water splashing against her toes. Gulls wheeled overhead and squawked as they circled. The sun bathed the creek in soft, honeyed light. For the first time I thought how pretty the sky was, reddish gold, pink with swirls of white and maroon. Though Jit didn't turn around, I knew she heard me. I hadn't tried to silence my steps as I walked up behind her, so close I could have touched her. "It is a good idea," I said. A motorboat sputtered around the point, its sound like the whining of a chain saw. "Jit, we can't stay here. You know that. We have to make decisions."

"I thought you wanted me to marry Johnny Turner." She turned, fixing me with a tight, fierce glare.

I laughed. I always laugh when I'm nervous. "Well, it did get me thinking. I thought—"

"Me too," she said, squinting at me, still frowning.

"Do you want to marry him?"

"Of course not. Don't be stupid."

"Well what do you want?"

She shook her head, gazing at the water, tugged back into silence. Her hair was tousled by the wind; she was wearing an old t-shirt, a baggy, shapeless green one. Suddenly she looked young and vulnerable, and I realized I had no idea where she'd spent the night, if she'd gone to Josie's, as I suspected, or if she slept right here on the pier. "I don't know," she said, her shoulders slumping. "It's all happened so fast, I just don't know."

For a moment I felt sympathetic, but there was something in the sag of her shoulders that irritated me. It was just like Jit to be passive and resentful, to think we could stay here by retreating like turtles inside our shell. "Well, you better think about it," I said. "You better—"

Before I could finish, she launched headfirst into the creek, cool water splashing against my words.

JIT SOLDIER

40

I woke to a cloak of fog, thick as smoke, obscuring the trees just outside my window. When I first opened my eyes, I longed only to shut them again, to turn over and push back into a dreamless sleep. Then I saw her. "Mother!" I must have gasped because she turned from the window as I scrunched farther into the bed, frightened of her nearness. My heart beat wildly. Instinctively, I hugged my arms to my chest.

"I'm sorry, I didn't . . . didn't mean to frighten you," she stammered, looking confused.

Only then did I sit up facing her, frozen.

"I . . . I haven't slept well lately," she continued. "And I don't know how—" She took a step closer to me, but silence yawned between us. I smelled the musty air rising up from the creek, a close, clammy smell like mildewed clothes. There was no breeze, and the curtains hung limp in the air. I clutched my knees tighter as if protecting myself. From what I didn't yet know.

Mother turned toward the door, her look strained, listening. I imagined she was worried about Amanda, afraid Amanda would hear her voice and burst into my room. "I didn't mean to scare you," she said, staring at my knees held tight to my chest. Again she paused, distracted.

"What is it you want?" I surprised myself by asking. I'd never said such a blunt thing to Mother before, and I half expected her to turn on her heels, astonished at my rudeness. Instead, she edged closer.

"Amanda has to have hope," she said. And then quietly. "I depend on that. I know I do." Then she looked at me with a look of entreaty as if she wanted my understanding. "And I know it's not been fair."

In another life, I might have cried, tears streaming down my face, my body curled up in a knot. In another life, this might have been the moment when we began, tentatively, to unburden ourselves, but today I simply said,

"I'm not going." I hadn't planned to say this, but now that it was said I knew it was true. I wasn't going to Tuscaloosa.

"We can't leave you here," Mother said. "We can't—"

"I'm not going," I repeated and turned my face toward the window, toward the white drifting fog.

When I came downstairs an hour later, I heard Mother and Amanda arguing in the kitchen, their voices a high-pitched fever in the air. "That's ridiculous," Amanda said, pointing a piece of toast at Mother. "I don't know why you're saying such things. You're being ridiculous."

"I can't, Amanda," Mother said. She was standing in front of the coffeepot, staring at Amanda with wet, glittering eyes. "I just can't." She looked resolute, determined.

"But Mother, you won't have to."

When they saw me standing in the doorway, Mother gasped and Amanda visibly stiffened. "Won't have to do what?" I said finally because I had no idea what they were fussing about. In the past when they argued, Amanda would simply deny Mother attention and Mother would easily capitulate. This was something new.

Amanda glared at me. "Just look what you've done. Mother says she won't go to Tuscaloosa unless we all agree to go, but I told her that's ridiculous because we're all three going."

They stared at me as if waiting for a reprieve. I listened to the coffee perking in the background, the hum of the refrigerator. I'd never felt so alone, so isolated. The light behind them was milky, thick with swirling dust. "I'm not going," I said.

"That's ridiculous!" Amanda exploded. She started toward me, her hands clenched, and for a moment I thought she meant to hurt me. "You know it's a good idea, the best possibility for all three of us." But then she stopped, collected herself. Her face smoothed out. She looked earnest, attentive. "You need to think about this," she said. "I know it's sudden, but look, I'm taking on extra work. I can work weekends at the nursing home. With that and my hospital job I can make enough to get us moved. But I need your help. You know that, Jit. I need your help."

It was the softness that frightened me, turned me to jelly. It made my knees shake, my thoughts go blank, my heart pause. "I'm not going," I repeated, but my voice was low, frightened, an animal caught fast in a trap.

When I was little, my father used to take my hand and walk with me down to the pier or deep into the woods where he'd tell me about the woodpecker's habits or the seasonal tides in the creek or the names of the trees—pine, water oak, ash, magnolia, maple, cottonwood, sassafras—and in this way he let me know that I mattered. When I looked troubled or seemed too quiet, too still, he'd take my chin firmly in his hand and make me look at him. "Now, tell me what's wrong," he'd say. And then I'd blurt out whatever was bothering me. If I told him some problem between Amanda and me—maybe Amanda had been bossy at supper or had told me I'd better start speaking at school so people wouldn't think I was a retard—he'd hear me out.

"It's okay to be quiet," he told me once, "as long as you're not using silence as avoidance. As long as you're participating inside, then silence is just fine. Because let's face it, some people are talkers and some people aren't." Then he squeezed my hand and said, "Look at the light through the trees," and I'd notice how the pale golden light bled rivulets of brightness through the branches shadowing our knees.

What I missed was kindness. Daddy's kindness. That memory led me out into the woods to a secret place we often went, though it wasn't far from the house. Pine needles crackled beneath my feet. I lifted my head just as a gull wheeled in circles against a vast gray sky

Yesterday I ran after Amanda's car, wanting to sit together on the floor and blab it all, everything that happened with Mr. Hesse, Johnny Turner, Teddy, Born Jones, and Aunt Katy, but I forgot how easily Amanda was distracted by new possibilities. It wasn't the idea of going to Tuscaloosa that shocked me, but the suddenness of it, the assumption that she could make the decision. I knew that what Amanda wanted would always have a strong pull for me, would seem sensible and right. She got so excited, she was like a pure ray of light. But now I wasn't looking at the light, but staring off to the side, wondering what I wanted. As I pushed through the branches into the secret place, another thought leapt into my head. Amanda might frighten me, but she doesn't want me to desert her. Amanda needed me. She needed me as a foot soldier, someone primed and ready to follow. But what would happen if I didn't?

"What are you doing?"

I was so surprised to hear Amanda's voice, I jerked around. "What?"

She pushed aside the branch that partially blocked her path. "God, it's freaky here."

"It's beautiful."

"Freaky."

We glared at each other until I turned away, embarrassed, not knowing why I should be embarrassed. When I looked up again, Amanda was watching me, her eyes like a pair of grabbing hands. I flinched, then steeled myself. "Where did you go the other night?" she asked as if it was the most innocent question in the world.

I didn't answer right away. Instead, I stared at her jawline, saw her finger her thigh in nervous agitation. This comforted me. I wanted her to be nervous too. "I went to Daddy's cabin," I said. "Where did you go?"

"To bed." She nodded defiantly, tilting her chin. She seemed proud of herself.

For a moment I felt as if I couldn't breathe. I thought of our fight on the pier, the two of us pushing at each other, sparring like men, our hands grabbing at flesh, shaking and pulling, then Amanda breaking loose, running back to the house. "That's sick."

"No sicker than sleeping in your dead father's cabin."

"That's ugly, Amanda." Anger bulged inside me, a new muscle. "There's no reason to be ugly about Daddy unless you just want to hurt me. And since you don't know a damn thing about what's happened to me in the last five months, you can just shut up." It was the longest string of words I'd uttered since I came home.

"Well, I'm glad you got all that pent-up hostility out!"

"Who says I got it out?"

"Great! I can't wait to hear the encore."

I stood up, ready to leave her to her meanness.

"Go ahead," she taunted. "Run away."

I shook my head. "I was here first."

"Well then, you'll just have to share." She plunked down on a tree stump as if claiming her place. I too sat back down and planted my feet solidly on the ground. I needed to do this because I was still frightened of fighting with Amanda. I watched as she looked around her, worried about bugs and snakes, lizards and frogs. "Listen," she said, leaning toward me, "I talked with Mr. Kirk today, and he thinks there's a way he might help. He knows the administrator up there, trained under him really, and he says he'll put in a good word, that he's been pleased with my work. Pleased, Jit. I haven't had much praise, if you know what I mean."

Her words sent a wave of unwelcome feeling through me. I knew how important praise was to Amanda, and I nodded, but had nothing to say.

"I know this decision is hard, but what we decide is important to all of us, and I want you to think about this, Jit, really think about the options we have. You've got to face reality."

I stiffened. Reality was the big bugaboo Amanda always held up to frighten me. "Whose reality?" I said.

"Very funny," she said. "Aren't you getting smart."

"Maybe," I said. And then we both slipped into a tense silence, a white stretch of time so quiet I could hear her breathing, the sullen intake of each breath. We kept our eyes pinned on each other as if we might wear each other down. Above, the sky looked as if it had been swirled with sugar.

"Oh, stop it!" Amanda said finally, standing up, drilling me with angry eyes. "Just stop it." Then she whirled around, picked up a pinecone and threw it hard at a tree. It made a loud whacking sound, then dropped almost silently into the pine straw.

"What about Mother? Does she have a vote?" I knew it was a cheap shot to use Mother, but I didn't know any other way to fight Amanda.

"You've got Mother so riled up she doesn't know what she wants to do."

"Maybe she does."

"Oh, Jesus, what do you know?" Amanda blurted. "She never even wanted you. She didn't want you to be born."

The air went loud with silence. A hawk circled above us, its dark wings spread. A branch crashed somewhere in the woods, the sound echoing through the trees. I sank deeper into myself as if I'd been punched, my lungs deflated, the breath sucked out of me, my vision blurred. "Jit, I didn't mean that," Amanda said, "really, I don't know why I said . . ." but already I was bolting through the woods, moving effortlessly through brush, a white sun drilling its heat through my back.

It was late afternoon, and I was walking toward town, not even bothering to stick out my thumb. I didn't really care if anyone stopped. I just needed to move. I touched my stomach, my shoulder, my thigh, rubbed the hard knob of my elbow. To see if I was really there. *She didn't want me to be born.* It wasn't that I couldn't imagine it; it was just that I hadn't imagined it. She didn't want me at all! I heard the cars whizzing past me, felt the hot surge of dusty wind. The cows behind a barbed wire fence raised their heads to moo at me as I floated past. They bunched together, thick and huddled, watching me with their foolish, frightened eyes. Soon, I'd be a shadow in the darkness, a moving blur, but for now there was a halo of light. Just at the edge of the horizon the earth looked like it was burning. I focused on that.

When a car pulled up behind me and honked, I didn't turn around. I was afraid I'd see a bunch of middle-aged men like the kind who showed up at Earl Ray's, but to my surprise a hoarse, warbly voice called out, "Hello, young lady, you going to Moss Point?"

I turned to see an older woman whose dark hair was threaded with gray. Suddenly town seemed like a good idea. "You not going to get anywhere fast walking," she said "That's why God made cars."

I smiled back at her. She reminded me of Josie.

"Com'on, I can take you," the woman said, waving me toward the front seat of her old Plymouth.

When she pulled into the parking lot of Randy's Pizza Parlor, Mrs. Wilkins said, "Now, you let your mama know you got here all right." She smiled at me, and I nodded, wondering what she'd think if she knew the truth. "That's a good girl," she smiled.

I walked through the front door of Randy's, near where the pay phone is. *Call Aunt Katy.* The line rang and rang, but when there was no answer, I realized Aunt Katy was probably at the day care center or picking up Henley from school; it was two hours earlier in Los Angeles, and I could see Henley airplaning out of his class, his arms spread wide like wings, his mouth buzzing like a motor, his feet propelling him in circles till he was giggly and dizzy and collapsed at Aunt Katy's feet. I saw her smile, tilting her head, then taking firm hold of his hand. "Well hello, Henley. Just when did you turn into an airplane?"

I was still holding the phone, thinking about the two of them, warmth spreading through me when I felt his presence behind me. I put the phone back in its cradle and turned in time to see a drunk man lurching toward me. I ducked, getting out of his way as fast as I could and walked out into the parking lot surrounding Randy's. At either end of the building spotlights blazed a sheet of brightness; a globe light hung over the door. Beyond that, there was only darkness and lines of parked cars.

At the end of the lot there was a big grassy field, and I walked quickly toward it, pushing between cars, almost running as panic welled up inside me. I remembered this feeling on the bus to Los Angeles, my mind cloudy, my thoughts jumbled. But then I thought of Born Jones nodding his head at me and offering me Cheetos, as if to say, "You'll be all right," and I breathed slower, remembering his rough, tender voice, the way he said to the bus driver, "Yes sir, everything's fine back here." Somewhere in the parking lot, a car motor started up, the rattle of an engine, then the squeal of tires. I moved closer to the field, squatting down in the grass, private, hidden in deep shadow. I needed to be quiet, to figure out what I should do next. I pulled out blades of grass, tearing them to bits. When I looked up, no stars streaked the sky. The moon was shadowed by clouds.

"Hey," a voice leapt out of the darkness. I jerked at the sound, fell back on my butt, and then stumbled quickly to my feet. When I turned toward the voice, I was surprised to see Johnny Turner hanging out the driver's side of his father's car. My first instinct was to run.

"I didn't mean to scare you," he said. He took a drag off a cigarette, blew a stream of smoke into the air. When my eyes adjusted, I saw he was squinting at me, curious, his dark hair falling across his forehead. He pushed it away, blew more smoke. "I'm sorry about your dad." His voice was low, but it still had that edge of defiance.

At the mention of my father, words stormed out of me. "You didn't even know him. You didn't know a thing about him. And he didn't kill himself either. He drowned!" Mosquitoes whined above my head. A dog barked from a passing car. I slid back into stillness.

"I'm sorry," Johnny said. "I didn't mean to hurt your feelings. You're right, I didn't really know him. How old was he?" His voice was softer now, almost tender.

"Forty-four."

"Man, that's too young."

I nodded. "I thought he'd die like everybody else's daddy, you know, have a heart attack at seventy-five. I thought he'd be old."

Johnny took a drag off his cigarette, his gaze flicking across my face. With the other hand he traced a finger over the car's door as if brushing it free of dust. "My old man will never die." Bitterness edged his voice. "He'll stay around just to get on my case."

I'd been staring off into the fields, a sea of high grass. "Do you hate him?" I asked, turning toward him. I had not meant to be curious, but I was.

He stabbed out his cigarette. "He's mean. He's mean as hell."

"I'm sorry." When I gazed at him, I saw something besides his football muscled arms and sexy smile. In fact, he wasn't smiling. He was frowning, his face shadowed with worry, thick and dark and foreboding. He looked tired.

"It's okay," he said, glancing away. A horn tooted nearby, a flash of lights, and then there was giggling, a high squeal, the slam of doors. Neither of us moved. "You want to sit down?" he asked.

I stared off into the darkness. "I don't know."

"You want me to take that?" he said, and it was only then I realized I'd been holding a candy wrapper, a piece of litter I'd picked up from the ground. When I handed it to him, I noticed he was wearing a long-sleeved white shirt with big sweat stains under the arms. I saw a tie slung over the front seat, a pizza box in the back. Even with the lid closed I could smell it. "Aren't you gonna eat that?" I asked.

"I guess. You want some?"

I hadn't thought about eating, but suddenly I was hungry. "Sure," I said, and without another thought I got into the passenger's side of his car. Johnny leaned over the seat and opened the pizza box, offering me the first slice.

Maybe it was inevitable that Johnny and I would drive around the back roads, drifting into our own secret thoughts. I didn't say a word about home, about Amanda or Mother, about why I was slipping around town tonight, alone and lonely. And Johnny didn't ask. He only asked where I ran away to. "California," I said, as if that answered it all. For about thirty minutes we rode in silence, driving out west of town toward the lagoon where the old drawbridge still opened to let barges float through. On the radio, a blues singer crooned about the hard times, the loss of love, and with the windows open, a warm breeze blew in, ruffling my hair.

"I like your hair," Johnny said as we made a loop at the bridge and turned back toward town. My hair was cropped short, and my neck felt sleek and cool. Johnny smiled at me, and for the first time that little place in my stomach jumped, sending its familiar signal to my brain. He seemed different tonight, not so cocky, so sure of himself. More isolated. Alone.

"Thanks." I smiled. And we returned to silence.

But it wasn't like that drive months before. Tonight, I was caught in a knot with Amanda, wondering why she'd said what she did. *She never wanted you.* I stared out the window at the trees and fields going past in a blur, and all I could think about was how mean Amanda could be. Was she always that mean? Did she always want to hurt me? But I knew she'd never been this way before because she hadn't needed to. I'd been ready to do her bidding, and I'd believed we wanted the same thing: for our lives to be normal. To do that, Amanda had managed Mother while I kept track of Daddy. We'd acted as a team, alert, intent, dedicated to survival. But now everything had changed. I gazed into the dark, featureless fields. Then I saw something.

"Look," I said. But we were moving too fast.

"What?" Johnny too seemed locked in a private dream.

"Can you turn around and go back? I've got to see . . ." But I didn't want to tell him. I wanted him to see it for himself.

At the first dirt road Johnny turned the car around and drove slowly back while I stared out the window, passing the dark fields that seemed to merge into a dark starless sky. "There!" I said. And then he saw it too, a field of softly blinking lights, fireflies hovering low over tall, weedy grass, flickering like tiny magic wands, like fluttering shadows. "I have to get out," I whispered as if we were in a sacred place; after we stopped, I moved quietly toward the field as if gliding through water. I heard Johnny's footsteps behind me in the grass, and I walked slowly, my feet seeping into the marshy dirt until I was in the middle of the fireflies. I stopped, silent, still in the darkness. Neither of us spoke. We just stared at the blinking light, and then I lay down in the grass, staring up at fireflies, the grass tickling my legs, poking at my neck. It felt reverent. Holy. Johnny lay down beside me and for long moments, neither of us moved, caught beneath this furious beauty.

"I've never done this before," he whispered. His voice was close to my ear. "Me either."

And then we lay still. Silent and still.

"The world beneath this world," Born Jones used to say, and though I'd liked the sound of that phrase, I didn't really know what he meant. Above me, the fireflies blinked and trembled. Beyond them, the black night was seamless, blurred. I lay quiet, barely breathing, reading the night like a pulse, a thin membrane of beauty enclosing me. This too was my world, the source of love. This too was mine. A world beneath this world. For so long I'd wanted my mother's love and secretly believed there was something I had to do to earn it, to make her love me. Now the thought of letting her go seared me with sadness. I saw her standing in my room this morning, frightened, worried, trying to talk. I heard her arguing with Amanda. I won't go unless she goes. I won't go. And I realized she was trying to claim me, the only way she knew how: by refusing Amanda.

Something eased inside me as if a weight had lifted. I sank deeper into the grass, breathed in the smell of dirt and grass and clover, watched the fireflies flicker and shimmer in their electrical light.

"I'm going to Vietnam," Johnny said softly. He didn't move, not even a finger.

"What?" I sat up, stunned by his announcement. I didn't know a thing about Vietnam except for those pictures on TV, the men sloshing through rice paddies, guns raised over their heads. They looked pale and frightened, too young to be fighting a war. "Why?" I asked.

"I don't know," he said. "Maybe because I don't know what else to do." He shrugged. "Maybe it's the only way to get back at my old man."

"Are you scared?"

He was still lying down, his hands cradled behind his head. "Nah," he said, closing his eyes, letting the silence spread between us, pale, endless. He opened them again. "Yeah." His eyes were wide and solemn. "Yeah, I am."

"I would be," I said. "But just about everything scares me. Or used to."

"You're different now," he said, watching me. "You're leaving too, aren't you?"

I was surprised at this. "No, Amanda is." And I told him how his dad was closing up the house, how Amanda was going up to the university in

Tuscaloosa, taking Mother with her so she could finish college.

"Sonofabitch!" he whispered, his whole body tense. "What about you?"

"I don't know."

"You could go with me to Vietnam," he laughed. And then I laughed too. We smiled at each other, surprised to be joking about such serious things. By now the fireflies had scattered, moved away to another field. There was only darkness, a low cloud cover, the steamy heat rising in waves from the ground.

"Will you kiss me?"

I looked at Johnny. For a moment he seemed awkward, puzzled as if he'd never asked this question before. But I couldn't help thinking about that other night, the drive to the old Parker place, the loss of my sweater. "What happened to my sweater?" I whispered.

He smiled, embarrassed. "I threw it out the window as I was driving home."

I covered my face, shamed, thinking how much trouble that sweater had caused.

"Com'ere," he said and touched my arm. It was his shyness that made me bold, the way his hand barely grazed my arm, though its pressure surprised me. He looked so serious, so stunned, as if he were swimming far out beyond familiar waters. I kissed him, leaning toward him, his hand still on my arm, but softly, then traveling up my neck, floating there, tentative, silky, rubbing lightly down my spine as if in retreat. I felt each stroke, each pause, and didn't know what to make of the pleasure. My body quivered and jumped with anticipation. Johnny pulled away from me, staring at me as if he didn't quite believe I was real, but in that pause something changed, electrified, and then he was kissing my throat, my neck, my ears, my hair, his hands pulling me down to him, down to the grass where we both lay as if we were always meant to be here, down to the clover field under a black, endless sky. His hand touched my breast, first tentatively, then urgently, his mouth opening to tongue the nipples through cloth, wetting each breast, then slowly lifting my t-shirt so that there was only the relief of air. Perhaps it was inevitable that I think of Mother again, Mother who was so frightened of the body, frightened of feelings, and I pulled away, stopped by the memory of her saying, "You find that sweater!"

I sat up, shivering, startled. Suddenly, I was chilled.

"I'm sorry," Johnny said, sitting up beside me. "Really I didn't mean this. I'm trying . . ." He sighed. "I'm trying to be . . ."

I shook my head as if I were shaking myself loose from everything that had held me in place. I thought of myself as a little girl, swimming away, swimming to some unknown freedom in my dreams. And then I did what surprised even me. I pulled the t-shirt over my head and leaned over to kiss Johnny, not on the mouth, but softly at the throat, feeling my breasts graze his shirt, his pocket, the tense, hard muscles of his arms. He barely breathed as I unbuttoned his shirt and sent it flying. It floated for a second, rising like a big, puffy cloud, then fell in a heap in the grass. We both giggled. And then lay down together, rising, floating, suspended in a cloud of our own while the fireflies flickered, then blurred in the distant fields.

I told Johnny to let me out at the creek road, and I walked in alone, caught between the reality of lights on in the house and the dreamy pause of lying in the fields with Johnny Turner. Silently I glided through the back door, holding the kitchen doorknob tight so it wouldn't squeak, closing it gently. Just beyond me, the refrigerator hummed. I opened it to get a glass of milk, conscious of the rattle of the shelves, the scrape of the carton. A branch brushed against the side of the house, a thrushing sound. The glass clinked when I set it down. I stood a moment in a circle of silence, then crossed the living room, instinctively stopping to look out the windows toward the creek. I felt instantly peaceful, serene until I saw Amanda huddled in a chair, staring at me. I jumped. "Jesus, you scared me!" My heart raced. A chill ran up my spine, settling somewhere deep inside.

"Sorry," Amanda said, "but I've been waiting all night for you. You ran off and didn't let me explain."

"There's nothing to explain," I said, and continued walking across the room. Of course, I was punishing Amanda, but what did she expect?

"Jit, there's an entire year to explain." Her voice sounded strained, exhausted.

"Not tonight." I passed the upholstered chair with the faded ottoman and turned toward the stairs, aware of the grass stains on my shorts, the disarray of my hair. I plowed my fingers through it, weeding out clover stems, dirt.

"Yes, tonight."

"I'm going to bed."

"No, you're not!" Amanda sat forward as if she might pounce.

"Good night." And I walked quickly up the stairs and into the bedroom I'd slept in for sixteen years, turning fast and locking the door. But I didn't go to sleep. Instead, I sat on the bed, thinking. I thought about the fireflies swirling above my head, about the soft swish of summer grass beneath my feet, about Johnny's lips on my elbows, my neck, my knees, and then about Amanda sitting in the dark, waiting. Usually when we fought, I felt frightened and guilty, my body cringing, the air around me shallow and thin as if it too was destined for punishment, but tonight I was being led down another path. I was too full of something, too caught in the swell of sorrow and that sudden opening of pleasure. Comfort, I knew, was what Amanda wanted to offer. She wanted to give me what Mother couldn't, a reason, a story for what had happened, a beginning, middle and an end. More than anything she wanted to take back her words, words that had hurt me, but those words I needed to hold onto.

Within minutes, I heard footsteps, then the rattle of the knob. "I know you're in there so don't pretend you're not."

"I'm not pretending," I said, conscious that I'd never before locked my door.

"Please, Jit." Her voice swelled with urgency. "Open the door."

"I don't want to talk to you right now."

Even through the door I could hear Amanda's breathing as if she were leaning against the door, breathing her strength into the wood. I steeled myself against it. Already I could feel some of the life force oozing out of me, but I didn't open the door.

When I heard her steps on the stairs, then a door slam, I took a big gulp of air. I wrapped my arms around my chest, reminding myself that my skin was breathing skin, my bones solid bones. I was a girl sitting in her room, looking out at Soldier Creek.

41

I flew down the stairs toward the darkness of the living room. Inside this darkness there was a deeper dark, a bitter turning I didn't want to comprehend. All my life I'd thought of Jit as part of me, a secret pocket of flesh tucked safely inside my boundaries. Always I was the pilgrim, the wayfarer, and Jit, like Mother, my ballast. She kept me on course, needy and demanding, but I'd never thought of her as separate, ready to make her way in the world. And now look at her, pulling free of my orbit, circling on her own. The little shit!

I didn't stop when I reached the living room but pushed out into the night, running down the bluff toward the creek. I tripped over roots and lay sprawled in the bush, but I picked myself up and went on as if carried by an invisible force. The boards of the pier were rough, uneven, but I didn't dare stop. In the night, the creek was solid blackness, and when I reached the end of the pier, I kept running as if throwing myself off a cliff. I shrieked in terror. And then to my surprise, I splashed down into water, sinking to the bottom, to the squish of sand, the flutter of seaweed. For a single instant, I felt free and alive as if I'd just shaken hands with the devil and survived, but that moment collapsed and I rose shivering, terrified, streaking toward the dock.

"Jesus!" I sat wet and trembling on the pier, my clothes dripping, water puddling between my breasts. There was no sound but the crickets in the trees, the occasional leap of a mullet. Darkness surrounded me. I imagined the trees unsettling from their roots and stepping closer, stalking me. A moth tickled my hair and I shivered, then relaxed as the boards beneath me softened, smoothing out into a hard, flat bed. There was a haze over the moon. Looking at it, I seemed to lose time, unscrambling myself from the here and now, falling backward into another place. I saw the gothic buildings of Trinity College, the busy silence of the library, the thick hungry talk of students moving out into the night. I'd jumped into Trinity College just as I'd jumped into the creek: compelled, unprepared, terrified. I'd wanted a pure leap into another world. If only I could jump over the past, surely I'd be free. But here I was.

Suddenly I was very tired. I lay down on the pier. And for the first time in my life I thought of my little sister having a life of her own, making decisions, picking herself up, moving on. Baby! I wanted to laugh. But I didn't. I didn't dare. I just never thought of her growing up, defining herself. I never thought I'd have to fight her. I crooked my arm under my head for a pillow and surprised myself by thinking, Maybe I won't. That thought amazed me: the idea of Jit doing whatever Jit wanted to do, letting her fall like baggage from my shoulders. I wondered if I could . . . I wondered . . . and then something changed inside me like a yolk breaking loose from an egg. I touched my eyes. Wetness. "You little shit," I kept saying, wiping at my eyes. "You little shit," because suddenly I didn't know which one of us got lost.

42

When I got out of bed, the fog was beginning to clear. I could see the roof of Josie's One-Stop, the bare outline of the point. I raised the screen and climbed out on the roof where last December I'd tied bedsheets together and slid to the ground. I remembered it as if it were yesterday, how frightened I was. Now I sat in my nightgown, the moisture dampening my legs, my skin, my hair. I folded myself over my knees and closed my eyes as if to blot everything out.

I couldn't believe I fell asleep, but when I opened my eyes, I was surprised by a flush of light, the sky red-tinted, edged with gold. It reminded me of the early mornings in California, the sun rising over the Pacific Ocean, and I thought of Aunt Katy and Henley and Born Jones. Looking west I wondered what they were doing in Los Angeles. It was still night there, and I imagined Aunt Katy and Henley snuggled together in sleep, Henley with his fluffy bear to hold, Aunt Katy roaming the back pastures of her grandfather's yard in her dreams. Born Jones would have tacked up a few new drawings and then fallen asleep with his clothes still on. While they were sleeping, I was wide awake, thinking.

I turned toward the side of the house where the entwined trees had grown so close together you couldn't spare one without killing the other. They were beautiful but monstrous, their trunks bound tight to each other like Siamese twins. Freaks of nature. I sat very still, staring, waiting, until, like the downflash of a knife, I thought, *like Amanda and me.* We grew tangled together, then trouble yanked us apart. Made us afraid. Maybe we were too fragile to be afraid before. Maybe we were too scared of hurting each other, killing the closeness. As I was thinking this, a brighter light spread through the treetops, golden streaks as if the sky was waking up. I saw myself standing on Aunt Katy's doorstep, hugging her, laughing and talking, and I knew, as if it had been buried in my brain all along, that I was going back to California, back to Aunt Katy and Henley in Los Angeles, back to a different life. It was such a radical thought I couldn't move. Not even wiggle my toes. "Running again," I heard Amanda say, but for the first time I understood how much the ground had shifted. I was choosing to leave. I hunched over, the sunlight slanting across my knees.

It was minutes later that I saw Amanda walking up the path from the creek. She looked bedraggled, wrinkled, as if she'd slept in a knot. I thought of my locked door, our angry words, and some ghost of worry pulsed in my throat. I imagined the roof crashing in, the wolf eating me up until I remembered the decision I'd just made and I hugged myself, tugging my nightgown around my toes, shivering with pleasure. Amanda was still coming up the path. She looked up, startled, stopping where she was, staring at me. To my surprise, she waved. "Can I come up?"

"Sure." I stepped into my room and unlocked the door, and then I was back on the roof beneath the trees. The morning was silent, still. The air smelled like lemons and seaweed, tart and calm, but the horizon was on fire, a single thread of flame at the tree line, the sky faded pink. I turned as Amanda crawled out, her shirt stuck to her back, her shorts wrinkled to her legs. My nightgown drooped against me, clinging with heat. For a long minute we were silent, sitting together, watching the sun come up.

"It's beautiful," Amanda said.

"Freaky," I said.

Amanda laughed, tapped her foot on the roof. "I wish you wouldn't be such a hard-ass," she said, but her tone was affectionate.

"Well, you never asked me why I didn't want to go. You never ask the most simple things."

"Why didn't you just tell me? Why do I have to ask first?"

I shrugged, staring up into the pine needles, so prickly and stiff. "I don't know. Habit, I guess."

"Okay," she said, looking closely at me, "I'm asking. I'm begging, for god's sake. Why don't you want to go with me?"

And then it all tumbled out: the bus ride to New Orleans, those awful soldiers, then Born Jones, Earl Ray, and the frantic rush to find Aunt Katy. To my relief, Amanda listened intently nodding and even laughing at Born Jones meeting Henley, and then to my surprise she told me about Teddy and Jeremy and this incredible professor, Dr. McKune. "I thought I'd do something wonderful up there, that I'd grow up, but it's either harder or easier than it seems."

We were both a little astonished at ourselves, as if we might fall off the roof. Neither of us had mentioned Mother. Neither of us had mentioned

Daddy's death. The loss of the house. Or the loss of each other.

"But you haven't really told me why you don't want to go to Tuscaloosa."

"Well, in a way I have." For a moment I imagined the roof tilting violently, tossing me to the ground, but then I took a deep breath and said it out loud. "I'm going back to Los Angeles."

The air swelled with meaning. Amanda was silent. She hunched over, pulled her knees up to her chest and looked out at the trees. The leaves shivered as a breeze floated up from the creek. "What about Mother?"

I didn't know what made me do it, but I took Amanda's hand in mine. Her palm was soft and cool, the fingers rough, even calloused on the ends. For the first time I felt the heat between us, all the anguish and love we couldn't reveal. "She'll go with you. You know she will. She was trying to pull us all together, but some things come too late."

"Jit," Amanda whispered. There were tears in her eyes.

I held tightly to her hand as I looked through the leaves at the creek, breathing deeply the smell of pine sap and algae, of crab bait and water lilies, watching the creek as it lapped against the shore, as it flowed past the point into the dark choppy waves of Perdido Bay.

ACKNOWLEDGMENTS

It has been an honor to work with Kim Verhines, editor at SFA Press, and her assistant, Shaina Hawkins. I'm delighted that my book was chosen for the SFA Fiction Prize. I feel gratitude for the friendship and narrative insights of so many people, especially Marilyn Abildskov, Beverly Blasingame Jean Bolton, Kate Bolton Bonnici, Kathryn Ann Ford, Robin Hemley, Jay Lamar, Robin Miura, Debra Spark, Patricia Stevens, Shirley Tarbell, Lynn Taetzsch, Kris Vervecke, and the late James Alan McPherson. I want to thank Michelle Tessler, agent extraordinaire, for her belief in this project and Robin Miura for her wonderful editing skills.

Continued thanks: to David, my husband, my confidante, always; to my family in Alabama, who provided me with the impetus to tell stories; to Susie, Wyline, Amy – and the late Louise Bouzan – who shared the beauty of Soldier Creek with me when I was a girl growing up on the coast of Alabama.

A short section of this book was published in *Stories from the Blue Moon Café*, edited by Sonny Brewer (MacAdam/Cage, 2002).